BAD MOVE

"*Bad Move* defies easy categorization, and bless Barclay for that. It is a mystery, yes, but there is a vein of humor that runs wide and deep through it. Barclay demonstrates a fine and steady hand, as well as keen insight and a canny knowledge of his subject matter. Combining those elements with an extremely readable writing style and a highly imaginative plot, you can't ask for any more." —Bookreporter.com

LONE WOLF

WITHDRAWN

LINWOOD BARCLAY

BANTAM BOOKS

LONE WOLF
A Bantam Book / October 2006

Published by Bantam Dell
A Division of Random House, Inc.
New York, New York

All rights reserved
Copyright © 2006 by Linwood Barclay
Cover design by Jae Song

Bantam Books and the rooster colophon are registered
trademarks of Random House, Inc.

ISBN 978-0-553-80455-3

Printed in the United States of America
Published simultaneously in Canada

www.bantamdell.com

OPM   10 9 8 7 6 5

To my Green Acres family,
those still with us and those not

1

TRIXIE SNELLING SEEMED TO BE working up to something over lunch this particular Tuesday, and really just killing time talking about scouring costume stores to find forehead ridges to please a client who liked to be dominated by a Klingon, but she never got to it because I had to take a call on my cell that my father had been eaten by a bear.

"There were those two Klingon chicks in the series where the bald guy was the captain, right?" Trixie asked me, because she knew that I was something of an authority when it came to matters related to science fiction.

"Yeah," I said. "Lursa and B'Etor Duras. They were sisters. They tried to overthrow the Gowron leadership of the Klingon High Council." I paused, then added, "Lots of leather and cleavage."

"I'm okay there," Trixie said, shaking her head at the useless information I had stored in my head. I wondered sometimes what important stuff gets crowded out when your brain is filled with trivia.

"My closet's so full of leather," Trixie continued, "I'm afraid it's all going to congeal back into a cow. I should show you sometime." Even though Trixie was dressed, at the moment, in a dark blue pullover sweater and fashionable jeans over high-heeled boots, it wasn't difficult to imagine her in full dominatrix regalia. I had seen her that way once—and not as a client—back in the days when we were neighbors. We'd kept in touch after Sarah and I and the kids had moved away, and even though we were just friends, and met regularly for lunch or a coffee, I never quite got over the novelty of what she did for a living.

She continued, "But getting these ridges onto my forehead, making them blend in with the rest of my head, then there's the makeup that makes me look like I've fallen asleep at the tanning salon, I mean, getting ready for this guy is a major production. Where are the guys who just want to be whipped by the girl next door? Plus, he wants me to torment him without wrinkling his Starfleet uniform."

"He wears a Starfleet uniform," I said. "What rank is he?"

"Captain," Trixie said. "There's these little gold dots on his collar that supposedly denote rank, but he just tells me to call him Captain, so that's fine. He's paying for it. I'm just glad he doesn't want me to call him Rear Admiral. Imagine what that might entail."

"I imagine that you are well compensated for your efforts."

Trixie gave me a half smile. "Absolutely." The

smile disappeared as quickly as it had appeared. Trixie picked at her spinach salad as I twirled some fettuccine carbonara onto my fork.

"What's on your mind?" I asked.

She shook her head. "Nothing." She picked at her salad some more. "What's going on with you? Things working out with Sarah as your boss?"

I shrugged, then nodded. I'd been working as a feature writer at *The Metropolitan* for more than a year now, having accepted the fact that I could not make a go of it staying home and writing science fiction novels. I'd been assigned to Sarah, whose responsibilities at the city desk included overseeing a number of feature writers, some neurotic, some egotistical, some neurotically egotistical, and then there was me, her obsessive, often pain-in-the-ass, husband.

"Oh sure," I said. "I mean, she wants to kill me, but other than that, the relationship is working well." I had a bite of pasta. "I'm on the newsroom safety committee."

"There's a surprise," Trixie said.

"It's no joke. We've got air quality issues, radiation off the computer screens, there's—"

"Let me see if I understand this. You work for a major daily newspaper, where they send reporters off to Iraq and Iran and Afghanistan and God knows where else, and they expose murderous biker gangs and do first-person stories about what it's like to be a skyscraper window washer, and you're worried about air quality and computer radiation?"

"You make it sound kind of weenie-like," I said.

Again, Trixie gave me the half smile. "Sarah okay with you and me being friends?"

I nodded. "I were you, I'd be more worried about my own reputation, hanging out with a writer for *The Metropolitan*."

"And how was your trip? Didn't you guys go someplace?"

"That was months ago," I said. "A little trip to Rio."

"Good time?"

I shrugged. "I found it a bit stressful." I paused, then added, "I'm not a good traveler."

"How's Angie?" Trixie asked. My daughter was nineteen now, in her second year at Mackenzie University.

"Good," I said. "Paul's good, too. He's seventeen now, finishing up high school."

"They're good kids." Trixie's eyes seemed to mist when she said it, and then she seemed to be looking off to one side, at nothing in particular.

"I keep getting this vibe that there's something on your mind," I said. "Talk to me."

Trixie said nothing, breathed in slowly through her nose. If she needed time to work up to something, I could wait.

"Well," she said, "you know the local paper in Oakwood? *The Suburban*? There's this—"

And then the cell phone inside my jacket began to ring.

"Hang on," I said to Trixie. I got out the phone, flipped it open, put it to my ear. "Yeah?"

"Zack?"

"Hi, Sarah."

"Where are you?"

"I'm having lunch with Trixie. Remember I said?"

"So you're not driving or anything?"

"No. I'm sitting down." My mind flashed to Paul and Angie. When you have teenagers, and someone's about to give you some sort of bad news, you know it's probably going to be about them. "Has something happened with the kids?" I asked.

"No no," Sarah said quickly. "Kids are fine, far as I know."

I let out a breath.

"So anyway," Sarah said, "there's this stringer I use sometimes, Tracy McAvoy? Up in the Fifty Lakes District? She does the odd feature, breaking news when it happens up there and we can't get a staffer there fast enough. Remember she did the piece about that seaplane crash, the hunters that died, last year?"

I didn't, but I said, "Sure." However, I could recall seeing the byline, occasionally, in the paper. Fifty Lakes is about a ninety-minute drive north of the city, lots of lakes (well, about fifty) and hills, cabins and boating and fishing, that kind of thing. A lot of city people had cottages up there. My father, for one.

"I just got off the phone with her," Sarah said. "She's got this story about a possible bear attack. Pretty vicious."

I could guess where this was going. Tracy was an okay reporter, she could file a basic story, but the city desk was wanting something more, some color, maybe a piece for the weekend paper. The sort of thing I was born to do. "Sarah, just get to it."

"Would you shut up and listen? It was in Braynor, well, in the woods outside Braynor."

"Yeah, okay. Braynor's where my dad's camp is."

"I know. Well, here's the thing. They found this body, this man, and I guess there wasn't a whole lot of him left to identify, and they found him right by Crystal Lake."

That was the lake where Dad ran his fishing camp. A handful of cabins, rental boats. I mentioned that to Sarah.

"I know, Zack. That's where they found the body. In the woods by your father's place."

"Jesus," I said. "I guess I should give him a call." I paused. "I can't even remember the last time I talked to him. It's been a while."

"Here's the thing," Sarah said, hesitating. "Nobody's seen your dad for a while. And they haven't identified this body yet."

A chill ran through me.

"I phoned your dad's place," Sarah added. "But there wasn't any answer."

I slipped the phone back into my jacket and said apologetically to Trixie, "Hold that thought. Something's sort of come up."

2

MY PARENTS WOULD TAKE ME and my older sister Cindy up to Fifty Lakes when we were kids. I guess we went up there two or three summers in a row, when Dad took a week off from his job at the accounting firm. There was a camp that rented out spots to people with travel trailers—Airstreams and the like—before everyone started going to Winnebago-style RVs that you didn't tow but drove.

We didn't have anything as upscale as an Airstream. Dad had gotten a deal, from someone he worked with at the accounting firm, on a tent trailer, which looked like a flattened box while en route, hitched to the back of the car. When you reached your destination, the contraption opened up with a canvas top, high enough to stand in, a big bed at each end, and a little sink with running water. Cindy and I weren't in our teens yet back then, so our parents had us sleep together on one side, while they took the other. I'd spend most of the night lightly running my finger along Cindy's neck so she'd think her sleeping bag was infested with spiders, and when she'd awake at midnight, screaming, I'd pretend to have been roused from a deep sleep just like my parents, who'd shout at her to be quiet, sometimes waking other campers in nearby spots. The hard part then was trying to roll over and not pee myself laughing.

That was probably the most fun thing about camping. The swimming and the fishing, those things were okay. But Dad spent so much time enforcing rules of behavior to keep us from hurting ourselves, or any of our secondhand camping equipment, that the appeal of vacationing was limited. Zip up the door fast so the bugs don't get in. Don't lean on the canvas or you'll rip it. Don't run on the dock with wet feet. Put on your life jacket. So what if the boat's still tied to the dock and the water's only two feet deep, put on your life jacket. Watch those fishhooks, for crying out loud, you get one of those in your finger and you'll get an infection and be dead before dinner.

He was something of a worrier, Arlen Walker was, and I'll understand if you find that amusing. His perpetual state of anxiety was as much of an annoyance for his wife and my mother, Evelyn Walker, as my conviction in the certainty of worst-case scenarios has been for my long-suffering Sarah.

"For God's sake, Arlen," Evelyn would say, "loosen your gas cap a bit and let the pressure off."

While family trips seemed to be sources of great anxiety for Dad, he still enjoyed his time in Fifty Lakes, away from the city, away from work. There

were rare glimpses of something approaching con-
tentment in this man who seemed unable to relax. I
remember seeing him once, his butt perched on a
rock at the water's edge, his bare feet planted on the
lake bottom, water lapping up over his ankles. His
shoes, a balled sock tucked neatly into each one,
rested perfectly side by side on a nearby dock.

I approached, wondering whether I could get a
couple of quarters out of him so Cindy and I could
buy candy bars at the camp snack bar, and instead of
reprimanding me for some misdeed of which I was
not yet aware, he reached out a hand and tousled the
hair on top of my head.

"Someday," he said, smiling at me and then looking out over the small lake.

And that was it.

"Someday" came eight years ago. Mom had been
dead for four years at the time, and Dad decided the
time had come to make a change. He retired from
the accounting firm, sold the mortgage-free house in
the city my sister and I had grown up in, and bought
a twenty-acre parcel of land up in the Fifty Lakes
District, south of the village of Braynor, that had two
hundred feet of frontage on Crystal Lake.

He hadn't just bought a getaway property. He'd
bought a small business, called Denny's Cabins
(named for the man who'd originally built them back
in the sixties). There were five rustic cottages, a few
docks, and half a dozen small aluminum fishing
boats with low-powered outboard motors bolted to
the back. There was always one available for Dad to
go fishing whenever he felt the urge, which actually

wasn't all that often. He liked the tranquility of living at a fishing camp, even if he didn't drop his line into the water every day.

I'd only been up there a couple of times, the first soon after he bought it, to see what he'd gotten himself into. There was a two-story farmhouse and barn on the property, a couple of hundred yards up from the lake, but Dad had chosen not to live in it, preferring instead to take the largest of the five cabins, fully winterize it and spruce it up with new furniture and flooring and appliances, and live year-round at the water's edge, even in winter, when the lake froze over and the winds howled and the only people you were likely to see were lost snowmobilers and the guy who plowed the lane that wound its way in from the main road. Living in the farmhouse, with all that room to roam around in, would have been a constant reminder to Dad of how alone he was.

The second time I went up, a year or so later, I took Paul. He was eleven, and I'd had this notion that a father-son fishing trip would be the ultimate bonding experience, which it was not, because children who have grown up accustomed to blasting space aliens on a TV screen are ill equipped to sit in a boat for five hours waiting for something to happen. Anyway, I had phoned Dad and asked about renting a cabin for a weekend, not knowing that he'd berate me for two solid days about not getting our Camry rust-proofed.

"You might as well take a power drill to it now, get it over with," he told me. "Honestly, you spend that money on a car and don't get it rust-proofed, it's beyond me."

"Dad, the new cars already have perforation warranties."

"Oh yeah, right, like they honor those things."

We talked on the phone now and then, but not much. He'd actually bought himself a computer and occasionally I'd get an e-mail message from him, usually just a line or two to explain an attached photograph of some big muskie or pickerel he'd caught. For an old guy who was resistant to change, he'd embraced some of the new technologies with enthusiasm. I think it must have been those long, cold winters that brought him around. He was tired of being isolated, and his computer connected him to the world in ways he'd never imagined possible.

And now, from the sounds of things, he could be dead.

I quickly explained to Trixie what Sarah had said, and, after she'd hugged me, she had but one word to say: "Go."

Once I was on the highway that led north out of the city, behind the wheel of our hybrid Virtue, pushing the little car as hard as it would go, I got Sarah on my cell again, asked her to tell me again what she knew.

The freelancer, Tracy, had learned of the incident about the same time as the authorities. She was being treated for a sore throat at her doctor's, an elderly man who should have retired years ago but still practiced because it was hard to attract new GPs to an out-of-the-way place like Braynor. He did double duty in Fifty Lakes as a coroner, and Tracy was there when the call came in that a body had been found up by Crystal Lake, that it had been mauled pretty badly, and the first thing that had come to everyone's mind was that a bear was to blame. Tracy offered to drive the doctor in her own car, and called *The Metropolitan*'s city desk when she figured she had a story that might appeal to an audience beyond the local paper she primarily wrote for, *The Braynor Times*. She'd had no idea, when she put the call in to Sarah, that there might be a personal connection.

Nobody knew for sure who the dead person was, but there was no sign of Arlen Walker.

"So listen, Zack," Sarah said, a note of caution in her voice, "this has really just happened. They may not even have moved the body by the time you get there. In fact, I think Tracy has told them you're coming, so they may leave things as they are so you can, you know, do an identification."

"Okay," I said. At the speed I was going, I'd probably be up there in a little more than an hour and fifteen minutes.

"I'll come up, too," Sarah said, and I knew she meant it.

"Why don't I get up there, find out what's actually happened," I said, "and then I'll let you know." Because I am not normally someone to look on the bright side, or wait for all the facts before panicking, I was already making a mental list of people to call. My sister. The funeral director. The lawyer. The real estate agent. Sarah would be good at helping with that sort of stuff.

"What about Cindy?" Sarah asked.

I said I would call my sister when I knew everything.

"If I find out anything more, I'll call you," Sarah said.

The landscape changed so gradually as I headed north that I almost didn't notice it happening, but when I was about half an hour away from Braynor I noticed, even in my preoccupied state, that the hills had grown more steep, the forests of pines more dense, signs of civilization less prevalent, and the road frequently walled on both sides with jagged rock where the highway had been blasted through a rise in the terrain. Every few miles the scenery would open up as the highway skirted the edge of a lake, and taking my eyes off the wheel for a moment, I could see small boats in the distance, some moving at speed, others sitting with middle-aged men hunched over their fishing poles.

I saw a sign reading "Braynor 5" and began looking for the lane into my father's camp. I knew he was about three miles south of town, and before long I spotted the crudely painted sign up ahead, yellow letters painted onto a brown background, reading "Denny's Cabins: Fishing, bait, boats. Next right."

I slowed, saw the opening in the trees where the lane wound down from the highway, and turned in. It didn't amount to much more than two ruts with a strip of grass growing in the middle, and I could hear the blades brushing along the bottom of the car as I navigated my way in. The grass on either side of the ruts was matted down, where drivers had pulled over when encountering a car coming from the other direction.

Not far down, the lane branched into two. You took the left to go to the farmhouse Dad had opted not to use, but I couldn't have driven that way had I wanted to, because only a few yards ahead the lane was blocked by a wide wooden gate that was flanked on both sides by a neck-high chain-link fence.

The gate featured a collection of signs, some made from wood and sloppily printed, others commercially available metal signs, dimpled as though shot with BB pellets. They read "Keep Out!" and "Private!!" and "Beware of Dogs!" That last one had originally said "Beware of Dog!" but someone had painted a snakelike "s" at the end to make it plural. As if all those weren't enough, there was another that said "No Trespassing!" and a homemade one reading "Tresppasers Will Be SHOT!"

I caught a glimpse of the two-story farmhouse and the large barn beyond it as I passed, taking the lane to the right and down over a hill, where the woods opened up and the five small cabins, lined up like little white Monopoly houses, presented themselves.

As did the police car, the ambulance, and a couple of other vehicles parked at random on the lane and on the lawn behind the cabins. The dome lights on the police car and ambulance rotated quietly.

As I pulled ahead, I saw several people gathered on the other side of the ambulance, a couple of them having a smoke, like they were all waiting for something. I parked, got out, my legs feeling a little rubbery not just from what I feared I was about to learn, but from the drive.

They turned and looked at me. Two were dressed in paramedic garb, there was a young dark-haired woman clutching a notepad I figured was the free-lancer Tracy, a gray-haired man in a dark suit, tie, and wire-rimmed glasses who had to be the doctor doing coroner duty, three other men in plaid and olive civilian attire that suggested fishing, and a woman in her sixties in a kerchief, hunting jacket, and slacks.

Finally, there was the law. A man in his mid-thirties, I figured, black boots, bomber-style leather jacket, and a felt trooper hat. He took a step toward me.

"Can I help you?" he said. I had a closer look at him, his receding jaw, thin neck, eyes that blinked almost constantly. There was something about him, at first glance, that seemed familiar, but I couldn't place it.

"I'm Zack Walker," I said, and cleared my throat. "I got a call. This is my father's place."

The young woman with the notepad spoke up. "Mr. Walker? Sarah Walker's husband?" She was bordering on cheerful.

"That's right."

"I'm Tracy McAvoy. This is the guy," she told the cop. "The one's whose wife is the editor? At the paper?"

The cop held up his hand for her to stop, as if to say, "I get it." He extended a hand my way. "I'm Chief Thorne. Orville Thorne."

We shook. His hand was warm, and damp.

I said, "I was told you haven't been able to find my father, and that you have a body to . . ." I seemed unable to find the words I needed. "That there's, that you have . . ."

Thorne nodded, poked his tongue around the inside of his cheek, pondering, I guessed, whether I was up to the next step.

"Mr. Walker, we have had an incident. A man's body was found in the woods just over there." He pointed. The trees looked dark and ominous. "One of the guests here was out for a walk and discovered him this morning. We haven't been able to determine just whose body it is, you see, but all the guests here at your father's camp have been accounted for. But," and Chief Thorne paused to swallow, "we've not been able to locate your father, Arlen Walker."

"Maybe he's away," I said. "Did you consider that?"

Chief Thorne nodded. "There's his pickup over there." I looked over by the first cabin, the one I knew Dad lived in, and spotted a Ford truck. "And there's no boats missing, according to the guests here."

"I see," I said.

"It's an awful thing to ask, but maybe, if you wouldn't mind, you could take a look for us." He tipped his trooper-hatted head toward the woods.

I felt weak.

"Of course," I said.

He led me toward the woods, everyone else following, silently, like we were already in the funeral procession. As I began to be enveloped by trees, the air felt colder.

There was a small clearing, and on the ground, a tarp, maybe seven by four feet, with something under it that couldn't be anything but a body.

"Are you okay?" the chief asked.

I definitely was not. I said, "Yeah."

Chief Thorne approached one end of the tarp, gingerly grabbed the corner, and lifted it up, revealing a body, as best as I could tell, from head to waist.

Like they say, nothing prepares you.

What I saw under that tarp looked like something that had been dropped to the ground through the blades of a helicopter. Flesh ripped away, bone exposed, blood everywhere.

Some flies buzzed.

I turned away. I wondered if maybe I was going to be sick. For anyone to die that way, it was unimaginable. But for my own father . . .

"I know it's pretty impossible to tell," Thorne said. "But did you notice anything, clothing, anything at all, that would tell you whether that's your father?"

The surrounding pines seemed to be waving back and forth, as if in a high wind, but there wasn't even a slight breeze. The blue sky was below me, the grass above, and then, seconds later, everything was back where it was supposed to be.

"No," I said.

"We couldn't find any sort of ID on him, so I was wondering . . ."

I came out of the woods like a man stumbling out of a burning building, desperate for air. I went to my car, threw my hands out and leaned over the hood, trying to catch my breath. One of the ambulance attendants was saying something to me, but I couldn't seem to hear it.

There was the sound of a vehicle approaching, of rubber crunching gravel, and I looked up the hill I'd driven down moments earlier, and saw a blue sedan with a sign attached to the roof. I blinked, saw that it said "Braynor Taxi."

It came to a stop behind my car, and a man I recognized got out of the back, came around to the driver, who had his window down, and handed him a couple of bills.

"Thanks," he said, then turned and took in all the activity. The ambulance and police car, all the people standing around.

"What the hell's all this?" he asked as the cab started backing up the lane. Then his eyes landed on me. "Zachary?"

I looked at him, stunned. "Hi, Dad," I said.

"That a new car?" he said, pointing at the Virtue that was still holding me up.

"Fairly," I said, just now taking my hands off the hood.

"Don't tell me," he said. "You didn't bother to rust-proof it."

"It's got lots of plastic panels," I said. "You don't have to."

"Yeah, well, we'll see." Now he'd noticed Chief Thorne. "Christ, Orville, what's all the commotion?"

"Hi, Arlen. Jesus. Have to say, it's a pleasure to see you today. Where the hell have you been?"

Dad bristled. "Uh, just in town, Orville." He sounded defensive.

"How early did you go in? We been here some time now." Orville Thorne was sounding a bit defensive himself. "Did you, were you in town overnight?"

Dad sighed with annoyance. "Orville, I have to paint you a picture, for Christ's sake? What the hell's going on here?"

The others—the ambulance attendants and the doctor for sure—were looking at Orville with some disapproval, like maybe he'd missed something he should have thought of. He must have sensed it, because he coughed nervously.

"Well, shit, Arlen, there's something here in the woods you should have a look at," he said tentatively.

As Dad glanced toward them, Orville took his arm to lead him that way, but instead, led Dad right over his foot, and Dad tripped, one of those fluky kind of things, and went down.

He yelped, and when he tried to get back up, couldn't.

"Jesus," he said. "My goddamn ankle. I think I must have twisted my goddamn ankle."

People shook their heads, rolled their eyes. "Nice one, Orville," one of the ambulance attendants said.

3

I RUSHED FORWARD, but moved aside for the older gentleman in the suit and tie, who creaked like an old door as he bent down to assist my father. Dad was on his side, his craggy face twisted in pain, raising himself up with one arm and reaching back with the other toward his foot, even though he couldn't get anywhere close to it. "Shit," Arlen Walker said. "Jesus, that hurts."

"Don't try to get up," I said.

"No chance of that," Dad said. "How ya doin', Doc?" he said to the man in the suit.

"Just take it easy, Arlen," he said. He glanced up at me. "I'm Dr. Heath. I'm your father's regular doctor."

"Hi," I said, moving farther back so Heath and the ambulance guys could do their thing. I drew back up next to Chief Thorne, who was looking uncomfortable and embarrassed.

"I'm really sorry, Arlen," he said. "It was an accident."

"Sure, Orville," Dad said, wincing. "I know. These things happen."

"I was just trying to help," the chief said. He suddenly looked very young to me, with soft white skin, a few freckles around his eyes.

The rest of the crowd was taking in the show. There was the sixtyish woman in the kerchief and hunting jacket, a guest I figured, her arm linked with a man of similar age, both of them on the short side. Her doughy face was clouded with worry, but he was a bit harder to read. Just watching. Next to him, only slightly taller, stood a man in a dark green felt baseball cap, with what looked like a basketball hidden under his unzipped windbreaker and striped pullover shirt. His clothes must have cost a bundle to make someone his shape look so good. Even in casual garb, he was the best dressed of all of us. I glanced back at the cabins, spotted a Cadillac STS parked at one of them, and knew that one had to be his.

Next to him, an old-man-of-the-sea. Tall, his face lined with deep creases, a toothpick dancing back and forth between his lips. He was dressed in olive pants and a plaid flannel shirt, and he smiled at me when our eyes met.

"Bob Spooner," he said, extending a hand. I took it. "I'm glad your dad's okay," he said.

"Me too," I said.

I turned to Chief Thorne and said quietly, "Didn't anyone call around to see if my dad might be in town? You two spoke to each other by first names, like you know each other pretty well. I had a two-hour-long heart attack driving up here, expecting the worst. You couldn't have asked around?"

Thorne's tongue poked around the inside of his cheek. He was taking his time to come up with an answer, like maybe he hadn't expected this to be on the final. After a few seconds, he said, "We're basically in the middle of our investigation here, Mr. Walker. Our first concern was finding out who this man over here is, and when we couldn't immediately locate your father, well, you can understand why we were concerned."

"You didn't answer my question," I said. "Couldn't you have made some calls?"

Thorne said, "We saw his vehicle over there, the boats were in, there was no reason to think he might be in town."

"And why would he have taken a cab back?" I asked. "Why wouldn't he have taken his truck into town?"

Thorne ignored that. A few steps away, on the ground, my dad said, "Christ on a cracker, that hurts!"

Thorne tipped his hat back a fraction of an inch and said to me, "I'm sorry if you've been inconvenienced, Mr. Walker."

"Inconvenienced?" I said. "Inconvenienced? Is that what you call dragging me into the woods to show me a corpse I had every reason to believe was my father?"

The chubby guy in the nice threads said, "Orville,

didn't you call your aunt, see if she might know where Arlen was?"

Thorne coughed again. I said, "Your aunt? Why would your aunt know where my father was?"

I suppose it didn't make a lot of sense for me to be as angry as I was. I mean, I'd just learned that my father was alive. I should have been relieved, perhaps even joyous. Leaping about, even. But instead I felt enraged at being made to look at that body hidden under the tarp, to have been led to believe by this incompetent rube, for however briefly, that it was my father, looking like he'd been fed through a meat grinder. Maybe, too, I was reeling from the shock of it all. Losing a parent and getting him back all within a matter of minutes. How often did that happen?

Whatever it was, I was losing my cool.

"Mr. Walker," Chief Thorne said, trying to put some authority in his voice and placing a hand on my arm, "I think maybe you need to calm down and—"

"Get your hand off me," I said, shaking it loose and—I honestly don't know how the hell this happened—shoving Thorne away from me at the same time as he actually grabbed on to my arm, and his foot caught on a small rock, and then he was going down and taking me with him. The guy was a one-man tripping industry.

I was just going along for the ride at this point, but from Thorne's point of view, I was attacking him, so he scrambled wildly to get out from under me, scurrying sideways like a crab, looking wild-eyed, his hat gone, and then, suddenly, there was a gun in his hand and he was shouting at me, his voice squeaking a bit, "Freeze!"

Well, I froze. Except for the parts of me that were shaking. I may not have actually appeared to be quivering, but I sure felt that way inside.

Thorne's gun was visibly shaking. He put a second hand on the gun to help steady it, both arms outstretched, and there was something very Barney Fife about him at that moment. Not as thin and spindly, but equally erratic. He might not intend to shoot me but end up doing it anyway.

"You just hold it right there!" he shouted, glancing at me and then over to his hat and then back to me.

"Don't worry," I said, a bit winded from the fall. I shook my head back and forth slowly, raised both my palms to suggest a truce.

"Christ, Orville, put that fucking gun away!" my father shouted from the ground. "That's my goddamn son, for crying out loud!"

"He started it!" Orville Thorne whined.

Even with a twisted ankle, my father had the energy to roll his eyes. "Orville, for God's sakes, put that thing away before you hurt yourself."

Thorne got to his feet, lowered the gun slowly and slipped it back into his holster, brushed himself off. I went over and got his hat and handed it to him.

"Sorry," I said.

Thorne snatched the hat away and put it back on, shielding his eyes, unwilling to look at me after being scolded by my father.

"Yeah, well," he said.

"It's just, I thought my dad was dead. And then he

drove in. I guess I went a bit crazy, having just seen that body and all."

"Sure," he said.

I stuck out a hand. Without being able to see Thorne's eyes, I wasn't sure he saw it, so I took a step closer.

"Go on, Orville," said Arlen Walker. "Shake his hand."

He took my hand, half shook it, then withdrew. We both had reason to be embarrassed, I guess, but Thorne looked particularly red-faced.

"Okay," said my father. "Now that that's settled, could someone tell me what the hell is going on around here?"

Bob Spooner spoke up. "Arlen, there's a body in the woods. A man's body."

"Jesus," Dad said. "Who is it?"

"We don't know," Orville Thorne said. "It's no one from here. Now that we've found you, everyone from the camp here's been accounted for."

"For a while," I said, "everyone thought that it might be you."

"I wasn't here," Dad said matter-of-factly. "I got a ride into town last night. I'd had a bit of wine with dinner so I didn't want to drive." That would be Dad. As long as I'd known him, if he had so much as a drop of wine, he wouldn't get behind the wheel.

"I don't understand," I said. "Where were you going? Who gave you a lift into town?"

He was up on one foot now, an ambulance attendant on either side of him, about to lead him in the direction of the ambulance. He winced instead of answering.

"I bet I can guess," said Bob, a sly grin crossing his face.

"Bob." My dad glared at the man, said his name like a warning.

Bob seemed unafraid. "I'm just saying."

I noticed that the older woman and her husband had slipped back into the woods. I could just make them out, standing by the tarp. Then I noticed him holding up the tarp at one end so that his wife—I guessed she was his wife—could take a closer look.

Ghouls, I thought.

"Hey, Doc," Dad said to Dr. Heath as the paramedics moved him closer to the ambulance, "couldn't I just go lie down and put an ice pack on it?"

"Arlen, just come in to Emerg. We'll get an X-ray, make sure nothing's broken, confirm that it's just a sprain." There was a small hospital in Braynor, I remembered.

"But I gotta run this place," Dad protested. "I've got boats to get ready, firewood to cut. Place like this doesn't run itself, you know."

"You're not gonna be putting any weight on that ankle for a few days," Dr. Heath said. "Longer, if it's broke."

Dad closed his eyes and grimaced. "That's great," he said. "That's just great."

The words were coming out of my mouth before I realized it. "Don't worry, Dad. I'll look after things. Until you're better. I can get a few days off."

His eyes settled on me, weighing this offer. "It's a

lot of work," he said. "It's not sitting around on your ass in front of a computer all day."

Well. He likes my offer so much, he's going to butter me up to make sure I don't withdraw it.

I ignored the comment and instead returned his stare, waiting for an answer. He drew in air quickly, like the ankle was flaring with pain, and looked away.

"Fine, okay," he said.

"And I'll come to the hospital with you."

"No, no, no, stay here. I'll just be sitting around for hours down there. You look after things here, I'll give you a call when I'm done, you can pick me up."

I nodded my assent as they put Dad in the back of the ambulance. They said that once they had Dad admitted they'd come back for the body, which they'd now been cleared to remove, the coroner having had a chance to give it the once-over. The light on top was flashing, but the siren was off. We all watched as it went up the hill and went round the bend in the driveway.

"Well," I said, standing next to my new friend Chief Thorne. "I guess that just leaves one thing."

"What's that?" said the chief.

I pointed back into the woods at the body. "Who the hell is that?"

4

AS IF TO ANSWER THAT QUESTION, we all decided, like some collective alien intelligence, to return to the woods for another look. The one Denny's Cabins guest who'd introduced himself, Bob Spooner, Tracy the reporter, the seemingly inept Chief Orville Thorne, Dr. Heath, who'd chosen to stay here rather than accompany Dad to the Braynor hospital, and the portly but well-dressed guy with the Caddy.

The older couple were still in the woods, standing by the once-again-covered corpse, watching us approach. We were walking all over the place, matting down grass under our feet, making a mess of what might, under other circumstances, be considered a crime scene, but Thorne didn't seem all that concerned. How much evidence did you really need to convict a bear, if it was, in fact, a bear that had done this, and not a band of rabid chipmunks?

I felt more up to it this time, since I now knew that the dead man under the tarp was not my father. Thorne gingerly took hold of the corner of the tarp and pulled it back, much farther than before, revealing all of the body this time, instead of from head to waist.

The woman in the kerchief glanced down again, not as repulsed as I would have expected, as if she was not unaccustomed to death.

"Tell them," I heard her husband whisper to her.

"Not my place," she whispered back, turning away. If anyone else heard their brief conversation, they gave no indication.

"I'm going back to the cabin," she said, loud enough now that anyone could hear.

"I'll go with you, lovey," the man said, and they slipped away quietly.

A second look didn't offer much more in the way of information. The man—as torn to shreds as the body was, its size and form did seem to indicate it was a male—looked about six feet tall. Much of his face was chewed away, as well as his neck, and his torso had been chewed at by something with considerable enthusiasm. Only his legs, below the knees, seemed largely untouched. The corpse wore a pair of black lace-up boots and camouflage-pattern pants. That didn't necessarily make this some military guy, considering that kids were buying camo-style pants off the rack these days.

"I don't know, Orville," said Bob Spooner. "There's not much there to look at, is there?"

Thorne said, "You come up here a lot, Bob. Doesn't look like anyone you've ever seen?"

"Don't think so."

"And it's nobody from here, we're sure about that?"

Bob nodded. "I'm in two, cabin three's unrented right now, the Wrigleys," and he nodded his head in the direction of the couple who'd walked away, "are in four, this gentleman here," and he pointed to the well-dressed heavy guy, "you're in five, right?"

"Yes," he said, agreeably. "I'm up here alone," he said to Thorne. "Fishing, and checking out some property for a project I have planned. I've got my eye on thirty acres just up the shore a bit, planning to put in a big resort for sport fishermen that will—"

"Yeah, whatever," Thorne said, holding up his hand as if he were halting a car in traffic. "So, that's everyone."

"Yup," said Bob. "I've been up here for three weeks now, gotten to know everyone who's up."

"And no one was expecting any visitors?"

Everyone muttered no under their breath. "Well, that's a puzzler," said the chief.

"What about up there?" I said, pointing up the road, where the farmhouse, hidden by trees from where we stood, sat beyond the gate with all the warning signs.

"I don't think it would be anyone from up there," said Thorne.

I thought, *Huh?* But I said, "How can you know that? Twenty minutes ago, we thought this was my father."

"I'm just saying, I don't think it's anyone from up there," said Thorne. "Doesn't look like it to me."

This was a baffler. A cop who didn't want to make

every effort, consider every possibility to learn the identity of a guy who'd been mauled to death? I kept pressing. "At least you should go up there and talk to whoever lives there."

"Orville," Bob said softly, "you're going to at least have to ask them a few questions."

"What's the deal?" I asked. "I don't understand. Why can't you go up there and talk to them?"

Bob smiled sympathetically. "Last time Orville talked to those folks, they hid his hat on him."

"They did not!" Chief Thorne said, putting his hand up to the top of his hat and shoving it down more firmly onto his head. "We were just horsing around, that's all, no harm done."

"Orville, no one blames you. They're a weird crew. Listen, I find them kind of intimidating, too. We can go up there with you. They won't take your hat if there's a bunch of us there." Bob tried to say this without a hint of condescension, but it still came off as a bit patronizing.

Even so, Thorne was mulling it over. It was clear that he didn't want to go up there alone.

"Okay, Bob," he said. "Why don't you come along, too."

"I want to come," I said.

"I don't think that's really necessary, Mr. Walker," Thorne said, glancing at me, and there was something in his eyes then, just for a second, that looked familiar to me. It was the second time since I'd arrived that I felt I knew him from someplace.

I wanted to ask him if, by some chance, we'd met before, maybe when I'd been up to see Dad here before, but instead said, "This body's on my father's property, and in his absence, I think it's appropriate for me to know what's going on."

This was, of course, bullshit. Thorne was the law, and he could take, and leave behind, anyone he damn well pleased. But, evidently, he wasn't aware of that.

"Okay, fine then," he said. The three of us started walking up the lane. No one spoke for a while, until Thorne said to me, in a tone that bordered on the accusatory. "So, you're from the city."

"Yeah," I said.

Thorne made a snorting noise, as if that explained everything. Bob Spooner gently laid a hand on my back, then took it away. "Your father's told me a lot about you," he said.

"Really?" I said.

"Says you've written some books, whaddya call it, that science fiction stuff. Spacemen, that kind of thing."

"Some," I said. "But not so much these days; I'm a feature writer for *The Metropolitan*."

Bob nodded. "Yeah, he told me that, too. Good paper. Don't see it all the time, but when I do, there's lots to read in there."

We were coming round the bend now, approaching the gate decorated with its numerous warnings for trespassers.

"I guess they don't like visitors," I said.

"They don't like much of anything," Thorne said.

The three of us stood at the gate, Bob resting his arms atop it. About fifty yards away stood the two-story farmhouse, and it didn't look much the way I'd remembered it from when my father first purchased the property. Back then, the shutters hung straight, there wasn't litter scattered about the front porch, there weren't half a dozen old cars in various states of disrepair, the lawn out front of the house was cut, the garden maintained. Now, none of that was the case. There was an old white van up near the barn, a couple of run-down pickups and a rusting compact out front of the house. There was an abandoned refrigerator shoved up against one side of the building, a rusted metal spring bed leaned up against it, a collection of hubcaps hanging on nails that had been driven into the wall, half a dozen five-gallon red metal gas cans scattered about.

"Has my dad seen all this?" I asked of either Thorne or Bob. "The place is a dump."

"It is a bit of a concern to him," Bob said. "And by 'a bit' I mean huge. But he doesn't exactly know what to do about it."

"How many live here?" I asked.

Thorne said, "It depends on the day, I think. But right now, I think there's the old man, well, he's not that old, but he runs the family. Timmy Wickens."

"Timmy?" I said.

"And Timmy's wife, Charlene, and they've got a couple of boys, early twenties. Arlen tells me they're her boys, from some other marriage. I think their last name is Dunbar. And there's a daughter, Timmy's actual daughter, she must be about thirty, thirty-two or so. Her name's May. She's got a boy of her own, he must be about ten, he lives here, too. I think she's got a boyfriend, lives here with the bunch of them, but I'm not sure. And they all got their like-minded friends, dropping in now and then."

"What do you mean, like-minded?" I asked.

Thorne shrugged. "They just don't like mixing with everybody else. I mean, look at the signs." He pointed to the ones we were leaning up against. "They think the world's out to get 'em, I guess. And they're not what you'd call fans of the government, large or small. They've had a few run-ins with other locals over things. Pissed so many people off the last place they moved that they had to come here. Sometimes, it's just easier to leave them alone out here than have to deal with them."

"Why would my father have rented to them if they're a bunch of whackos?"

Bob said, "I don't think he had any idea. Timmy came to see him when he saw the house was up for rent, all cleaned up, looking respectable. Wasn't till afterwards that your dad saw what he'd got him-self into."

"Oh man," I said, still surveying the landscape. I spotted an old washing machine beyond the fridge. "So, are we going in?"

"Why don't we just try calling them," Thorne said. He straightened up, cupped his hands around his mouth, and shouted, "Hello!" He waited a few seconds, then again, at the top of his voice: "Hello? Mr. Wickens? Hello?"

The house remained quiet.

"Can't you just go up to the door?" I suggested to Thorne.

He pointed to the "Beware of Dogs" sign. "Can you read?"

"I don't see any dogs," I said. "And I know you've got a gun. Can't you defend yourself against some puppies?"

Thorne said, "Let me try calling again." He took a breath. "Hello!"

Still no sign of action at the house. No one at a window peeking out. Nothing.

"If you're not going to go, I guess I will," I said. I had my foot on the bottom board of the gate, the other foot on the board above it, then a leg over the top in a couple of seconds. "I'll go knock on the door," I said. I was feeling a bit wired still. The discovery of the body, the drive up, the mistaken identity, it all had me a bit rattled, and I was eager to get some answers. Also, there was a part of me that was enjoying showing up Chief Thorne in a way I found hard to explain.

"Mr. Walker, I think you're making a mistake," Thorne said. But I had both legs over now, and had hopped down to the other side.

I had taken maybe a dozen steps in the direction of the house when, up by the barn, I saw two brownish-gray blurry things heading toward me. Blurry, because they were moving so quickly. They were low to the ground, galloping, coming at me like a couple of torpedoes, and as they closed the gap between us, I could hear their rapid, shallow breathing and deep-throated growling.

The sign was right. These were dogs.

"Yikes," I said, stopping for maybe a hundredth of

a second, then turning back and bolting for the gate. Never did such a few steps feel like such a great distance.

"Hurry!" Bob shouted. "Don't look back!"

I leapt at the gate, had my arms over the top, my legs looking for a purchase. My chest was over the top as the two dogs threw themselves at the gate, a combined frenzy of snarling and barking. I looked down, only for a second, saw one brown beast, one black, a bristly ridge of fur raised along each of their spines.

My leg jerked back as one of the dogs grabbed my pant leg, down by the cuff. The dog must have been in midair as he bit into it, and his own weight dragged my leg back down. I kicked wildly, heard the sound of fabric tearing, and now Bob and Thorne had grabbed hold of my upper body and were pulling me to safety. I fell into their arms, didn't even try to find my footing on the other side of the gate, then fell out of them and onto the gravel.

The dogs were going nuts on the other side, barking, biting at the wood, slobber flying in all directions as they tried to eat their way through the gate to get at me.

They weren't even particularly huge dogs—they wouldn't have come up much past my knee if I'd been standing next to them, which I had no intention of doing. But their boxy heads and ragged teeth seemed disproportionately large compared to the rest of their sinewy bodies. Their ears were short, their eyes large and menacing.

They were jaws on legs.

Thorne offered a hand to help me up, then pointed to the relevant sign again. "I told you not to go over," he said smugly.

The dogs had accomplished what Thorne's shouts had not. The front door of the house was open now, and there was a man approaching, followed by another, younger one, stocky with black hair, and then a young woman. She had dirty blonde hair, and the down-filled hunter's vest she wore over a plain blouse and jeans failed to hide her nice figure.

The man in the lead, late fifties I figured, was about six foot, broad shouldered, nearly bald with a glistening scalp, thick through the middle, 230 pounds, easy. He had the look of a football hero gone to seed. Not quite in the same shape he was thirty years ago, but still capable of doing a bit of damage. He trotted down in black military-style boots, and while not in camo pants like our dead friend in the woods, his pants and jacket were olive green.

"Wickens," Thorne said quietly.

"Gristle!" he shouted. "Bone! Halt!"

The dogs kept barking, oblivious. As Timmy Wickens got closer, he shouted the names again, and the dogs, hearing him this time, stopped their yapping and looked behind to see where the voice was coming from. At the sight of their master, they became docile and stood, patiently, awaiting instructions.

"Barn!" Wickens said, pointing back to the structure, and the dogs immediately took off, charging back to where they'd come from. "Dougie," Wickens said, speaking to the young dark-haired man who'd come loping along behind him, "make sure they stay in there. Did you not close that door like I told you?"

Dougie looked down. His arms hung heavy and straight at his sides. "It might have slipped my mind. I was doing some other stuff."

Wickens sighed. "Go do it now," he said, and Dougie turned and walked off as obediently as Gristle and Bone.

That dealt with, Wickens approached the gate with a relaxed swagger, like having the law and a couple of other men waiting to see him was no big thing. His eyes narrowed as he looked at the three of us, settling finally on Thorne.

"Chief," he said, a somewhat bemused expression crossing his face. "What can I do for you today?"

"Mr. Wickens," Thorne said, nodding, removing his hat and tucking it firmly under his arm. Any other time, I might have interpreted that as a gesture of respect, but odds were he just wanted to hang on to it. "How are you today?"

"I was pretty good up to a moment ago when you got my dogs all riled. Who's this man was about to trespass on my property?"

I let Thorne do the talking. "This here's Zack Walker, Timmy. He's Arlen's son. Arlen twisted his ankle, has been taken to the hospital, and Zack here is trying to help out. And you may know Bob here, he's renting one of Arlen's cabins."

The woman—I guessed she was the daughter, May—inched forward, holding back a step or two behind her father.

"Is this about Morton?" she asked. "Has someone found Morton?"

Timmy Wickens turned and said, "Just hold on, May, and let me see what this is all about."

"Is someone missing?" Thorne asked. "Who's Morton?"

"My daughter's boyfriend," Wickens said, not yet appearing concerned about anything but my going onto his property, which, when you thought about it, it really wasn't. This was all land rented from my father. "Morton Dewart. He's been gone awhile, doing a bit of hunting."

"What's he hunting for?" Thorne asked.

Wickens ran a hand over his bald head, paused a moment as if to collect his thoughts, and said, "Well, there's been a bear out there he's been looking for. It's been nosing around the house, Morton's been saying he wants to teach it a lesson, make sure it don't come around here no more. My daughter, she's got a young son, Morton wants to make sure it's safe for him to play outside. So he grabbed his shotgun and said he was gonna go looking for it."

"You've seen this bear?"

Wickens nodded slowly. "Big bastard." Another pause. "Has one ear missing, left one I think, like it got cut off, or he lost it in a fight with another bear, which is more likely."

Bob raised an eyebrow, imagining a bear fight, maybe.

"What's going on?" May asked. Her voice was filled with worry. "Why are you here? Has something happened to Morton? He's been gone a long time."

Thorne swallowed hard, put the hat back on his head. He must have been confident that no one would hide his hat when there were life-and-death matters to be discussed.

"Mr. Wickens," Thorne said, "there's been a bit of an incident, just down over the hill a ways, by Arlen's cabins."

"This to do with Arlen's ankle?" Wickens asked.

"Uh, no, not exactly. But I wonder if you'd mind coming to have a look with me at what we found." Tentatively, he added, "You might want to leave your daughter here."

May stepped forward. "No, I'm going, too."

"Ma'am," said the chief, "I don't know that that's such a good idea."

"I'm going," she said again, her teeth clenched in determination.

Timmy Wickens produced a set of keys and undid the padlock on the gate. He swung it open a couple of feet, enough to let himself and his daughter out, then closed it, hanging the padlock in place without driving it home.

We walked back, the five of us, no one saying anything. Thorne led the way back into the woods, and when the tarp became visible, May put her a hand to her mouth.

"It's a man, that much we're certain of," said Thorne. "But he's a bit hard to identify. I wonder, this Morton fella, did he have any what you might call distinguishing marks?"

May was staring straight ahead, slowly shaking her head from side to side, as if she could deny what was about to unfold. Wickens said to her, gently, "Miss, uh, May, does Morton have some kind of mark, maybe a tattoo, anything like that?"

I was thinking, if he had a tattoo, it had probably been eaten off him, if this was Morton Dewart.

"He's, he's got a dagger tattoo on his, his . . ." She was thinking now. "His left chest, on the left side, his left."

Thorne breathed in through his nostrils. Clearly, that was not going to be adequate. "He got any markings or tattoos anyplace else?"

"Uh, um," said May, tears already starting to form. "His ankle, like, a little ways up, a snake. I think, his right leg."

Thorne nodded. This was a possibility. I sidled up next to him, alongside Dr. Heath, who'd been waiting around for our return. He lifted the tarp from the other end, revealing the dead man's boots. Gingerly, he rolled down the thick, gray, bloody work sock, and there it was. A snake, shaped like an S, about two inches long.

Wickens and his daughter couldn't see the leg from where they were standing, but when Thorne looked over at them, I guess it showed in his face, and he said, "I'm sorry."

May threw her arms around her father, and began to wail.

5

IN THE FOLLOWING COUPLE OF HOURS before Dad phoned for me to come and pick him up at the hospital, I accomplished a fair bit.

First, I went into his cabin, the first in the line of five nearly identical buildings along the shore, and bear-proofed it. No way Yogi was coming in to get me for dinner. The cabin consisted of one large room that was a combined kitchen, living, and dining room; two bedrooms, one of which Dad used as an office; and a bathroom. I went to each window in every room, made sure they were all properly latched. Lakeside, there was a screened-in porch with a door, then a second door into the cabin itself. I figured screens didn't offer much protection against a bear, so I didn't worry too much about that door, but the one from the porch to the cabin I made sure was locked, as well as the door that came in from the back. I didn't know whether bears had the smarts to turn doorknobs, but no way they had keys.

I rummaged around in the kitchen cupboards

until I'd found a kettle and some teabags, and made myself some tea. I was feeling a bit chilled, which I attributed as much to the whole experience as the weather. In the living room area, where an old couch and a couple of worn easy chairs were positioned around a television, there was a woodstove, a pipe running straight up from it and through the ceiling. Dad had outfitted this cabin with a furnace for year-round living, but the stove was a nice touch. I crumpled up some newspaper in the bottom, laid on some kindling followed by logs that Dad kept in a neat pile next to the stove, and got a fire going.

The cabin screamed Dad. Wood piled neatly, out of the way where you couldn't trip on it. A fire extinguisher hanging on the wall by the back door. No knives pointing up in the cutlery basket of the dishwasher. A textured floor in the base of the tub so as to prevent slipping.

Once I had my hot mug of tea, I took it with me into Dad's office. There was a computer on the nearly empty desk. Dad, being something of a neat freak in addition to a safety freak, kept the desk uncluttered. Shelves that lined one wall of the room contained, among other things, neatly labeled file boxes. I jiggled the mouse and the computer screen came to life, the on-screen desktop as tidy as his real one. I clicked on the round blue "E" at the bottom and opened up the Internet.

I entered "bear attack human" into the Google box and was reading my third article when the phone rang.

I grabbed the receiver. "Hello?"

"Zack?"

"Sarah, hi," I said.

"I've been trying your cell, but you haven't been answering." She was worried, and pissed.

"I guess you can't get much of a signal up here," I said. "Sorry. I was just about to call you." I was, honestly, about to do just that.

"What's going on? Is your father, is he . . ."

"He's alive," I said. "He's okay. Well, he's got a twisted ankle, but that had nothing to do with a bear."

"Then who—"

"A neighbor. Or a friend of a neighbor. Went out looking for a bear, guess the bear found him first. Who was that writer? Said, sometimes you get the bear, sometimes the bear gets you?"

I gave Sarah more details, how Dad had hurt his ankle, the confusion, the confidence-inspiring Chief Orville Thorne.

"So, does this mean you're coming straight back?" Sarah asked.

"Here's the thing," I said. "I sort of offered to stay a few days, help my dad until he's back on his feet again."

"Oh," Sarah said, clearly some hesitation in her voice. "Is that such a good idea? I mean, isn't there a bear wandering around there?"

"Yeah, well, I'm going to be careful. I've already been on the net, reading up on bear attacks, and when I go into town, to get Dad, I'm going to get some bear spray."

"Bear spray?"

"They've got this stuff, I just found it on the net, it's like pepper spray, you shoot some in the bear's face, he leaves you alone."

"Really."

"The main thing, they say, is don't run."

"Don't run," Sarah said. "So a bear's coming at you, you're supposed to just stand there. What are you supposed to do, tell him you're a close personal friend of Smokey?"

"Throw something at him," I said. "Scare him off."

"Uh-huh."

"Or punch him. Right in the nose."

Sarah was quiet for a moment. Then, "You. Punch a bear in the nose. I can see that."

"The fact is, bear attacks on humans are very rare," I said, quoting from an article on the screen. "Bears don't naturally want to attack humans, will even try to avoid them most of the time. Unless, you know, they're hungry or something."

"Isn't there someone else up there who could help your father?" Sarah said, changing gears.

"Maybe," I said. "But at least for a couple of days, I think I should hang in. You think you can swing them into letting me have a few days off?"

"Yeah, I imagine. What are you working on, anyway?"

Although Sarah was often my editor when I was doing a story for cityside, I also reported to editors for other sections that ran features. Such was the life of a reporter at *The Metropolitan*, that you served several masters all at once who wanted different things and conspired against one another in their bid to get them. In just a year I'd seen several reporters gunned down in editorial crossfires.

"A feature on people never going out anymore, they've got home theater systems, Jacuzzis, all that shit, the whole cocooning thing."

"Wow, great idea," Sarah said. "I don't think we've done that in, I don't know, two months, at least. We've done that story twice a year for the last ten years."

"It's for Weekend," I said. "I think they just heard about it."

"I'm going to talk to Magnuson about this," Sarah said, invoking the name of our much-feared—at least by me—managing editor. "This is stupid."

"So you're saying don't worry about it."

"That's exactly what I'm saying. Just promise me you'll be careful."

"Have you forgotten who you're talking to?" I said.

I sensed Sarah smiling at the other end. "I know," she said tiredly. "But you have had lapses."

Not more than a minute after I hung up, the phone rang again. "I'm finally done," Dad said. "Can you come get me?"

"Sure."

"Are you planning to pick me up in that little car of yours, or are you going to bring my truck?"

I did a brain-sigh. "It's a safe car, Dad. It's also good for the environment. It's a hybrid."

"Oh jeez, say no more. Why don't you come in the truck. Extra set of keys in the drawer. I'll have more room to stretch out my leg, which hurts like the bejeezus."

"Twenty minutes," I said. "But we have to pick up some things on the way back."

"Like what?" Dad asked.

"I'll tell you later," I said, and hung up.

Dad's truck was like his cabin: immaculate. Except for a few dead leaves on the driver's floor mat, it was spotless inside, and the gas gauge was only a needle's width from full. Dad had never let the tank on any vehicle he'd ever owned go below the halfway point, and any time I'd ever borrowed his car as a teenager, I made sure to never leave it with anything less than three-quarters of a tank of gas. "It's simple preparedness," he'd say. You get an overnight oil crisis, and you're all set.

Braynor District Hospital wasn't hard to find. It sat on a hill on the road going out of Braynor to the north, and driving into town from the south you could see the blue "H" atop the building in the distance. I swung through the entrance to Emergency and saw Dad waiting for me behind the glass doors, sitting in a wheelchair with a pair of crutches in front of him, propped on his shoulders.

I left the truck running, exhaust spewing out the tailpipe, and as the electric doors parted, Dad said, "What are you doing, leaving the truck running?"

"Dad, I'm right here, I can see the tr—"

"Someone could just run up and make off with it," he said.

"For Christ's sake, Dad, we're like, twenty feet away from it," as I reached over to take the crutches. "Can you just crank it down for a second?" I went back to the truck, slipped the crutches in the short cargo area behind the seats, then returned to my father.

"We taking the wheelchair?" I asked.

"No, just wheel me to the truck, and then you leave it here."

I nodded, pushed the chair close to the truck, opened the passenger door, then wheeled the chair a bit closer. Dad reached out, grabbed the truck's inside door handle, and started hauling himself out of the chair, resisting my attempts to assist him. "I've got it," he said, putting his weight on one foot only. The other was clad in just a thick sock, which was pulled up over whatever bandaging they'd wrapped around his ankle.

Once he was in the truck and seatbelted in, I closed the door and returned the wheelchair to the lobby. Then I was back in the truck.

"Where's a good sporting goods store?" I said, putting the truck into gear.

"What?" asked Dad. "You're not going to help me? You're just up here to do a little fishing?"

Just hold it together, I told myself. "Bear spray," I said. "It's like pepper spray. It was a friend of your neighbors became dinner for a bear in your woods. So I figure, unless you want to be his breakfast tomorrow, maybe we should get ourselves a can or two."

My father considered that a moment. "That's a good idea," he said, apparently surprised that I could come up with one. "You can't be too safe, you know."

"My thoughts exactly," I said.

6

WE DISCUSSED BUYING FIVE CANS of bear pepper spray—
one for each of the cabins—but when I ran into the
sporting goods store and found they were about fifty
bucks each, I knew Dad would be relieved to find
that they only had a couple cans of the stuff left.
There was dust on the tops, indicating that the prod-
uct was not exactly flying off the shelf.

I popped into a men's shop on the main street for
some extra underwear and socks, since I'd left the
city without packing. When I got back into the
pickup, Dad said he was thinking about inviting
everyone from the other cabins to his place for dinner and beer.

"Everyone's probably kind of shook up, with what
happened and all," Dad said. "That poor son of a
bitch, getting eaten by a goddamn bear. And I don't
want everyone bailing on me either, leaving me with
a bunch of empty cabins. Cabin three's already
empty. You can help yourself to that one."

"Thanks," I said.

Dad pointed up the street to Henry's Grocery, said I could get everything I needed there while he sat in the truck and nursed his ankle. "You know how to buy groceries?" he asked. "Or is that something Sarah does?"

"Sometimes she takes me with her, puts me in the little seat so I can pick up some tips," I said.

Dad said that if Bob did well out on the lake today, he'd bring some fish that could be fried up. But Dad also wanted frozen hamburger patties, buns, stuff for making salad, chips, plenty of beer. He was very specific. "Not those buns with the sesame seeds on top. They get caught in my teeth. I hate that. And get the frozen sirloin burgers, not the mystery meat stuff."

"Okay, Dad."

"And none of that light beer. Nobody wants to drink that pony piss."

"Got it, Dad."

"Did I mention about the sesame seeds?"

"Yes, Dad."

"I don't want you to make a mistake, that's all."

"Hey, what about the Wickenses?" I asked. "You inviting them to this shindig? They really took the hit on this one. It was the daughter's boyfriend the bear decided to have for lunch."

Dad looked straight ahead through the windshield. "I think the best thing would be to let them deal with their grief in private."

"What's the deal with them anyway?" I asked. "The Keep Out signs and the gate and the barbed wire. Isn't that your property they're on?"

Dad swallowed, kept looking out the window. I noticed him clenching his right fist. "That's none of your concern, Zachary."

"All I'm saying is, who *are* these people? The property looks like it's going to ratshit. Old cars, a fridge outside, and Jesus, have you seen those pit bulls? They nearly took a leg off me when the chief and Bob and I went up there to talk to them. Who keeps fucking dogs like that? Nutcases, that's who. Have you seen the teeth on those things? I'd rather go swimming with sharks than knock on their front door if—"

"Zachary!" Dad bellowed. "Enough!"

"Dad, look, they're on your property. They're renting your farmhouse. If you've got some problem with them, you should do something about it."

He turned and glared at me. "Did I say I had a problem with them? Have I complained to you about them? Have I said one damn thing to you about them?"

I slammed the truck door and headed up the street for Henry's Grocery. I noticed along the way, taped to the light standards, flyers for the fall fair, which kicked off with a parade four days from now, on Saturday. And some other posters, taped just above or below the ones for the fall fair, headlined "Keep the Parade Straight!"

I didn't know what that meant, exactly. Perhaps, other years, it had taken a roundabout, serpentine route through Braynor that had somehow made the fall fair parade a less than spectacular entertainment.

I didn't bother to read the rest of the poster to find out. I was on a mission.

Once inside Henry's, I grabbed a cart with two front wheels so badly aligned and balanced I wondered briefly whether Braynor was built on a fault line. Working without a list, I made my way through the store, picking up a head of romaine, some croutons, a bag of hamburger buns without sesame seeds, God forbid.

I was coming around the end of the aisle when I nearly ran the cart into a thin, white-coated man who at first I thought had escaped from some laboratory, but the absence of a pocket full of pens and the presence of blood splotches identified him as someone who had recently been behind the meat counter. Then I noticed the name "Charles" stitched to his jacket, and the clipboard in his hand.

He peered at me over his wire glasses.

"Hello," he said.

I nodded.

"Charles Henry," he said, offering a hand. I didn't have a chance to check it for blood before I took it. "Manager, Henry's Grocery. I don't believe I know you."

I thought, why would he? But then, in a small town, I guess if you're the local grocer you get to know all the local faces.

"No," I said. "I'm just staying at my father's place."

Henry's face was screwed up like he was detecting a bad smell, but since I couldn't smell anything, I figured that was his normal expression. "That doesn't mean you can't sign the petition," he said. "It's open to anyone."

"I'm sorry?" I said.

He shoved the clipboard at me. "To keep the parade family-friendly," he said. "Just sign down there. We're getting a lot of names, but we need more if we're going to be able to get the mayor to back down."

I smiled politely and waved my hands in front of me. "I don't really know much about all that, but thanks, and good luck, okay?"

As I tried to wheel the cart around him he said, "Don't you believe in decency?"

I honestly thought it was a bit overrated, but had a hunch this was the wrong time to say so. "Listen, really, good luck, but I'm really a bit pressed here," I said, and got the cart around him, feeling his glare all the way down the aisle.

When I returned to the pickup with the groceries, I knew Dad wanted to look in the bags, see whether I got the order right, so I put them right behind my seat where he couldn't reach them. I saw him glance back there a couple of times, the anxiety plainly visible on his face, but with his ankle so sore, he couldn't shift around very far.

"Met Mr. Henry," I said, turning the key and pulling the transmission down into drive.

"Oh," said Dad, still pissed over our earlier argument.

"His face always look like that?"

Dad didn't respond, and we didn't talk the rest of the way back.

A small crowd gathered when we came down the hill and to a stop behind Dad's cabin. At a glance, it looked like most everyone I'd seen earlier. The older couple, the well-dressed heavyset guy, and Bob Spooner.

They gathered around Dad's side, opened the door for him, helped him out. Spooner saw the crutches behind the seats, grabbed them, assisted Dad in getting them under his arms. "Come on, Arlen, let's get you inside."

I got out the driver's door, not rushing. Everyone else wanted to help. They seemed to have a genuine affection for Dad, particularly Bob and the older couple. This, I was learning, was not your typical fishing camp where the guests were strangers. This was some kind of family.

I brought in the groceries and my new clothes and the bear repellent, glancing over my shoulder into the woods as I approached the cabin. It was dusk, and the trees were losing their distinctness and blending together into a single shadow against the darkening sky. I stopped a moment and listened, hearing nothing but a light breeze blowing through the pines. Now, with daylight fading, it was hard to tell where, exactly, the body had been. It was long gone now, taken away shortly after May Wickens fell into her father's arms, and the entire incident, in many ways, seemed part of the distant past. Almost as if it had never happened.

Dad was inviting everyone to come back in an hour. Bob Spooner said he did, indeed, have a stringerful of pickerel hanging off the dock that he could clean up before then, and the others were making offers of what they could bring. Before they could head back to their respective cabins and get ready, Dad wanted to introduce me formally to everyone, even if I'd already made their acquaintance.

"Bob I know," I said, shaking his hand again. Then Dad introduced me to Hank and Betty Wrigley, the older couple, who came from Pennsylvania every fall to rent cabin 4 for three weeks, and finally, the plump guy decked out in Eddie Bauer, who pressed his sweaty palm into mine and shook it for at least three seconds longer than he should have. Everything about him screamed "sales."

"I'm Leonard Colebert, and I'm in diapers!" He beamed.

The others either shook their heads or rolled their eyes, or both. I guessed that they'd heard this one before.

"No kidding?" I said.

"That's right. I own Colebert Enterprises, makers of diapers for infants, toddlers, bedwetters, adults, you name it. If you can't hold it, we will." He laughed.

I found myself discreetly wiping the sweat from his hand on the backside of my jeans. I wondered if I was starting to develop a phobia about handshaking.

"Well," I said. "You been coming here long?"

He shook his head. "Only a couple years. Not as long as Hank and Betty here, certainly not as long as Bob. Bob, how long you been coming up here?"

"Thirty, thirty-two years," Bob said evenly. "Right back to when Denny himself had it. Didn't have running water or toilets in the cabins back then, but then Denny sold the place around 1980, and Lyall Langdon bought it, did a bit of upgrading, and he was the one sold the place to your dad. But they've always hung on to the name Denny's Cabins. Everyone knows it by that, and it's a name with a certain recognition factor."

"And you?" Leonard said to Hank and Betty Wrigley.

Betty, quietly, said, "Well, I guess nearly twenty years. We used to come up for a week every summer, but once Hank and I were both retired, we made it three weeks."

"What sort of work did you retire from?" I asked, already weary of Leonard leading the conversation.

Betty said, "I was a nurse, and Hank here was in construction."

Hank nodded. "I had my own crew. We built houses, mostly."

"Me," said Leonard, "I don't think I'll ever retire. I just love it too much. Love it love it love it. But I like to get away from it all, too, you know. I could afford to stay anywhere, but I like it here."

Dad shot Leonard a look that said "Asshole."

Bob Spooner said to Dad, "You want to give Orville, and, you know, a call, see if they want to come out."

Dad waved a hand dismissively. "We'll see." He changed the subject. "Hey, we picked up some cans of anti-bear spray. Anybody wants to borrow a can, let me know."

Bob smiled. "I keep my Smith and Wesson in my tackle box. Maybe I'm gonna have to start carrying it with me everywhere I go."

Terrific, I thought. We could all get guns and wander around the place packing heat.

Everyone agreed to meet back at Dad's place within the hour, and once Dad was settled inside, Bob motioned for me to join him.

"It's a good thing you're here, your dad really needs you right now," he said. Bob was a tall guy, an inch or two over six feet, and even though he was twenty or more years older than I, I had to work to match his stride.

"Yeah, well, he's not always the best at making one feel welcome," I said.

"He does like things just so," Bob conceded. "But he's really improved this place since buying it from Langdon. Langdon, he fixed the place up when he first bought the camp, but in those last few years he had it, he let it run down. Broken boards in the docks, busted steps into the cabins. You had to be careful you didn't trip and break your neck."

"If it was a safety issue, I'm sure Dad was all over it," I said. I don't know whether I was comforted or distressed by the fact that I might have come by my own safety phobias honestly.

We were walking along the lake's edge, listening to the water lap up against the shore. We passed a high, small wooden table with a hole cut in the center, and positioned directly under it, a short metal trash can with a lid on it.

I pointed. "What's this?"

"That's where we clean our catch," Bob said. "Scrape what's left into the hole, falls into the bucket. Has to be emptied every day. That right there would be incentive for a bear to wander down here. Need to mention that to Arlen."

My eyes darted about nervously. I reached under the table and gingerly lifted the lid for a peek inside. An eye, still tucked into a fish's severed head, glared at me.

I put the lid back on.

"Anyway," Bob continued, "your dad's kept what was good about this place, and fixed what was bad, and I'm grateful to him for that. This lake, it means the world to me, coming up here year after year. The fish don't bite quite the way they used to, there's a few more people fishing out of this lake than used to, but it's still beautiful up here. I'm up here three weeks of every year, and the other forty-nine I'm wishing I was. I'm thinking, now that my wife is gone—she passed four years ago from cancer, awful thing—that maybe I'll spend my whole summer here. If I thought your father would go for it, I'd sell my home in the city, get cabin two winterized like the one your dad lives in, just live up here year-round."

"You should talk to him," I said. "I bet he'd go for it."

"Yeah," he said. "But first, he's going to have to figure out what to do about them." He nodded his head back in the direction of the farmhouse. "They're trouble."

"Dad doesn't want to talk about them."

"That's 'cause he don't know what to do about them. And that embarrasses him."

"Just what's the problem?"

"They remind me of that bunch at Waco, remember them?"

I nodded.

"Cutting themself off from the world, thinking everybody's out to get them, getting themselves ready to defend themself against attackers."

"What attackers?"

"The government, most likely. But if not them, black folk, homosexuals, Communists, who knows? That woman, the young one whose boyfriend got eaten by the bear? She's got a ten-year-old boy. He don't go to school. They teach him right there, up at the house. Y'imagine the kind of poison that's going into that boy's head?"

A hopeless feeling washed over me.

Bob led me out onto one of the five docks. On one side, secured with braided white nylon rope, bobbed an aluminum boat, about fourteen feet long, loaded with fishing poles, tackle boxes, nets, and life preserver cushions. "That's my rig," Bob said. The other side of the dock was empty, and Bob reached for a metal chain slipped around one of the posts. I recognized it as a stringer, with oversized hooks that closed like a baby's safety pin through a fish's jaw and kept your day's catch fresh, and underwater, until such time as you wanted to bring it in and clean it.

Before Bob pulled the stringerful of fish out of the lake, he said to me, "Whaddya say, tomorrow morning, I take you fishing? We'll go out early, before you have to start helping your dad with camp chores."

I shrugged. "Sure," I said. It actually sounded like a fun thing to do. More fun than with my son Paul, griping about not having his Game Boy with him.

Bob gave me a thumbs-up. "Wait'll you see what I got today. We got some good eatin' here, that's for darn—"

He pulled the stringer out, and there was nothing there but five pickerel heads that had been raggedly, savagely separated from the rest of their bodies.

"Jesus H. Christ," Bob said, shaking his head slowly. "Those fucking dogs. Again." He looked back in the direction of the farmhouse. "They love their fucking fish."

7

"SORRY," BOB SPOONER SAID when he came into Dad's cabin later. "No fish. They made a break for it."

"You're shittin' me," Dad said, sitting at the kitchen table, breaking up romaine leaves into a bowl. "They got off your stringer?"

"It's amazing," said Bob. "I must notta snapped the clips shut. I'm an idiot."

Bob had told me he wasn't going to tell Dad about the pit bulls eating his fish. Dad had had a bad enough day, what with a dead guy being found on his property and wrecking his ankle. When I asked him how he could be sure it was the Wickenses' dogs, Gristle and Bone, Bob explained that Timmy Wickens, or one of his grown sons, often brought the dogs down by the lake, letting them off the leash to splash around in the water.

"Couple times, I've seen those little bastards coming out of the water, fish in their mouths, chewing them up and swallowing them like dog biscuits. And then we go out, check our stringers, there's nothing there but the heads."

"You complain?"

Bob smiled at me, like I was a poor, simple soul. "You try talking to those people."

Sooner or later, I felt, I was going to have to.

Before Bob came over with his fish story, I went back to Dad's cabin and found him leaning up against the kitchen counter, slipping a key off one of four nails that had been driven into the wall. He tossed it to me, and, not being particularly sports-inclined, I panicked as it flew through the air toward me. You don't want to miss a toss from your father. Somehow, I got it, and he said, "That's for cabin three. You can use it long as you want."

"Okay. But I don't mind camping out here on the couch, in case you get a chance to rent it. Besides, you could probably use the help around here, like grabbing you the TV remote."

"No, it's okay. You take it. You should have some privacy. There's some sheets and blankets in the closet in my bedroom you can use."

Fine, I thought.

"Tomorrow, I'll show you what needs to be done around here. Couple days, I should be back to normal."

"I can take as much time as you need," I said, although I knew I couldn't stay away from work that long. With only a year in at *The Metropolitan*, I didn't have much rank and hadn't earned many favors. "I talked to Sarah, she said she'll clear it for me with the other editors."

"How's she doing? You still making her life hell?"

"Like father like son," I said.

The words were out of my mouth before I could get them back. They just slipped out. You could almost see them hanging in the room. I wished there were some way to reel them back in, stuff them back into my big, fat mouth.

Dad looked at me, and I was expecting him to give me a blast, but instead, he turned his back to me and washed his hands in the sink.

"Dad, I'm sorry, I didn't mean that."

"Don't worry about it," he said, studying his hands as though getting them clean was the most important thing he'd ever had to do.

"Really, I'm sorry. That was a cheap shot. That's not how I feel."

Dad grabbed a towel, wiped his hands off. "Sure it is," he said. "You've always thought I was hard on your mother. I know that."

"No, no, that's not true. When I was little, yeah, you could be a bit tough on her, on all of us, but later on, when we got older, I don't know."

"I know you blame me for that time . . ."

I paused. "What? You mean when she went away? When I was twelve?"

Dad turned away, pivoting on one foot so as not to put weight on his bad ankle, and hung the towel back on the rack on the oven door. He said nothing.

I said, "She was gone for, what was it, six months?" Still no response from Dad. "I remember she phoned all the time, to talk to me and Cindy, but

I never saw her once for, like, half a year. All you'd tell us was that Mom needed some time."

"I don't want to get into this now," Dad said. He turned, and started to slip when he lost his balance trying to keep his weight off his injured ankle. I ran forward, but Dad caught himself before I got there. I handed him his crutches and he made his way over to the table.

"Pass me those buns," he said. "I'll butter them."

Not long after that, Betty and Hank Wrigley showed up. He'd brought some booze, and she had a bowl of potato salad covered with Saran. Then Bob arrived, telling his lies about what happened to his fish, and soon after that, Leonard Colebert, the diaper magnate, came through the door that led to the porch, two pie boxes tied with string hanging from his index finger. He must have done a fast pastry run into Braynor.

It was a party.

We cooked and ate and drank, and drank some more. At one point, I was sitting on the porch, Colebert in a chair to my left and Bob on my right. Colebert, it seemed, had one topic he liked to talk about more than any other.

"There's millions in diapers," Colebert said. "We've barely tapped the market."

"What are you talking about?" I said. "You got all the old people thinking they need 'em now. I see all these commercials, these women, they don't look a day over forty, running along the beach, getting their toes wet, prancing about, liberated from having to find a bathroom in a hurry. What else do you want?"

"Listen, this is just the beginning," Leonard said, lowering his voice conspiratorially. "It's all in the marketing. As you say, we've created this need among old people who might actually have been able to hold it, but now figure, what the fuck, who needs to, right? Let 'er rip. I mean, sure, there's lots of people got a genuine need, but that's a limited market. But what about everyone else, middle-aged and younger, who figure they don't need a diaper? You for instance."

"Me?" I said. "What about me?"

"Say you're on a trip, you're doing the interstate, you want to make good time, you don't want to have to stop to take a whiz, so you wear a diaper, you can drive for hours. You've got your family with you, everyone whining about taking bathroom breaks, but you put them all in diapers, you get to where you're going sooner, which means you can start having fun sooner." He pointed his finger at me for emphasis. "We're talking convenience. Like take when you're watching TV, say, like, a Super Bowl, you don't want to miss a touchdown while you're standing over the can, shaking that last drop from your dick."

Bob looked across at me, then gazed back at the reflection of a full moon in the rippleless lake.

"Gamblers, of course, have been wearing them for years," Leonard informed us casually, like he figured everybody already knew this. "Say you're playing a slot machine, you don't want someone else taking your place when you go to the bathroom, that machine is yours, right? You know your win is just a crank away, you can't afford to walk away. Or you're at the blackjack table, you're on a streak, you gonna walk away from a thousand-dollar payoff? When you're in a diaper, you keep shoving in those nickels, you keep playing those hands."

He rubbed his hands together avariciously. "The trick is to remove the social stigma around wearing a diaper, so that anyone can do it and not feel ashamed. Like, if you're elderly, and you've got a weak bladder, if you've got a real need, you shouldn't have to feel badly about wearing one, but other people, you know, young adults, they might feel uncomfortable about it at first."

"You think?" I said.

"Advertising's the key. You do a campaign, sign on somebody like Brad Pitt or Angelina Jolie or like Bob Dole, remember when he did the Viagra ads? Somebody like that, respectable, big name."

I looked at Bob and we both shrugged.

"Anyway, you get someone famous, the viewer knows they're doing it in their pants, they think, 'Hey, I can get my head around that.'"

Bob grabbed his beer by the neck of the bottle and took a very long swig.

"And let me tell ya," Leonard said, "there's more in diapers than what you think. There's millions. Enough to build a first-class resort up here."

Bob turned his head. "What resort is that, Leonard?"

"I've got a proposal for a chunk of land just up the lake"—he pointed north—"closer to Braynor. Sometime, we'll take a walk, we'll drive up there and hike in, I can show you. Both of you."

Bob persisted. "What are you talking about, a resort?"

"A fishing resort. It'll be beautiful. Like nothing this lake or any of the Fifty Lakes up around here have ever seen. First class all the way. Five hundred rooms by the time it's done. First phase, we'll have a hundred rooms I figure, then gear up the rest, a hundred at a time. Gives us time to get the waterfront redeveloped, put in a wharf—"

"Wait a minute, hold on a sec," Bob said. "What lake are you talking about? You don't mean this lake?"

"What lake you think I'm talking about?" Leonard said. To me, he said, "I don't want you getting the idea I'm trying to put your dad out of business. There's always going to be people, you know, people on a budget, need to come to a place like this."

"Of course," I said.

"My place'll be first-class all the way. And we'll hire first-class guides, to run charters. Get half a dozen guys on a boat, take them out to the lake to fish. Maybe have a dozen boats or more. That should be enough. You figure, a lot of people, they'll bring their own boats up. We'll need a marina, to sell gas down by the water. Say, I just had an idea, Bob."

Bob looked almost too horrified to speak. "What?"

"I could hire you on, to run charters. You could spend your whole summer up here, running fishing tours. No one knows this lake better than you. You'd know every little nook and cranny where someone could find a fish."

"If there are any left," Bob said. "There's already

fewer fish in these waters now than five years ago, ten years ago. You put up some big resort, this lake'll be fished out in no time. You'll ruin it."

Leonard waved his hand dismissively. "Don't worry about that. There'll always be fish. And listen, I gotta spend all this diaper money somehow!" He laughed.

"Let me ask you something," I said.

"Shoot," said Leonard.

"Are you wearing a diaper right now?"

Leonard smiled. "You can't tell one way or another, can you?"

Bob got up abruptly. "I'm turning in," he said. He looked at me, a sadness in his eyes. "We still on to go fishing in the morning?" He was asking like it was the last time he'd ever be able to do it.

"Yeah," I said. "What time should I be ready?"

"Six-thirty?"

I swallowed. "Six-thirty?"

Bob smiled. "You want to catch fish or not?"

I sighed. "Sure, I'll be ready."

"And we'll take a walk up there, right?" Leonard said to Bob. "Before the week's over? Show you where the hotel's going, the dining hall? Maybe, someday, even a casino? If I can get the license."

Bob left without responding. Leonard watched Bob walk back to his cabin, then said to me, "He seems a bit upset about something, doesn't he?"

"Maybe," I said. "Hard to know what it could be."

"Anyway," Leonard said, recovering quickly from Bob's slight, "my company's also going to sponsor this new reality show. It's just a blast, listen. They take this guy, and they tell him, you're gonna love this, they tell him his parents are dead, killed in an accident, whatever. But the parents are alive, and in on the joke, and they get to watch their son planning the funeral arrangements, going to the funeral. It's absolutely hilarious. Then, at the reading of the will, the guy finds out he's been stiffed, he's not getting anything, and then they bring in the parents, who are really alive, and, here's the best part, because we're the sponsor, it's worked right into the whole plotline that everyone has to wear a diaper, because when this guy sees his parents are still alive, you know he's going to shit his pants, right? So when . . ."

I went back into the cabin, unconcerned about seeming rude to Leonard. He seemed impervious to offense, giving or receiving.

Dad and Betty and Hank were sitting at his table, dirty plates stacked to one side, a dozen empty beer bottles here and there. I said, "I think the bear got the wrong person."

Betty said, "That's sort of what we were talking about."

Dad said, "Come on, Betty, this doesn't make any sense."

I grabbed a beer, twisted off the cap, and took a chair at the table. "What doesn't make any sense?" I asked.

"You knew Betty was a nurse, right?" Hank said.

I nodded. "You guys told me, you're retired now."

"Don't even tell him," Dad said. "He'll just make something of it."

"Arlen, I'm just telling you what I saw," Betty said.

"What did you see?" I asked. I remembered how Betty and her husband had gone back into the woods alone, how he'd held up the tarp for her so she could get another look. I'd branded them ghouls at the time.

Dad shook his head, gazed down at the table, realizing it was pointless trying to keep Betty from telling me whatever it was she wanted to.

"I worked in Emerg for years," she said. "Off and on, but I was down there a lot. In a lot of different hospitals, too. Most of that time, down in the city, but when we first got married, Hank and I, we lived up in Alaska."

"No kidding?" I said. "I've never been up there, but have always wanted to see it. Ever since I saw that movie, with Pacino and Robin Williams, he's the killer, and Pacino can't get to sleep because the sun never goes down."

"It's beautiful," Hank said. "You should go."

"Sarah would love it, I bet. Can't you take one of those cruises, see whales or something?"

"Can I tell my story?" Betty said. Hank and I shut up. Betty continued, "So I've seen the whole gamut, you know? From guys who've fallen off their fishing boats to teenage gang members who've been knifed in the head."

"Yuck," I said.

Betty shrugged. "A few times, in Alaska, I helped treat people who'd been attacked by bears. Maybe you saw that documentary, the one about the guy who lived with grizzlies, got killed by one?

Remember how they brought bits of him back in garbage bags? I've seen that kind of thing. I've seen what bears can do, when they attack, which is still very rare."

"I read that on the net," I said. "They'd just as soon avoid people as have a run-in with them."

"But when they do," Betty went on, paying little attention to me, "they maul their victims, swat them about, and they've got these huge paws, with claws. Person gets swiped with one of those, they've got scratches a couple inches apart. And bears got big jaws. They take a bite out of you, you notice something's missing."

"Okay," I said, getting interested.

"I took a long look at that body, of Morton Dewart. And you know, I could be wrong, but he didn't look to me like someone who'd been killed by a bear."

Dad said, "It could have been a wolf, you know. Maybe a cougar. They've got cougars up here, I'm pretty sure of that."

"Dad," I said. "Let her tell it."

"And when I've worked in ERs in the city, I've seen things there, too, that reminded me of how this Dewart guy looked. He was torn apart, in a frenzy, by an animal, or animals, with jaws a lot smaller than a bear's."

A tiny shiver went down my spine. "Let me guess," I said. "Dogs."

Betty nodded. "Like I say, it's not like I did an autopsy out there in the woods or anything, but based on what I've seen over the years, and believe me, I've seen a lot, I'd say so."

Suddenly, we were interrupted.

Leonard Colebert stepped into the cabin, threw his arms proudly into the air, like he'd scored a touchdown. "I'll bet you can't tell, to look at me, what I've just done."

8

I TURNED IN SOON AFTER THAT, but didn't sleep very well in my bed in cabin 3. The mattress sagged a bit in the middle, but that wasn't the problem. I couldn't stop thinking about what Betty had to say, that the death of Morton Dewart might not be as straightforward as it looked, plus there was something else that was gnawing at me in the middle of the night. I kept wanting the sun to come up so I could go outside and look for something I thought should be there, but which no one had found.

So when it got to be six, the time I'd hoped to wake up to join Bob to go fishing, I was already awake. I sat up in bed, tired and logy-headed.

The sun was streaming into my bedroom window from a low angle as I threw back the covers and touched my feet to the cold plank floors. I padded into the bathroom, where I had a quick shower. I'd grabbed a couple of towels, in addition to bedding, from Dad before heading over to my own, private accommodation. Other than my new socks and underwear, I had nothing that you could call a travel kit. I wished I had thought, when I'd bought my clothes, to pick up a toothbrush, razor, shaving cream, and a few other items.

My teeth felt furry.

Some stuff I could probably borrow from Dad, but the rest I'd need to get next time I was in Braynor. Once I was dressed and had combed my hair with my fingers and run my index finger over my teeth, I went outside. Rather than head down to the lake, or over to Dad's cabin for some breakfast, I went straight into the woods.

It wasn't hard to find where Morton Dewart's body had been. The grass was tramped down in the area around where the tarp had been draped over him. I'm no tracker, but I looked off into the forest, as if the location of the body were the center of a wheel, and imagined spokes leading off from it. All the possible routes Dewart might have taken to reach the point where he'd met his end. I was looking for disturbances in the pine needle–covered forest floor, or broken branches, anything to indicate what path he, or a bear, might have taken here.

I didn't see a damn thing.

So I began walking in ever growing circles, starting at the point where the body had been found, searching the ground, scanning back and forth ahead of me. I ducked under branches, stepped over rocks, hopped over small dips in the terrain.

I did not find what I was looking for.

I walked back down to the lake, which was still and shimmering from the early morning sun. Down by the dock, Bob was sitting in his boat, examining lures in his tackle box, getting ready.

"Morning!" he called. Very cheerful for so early in the day.

"Be over in a minute," I said, heading for Dad's cabin. If I could get a dab of toothpaste, I'd take another run at my teeth with my finger.

Dad's cabin was unlocked and I opened the door quietly, figuring he'd still be asleep. There was no radio going, no sounds of bacon frying in a pan. But there was snoring. As I passed by Dad's open bedroom door, I caught a peek of him in there, on his back on the far side of his double bed, making noises like a Union Pacific freight. Dad had done me a favor, putting me in cabin 3, instead of letting me crash on the couch and try to get to sleep with that racket going on.

I crept past his door to the bathroom. The door was barely ajar, and I eased it open with my hand, hoping it wouldn't squeak too much on its hinges.

"Hey, sweetie," came a voice from inside the bathroom. A voice that sounded very female. "I didn't wake you up, did—"

And then, when she saw who was coming in to see her, this woman with brown hair who looked, at a glance, to be about my father's age, standing there in a white bra and black slacks that she was in the process of zipping up, screamed.

Not a blood-curdling, oh-my-God-you've-come-here-to-kill-me scream, just a short one, of pure surprise. More a whoop, really, than a scream.

I didn't scream myself, although I might easily

have done so. Instead, I was blabbering, "Sorry! Sorry! Didn't know anyone was in here! Sorry!" I grabbed hold of the doorknob and yanked so hard on it that I slammed the door into my head, knocking myself back into the main room, almost stumbling over the couch before I caught myself.

Dad was hopping out his bedroom door now, shouting, "Lana! What's wrong?" And then he saw me, then clutched at the wall for support, and even in his barely awake state, started putting it all together. "Oh shit," he said, looking at me. "What are you doing up this early?"

"I'm going fishing," I said. "I just wanted to rub some toothpaste on my teeth and jeez I didn't know you had someone here why didn't you tell me you were having company and I wouldn't have walked in?"

"Didn't you bring a toothbrush?"

"No, I did not bring a toothbrush. When I heard you were dead, for some reason, my first stop was not for a toothbrush and floss."

"You don't have any floss either?"

"Dad."

"What about when we were in town yesterday? Couldn't you have picked up what you needed then? Honestly, can't a person have even a little privacy around—"

The bathroom door swung open and Lana stepped out, a pink button-up-the-front blouse pulled on, her fingers doing up the top button. "Arlen, stop, please, it was just an accident."

Again, I said, "Listen, I'm sorry, I had no idea anyone was in there. I just wanted to brush my teeth was all and—"

"Yeah, well, the bathroom's free now, so why don't you do what you have to do," Dad suggested.

"I'm Lana," she said, extending a hand. "You must be Zachary."

"Yeah, Zack, yes," I said, shaking her hand. "It's a pleasure to meet you, Lana."

"Lana Gantry," she said. "I'm a friend of your father's." She smiled. "Although you probably figured that out by now."

The implications of what I'd stumbled into were now starting to sink in. This woman was a friend of my father's. She was in his cabin at 6:20 in the morning. No one came to visit at 6:20 in the morning. Which meant that she must have arrived late last night, after the party broke up. Which meant that she must have spent the night with my father and oh God there are just some things you don't want to think about why did I have to walk in here and how do I get out of this gracefully?

"I know all about you." Lana smiled. "You're a writer for *The Metropolitan* now, aren't you?"

"Yes," I said, looking at her closely for the first time now. She was probably in her early sixties, trim, a pretty impressive figure, which I was able to discern even now that she had her top on. A beautiful face with full, already red, lips, high cheekbones, brown hair with subtle streaks of silver in it that would probably have fallen just to her shoulders if she didn't have it pulled back and clipped.

"It's a real treat to see you again," Lana said. "Needless to say, you've sure grown up."

A puzzled looked must have crossed my face. "I'm sorry, I'm having just a bit of trouble placing you . . . Wait a minute."

Dad shook his head, annoyed, and was about to say something when Lana turned to him, putting a finger to her lips. "Let's see if he remembers."

Dad said, "Lana, it's really not necessary that—"

"Shhh," Lana said to him.

There was something about her that was familiar. "What did you say your last name was?" I asked.

"Gantry."

"Mrs. Gantry?"

"I think he's getting warm." Lana smiled at Dad.

"You used to live down the street from us? And moved away, when I was, like, thirteen?"

She smiled, stepped forward and gave me a hug, followed by a peck on the cheek. "Good memory."

"Lana's husband, Walter, died a few years back," Dad said. "We both ended moving up this way, ran into each other in Braynor. It was, uh, sort of a coincidence." Dad reached around behind the bedroom door and came out with his crutches, which he tucked under each arm so he could come out into the room.

"Have you had any breakfast?" Lana asked me.

"Uh, no, but listen . . . I have to get going anyway. Bob's taking me out fishing this morning, and I don't want to intrude."

"Nonsense. Let me make you up something. You can take it out with you, if you want." She was already heading over to the kitchen counter. "How about peanut butter and toast? Or a fried egg sandwich? That would only take a moment."

Dad said, "Do you really have time, Lana?" To me, he said, "Lana runs the café in town."

"This'll only take a sec," she said. "I've got the girls trained to open up, I don't have to be there first thing. So how about a fried egg sandwich?"

"A fried egg sandwich would be great," I said. She had a small frying pan out before I could finish the sentence, and now was in the fridge getting out a carton of eggs.

"That's something, the two of you running into each other, years after you left the neighborhood," I said.

"Yes, it is," Lana Gantry said, putting two slices of bread into the toaster. "By the way, I think you've met my nephew, Orville?"

I blinked. "The chief? Of police?"

"I know he was out here, what with that horrible business of the man who was killed by the bear. What a terrible, terrible thing that was."

"Yes, we met," I said. *And he pulled a gun on me*, I could have added. *And he seems like a bit of a twit*, I might have mentioned.

"I'm so proud of him. He's turned into quite a young man himself," she said. I nodded, not sure what I could possibly add to that. My toast popped and Lana buttered the slices, then slid a fried egg onto one of them. "Salt and pepper?" she asked.

"Sure," I said, still processing so much information being delivered in such a short time.

"I didn't cut it so the yolk wouldn't run all over the place," she said, handing me my breakfast in a sandwich bag.

Lana gave Dad a light kiss on the lips, which embarrassed him. "Gotta run," she said. "Come in for a piece of pie if you get a chance." She smiled at me, grabbed a set of keys on the kitchen counter, and was out the door.

"She seems nice," I said. "I hope you kids are using protection."

Dad scowled. "I think Lana gave you that sandwich to go."

I smiled. "Okay, I'm off. When I get back, you can start showing me what needs to be done around here." He was still scowling as I slipped out the door and ran over to the dock, where Bob Spooner was sitting patiently in his boat.

"Ready?" he said.

I stepped carefully into the boat, putting my foot toward the center so as not to tip it.

"Meet Lana?" Bob asked, grinning. "I just saw her car take off for town."

I nodded. "I kind of walked in on her in the bathroom. I could have used a heads-up on that one." I was thinking as Bob unhooked the boat from the dock and, with an oar, pushed us a boat length out, where it was deep enough for him to lower the outboard motor. "Is that where Dad was night before last, when we thought he was under that tarp?"

"Think so," Bob said. "I figured Orville would have thought of that, or called, or something, but I guess he didn't."

"Would Orville know a clue if it bit him in the ass?"

Bob shook his head, said nothing, and dropped the motor into the water. He primed the squeeze bulb on the gas tank, then yanked the cord—just once—to bring the motor to life.

We didn't do much talking as we headed out into the lake. We were the only noisy thing out there, and I didn't want to make it worse by shouting over the motor. It had been a few years since I'd been out here, and I'd forgotten how beautiful it was. It wasn't a huge lake; about two miles across and six or seven miles long, surrounded by forest. There were cottages here and there, a trailer park at the south end, but it wasn't an overdeveloped lake. You could still come up here and feel you were getting away from it all.

Bob turned back on the throttle as we approached the shore a mile or so north of Denny's Cabins. We were maybe fifty yards away from an awe-inspiring stand of pine trees. He pointed, raising his voice slightly over the outboard. "Must be over here somewhere."

"What?" I said, leaning toward him from my perch on the middle seat.

"Leonard's resort," he said, shaking his head.

"That guy's something else," I said. "Do you think he was actually taking a piss while he sat there and told us about it?"

Bob shrugged. "Won't be long before I'm wearing those goddamn diapers myself. Just got to make sure I don't buy his brand."

He killed the motor and released two fishing poles from brackets built into the side of the boat, handed one to me. "This is one of the best places to fish in the whole lake. There's weed beds run through here, great feeding area. Every time I come out, I usually troll through here once, or drift and cast."

"I can't believe any local government would okay a guy's plan to build a resort that huge on a lake that has so little development on it already. They must have to go through some sort of environmental study to build something like that. Surely the local council wouldn't let it go ahead."

"You really think that? That it would never be approved?"

I thought about that. "No. Sometimes, the worse something is, the more likely it'll happen."

"That's kind of how I feel, too. If the money's right, if Leonard can convince them this will bring new jobs to the area, people will go along with anything."

"But then again, I could be wrong. I mean, look around. Because there is so little development on this lake, and a huge resort would have such an impact on it, maybe the people in charge will show some sort of common sense, some concern for the environment."

Bob hooked a lure to the end of his line, what looked like a four-inch fish with froglike coloring and three sets of hooks dangling off it. "How about something like this?" he said, lifting out of the tackle box a similar lure, but it had more yellow in it. ·

"Looks good," I said, and he handed it over. I struggled, taking a couple of minutes to open the clip at the end of my line and attach it to the lure. I nearly jabbed myself twice, but did my best to keep Bob from noticing. Bob whipped his pole back over his shoulder, then cast out, the plug landing in the water thirty to forty feet away.

"We'll drift this way"—he pointed—"so cast out the other side."

I was worried about how this was going to go, but surprised myself when the pole whipped back over my head, I released the tension on the line, and the plug went sailing through the air, plopping nicely into the water not far from where Bob's had gone.

"Juanita would've loved a morning like this," Bob said.

"Juanita?"

"She was my wife. You're thinking, a name like that, what was she? She was from Mexico, originally. She loved to come out here, especially early in the morning, with the water smooth as glass, the mist still not all burned off. At first, years ago, when we first started coming up, I thought she did it just to keep me happy, which made me feel sort of bad. Didn't want to think she was sitting out here for hours just tolerating it, you know?"

"Sure."

"So one year, I decide, without telling her, to book something different for when we usually come up here. Put aside some money, to take her to San Francisco. Ride the trolley cars, see the Golden

Gate, that kind of thing. Well, she finds out I've done this and doesn't talk to me for two days. All she wants, she says, is to come up here and sit on a lake with me. Made me cancel the Frisco trip."

"She liked fishing?"

Bob Spooner shrugged. "Liked it okay. It was sitting out here that she liked most. Sometimes, she'd bring a book, curl up right there, on the floor by the front seat, and just read while I fished. One time she read one of your books."

"Really?"

"Yeah, your dad had a copy, she borrowed it. About these guys, they go to another planet, they're like missionaries, only backwards? They try to spread the word that there's no God, but then something awful happens to them. That one."

"How'd she like it?"

Bob pondered. "I don't know. She didn't finish it."

I reeled in, cast out again. "You miss her," I said.

Bob nodded. "Awful thing, that cancer. Took her a long time to go. Didn't want to lose her, but at the same time, wished I could have ended it for her sooner."

For a long time, we said nothing. We sat there in the stillness of the morning, watching the last of the overnight mist burn away. I understood what had drawn my father up here to stay, how up here, there was much less to worry about, much less to get your shorts in a knot about.

Except, maybe, for the Wickenses.

"I'm thinking," I said, breaking the silence, "of taking Dad into town to see a lawyer, see what he can do about those people renting his farmhouse. Maybe he could get them evicted. Look what they're doing to the place."

"Worth checking into," Bob said, studying where his line disappeared into the water. He turned his reel a couple of times, then let it back out again.

"A lawyer could at least let Dad know where he stands, tell him what his options are regarding—"

And then my line took off. The reel started spinning.

"Jesus, what the hell's that?" I said. "I must be caught on a log."

"That's no fucking log," Bob said. "You've got hold of something." He began reeling in his own line so he could concentrate on what had hold of mine. "Just play it," he said gently. "Keep him busy."

I pulled back on the pole, then eased it forward again, turning the reel furiously to pick up the slack and bring the fish closer to the boat.

Something dark and oily looking broke the surface of the water. Something long and slender and black, and at least three feet long. With a broad fin toward one end.

"Whoa," said Bob.

"What? What is it?"

"It's a muskie, that's for sure. Probably go four feet, maybe more."

And then the fish's snout appeared above the surface, my lure caught on the edge of its lower lip, and it shook its head vigorously back and forth a couple of times before disappearing under the surface.

"That's not just any muskie," said Bob. "I think that just might be Audrey."

"Audrey?"

"Just then, I noticed a scar on her snout, just under the right eye. I know that fish. I've hooked into her a couple times over the years. Biggest fish I've ever seen out here. Keep reeling in."

"I'm trying but she's putting up a hell of a fight." Truth was, I couldn't manage to turn the reel. "You want to take it?"

Bob shook his head. "She's your fish. You either land her, or you don't. I hooked into her three years ago, and two years before that. It's in my diary. That bitch is still out here. I don't believe it. Last couple times I hooked into her, it was right near here."

The pole was bent over sharply, the line taut. "Why Audrey?" I asked.

"My grade two teacher. Used to whack me with a ruler every day. Meanest bitch ever to stand in front of a classroom." He paused. "I've thought, if I could ever land Audrey, I could retire from fishing altogether and die a happy man."

"It's not right that she's hit my line," I said. "Really, take the pole and—"

And suddenly, my fishing pole sprang upward, the tension going out of it instantly. The line went slack.

I reeled in as quickly as I could, until my lure appeared above the surface of the water, nothing attached to it.

Bob smiled. "Audrey's as smart as she is mean. Maybe, next time we're out here, she'll hit my line instead of yours."

When I got back to Dad's cabin, Dr. Heath was taking a look at Dad's ankle. Dad was stretched out on the couch, and the doctor had perched himself on the big wooden coffee table, looking at the bandage, lightly touching it.

Dr. Heath turned when he saw me come in. "Why, hello," he said. "Just thought I'd take a run out here and see how your father's coming along."

"And how's that?" I asked.

The elderly doctor nodded wisely. "I'd say just fine. If he can keep his weight off it, I'd say another week he'll be in pretty good shape."

Yikes. A whole week? Taking that much time off from the paper might be pushing it. Best to take this a day at a time, I told myself.

"Arlen," he said to my father, "you have to promise me you won't do anything stupid."

"Fine, fine, don't worry," he said, pulling a thick sock back up over the wounded ankle. "Zachary's hanging in for a few days."

The doctor grabbed his medical bag, headed for the door.

"I'll walk you to your car," I said.

We were approaching his black Buick, and I said, "Can I ask you something?"

"If you're worried about your father, you shouldn't be. He's going to be just fine."

"That's good, but that wasn't what I wanted to ask you about. It's about Morton Dewart."

"Awful thing," Dr. Heath said.

"Did you do an autopsy on the body?" I asked.

"Of course," said Dr. Heath. "I had to declare a cause of death."

"And what did you determine that to be?"

Dr. Heath made a small snorting noise. "Misadventure, with a bear."

"So that was your conclusion, that he was killed by a bear?"

Dr. Heath looked puzzled. "Of course. You saw him. Didn't he look like he was killed by a bear to you?"

"But isn't that just an assumption?"

"You heard what Mr. Wickens said. He made a statement that Mr. Dewart had gone out, specifically, to find that bear, and shoot it. Then he's found as he was. It doesn't take much to put that together, Mr. Walker."

"But when you did your autopsy, did your examination of the wounds support the contention that he was killed by the bear? Did the bite marks match the size of a bear's jaw, that kind of thing?"

Dr. Heath was shaking his head, getting irritated. "Look, I don't understand what the point of your question is. We saw the body, we have Mr. Wickens on record as saying the deceased was hunting for a bear. I think you put all that together and you conclude that Mr. Dewart was killed by a bear. That's what I did, and now the body is being released to his own family, not the Wickenses."

I looked into the doctor's face, made an awkward smile. It wasn't my intention to be disrespectful. Dr. Heath seemed like a nice old gentleman. But I had to ask.

"You didn't really conduct a thorough autopsy, did you? You figured it was a bear that killed him, as opposed to, for the sake of argument, a couple of dogs, so you didn't look for any other possibilities."

His face was getting flushed. "I totally resent the implications of that remark."

"I'm sorry," I said. "I'm asking you these questions with the utmost respect. But there's another wrinkle to this I want to get your thoughts on, and I admit, it may be more in Chief Thorne's area than yours."

"And what's that?" Dr. Heath said, his hand on the car door, eager to leave.

"Where's the rifle?"

Dr. Heath's brow furrowed. "What rifle?"

"If Morton Dewart ran into a bear while he was out hunting for one, where's his rifle? I searched the woods this morning, went all around the area where the body had been found, and there's no rifle, no shotgun, whatever you want to call it, anyplace."

He opened his car door, tossed his case over to the passenger seat, and said to me, "I have no idea where it is, and it isn't any of my concern. I've done my job and I've done it to the best of my ability, and you've got a lot of nerve questioning me this way."

"Please, I mean no disrespect. It's just, if it wasn't a bear, and if it was, say, a dog, or more than one—"

"Your father's a good man," Dr. Heath said, "and he'd be ashamed of how you've just spoken to me. How dare you."

And he got in his car and drove off, kicking up gravel as he drove up the hill.

As I listened to his car hit the paved highway with

a squeal of the tires, I thought about the implications of the questions I'd been asking, what it was they might add up to. I was starting to wonder whether I wouldn't feel more at ease with the notion of a murderous bear in the woods.

9

"SO WHAT WERE YOU AND THE DOC talking about?" Dad asked when I returned to the cabin. He was still on the couch.

"We need to talk," I said.

"Look, if this is about Lana, I don't need any lectures from my son about my sex life."

I closed my eyes, but then, when the images started appearing, I reopened them. "God, no, I do not want to talk to you about your sex life."

"Because it's my business," Dad said.

"I don't want to talk about your sex life, okay? I can't imagine anything I want to talk about less."

"But in case you're wondering, it's pretty good," Dad said. He made a fist and shoved it forward slowly. "I still got it. Although this ankle's gonna slow me down a little bit for a while."

"That's great, Dad. I'm thrilled. You can do ads for the little blue pill."

Instant umbrage. "Who said I need that? Did Dr. Heath tell you I need that, because he's got no business spreading that kind of thing around. There's such a thing as doctor-patient confidentiality, you know."

"Dad! I don't give a shit about your sex life, okay? There are more important matters to discuss than that."

Dad sat quietly, waiting.

"I'm not totally convinced that you've got a bear problem," I said.

"Aww, jeez . . ."

"Listen to me. I couldn't sleep all night, thinking about what Betty said. She's seen a lot, you know, in her line of work. She doesn't think it was a bear at all—"

"Okay, so maybe it's a wolf or a coyote or something like that?"

"Have you seen a lot of wolves and coyotes? And when's the last time you heard of them bringing down a man and killing him? But if it was dogs, like Betty seemed to think, well, you don't have to look far to find a couple of those. You weren't there yesterday, you didn't see how those little beasts came after me, they were—"

"Look," Dad protested, "Betty doesn't know what she's talking about. She means well, but really, I've known her a few years now, and she's a worrier, that's all. That was a bear that did that, and we've got our bear spray, so if he comes around again, we'll be okay. And Lana was telling me that Orville, her nephew, is talking to the wildlife people, maybe getting some people to hunt down this bear before it hurts anyone else."

"There's another thing, Dad. I walked around out there this morning, where they found the body. The Wickenses, they say he'd gone out hunting for a bear, but if that's true, then where's the rifle? I don't think Orville found one, and I kind of doubt the bear took it with him."

"Aw, you're full of it. Did you come up here to help me or make my life difficult?"

"You know what I think? I think you'd rather have a killer bear out there than a couple of killer dogs, because if it's a bear, it's out of your hands. But if it's those dogs, acting with their owner's blessing, living in a house that belongs to you, right up there on your property, it's a problem you have to deal with."

Dad said nothing. He bit his lip, looked away from me and out the window, toward the lake. I took a seat in a recliner across from the couch, leaned back, made no attempt to interrupt the silence. We sat there, the two of us, for about a minute, until Dad finally spoke.

"I got some coffee going over there. You mind getting me a cup? Help yourself if you want some."

I got up. "Black, right?" Dad nodded. I poured us two cups of coffee, brought them back over, and plopped back into the recliner. I took a sip. "Good coffee," I said.

Dad drank some of his. "Catch any fish with Bob this morning?"

"No. But Audrey hit my line."

"Jesus, seriously? Bob's been after Audrey for years."

"Didn't get her, though. We each caught a pick-erel, otherwise nothing. Nice of him to take me out, though."

"Yeah," said Dad. "He's a good guy, Bob is."

Then we were quiet again for a while. Dad took another sip, looked out over the lake again, and said, "I don't know what to do."

I nodded. "I can understand that. It's a tricky sit-uation."

"I want them out," Dad said. "I can't sleep."

I didn't say anything.

"There's always gunfire up there," he said. "Shooting all the time, like, target practice or some-thing. I can handle a bit of that, you know? You have to expect it, up here in the mountains. But it goes on and on some days. One time, I thought I heard a ma-chine gun. Who needs a fucking machine gun? And they wear all this camouflage garb? What do they think they are? Who do they think's coming to get them? What are they taking a stand against?"

"Have you done anything about this so far?"

Dad sighed. "A few weeks ago, after an afternoon of nonstop shooting, I called Orville."

"Oh."

"Look, it's kind of complicated. He's Lana's nephew, and, well, there's more to it than I can ex-plain. He tries to do his job, but he's a bit lacking in the intimidation department."

"What happened when you called him?"

Another sigh. "He went up there. He thought it would be better, I didn't go with him, maybe the Wickenses would hold it against me if they knew I'd

placed the call. Orville said he could say that there'd
been some general calls about gunfire, without men-
tioning my name, and he was just checking into it. I
kind of walked up through the woods, watched what
happened. They let him inside the gate, and those
boys of Charlene's, Timmy's wife, Darryl and Darryl
I call them, although not to their faces, their real
names are Wendell and Dougie, they took Orville's
hat, started tossing it back and forth, Orville running
back and forth between them."

"Monkey in the middle," I said.

Dad nodded. "It was pitiful to watch. The boys
were giggling and laughing, and finally their old
man, Timmy, he says, okay now, boys, let's stop this.
And he hands Orville his hat back, but not his dig-
nity. He scurried out of there with his tail between
his legs."

"God," I said, picturing it. "There's something
about Orville, Dad."

"What? What do you mean?"

"I don't know. When I first saw him, he reminded
me of someone, and he still does. Did he hang
around in our old neighborhood, visiting his aunt
Lana? But he looks ten or more years younger than
me anyway, so he'd only have been a baby."

"I don't know," Dad said cautiously. "Who does he
remind you of?"

I shrugged. "I just feel I know him from somewhere. Maybe from the city? I worked for that other
paper years ago, maybe I interviewed him back
then."

"Could be," Dad said. "What difference does it

make?" He seemed annoyed by how I'd sidetracked the conversation.

"Forget it," I said. "Okay, let's get back to the matter at hand. There may be other avenues to pursue with regard to the Wickenses without dragging Orville into it. You should see a lawyer. Get a letter drawn up, tell them they have to leave. Give them a month's notice, after that, they're in violation of a court order, anything."

Dad mulled that one over. "A lawyer."

"Yeah."

"I hate lawyers."

"Everyone does, Dad. Sarah maybe even more than you. But this might be one of those times when one could be useful."

"I guess it's an idea. Suppose it wouldn't hurt to talk to someone."

"Sure," I said. "There must be a few lawyers in Braynor."

Dad nodded, thinking. "There's the one who handled this real estate deal for me. I guess I'd start with him."

"Why don't you call him, see if you can get an appointment, maybe tomorrow?" I suggested. "Where's your phone book?"

"Just leave it with me. It's in my study. I'll do it, I'll call him." He took a deep breath, let it out slowly. "Okay. That's good. I feel like we're making progress."

He reached for his crutches, got himself up off the couch. "Yeah, this is a plan." He shoved the crutches under his arms, moved toward the door of his study. Suddenly, he was a man with a mission. "I think his name's Bert Trench. That's it. He's got an office on the main street of Braynor."

He was in the study now, settling into his chair in front of his computer, reaching for the phone book. He was shouting, figuring I couldn't hear him fifteen feet away by the kitchen counter. "I'll bet he can get some kind of injunction! No, not an injunction. An eviction! He can get an eviction notice! You think?"

"Possibly," I said.

"Okay, here's the number." I heard Dad pushing some buttons on the phone, then, "Yeah, hi, it's Arlen Walker? Mr. Trench handled everything when I bought Denny's Cabins. . . . That's right, yeah. . . . I was wondering, could I make an appointment with him, soon as possible? . . . Tomorrow would be fine, sure. . . . That's perfect, thank you so much."

He hung up. "Tomorrow at ten-thirty!"

"That's great, Dad. I'll drive you in."

"You'll come in, too, won't you? To talk to the lawyer with me?"

"Yeah, sure."

"This is very good. Maybe I can get rid of those bastards once and for all, the whole goddamn lot of them! Then, once the house is empty, I'll get it cleaned up. We'll have to rent a Dumpster, throw out all that crap up there, the rusting appliances, that old rusty bed, Jesus I can't believe the way they've let the place—"

There was a knock at the back door. I walked the two steps over and swung it wide.

It was Timmy Wickens.

Dad was still shouting. "Those sons of bitches will just have to look—"

"Dad!" I shouted.

"Huh?"

"Mr. Wickens is here."

Wickens, in black boots, work pants, and a padded hunting vest, his bald head gleaming, smiled. "I wanted to have a word with Mr. Walker."

"Sure," I said. Dad was already hobbling out of the study. "Won't you step inside?" I said to Wickens, who accepted the invitation.

"Mr. Walker?" Wickens said as Dad made his way to the door. "How's your ankle?"

"Oh, you know, it smarts a bit," Dad said. "I'm sorry to hear about your trouble. That young man."

Wickens nodded. "Tragic," he said. "Just tragic. Can't ever remember something like that happening up here."

"Yeah," I said. "How's your daughter doing?"

There was a glint in Wickens's eye, like maybe I'd crossed some line, daring to ask a question about her.

"She's good," he said. "She's going to be just fine. May's a strong girl. So you're Mr. Walker's son, right?"

"Yes," I said. "I'm staying with Dad a few days, helping him out till his ankle gets a bit stronger."

"He's taken over cabin three," Dad said. "Making himself right at home."

"What I was wondering," Timmy Wickens said to Dad, "Charlene and I, that's my wife," he looked at me when he said it, "we were wondering could you join us for dinner tonight? The two of you."

I looked at Dad.

"I know it's short notice and all," Timmy said, "but we'd be much obliged if the two of you joined us for dinner. Our misfortune kind of turned your life upside down, too, and we'd like to make it right."

Dad appeared stunned. "Zachary, are we, are we doing something tonight?"

I shrugged. "Not that I know of."

Dad's eyes widened. "I, I guess, I don't think we've got anything on for tonight."

Wickens smiled. "That's great, then. Why don't you stroll up around six-thirty or so?"

"That sounds great, Timmy," Dad said. "Isn't that great, son?"

I nodded. "Sounds terrific."

"Settled then," said Wickens, turning and heading back out the door.

Once I had it closed behind him, Dad and I stared at each other for several seconds without speaking.

"Sarah," I finally said, "would tell me, in social situations like this, that we should take some kind of hostess gift."

"Okay," Dad said. "Got any ideas?"

"I was thinking, a case of Alpo. We give the dogs something to eat, maybe they won't eat us."

10

IT WAS TIME to set other problems aside temporarily and start tackling the chores at Denny's Cabins. Helping out around the place was, after all, the initial reason for my decision to hang in, although other things that threatened to keep me here longer seemed to be growing exponentially.

"This is dump day," Dad informed me.

"Shit," I said. "I forgot to get you a card."

"Do you want to help, or do you just want to be a smartass?" Dad asked. It was, I had to admit, a tough question. I believed it was possible, with some effort, to do both. I had been pissed at him ever since Timmy Wickens's visit for not being creative enough to come up with an excuse to get us out of dinner with people we were trying to find a way to evict.

"You could have said something," he said accusingly.

"He was inviting you," I said. "I was just an afterthought."

We bickered about that for a while, got nowhere,

finally decided to move on. "Tell me what needs to be done around here," I said, which had brought us to the exciting news that it was dump day.

But there was more. "Once you do a run to the dump, there's grass to cut, fish guts to bury, we need to make sure we've got worms, there's—"

"See if we've got worms?"

"Night crawlers, bait, for crying out loud. I keep 'em in a fridge out in the shed."

I sighed. "And the fish guts?"

"You've seen the bucket under the fish-cleaning table down by the docks?"

Who could forget?

"Well, they won't let us put raw fish guts in the municipal dump, so we have to deal with them ourselves."

"I'm guessing they won't flush."

"You have to take them out to the woods and bury them."

"Are you kidding?"

"There's already a hole dug out there. There's a big board over it. Take the guts up, dump it in the hole, throw some dirt in over it, put the board back over."

I nodded tiredly. "Okay, you stay here, I'll get these things done."

"You know how to drive a garden tractor?" Dad asked. " 'Cause the grounds are really looking a bit unkempt. I would have done it yesterday if it hadn't been for all this other shit happening."

"I think I can figure it out."

"Because it's a bit special, this tractor, because—"

"Dad. I can figure it out."

Dad held up his hands. "Okay, okay, you're the expert, I don't know a goddamn thing."

"Whatever," I said, heading out the door.

"Yeah, whatever!" Dad shouted as the door slammed shut. I was tempted to go back, say "Good comeback!" but decided someone had to be the mature one. An hour ago, I was a genius and a hero, coming up with the plan to talk to a lawyer about evicting the Wickenses, but now I was an idiot again.

I decided to tackle the garbage run first, loading half a dozen plastic cans jammed with green garbage bags filled to bursting into the back of Dad's Ford pickup. Leonard Colebert strolled over, hands parked in his front pockets so as to reduce the risk of being asked to lift something.

"So, this is garbage day?" he asked, smiling. I decided Leonard was probably undeserving of a smart-ass response—although that could change—so I merely nodded. "That was a good time last night," he said, referring to the party at Dad's cabin. "I didn't get a chance to tell you even a fraction of what's involved in the diaper business, or all the plan for my big resort."

"Well, it was pretty busy," I said, loading a can into the back of the truck and making sure the lid was secure.

"You mind if I tag along with you?" he said, one hand already on the passenger door. I couldn't think of a way to say no, so I motioned for him to hop in.

"I rode with your dad to the dump one day," he

said. "You pass right by the property I'm getting to build my resort on. I'll show you."

Oh boy.

When we were on the highway, Leonard said, "God, I love it up here. I could go anywhere, you know, Club Med, you name some fancy place, I could afford it. But there's nothing like being up here."

"There a Mrs. Colebert?" I asked.

"Not at the moment, but you never know, that could change," Leonard said, puffing out his chest. "I've had my share of ladies over the years, that's for sure. But never really found the right one."

There had to be a girl somewhere, I figured, who wanted to listen to diaper talk all day.

The road took a slight bend to the right when Leonard shouted, "Here! Here's the spot! Slow down."

I pulled over onto the shoulder and brought the truck to a halt, leaving it running in drive with my foot planted on the brake. Leonard was pointing into dense forest. The lake was probably no more than a couple hundred yards away, but you couldn't see it.

"Okay, this is where you'd drive in, there'd be a big sign here, maybe something like 'Colebert Lodge,' I don't know, and a huge neon fish jumping out of the water, a line coming out of its mouth. Can you picture it? It'd be super vivid, like a Vegas sign, but tasteful, you know?"

"Right," I said.

"It'd be bright in the daytime, but at night, it would

light up the sky, you know? There's nothing like that around here, let me tell you."

"You're right about that."

"So we take down about two acres' worth of trees over there to put in some parking, and once we do that, you'll be able to see right through to the lake, where there'll be the main hotel, about five stories high, I figure, and restaurants and snack bars, a huge bait shop. Just huge." He shook his head in wonderment. "Can you imagine it? Huh? Can you?"

"Actually, yes," I said, doing a very good job of concealing my excitement, and wondering, for the first time, what Leonard, sitting next to me, was wearing under his khakis.

"Come on," Leonard said, already opening his door. "I'll show you."

He was out of the truck before I could say no, so I killed the engine and followed him through the tall grass at the edge of the highway and into the forest. For a short, not particularly fit-looking guy, he was hard to keep up with.

"You think we're going to need the bear spray?" he called back to me.

"Let's chance it," I said.

"Okay," he said, once we were shrouded in trees. "Okay, hotel over there, maybe a swimming pool over there, although we'll have lakeside swimming, too. There's some weedy areas, a bit of marshland along the shore, but we can backfill that in, land-scape it, you'd never know there was anything natural there before."

"Well," I said.

"Hey, here's an idea," Leonard said. "Looks like I've already got Bob Spooner talked into working for me, running a charter."

"I wouldn't be so—"

"But there'd probably be something here for you, too. You could help me write up press releases, the literature, that kind of thing? Be my PR guy, my media relations officer. Because every big resort, you gotta have one of those. I'd make it worth your while."

"I don't think so," I said.

We were climbing now, the ground gradually sloping upwards. When we got to the top, I instinctively leaned back. We were standing at the edge of a sharp dropoff. It was a good thirty feet down to another section of heavily wooded forest.

"Down there, we clear the trees, that's where I'm going to put in the children's playland. I'm thinking of a huge model of a whale, the kids can run through it, pretend they've been swallowed by Jonah. And there'll be a fountain, shooting water out of the blowhole, the water'll come down the side, like one of those splash pads. Even from out in the middle of the lake you'll be able to hear the kids laughing and screaming." He smiled with self-satisfaction. "I've got lots of conceptual drawings, if you'd like to see them."

"Maybe sometime," I said, turning and heading back to the road. "I've got a lot to do, Leonard."

He came after me. "I'm going to bring Bob out here, win him over. I don't think he's quite sold on the idea yet."

Back in the truck, I let Leonard guide me to the dump, which amounted to an excavation in the middle of the wilderness overseen by an old guy sitting in a small metal shack. Leonard wouldn't shut up about his dream, the resort, the diaper business, his reality show where a mother and father trick their child into thinking they're dead. But I had pretty much tuned him out, and merely nodded mechanically every minute or so, like a fake dog in a rear car window.

I was grateful Leonard had decided to go fishing the moment we returned, so once I had the truck parked I was able to head over, alone, to the outbuilding that sat back behind the fourth cabin. A small, open-air garage was attached, and inside were a green lawn tractor, stacks of cottage shutters, wood scraps, old gas cans. Inside, I found a freezer and an old refrigerator. There were a few bottles of beer inside, a couple of cans of Coke, and a plastic container that appeared to be full of dirt.

I hauled it out, set it on top of the freezer, took a deep breath, and then dug my fingers in. As I raised out clumps of dirt, dozens of worms squirmed out between my fingers, slipping back into the bin.

"Okay," I said. "We got worms. We got more than enough worms." There was a roll of paper towels hanging from the wall, and I tore off three or four to wipe the dirt from my hands just as Hank Wrigley rapped on the door, wanting a dozen of the little wigglies for his bait can. I counted them out, then wiped my hands off a second time. "Just put it on my tab," he said. I wished him good luck, then went around to the garage and planted myself into the seat of the lawn tractor.

There was a floor-mounted gearshift in front of me, a throttle lever on a panel under the steering wheel, and a single, tiny key inserted in the ignition. I guess Dad wasn't too worried about tractor thefts up in these here parts.

I turned the key and the tractor roared to life. It was fitted with a variety of switches and levers for lowering the housing that enclosed the lawn-cutting blades, but before dropping it down, I wanted to drive over to where I was going to be doing the cutting. The area where the camp first came into view when you rounded the last bend as you came in from the highway was looking pretty shaggy, I'd noticed.

I grasped the throttle lever and shoved it ahead.

It had never occurred to me that a lawn tractor might benefit from a headrest. It was not the sort of vehicle that one would expect capable of inflicting whiplash.

The tractor shot ahead like a launched pinball. My body flung backward as my left hand lost grip of the wheel. The tractor became an unguided missile, coming out of the garage like the Batmobile emerging from its secret underground exit. It took a moment for me to struggle against the g-forces and lean forward enough to resume my hold of the wheel.

Dad was watching from the window as I shot past, my face no doubt frozen in terror. I had, for reasons I find totally reasonable, expected a lawn tractor to behave like a lawn tractor, and not a Ferrari.

I shoved the throttle back down, stomped on the

brake pedal. Once the tractor was no longer moving, I turned the key to shut down the motor.

Dad approached on crutches.

"I can see why you didn't want any advice," he said. "Looks like you were born to drive one of these babies."

I was still catching my breath. Finally, I said, "When did they start installing turbochargers in these fucking things?"

"It's a bit modified," Dad said casually. "I did most of the modifications myself." He beamed with pride. "They do lawn tractor racing up here. At the fall fair. And it still cuts the grass pretty good besides."

I swung my right leg over the wheel, and got off. "I think I'll do the fish bucket instead," I said.

"If my ankle doesn't heal up before the fair," Dad said, "maybe you'd like to race it for me. I wouldn't be able to put much pressure on the brake."

"Why not just install a parachute on the back?" I said, heading for the lake and not looking back.

This was terrific. Not only was I doing the camp chores and assisting my father in finding a way to save him from his whacko tenants, but I was now expected to sub for him in a race in which all the entrants employed John Deere emblems as protective headgear.

The garbage pail under the fish-cleaning table hadn't been emptied since I'd seen it the day before, and it was as disgusting a bucket of anything as I could ever recall witnessing. Fins and scales and guts and heads and eyeballs, all swimming in an ooze that gave off a stench that made me want to lose the fried egg sandwich Lana had been good enough to make for me earlier that day.

I grabbed the gut-splattered handle gingerly and carried the pail as far from my body as possible, not eager for it to brush up against my pants. On my way back from the lake I saw a police car parked near the tractor, and Chief Orville Thorne engaged in conversation with Dad, who'd propped his crutches up against the tractor hood and dragged himself into the seat.

"Chief," I said.

Thorne touched the brim of his hat, like he intended to tip it but ran out of gas. He glanced at the bucket. "Whatcha got there?"

"I heard you were coming so I made lunch," I said.

"Orville here says he's got a couple people rounded up to hunt down that bear and kill it," Dad said.

"That so," I said. I pictured Orville and others with skills equal to his roaming the woods, armed to the teeth. Put the ambulance on standby now, I thought.

"Your dad says you might be questioning whether that's really necessary," Orville said, a hint of a smirk on his lips. I wanted to take his hat and subject the top of his head to a noogie attack. "And I heard you had a few words with Dr. Heath. He's not very happy with you."

"Look, he's a nice man," I said, "but I don't think he conducted a very thorough autopsy on Morton Dewart. Betty Wrigley doesn't think it was a bear killed him. But it might have been dogs."

Orville rolled his eyes. "And what's she, a nurse or something?"

"Yes," I said.

That caught him off guard, so he adjusted his hat while he figured out what to say next. "Well, if I listen to you, and do nothing, and it turns out you're wrong, and that bear kills again, then I'm gonna end up with egg on my face."

"Do what you want," I said. "Just let me know when you and your friends are combing these woods so I can run into town and get fitted for a Kevlar vest."

"Zachary," Dad said, "would you stop being an ass? Orville's just doing his job."

"I've got work to do," I said, lifting up the bucket of fish guts.

Dad pointed into the woods beyond the fifth cabin. "Back in there. You'll see a mound of dirt, a shovel, and a board. An old cottage shutter. Make sure you cover it up with lots of dirt. That's really important." He paused, and smiled. "Okay, chum?" He started laughing. He turned to Orville. "You get it? Chum?"

"No," said Orville.

The scene was just as Dad described it. I set the pail down and hooked my fingers under the shutter that lay on the ground. It revealed a round hole, about two feet across and two feet deep. I'd expected to see maggots feasting on guts, but there was nothing visible in the hole but dirt. I dumped in the bucket's contents, which slid out with a gag-inducing *sloosh*. Then I grabbed the shovel, buried the guts with an inch of dirt, and slid the shutter back over the hole.

Orville was nowhere in sight but Dad was still perched on the tractor seat as I did my return route with the empty bucket. "You got it, right?" he asked. "Chum?"

I was thinking, he better get well soon, before I kill him.

11

It wouldn't have been a long walk up to the Wickens place, but with Dad on crutches, it wasn't hard to talk him into letting me drive us up there. I got him into the passenger seat of my Virtue, the hybrid car I'd bought at an auction some months ago, and even though we weren't traveling more than a couple of hundred yards on a gravel driveway, and wouldn't even get anywhere near the main road, Dad buckled his seatbelt.

"Are you kidding me?" I said..

"It doesn't seem to offer the same kind of protection as my truck," he said.

"Your tractor can outrun a Porsche and it doesn't have a seatbelt."

When we got to the gate of warning signs, I got out and waved at the Wickens house, figuring someone would probably be watching for us. One of the Wickens boys came running down and unlocked the gate, blond-haired, shorter than the one I'd seen when I'd walked up here with Orville and Bob.

"Wendell," Dad said. "The less stupid one."

As we pulled in, Dad cast a disapproving eye at the abandoned appliances, bits of furniture, bits and pieces of junk. "If I ever get them out of this house, there's going to be one hell of a cleanup to do." I glanced over to make sure his window was up, not eager for any of the Wickenses to hear that kind of talk.

Timmy strode out onto the porch, took the two steps down, and opened the car door for Dad, even reaching into the backseat to grab his crutches. Dad handed him a six-pack of Bud we'd brought along as a gift.

"That was a nasty fall you must of took," Wickens said, handing Dad his crutches.

"Yeah, it was pretty stupid," Dad said. I came around, took Wickens's hand when he extended it. He introduced me to the boy—not a boy really, but a young man in his twenties—who'd opened the gate for us. He was broad shouldered, with blunt, angular facial features. "This is Wendell. His brother, Dougie, is around here somewhere."

I shook Wendell's hand, which, while huge, was strangely limp and doughy in mine, like he couldn't be bothered to squeeze. "Hi," I said. Wendell only nodded.

Timmy led us inside. I was looking around nervously beyond the open door, and Timmy sensed something was troubling me. "What's the problem?"

"Well," I said, "I'm just a little worried about the dogs."

"Gristle and Bone?" Timmy grinned. "They're just

playful, is all. They're in the kitchen. They spend most of their time in there, waiting for scraps when they're not snoozing."

I laughed nervously. "They, uh, gave me a bit of a scare yesterday."

"Tell ya what," Timmy said. "I want you to be able to relax, so I'll have the dogs put out in the barn."

"I'd be most grateful," I said.

"Wendell," Timmy said, "take the pups out, okay?"

"Sure thing, Timmy," he said, and disappeared toward the back of the house.

A heavyset woman, about Timmy's age I guessed, appeared. She was dressed in a dark T-shirt and stretch slacks, her graying hair pulled back with pins. Her neck was jowly, her nose red and splotchy. "I'm Timmy's wife, Charlene," she said, motioning for us to take a seat in the living room, which was littered with mismatched chairs, plaid couches, coffee and end tables buried in car and sporting and gun magazines.

Dad settled into a chair and I was about to take a spot on the couch when I was distracted by something.

Hanging above the fireplace mantel, slipped into a cheap black frame, was a military dress photograph of Timothy McVeigh. The Oklahoma City bomber. The man convicted, and ultimately put to death, for murdering 168 people when his rental truck, loaded with explosives, destroyed one side of a federal government building on April 19, 1995. I instantly recalled that less formal shot of McVeigh, in his orange prison jumpsuit, being paraded before the press on his way to a police van while an angry mob screamed out what they wanted to do with him.

The very idea that someone would frame that man's picture and put it on a wall left me numb.

For a moment, I didn't realize Timmy was attempting to make another introduction. "I want you to meet May," Timmy said, and I turned around to see, standing shyly next to him, the young woman who'd fallen, weeping, into his arms the day before. If it weren't for her tired and vacant look, she would have been a lovely woman. Her dirty blonde hair half hung over her eyes, which probably suited her at that moment, since she didn't seem to want to look me or Dad in the eye. She tried to force a smile as she was introduced.

"I'm very sorry," I said. "I understand you and Mr. Dewart were close. He was your boyfriend?"

Her smile cracked. "We were friends," she said.

"Awful, awful thing," said Charlene, and Timmy nodded along with her. "Just awful. Terrible for his family."

"Daddy says he was looking for a bear," May said, without, it seemed, much conviction. "It just, it just doesn't seem possible."

Timmy Wickens slid an arm around his daughter's shoulder. "Honey, why don't you go help Mom with dinner."

She turned obediently and sleepwalked her way to the kitchen, Charlene following her.

"She's very upset," Timmy said, once the women were out of earshot.

"I can imagine," said Dad.

I was about to sit down on the couch for a second time when another man, the one Timmy had referred to as Dougie the day before, strode into the room with a young boy.

"Well, now you can meet everyone," Timmy said. "Charlene's son Dougie, and May is my daughter, and this here is my grandson Jeffrey, May's boy."

Dougie nodded and continued on to the kitchen, but Jeffrey approached with his arm extended. He was holding, in his left hand, a TIE fighter, a model spaceship with two hexagonal wings connected to a round pod, from the *Star Wars* movies.

"Pleased to meet you," he said, shaking my hand and then Dad's.

He was a handsome young boy, shiny blond hair swept to one side, a look of innocence in his eyes.

"Hello," I said. "Nice TIE fighter. You got an Imperial soldier inside the cockpit there?"

Jeffrey brightened. Imagine an adult knowing such a thing. "Wow. No, I haven't got one of those yet. You like *Star Wars?*"

"I love *Star Wars,*" I said. "I love all sorts of science fiction. I've even written a few science fiction books."

"No kidding? Were they made into movies?"

"No," I said.

"But they were optioned, at least, weren't they, son?" Dad asked.

"No, Dad, none of them were optioned." To Jeffrey, I said, "My whole office at home is filled with sci-fi toys. *Star Trek, Lost in Space,* all kinds of stuff. I've never really grown up."

Jeffrey giggled at that. "I haven't seen you around very much," he said. He nodded toward my dad. "I've seen Mr. Walker down by the cabins, but not you. Are you renting a cabin?"

"I'm borrowing one. I'm Zack Walker. That's my dad."

Jeffrey nodded, then frowned. "I guess you heard about Morton."

"Yes," I said. "We have."

"He was looking for a bear and it killed him. That's what happened." He said it with conviction.

"How old are you, Jeffrey?" I asked.

"I'm ten," he said. "I don't go to school. I learn right here at home. My mom teaches me, and Grandpa helps prepare lessons for me."

"Isn't that great," I said.

Jeffrey said he had to go and ran off after Dougie. Timmy smiled proudly as I sat down on the couch. "He's a great kid."

"Who's that?" Dad said, pointing to the McVeigh portrait. *Jesus, Dad, don't go there*, I thought.

Timmy smiled reverently. "That's Timothy McVeigh, a famous fighter for freedom. You must have heard of him."

Dad, who's never been quite as plugged into the news as I, might not have recognized the picture, but he had no trouble with the name. "Christ, he's the one blew up that building, isn't he?"

Timmy shook his head sadly. "That's what they'd have you believe, but there are a lot of interesting questions about that day. Did you know that?"

We shook our heads.

"Well, one big question is, why did some federal employees who did FBI work not come to the Alfred P. Murrah Building that day? Huh? Did you know that a lot of them didn't report for work? Pretended to be sick? Do you know why? It's because they knew something was going to happen, that's why."

I leaned forward on the couch. This was not something I'd heard before. "What are you getting at, Timmy?"

"What I'm saying is, they had to have been tipped off by the military. You see, the amount of damage done to the building could never have been accomplished with the kind of bomb they say Mr. McVeigh had in that cube van. Absolutely impossible. Had to be something much bigger, something that detonated either instead of, or in addition to, that rental truck."

"I'm a bit confused," I said. "You're saying the military, the U.S. government, knew the bombing was going to happen, and got some of its people out of there, but let the rest die?"

"They didn't just know about the bombing," he said, and paused. "They're the ones that did it."

I was speechless for a few seconds. "The government bombed its own people?"

"It's incredible, isn't it?" Wickens said, as if sharing in my astonishment. "There are a lot of parallels between that event and what happened at the Twin Towers. You know how they pancaked down, one floor collapsing on top of another?"

The unforgettable images flashed in my mind. "Yeah," I said.

"That was because there were already bombs in the buildings. That's how they came down so perfectly, like when those demolition experts go in and drop a building, you know."

I paused. "You noticed those two planes, right?"

Timmy smiled and waved his hand at me. "Anyway, with the Oklahoma City thing, it just shows you what lengths the government will go to."

"To do what?" I asked. "What lengths?"

"To discredit honest, hardworking people, patriots, people like Timothy McVeigh, people like us and yourselves. You know," he said, smiling, "I've always found it a curious coincidence that he and I share the same first name."

"I'm still not sure I follow," I said. "How did this discredit people like McVeigh, and you?"

Timmy Wickens nodded patiently, as though he'd had to explain this to others many times, and was willing to go through it as often as was necessary to get his message out there. "The government, when it becomes too powerful and strives to interfere too much in people's lives, by tracking their movements, their financial transactions, by taking away their ability to defend themselves by bearing arms, will go to drastic measures to turn the public against those people who are fighting back to reclaim their constitutional rights and stop this country from slipping into moral bankruptcy and the watering down of the races." He was jabbing a finger in the air at me to make his point. "What are we to make of a world that lets colored people run rampant and turn our cities into jungles, that lets faggots get their own TV shows and lets them live together without no shame at all? Did you know, right here in Braynor, the faggots want to put a float into the parade? And that the town, our white mayor, who is married to a colored, is probably going to let them? Can you imagine such a thing? They'll probably build a huge purse and ride in it." He chuckled at his own joke.

"So," he continued, "they find people like Timothy McVeigh, who fight back against the government, who fight against the suppression of the truth, who fight to preserve decency and the family and preserve moral values, and frame them for monstrous acts like what happened at Oklahoma City. Mr. McVeigh was the kind of person with the courage of his convictions, who was willing to strike back at the government to let them know that they can't get away with these kinds of things."

"What you're saying is," I said slowly, "Timothy McVeigh didn't do it, he was being framed, but it was the sort of statement he would have wanted to make, and if he had, that would have been okay?"

Timmy thought about that for a moment, pursed his lips out, and nodded. "I think you're starting to get the idea." He slapped the tops of his thighs as though congratulating all of us. "Some people, it takes them a lot longer to get their head around this. You got it right away."

"Dinner!" shouted Charlene from the kitchen.

Timmy motioned for Dad and me to follow him. When Wickens's back was turned, Dad sidled up next to me and twirled his index finger beside his head, the international "they're crazy" gesture.

"Stop it," I whispered.

There was a long wood table in the oversized kitchen, up close to an open window that looked out toward the barn. Everyone was gathered there, taking their seats.

Timmy glanced out the window, toward the barn. "Dougie," he said, "is that the van I see sitting out there?"

Dougie craned his neck to look. "Appears to be."

"Didn't I ask you to back it into the barn?"

Dougie, in an exaggerated display, bounced his fist off his forehead. "I forgot."

"Jesus, Dougie, you'd forget your ass if it wasn't already in your pants."

Charlene, at the stove, whirled around. "You leave him alone!"

"Fine, fine, whatever," Timmy said. "Dougie, run out there, put away the van, and let the dogs out of the barn. We can toss them some dinner scraps out the window."

Dougie excused himself, and a few minutes later I could hear Gristle and Bone charge toward the house, then gather under the open window, growling and snorting. Then there was scratching outside, as the dogs jumped up against the house, high enough that their slobbering snouts appeared briefly at the window, then disappeared.

"Down!" Wickens shouted, and the jumping stopped.

When Dougie came back in, we all took our seats, Wickens at one end, his wife at the other, her chair backed up to a pantry door with a lock on it. The rest of us filled in the spots between, May at one corner by her father, head down.

Wickens lowered his head. "Dear Lord, please bless us and lead us into righteousness, and welcome the guests at our table, and we thank you for this food, and ask that you say a special prayer for our friend Morton, who was taken by one of your creatures, and we trust that it is all part of your divine plan, amen."

"Amen," said the rest of the family, all except for May, who had started to cry.

"There, there, sweetheart," said Timmy, slipping an arm around her.

"It was an awful thing," said Dougie. "I remember him saying to me, just before he went out, that he was going to find that damn bear once and for all. Who could have guessed that it would be the bear who got him."

How many more times, I wondered, would it be drilled into us how Morton Dewart had come to an end?

The family started passing around food. There was a roast of beef, a few rare slices already cut and lying in a pool of watery blood, some breaded fish fillets, boiled vegetables and mashed potatoes, slices of white bread stacked on a plate. Wickens produced, from his pocket, a jackknife that he used to spear slabs of meat and drop them onto our plates. It was plain fare, basic home cooking, and it was, to be honest, pretty good. I didn't realize, until I started digging in, just how hungry I was from working around the camp all day.

I reached for a slice of bread, slathered it with butter. "You'd seen the bear around here before, had you?"

Jeffrey piped up. "Not me, but Grandpa says it was around a lot."

Timmy smiled. "And it's a good thing you didn't run into him, or he'd of had you for breakfast, young man."

"Chief Thorne's talking about getting a party together to go after him, kill him," Dad said. "Was that your idea?"

"Uh, nope, but it's a darn good one," said Wickens. "Isn't that a good idea, everyone?"

Much nodding around the table.

"You know what's funny," said Dad, and every time he opened his mouth he was making me nervous, "is that they didn't find a rifle anywhere near where they found Morton. He must have taken one with him, right, if he was going out to kill a bear?"

What on earth was he doing?

I'd never have told him this had I thought he was going to bring it up with the Wickenses. This was the sort of information you held back until the time was right.

The table suddenly became very quiet. Wickens glanced at Wendell and Dougie, his wife looked at May, and May kept her head down. Only Jeffrey had something to say. "That's totally weird, huh? Where would his gun go? Where do you think it went, Grandpa? Do you think the bear would have taken it? Can you imagine that, a bear walking through the woods with a shotgun?" He cackled, then noticed that no one else was laughing. "Sorry," he said.

"That's okay, Jeffrey," said Timmy Wickens. "But you know, he might actually have picked it up, walked a ways off into the forest, and dropped it. I'll bet you it'll turn up eventually."

I was betting he was right. And I was willing to bet that it would be in the next day or so.

"Tell me about Mr. Dewart," I said.

May would have been the logical one to answer this, I figured, but she looked too distraught, so her stepmother Charlene stepped in. "He was a nice boy. From the city, but he was working up this way and got to know May, and it was just like having a third son around here. They was really hitting it off nicely. He was lots of help around here, good at fixing things, tuned up our cars and everything."

"He seemed a bit funny lately though," said Jeffrey, making a butter puddle in his mashed potatoes.

May spoke. "Jeffrey, eat your dinner. You've had enough to say tonight."

"I was just saying, that's all. He—"

"I said, eat your dinner and keep your thoughts to yourself."

Jeffrey frowned, took a forkful of mashed potatoes, the dam breaking and the butter flowing out.

It was quiet for a while after that. Periodically, Wickens or one of the boys would sling a piece of fat or a scrap of bread out the window, and the dogs would fight over the snacks, snarling and barking. "Let's give 'em some fish," Wickens said, sticking a fork into a fillet and tossing it out the window. The dogs went into a frenzy. I thought of Bob's stringer, empty but for some severed pickerel heads.

"Oh no," said Charlene, looking down. "There's another one of those goddamn field mice." She pointed down by the baseboard, where a small gray mouse was inching along tentatively.

"Everyone quiet," Wickens said, and a hush came over the room. He reached for the knife he'd used to serve the roast, held it by the blade between his thumb and forefinger, then, faster than you could blink, launched it and hit the wall. The blade went through the mouse, pinning it to the baseboard, where it twitched and wriggled.

"Awesome, Grandpa!" said Jeffrey, who scrambled out of his chair to yank the knife out of the wood, the mouse still impaled on the end of the blade. He handed it triumphantly to his grandfather. Wickens flicked the knife with his wrist, sending the nearly dead rodent sailing out the open window. Outside, the dogs growled at each other, fighting for the tidbit.

Wickens wiped the blade on his pants, then used it to spear another piece of meat on the table.

"Anyone for seconds?" he asked me and Dad.

"Nothing for me," I said.

"I'm stuffed," said Dad.

12

AS I DROVE DAD to the lawyer's the next morning in his pickup, he said, "I feel a bit bad, talking to Bert Trench about evicting the Wickenses, when they had us to dinner last night and all. I mean, it's not much of a way to show one's gratitude."

I glanced away from the road long enough to look at him. "Are you kidding me? Were you at the same dinner I was at?"

"It just doesn't seem very grateful, that's all."

"Dad, we've been over this. You think they had us for dinner because they like us? They were putting on a show. It was like opening night on Broadway. How many times did someone remind us that Dewart was killed by a bear? The whole fucking family was in on it—well, May didn't really have that much to say. But even the kid mentioned how Dewart had been killed by a bear. It's like they were trying to implant memories. By the time the evening was over I was convinced *I'd* seen Morton Dewart head out to kill that bear. And why do you figure they wanted to do that?"

Dad gazed out the window.

"Dad?"

"Well, it could still be because he *was*. And they need to talk about it. Wouldn't you feel the need to talk about it? I mean, from the very beginning, ever since those damn dogs chased you back over the fence, you've been just bound and determined that those dogs killed that man, that they've been covering it up. It's like you think Wickens meant to kill that man with those dogs, that it was deliberate, and you're basing that on what? Betty's glance at a corpse, and some feelings you've got, and a missing rifle."

"Oh, and while we're on the subject, what the hell were you thinking?"

"What?"

"Last night? Bringing up that thing about the rifle? Were you out of your mind?"

"What are you talking about? You've been going on like it's a big deal, so I thought I'd mention it, see what they thought."

I took a deep breath. "Dad, if there's no rifle, that's because Morton wasn't out hunting for a bear, and if he wasn't out hunting for a bear, that means everything Timmy Wickens and his family of nutcases is telling us is a lie, which is exactly why we don't bring up the thing about the rifle, because it tips them off."

"Oh," Dad said. He tapped his fist lightly on the dashboard. "Well, okay, let's say we go on your theory. Why the hell would Wickens want his own daughter's boyfriend ripped apart by those dogs?"

I thought of my daughter Angie, now in her second year at Mackenzie, majoring in psychology. I could imagine releasing the hounds on some of her boyfriends.

"I don't have an answer for that," I said. "Maybe that's something we should start looking into."

"We?" Dad said, glancing over at me. "That's something that *we* should look into? *We* should start looking into why the Wickenses would have wanted to kill that man? You know, that's why they have police forces, Zachary. They look into that sort of thing."

"Okay, let's turn on the Bat signal and Orville'll get right on it," I said.

Dad clenched his fist tighter. "Stop picking on him," he said.

"What do you care? What's he to you that you defend him? Is this because he's Lana's nephew? You don't want to point out what a doofus he is because it'll hurt your chances of getting between the sheets with her?" Dad's eyes widened. The angrier he looked, the more I felt egged on. "And you never did tell me whether you two are taking precautions. The last thing I want is a little baby brother."

"Shut up! For God's sake, just shut the hell up! Pull over! Pull over! I'm getting out!"

"Dad! You're not getting out! You're on crutches, for Christ's sake!"

"I don't care. Stop the car!"

I wanted to point out that, technically speaking,

we were not in a car, we were in a truck, but did not. "I'm not stopping," I said. "Look, I'm sorry. I won't make fun of Orville anymore." Dad eyed me warily, perhaps to see whether I looked sincere. I was not sure just how convincing I looked. The truth is, I was trying very hard not to laugh, not unlike when Sarah stubs her toe, and I try to look concerned, but she sees something in my eye and says, "You think this is funny, don't you?" At which point, I pretend to have a coughing fit.

I said, "I'll behave myself. I'm not saying it'll be easy, but I'll do my best. I'll treat the uniform with respect, even if I have some reservations about the guy inside it."

Dad looked at me for another second, decided, I guess, that that was the most he could expect for now, and turned his eyes front. We came down the hill into Braynor, traveled through the three blocks of downtown and came out the other side, and parked along the street outside a beautiful, old, three-story, if you counted the dormers, Victorian home that had been turned into a law office.

I got out, went around to help Dad step down, and noticed staple-gunned to the wooden light standard by the truck more Braynor fall fair flyers, listing, in print too small to see unless you went right up to it, some of the big events, including a parade, the lawn tractor races Dad had already warned me about, a massive roast beef dinner, various rides and games.

"This is what you want to involve me in?" I said, nodding my head at the flyer.

"I don't want you doing any damn thing you don't want to do," Dad said.

We mounted the steps of the old house and walked right in, since it was an office and not a residence. Inside, the charm and architectural significance I imagine must have once been there had been eradicated. The place looked more like, well, a lawyer's office, with a receptionist's station, some chairs and magazines.

I approached the middle-aged, slightly frumpy woman at the desk and told her we had an appointment to see Bert Trench, and she said he would be right with us. Dad plopped awkwardly into one of the chairs and I took one next to him.

"Look how old these magazines are," Dad complained. "Hey, look, they're going to impeach Nixon."

A heavy wood door opened and a short, mostly bald man in glasses strode out, hand extended toward Dad. Bert Trench looked to be in his midforties, and judging by the lopsided roll of flesh that hung over his belt, spent more time behind his desk than at the fitness club, if Braynor even had a fitness club.

"Hey, Arlen, how nice to see you," he said. His voice squeaked. "I don't think you've been in here since we did the paperwork on your place. Good heavens, what's happened to you?"

Dad struggled to his feet to shake hands. "Just something stupid," he said. "Slipped."

"Let's help you into the office here."

"This here's my son Zachary," Dad said.

"Nice to meet you," I said as the three of us went into the office. Bert made sure Dad was comfortably settled in one of the two leather padded chairs opposite his desk before he went round and took his spot. I sat down, glanced at a framed photo on Bert Trench's desk of a stunningly beautiful, dark-haired woman I guessed was in her late thirties.

Trench saw how the picture had caught my attention, then looked back at Dad. "Arlen, I read the piece in the paper today, by that Tracy girl, about the trouble at your place. A bear?"

Dad glanced at me, looking for a signal as to whether we were going to get into this. I did a small shake of the head. That wasn't why we were here, exactly.

"Awful thing," Dad said. "Just terrible."

"I can't imagine," Bert Trench said. He turned to me, reached for the framed picture. "This is my wife, Adriana. Arlen, her picture wouldn't have been here when you were last in."

Dad smiled, sort of shrugged. "I don't exactly remember, Bert."

"Adriana and I got married a year ago. This is number four! One of these days I'm going to get it right, and I think she's the one. Although I said that with numbers one, two, and three! Had you seen my other wives, Arlen?"

Dad shook his head, so Bert got pictures out of his desk, displayed them for us. They all looked like beauty queens. Bert must have had something that appealed to the ladies, besides his lumpy tummy, bald head, and squeaky voice, that was not immediately evident.

"Anyway," Bert said, gathering up the photos of his exes and tucking them away, "it's good to see you. Exciting times all around, huh? You see the paper today? Looks like they're going to let the gay boys into the parade. Council couldn't find a way to say no. Either let 'em in, or cancel the parade altogether, and if you ask me, it would have been better to take a stand and cancel the parade."

"What's the story here?" I asked, recalling Timmy's remarks about this, and the manager of the grocery store with the petition he wanted me to sign.

"Oh, sorry," said Bert Trench. "You're not from around here, are you?"

"The city," I said. Dad and Trench shared a glance, as though this would help explain a lot of things that might come up later in the conversation.

"There's always a fall fair parade," Dad said. "Beecham's Hardware, the high school band, the local cattlemen's association, the racing lawnmowers, 4-Hers, Henry's Grocery, Braynor Co-op, that kind of thing, they're all in it. There's these homo activists want to put a float in the parade, or march, or do synchronized wrist flicking, I don't know. The town council said no, so the gay boys were going to make a civil rights case out of it, so the town backed down, decided to let 'em in."

"They were going to go to court to be allowed *into* a parade like that?" I asked. "You'd think you'd do everything in your power to get *out* of a parade like that."

Bert Trench cocked his head, offended. "Pardon?" He eyed me curiously. "The fall fair parade is a tradition around here."

"Don't pay any attention to him," Dad said to Bert. "He makes fun of everything. The whole world's a joke to him."

"Listen," I said, turning to Dad, not Bert Trench. "I have a very good friend, a private detective, who just happens to be—"

"So, Bert," said Dad. "I wonder if you could help me with a little problem I got."

"What would that be, Arlen?" He wasn't even looking at me now. I'd mocked the fall fair parade. Even now, he was probably pressing a silent alarm button under the desk, summoning Orville.

"Uh, it's about my neighbors, Bert. My tenants, actually."

Bert squinted. "Refresh my memory."

"You wouldn't probably even know. It's just been in the past couple of years, I've been renting out the farmhouse, fixed up the best of the cabins for myself. Rented it to some folks named Wickens. They moved down from Red Lake way."

"Wickens," Bert Trench said quietly. "Wickens. That'd be Timmy Wickens, and his boys."

"Stepsons. There's his wife, and he's got a grown daughter, and her boy. It was the daughter, her boyfriend that got killed."

"I see," Bert Trench said, picking up a pen and making circles on a yellow legal pad.

"Bert, they scare the shit out of me. They're shooting guns up there, they've got No Trespassing signs all over the place, and these pit bulls, they're eating my guests' fish right off the stringers, and they're running the place down, it's going to cost me a fortune to get it back in shape when they leave."

"They're leaving, are they? Packing up?' Trench swallowed. "That'd be a load off, wouldn't it?"

"Well, that's what I'm here to see you about. I want them out. And I wanted your advice on how to go about that. How would I go about evicting them? How much notice do I have to give? And can I tell them, I don't know, that it's because I want to fix the house up and move into it, so they don't think it's personal? Because, I don't want them getting angry with me. I don't have a good feeling about them."

Bert Trench was studying his doodles. "Well, I don't know, Arlen, I don't exactly know . . ."

"Can you write them a letter, sort of a friendly eviction notice?" I tried not to roll my eyes. Dad went on. "Something kind of official? I've got the right to do this, right? I mean, it's my place and all."

"Sure, sure, you've got rights, Arlen. But, what have they actually done?"

"Done?"

"I mean, have they threatened you? Caused any significant property damage?"

Dad paused. "Not exactly. But it's a lot of little things, they add up, you know?"

Trench doodled a bit more, and then, in what looked like a staged gesture, glanced at his watch. "Oh my, goodness, I wonder if you could excuse me for a moment."

He got up, left the room, and closed the door behind him. Dad and I sat in the office, alone, nearly a minute, before Dad said to me, "The hell's wrong with him?"

"He started looking a bit pasty from the moment you mentioned the name Wickens," I said.

"He did seem a bit funny, didn't he?" Dad said. "I wonder what—"

The door opened again, and Bert Trench strode in, but he didn't head for his spot behind the desk. He had his hands in his pockets, and tried to look at us, but mostly was looking at the floor.

"Listen, Arlen, and Mr. Walker, Zachary, is it?"

I said nothing.

"I feel terrible about this, but I should have told you when you booked your appointment that I'm just not in a position to take any new business on at this time. I'm really pretty swamped with things, I've got a very large client base, and what you're asking for, what you'd want me to take on for you, that could run into a lot of hours, and I just don't think I could give you the kind of service that you deserve."

"I'm just talking about a letter," Dad said. "You haven't got time to write them a friggin' letter?"

"Like I said, I'm just not able to take on new clients at the moment," he said, trying to smile.

"I'm not a new client," Dad said. "I've already done business with you."

Bert Trench pretended not to hear. "There are some other law offices in Braynor, or you might want to try in Smithfield, or Jersey Falls, maybe someone there would be able to help you, I'm sure." He'd moved to the door and was holding it open for us.

We stood. Dad got his crutches under his arms and as we were going out the door he stopped and looked Bert Trench square in the eye. "Where are your balls, Bert?"

I noticed beads of sweat on Trench's forehead.

"I'm sorry, Arlen," he said. "I can't do this for you."

"Why not?"

Trench swallowed, bowed his head. "Couple years ago, there was a lawyer in Red Lake, he had this client, a plumber, did a lot of work at this house where the Wickenses used to live, before they moved this way and rented your place."

We watched him.

"So he'd done at least a thousand dollars' worth of work, gave the Wickenses their bill, they never paid, so this plumber, he goes and sees this lawyer, asks him to take care of it for him. And the lawyer, he sends them a letter."

"The Wickenses," I said.

"Yeah. So he sends them this letter. And the next night, his house burns down."

Dad and I said nothing.

"Nearly lost his family. Got them out just in time. Nearly lost his daughter, she's paralyzed, fell off a horse when she was fifteen, can't move on her own, and he carried her out just in time."

"It could have just been a coincidence," I said.

"The plumber, he gets a phone call the next day. Caller asks him, does he want his place to be next?"

Dad, shuffling on his crutches, and I moved for the door.

"I'm real sorry," said Bert Trench. "I just don't need that kind of thing. But, Arlen, any time you've got a basic real estate deal, you call me and I'll look after you."

"Sure, Bert," said Dad. "You'll be the first."

13

"SO, WHERE DOES THAT LEAVE US?" I said, sitting at the counter next to Dad in the coffee shop owned by Dad's main squeeze, Lana Gantry. We were still reeling from our meeting with Bert Trench as we hauled our butts up onto the stools.

"Hey, boys," said Lana, her elbows on the counter, leaning in intimately toward us. As she leaned, I could see Dad trying not to be obvious about peeking down her blouse.

"Hi, honey," Dad said.

"Lana," I said, smiling.

"How's your ankle, sweetie?" Lana asked Dad. He turned red, being called "sweetie" in front of his son.

"It's okay," he said quietly.

"If I didn't have this place to run, I'd come out there and stay with you till you get better." She smiled. "I could give you everything you need."

Dad kept blushing, swallowed, and said, "You know Bert Trench?"

"Yeah, sure, he has lunch in here all the time."

"Does he strike you as an attractive man?"

Lana smiled again. "All those hot wives he's had, that what this is about?"

"Yeah."

"Well, from what I hear, what he lacks in the looks department he makes up for in technique."

My eyebrows went up.

"And when he gets tired of one, he unloads her and gets another, and rocks her world, too. They don't even mind it that much when he wants a divorce, they're so exhausted. Don't you worry, though," Lana Gantry said, patting Dad's hand. "I won't let him lure me away from you."

"Um, Lana, I wonder if you could get me and my boy some coffees."

I looked beyond Lana at what was behind the glass. "I wouldn't mind a piece of coconut cream pie, too, if that's what I see there," I said. Lana was back with coffees in a moment, a couple of creams tucked into my saucer, Dad's black, and then she went for my pie.

"This looks fantastic," I said as she placed it in front of me. I put a forkful into my mouth. It was heaven.

"You boys need anything you give me a shout," Lana said, and headed over to the cash register to confer with one of the two waitresses working the room.

"Maybe there's other lawyers with some nuggets in their shorts who'd be willing to take this on," Dad said.

"Try some from some other towns, but not Red

Lake," I said. "Someone who's not likely to run into Timmy when he's getting gas or buying a loaf of bread. You could make some calls when we get back to the cabin," I said, pouring some sugar from the glass dispenser into my cup.

Dad nodded, looking down into his porcelain mug.

"And I have a friend I might call," I said. "He's had a bit more experience with these kinds of things than I have."

Dad looked over at me. "A lawyer?"

"No," I said. "An ex-cop. He works for himself now. Name's Lawrence Jones. He sort of owes me one. I'll call him when we get back."

The door jingled and in walked the law. Orville Thorne took off his hat, set it on the counter, and took the stool next to Dad, even though the one next to me was empty as well.

"I saw your truck outside, Arlen," Orville said, not even bothering with a nod in my direction. I felt an overwhelming urge to give him a nipple-twister. "Wanted to tell you I've got a couple folks together to hunt down that bear. Probably be tomorrow I should think, we'll get started first thing in the morning."

I shook my head, took a sip of coffee.

"What's the matter with him?" Orville asked Dad.

Lana appeared, leaned over the counter and gave her nephew a kiss on the forehead. "Hey, sweetie. Usual?"

"Sure, Aunt Lana."

She poured him a cup of coffee, black, then placed a chocolate dip doughnut on a plate for him.

Orville took a big bite, washed it down with the hot coffee. His mouth still full, he said to me, "So what's your problem?"

"He remains skeptical," Dad cut in. "About there being a bear. That it might be those pit bulls instead."

"That again?" Orville said, unaware that a huge doughnut crumb was hanging on to the corner of his mouth, undermining his authority.

Dad shrugged. "Well, Orville, he does raise an interesting point. Where's the rifle? If Morton went out to kill this bear, then where's the rifle?"

I leaned forward and turned so that I could see Orville's response. I was surprised to see that he was smiling.

"It's in my car," he said.

"What?" I said.

"Timmy Wickens dropped by the station half an hour ago and gave it to me. Said I'd probably want it for the investigation."

"Way to go, Dad," I said. "So, Orville, you're saying he came in, this morning, and gave you the rifle?"

"Yeah, Mr. Smartypants," Orville said. "He did."

"Mr. Smartypants," I said, nodding as though impressed. "Is that part of the police training up here? They give you a list of snappy comebacks? What about Mr. Poo-Head? You should try that one. Leaves people speechless."

"You just remember who you're talking to," Orville said. "And I could still have you charged with assaulting me, don't forget that."

"Jesus, I didn't assault you, I fell on you. Right

after you tripped my dad and fucked up his ankle. After we found out he was alive, which you should have been able to figure out before he actually showed up." I leaned in, whispered, "Had it ever occurred to you to give your aunt a call and see if maybe he was with her?"

"Jesus!" Dad said under his breath. "Do you mind? We're in her café, for crying out loud."

"I *did* do that," Orville whispered back. "There was no answer, and Aunt Lana wasn't at the café either."

We both looked at Dad. He sat silently for a moment, feeling both sets of eyes. He muttered something.

"What?" I said.

"Actually, we went to a motel, after she'd been out to the cabin for a bit, after everyone went home," Dad said. "And then she took the morning off from the café, let the girls handle it." He nodded his head toward the waitresses.

"A motel?" Orville said. He looked shocked. "Why are you and my aunt going to a motel?"

Dad rolled his eyes. "Look, Orville, we just wanted some time alone without interruptions, that's all. You know your aunt loves you and loves to have you drop by, but sometimes, it's just . . ."

Orville looked like he'd just found out there's no Easter Bunny. His aunt and my dad, messing around in a motel. How incredibly sordid. And on top of that, learning he might not be totally welcome to drop by her place whenever he wanted because she and Dad wanted to get it on.

It was a lot to take.

"Look," I said, "could we move this back to the rifle?"

"What about the rifle?" Orville said.

"What did Timmy Wickens tell you about the gun?"

"He said he found it only a few feet away from where we found Morton's body, under some bushes. I guess we just missed it."

"Shit," I said.

Dad looked into his coffee. "Sorry," he said.

"You tipped him off," I said. "I could have guessed Wickens would produce a gun, but I never expected it to happen this quickly. Don't you see? The fact that he came up with a gun so fast just proves that Morton never went hunting with it in the first place."

Dad and Orville looked at me like I was speaking in some other language. "So let me see if I get this," Orville said. "Timmy finds Morton's rifle, which proves Morton didn't have a rifle. Is that what you're saying? You know what? You know what? Maybe, instead of a bear, Morton Dewart was killed by aliens." Orville snickered, slapped his hand on the counter. To Dad, he said, "He writes science fiction books, right? Didn't you say that?"

"Orville," I said, "I'll say this really slowly so there'll be less chance that you'll misunderstand." Dad shot me a look. "What's it to Timmy Wickens whether we have Morton's rifle or not? If Morton was killed by a bear, well, he was killed by a bear. But if he wasn't, but it's in Timmy's interest for us to think he was, then Timmy's going to be doing whatever he can to make sure you don't start considering any other theories."

Orville looked me in the eye for a good three seconds, then did, I have to say, a pretty good impression of the sound a flying saucer might make, coming in for a landing. "Voo-ooo-ooo," he said, making his hand flat and gliding it toward the counter. Then, he walked two fingers toward Dad's coffee mug and, in a nasal voice, said, "Take me to your leader."

I chuckled, took another drink of my coffee. "Okay, Orville, I got nothin'. You're too clever for me. And besides, I guess I'd believe anything Timmy said, too, if I thought it meant he wouldn't take my hat again."

Now Orville had murder in his eyes, and he was lunging in front of Dad, knocking over his coffee and the sugar dispenser, which plunged to the floor with a great crash on the waitress's side. "You take that back," he said, attempting to grab hold of the front of my jacket, but I had leaned back, and as Orville tried to get me, he pushed Dad back and off his stool.

"Oh fuck!" said Dad, unable to swing around and save himself because of his one weak leg. As he began to plummet toward the floor Orville and I both jumped to catch him, getting our arms under his back before he hit the cracked linoleum.

"You two just knock it off!" Dad bellowed, and both of us felt chastened, catching the look of shame in each other's eyes for a second before lifting Dad back onto his stool. Lana was running over from the cash register.

"Good God, what have you fools done to him?" she said. "Arlen, are you okay?"

He grumbled something.

Lana noticed the spilled sugar, the knocked-over coffee cup, and peered over to the other side of the counter. "And who do you boys think is going to clean up this mess?" she asked me and Orville.

Orville and I craned our necks over to inspect the damage. The dispenser had shattered, spreading sugar everywhere.

"He did it," I said, pointing my thumb toward Orville.

"You started it!" he said.

"For the love of Pete," Dad said.

And then we heard a cell phone. Orville looked bewildered by the interruption, then reached into his jacket for his phone.

"Hello?" he said. His eyes grew wider as he listened. "Okay," he said. He folded the phone shut and said to Dad, "You know Tiff, over at the Braynor Co-op?"

Dad nodded slowly. "I think so. Tall guy, kind of goofy looking?"

"I know him," said Lana.

Orville nodded. "Yeah. Well, he's dead."

Lana gasped, put her hand to her mouth. "Oh my Lord. That's terrible. He was a relatively young man, wasn't he? Was he sick? Because I think I saw him in here just a few days ago."

"He wasn't sick," Orville said.

Lana was puzzled. "Was it an accident? They have all that farm machinery over there. Was it a thresher? Was he caught in a thresher?"

"Sounds like somebody put a knife in him," Orville said. He glanced at the mess we'd made. "I'm sorry, Aunt Lana, but I have to go." He picked up his hat, and strode out.

"I don't believe it," Lana said.

"What's the Braynor Co-op?" I asked Dad.

"Farm stuff. Feed, grain, tools, all that kind of thing."

"Seems like a funny place for someone to get killed," I said. "A bank, a liquor store, a gas station, that's where people get killed."

Dad just shook his head, like it was all getting to be too much. "What the hell is happening around here?"

"Why don't we go find out?" I said.

"What do you mean?"

"Let's go over to the co-op, see what's happened."

Dad thought about that. I expected him to say no, that we should head back to the camp, that there were things he didn't need to know about, but to my surprise, he grabbed hold of his crutches that had been leaned up against the counter, and said, "Yeah, okay. Bye, Lana."

Dad directed me to a building nearly a mile north of town, set back a little from the road, with a parking lot out front. There were half a dozen lawn tractors on display out front, some decorative hay bales, rolls of chain-link fencing. "This is where I got my tractor," Dad said. Like a lumber operation, there was an enclosed store up front, and a huge warehouse out back. We saw Orville's police car down around the side of the building, so we drove down there and got out. A small crowd was gathered at the open garage door that led into the warehouse. There were co-op employees—they all wore jeans and the same dark green shirts with "Braynor Co-op" stitched across the right breast—plus Orville and one of his deputies, the coroner I'd offended, Dr. Heath, and Tracy from the local newspaper. The usual crew.

Tracy came over to us. "How ya doin'?" she said. "You think Sarah would take another story from me this soon?" she asked me.

"Looks like all the news is happening up here," I said. "Maybe we can set up a bureau, you and I can run it. What's happening?"

"Tiff Riley didn't show up for work this morning, or so they thought. He was on late last night, was supposed to be here first thing this morning, nobody could find him, so they called home and got his wife, Edna—that's why they called him Tiff, because he was always arguing with her on the phone, his real name was Terrence—and she said he'd never come home the night before. She figured he got drunk or something. Anyway, someone was putting together a fertilizer order, went around to where they store it, they find Tiff there."

Tracy was pretty excited as she told it. Clearly, what with Morton Dewart and now Tiff Riley, she was having a terrific week, journalistically speaking.

"What happened to him?" I asked.

"He got stabbed." She pointed to her own stomach. "Right here. Couple of times. I took a peek in there. There's all kinds of blood on the floor. The guy who got eaten by the bear? That was the first dead body I ever saw, and now, like two days later, I get to see another one. Do you think there's any chance *The Metropolitan* would hire me on? Like, as staff? I could move to the city, no problem. I know you get a lot of dead bodies down there, and I could look at one every day if I had to."

"You'd probably be best talking to Sarah about that," I said. Just inside the garage door I could see Orville questioning an older man in a green shirt. "Excuse me," I said. I walked over, approaching from Orville's blind side so I could hear what they were talking about without him having a big hissy.

The man in the green shirt was saying, "He was on late last night. It's not like we have a security guard or anything, we've never had much need for anything like that, but Tiff was always happy to work late if that meant not going home to Edna, and there was a lot of tidying up to do, so he offered to hang in and make a bit of overtime, lock up when he was done. Got here this morning, didn't notice much out of the ordinary, but Tiff was due in at nine, and by ten-thirty there's still no sign of him, so I called Edna, and she hadn't seen no trace of him either. So we started to wonder where he was."

"Who found him?" Orville asked.

A young woman in a green shirt took half a step forward. She looked rattled, like she'd been crying earlier. "I was just doing some inventory work when I found him, found Tiff, down aisle nine. He'd been, like, stuffed in between some bags of fertilizer so you wouldn't see him if you were looking down the aisle, you'd only see him once you got there."

"Tiff have any enemies?" Orville asked.

The older man and the other employees shrugged. "Not really," said one. "Everyone liked Tiff," said another.

"Is there anything missing?" I asked.

Orville whirled around. "What the hell are you doing here?"

I said nothing, hoping maybe someone would answer my question. I guess the employees sensed the instant tension between us and decided it was better to answer questions posed to them by the police chief, rather than strangers.

Orville turned his back on me, hesitated a moment, and said, "Well, is there?"

"Uh, we haven't really done a complete check yet," said the older man, who I figured must be a manager or owner, or both. "We're going to do that, just as soon as we can. We're all a bit shook up."

"Some of the fertilizer's gone," said the woman who'd found him.

"Fertilizer?" said Orville.

"Quite a bit," she said. "Twenty, thirty bags, I'd say. I'll have to check."

Orville scribbled down some notes. "What the hell would anyone steal bags of fertilizer for?"

I said, "Maybe so there wouldn't be a way to trace that kind of stuff to the purchaser."

Orville turned around slowly, let out a sigh. "Okay,

why would anyone not want somebody to know they'd bought a lot of fertilizer?"

"Maybe because of what it contains."

Dad had worked his way over and had heard the last few exchanges. "Ammonium nitrate," he said. Dad, I seemed to recall, was fairly good at chemistry back in his high school days.

"What the hell is ammonium nitrate?" Orville asked.

"If Timothy McVeigh were still alive," I said, "you could ask him."

14

DRIVING BACK INTO TOWN, I said to Dad, "Wasn't one of the reasons you moved up to Braynor so that you wouldn't have so much to worry about?"

Dad snorted. "Wasn't that why you moved to the suburbs?" We hadn't talked a lot over the years, Dad and I, but he knew all about what had happened when I moved my family from downtown to the suburban enclave of Oakwood, where my friend Trixie still lived and plied her trade. The plan had been to find a safer place to live, and it had backfired rather spectacularly.

"Things don't always work out the way you expect, do they?" I said, offering him a grin.

"I didn't move up here trying to avoid a high crime rate," Dad said. "I just wanted a simpler life."

"I was remembering that time we came up around here with the tent trailer," I said. "I found you down by the lake, your feet in the water, just sitting there, and you looked more peaceful than I'd ever seen you. And then, once we got home, you were your old, cranky self."

Dad smiled. "I don't know how I did it for so long. The whole nine-to-five, Monday-to-Friday thing, commuting, the suit and tie, the ass-kissing, day after day, week after week, month after month, year after year of numbers. Numbers, numbers, numbers."

"I'm guess you get a lot of those in accounting," I said.

"And I loved numbers. I guess I still love numbers. Numbers impose order. They make everything work. They create this, this sense of balance in the universe. There's nothing quite so satisfying as when things add up the way they're supposed to. But one day, I'm sitting at my desk, doing the Fiderberg account, they had this chain of office supply stores, and I'm looking at the numbers, and it was like I'd never seen them before. I was looking at a three, the way it's like two incomplete circles stacked atop each other, and I thought, why is that a three? Who decided that three things would be represented by a symbol that looked like that? Why couldn't it have been a straight line coming down into a semicircle, like a cup? It would have made just as much sense. And then I started looking at all the numbers that way. Why is a seven a line across and then down on an angle? What does that have to do with seven things?"

"You're scarin' me, Dad," I said, but when he looked at me he could see that I was kidding.

"I decided I'd had enough. Your mother was gone, I was ready to do something else, to leave all that bullshit behind. And I remembered how at peace I felt up here, how I might be able to relax in a way I'd never been able to before. I found Denny's Cabins, and I liked the fact that there was just five of them. A single digit. Something manageable." Dad pointed to Henry's Grocery. "We need a couple things."

"Perfect," I said. "I can get a toothbrush."

I pulled over to the curb, put the truck in park, killed the ignition, but made no move to open the door.

"Do you think Mom would have liked living up here?" I asked.

Dad lips went in and out while he pondered that. "I've thought about that. Because," he struggled for a moment here, "I still miss her. I mean, Lana's terrific, and we have fun together."

I smiled, and resisted the temptation to tease.

"But there was only one woman like your mother." Dad blew his nose into a handkerchief, shoved it back into his pocket. "She put up with a lot with me." He looked out his window so I couldn't see his face. "And anything she ever did, it was nothing compared to what a pain in the ass I could be to her. That's why I think she might have liked it up here, because living here has made me a better person, I think."

"We all have our moments," I said. "You should talk to Sarah about me."

Dad nodded, still looking away. "I don't know whether you've ever noticed this," he said, "but I can be a bit difficult to get along with at times."

"Really," I said. "Where I work, this is where someone would shout 'Stop the presses!' "

He smiled tiredly. "Yeah, that's a bulletin all right. I just kind of like things done a certain way, and all the things I've ever done, as a husband and as a father, it's been to make sure you and your mom and Cindy were safe."

"Yeah, well, I think I understand."

"And that meant that sometimes I may have nit-picked a bit," Dad said. "I was hard on your mother."

He was being so forthright, I thought maybe I could broach that period of my youth that remained the most shrouded in mystery, when Mom left for six months.

"Is that why Mom went away, that time?" I said. "Why she walked out on us?"

Dad seemed to be focused on the lock to the glove box, staring at it. "That's hard for me to talk about."

"This is going to come out sounding, you know, accusatory," I said, hesitantly, "but what did you do that made Mom leave?"

Dad kept looking at the glove box, poking his tongue around the inside of his cheek. "Let me tell you what we need," he said.

"Hmm?"

"We need some milk, some cream for coffee, since that's the way you take yours, something for dinner. You pick something. I don't care. Pork chops, a roast chicken, whatever the hell you want. I'll just wait here and listen to the radio. Wait, let me give you some money." He was reaching around to his back pocket for his wallet.

"Don't worry about it," I said.

"No, no, you're my guest. I can pay for the damn groceries."

"Dad, forget it." I had the door open and was crossing the street before he could protest any further.

I grabbed a small plastic basket, figuring I wouldn't be buying enough to justify a big wobbly cart. I bought myself a toothbrush and toothpaste and a basic plastic comb, then headed for the meat section. I looked at steak and pork tenderloin and cuts of chicken, settled on some thick butterfly chops, then checked out the varieties of instant side dishes. I had a package of Uncle Ben's wild rice in my hand when I noticed, out of the corner of my eye, something short standing next to me.

I turned and saw young Jeffrey Wickens standing there, and not far behind him, pushing a cart, his mother, May.

"Hi," said Jeffrey. "Remember me?"

"Of course I do," I said. "You're my *Star Wars* guy. How are you, Jeffrey?"

"Good." He nodded. "I've already done all my school for today."

"Isn't that great," I said, smiling at May as she drew closer. "Most kids, they're probably still in school now, will be for a couple more hours."

"I know," he said. "Sometimes I wish I got recess, though, so I could play with other kids."

I nodded my understanding. May, a smile still evidently beyond her, said, "Hello, Mr. Walker."

"Zack, please," I said. "Nice to see you again. Picking up a few groceries?" A keen observer, that's me.

May Wickens nodded. "We need a few things," she said flatly. "Jeffrey likes to come with me when I shop. It's nice for him to get away from the house." She paused. "Nice for all of us."

There was something about her eyes. A pleading quality. They were tired, and sad, and it wasn't hard to figure out why, losing her boyfriend earlier in the week. But there was more than mere grief in May Wickens's eyes. She had the look of a hostage who doesn't expect the ransom will ever come.

"I'd just like to say, once again, thank you for dinner last night," I said, putting the image of the impaled mouse aside for a moment, "and tell you how sorry I am about Mr. Dewart."

May's eyes looked down. "Thank you," she said. She seemed to be wanting to say something else, her lips parting, then closing.

"Jeffrey," she said, "why don't you go pick out a cereal and maybe some cookies?"

"Sure," he said, and scurried off.

I leaned in a bit closer. "Are you okay?"

She raised her head, looked to the side, avoiding direct eye contact. "I, I just . . ."

I waited. I was about to put a hand on her arm, up by the shoulder, but held back, not sure whether that was the right thing to do, especially in a place as public as this grocery store.

"What is it again that you do, Mr. Walk—Zack?"

"I'm a writer," I said. "I work for *The Metropolitan*. I write features, mostly. And I've written some books."

"So you work for a newspaper?"

"Yes."

"I don't know if I should be talking to you." Her eyes darted up and down the grocery aisle.

"I'm not interviewing you," I said. I gave her my friendliest smile. "We're just talking. That's all."

"I just, I wish I had someone to talk to."

"Sure. Listen, would you like to go get a coffee? Lana's is just a couple of doors down. It's good coffee, and I can recommend the coconut cream pie."

"I don't know," she said.

"I'd be happy to buy you a coffee. I'd even like to, if it wouldn't upset you too much, ask you a couple of questions about Mr. Dewart, about Morton. I mean, there's been so much activity around our place related to what happened to him, but I don't feel that I know a single thing about him."

"Maybe, if we went quickly," May Wickens said, her eyes still scanning. "Let me, let me figure out what to do with Jeffrey. He can't know, he'll tell them, I mean—"

"Sure," I said. "If you don't want to be seen leaving with me, I'll just head over and meet you there."

Suddenly, Jeffrey was back, dumping two boxes of sugary cereal and a bag of Oreos into May's basket. "What else can I get?" he asked.

"Very nice seeing you again," I said to May, and then to Jeffrey, "You take care, okay? You get any more cool *Star Wars* stuff, you show me, okay?"

"I've got a Millennium Falcon," he said.

"And a Han Solo figure?"

"Yup."

I put a hand on his shoulder. "You take it easy, okay? And take good care of your mom. She's had a tough week."

"Sure thing," Jeffrey said.

I got to the checkout and tossed a local paper and a magazine onto the conveyor belt with my few items. While the cashier was ringing them through, the white-coated Mr. Henry reappeared with his clipboard.

"Would you like to sign our petition to—"

And then he recognized me as the son of a bitch who wouldn't sign it the last time I was in.

"Oh, you," he said, still looking like he was picking up a bad smell off of everyone around him.

"Still not interested," I said.

"So you don't care that our parade, this town's traditions, are being hijacked by special interests out to promote their agenda?"

"What are you talking about?"

"Those gays, and the lesbians. They want to ruin our parade."

"I see," I said. "Can I ask you something?"

"Sure."

"You've heard about those starving kids in Africa?" He nodded.

"Global warming and the depletion of the ozone layer and how the polar ice caps will probably all melt someday and we'll all be underwater?"

He nodded again, but his eyes were narrowing.

"Crack babies? The shortage of safe drinking water in the next few years? Rogue nations with nuclear bombs? You've heard of those things?"

Henry nodded a third time, and this time he spoke. "What's your point?"

I tapped the petition on his clipboard with my finger. "And this is what you're collecting signatures for? This is what's got your shorts in a knot?"

I handed over a twenty to the cashier, grabbed my bagful of items, and said to Henry, "I'd love to chat longer, but my boyfriend gets very pissy if his lunch isn't on the table on time."

I walked out of the grocery store, past a phone booth, crossed the street and opened the door to the truck.

"Tell me how much you spent and I'll reimburse you," Dad said.

"I don't think I'll be able to shop there again," I said. "In fact, *you* might not be able to shop there again."

"What are you talking about?"

"Dad, you okay here for a while?" I said. "I ran into someone in the store, I'm just gonna grab a quick coffee, I'll just be a few minutes."

"Who?"

If I told him, he might object, or at least have more questions than I had time to answer. "Just sit tight, okay? Here, I bought you *The Braynor Times*, and a *Newsweek*."

"I could stand to pee," Dad said.

"We all stand to pee, Dad," I said. "That's what makes us men."

"Are you going to be long?"

"Can you last fifteen minutes or so?"

"Just try to be quick."

I ran down half a block to Lana's, caught her eye as I walked in, and took a table in the back corner. There was no sign yet of May Wickens.

Lana strolled over. "Where's your father?"

"I ditched him," I said, giving her my just-kidding smile. "Listen, could I trouble you for a couple of coffees? I'm supposed to be meeting someone."

"Comin' up."

The door opened and May Wickens came in, head down, jacket collar up, acting like she thought she could make herself invisible. I raised my hand and she slid into the booth opposite me. The seat backs were high, and she slid over to the far side, slunk down so she was barely visible from the window.

"Where's Jeffrey?" I said.

"My father would kill me, but I gave Jeffrey a bunch of quarters to go to the video arcade at the corner. He's always begging to go and I'm always saying no. He thinks I'm at the drugstore."

Lana Gantry showed up with two mugs of coffee. She smiled at the two of us, but no small talk. Her eyes did a little dance as she wondered what I was up to, having a coffee with a young woman. She'd know, of course, that I was married.

"Thanks," said May. She wrapped her hands around the mug, as though taking strength from its warmth.

"You seem," I said, trying to find my way, "frightened."

May tried to take a sip of coffee, but it was still too hot for her. "You don't have any idea," she said. "He's, he's poisoning my son."

"What?"

She shook her head. "Not, I mean, I don't mean that he's actually poisoning him. It's with his ideas. He tells me what to teach him."

"We're talking about Timmy, your father," I said, just to be sure.

May nodded. "He decides what Jeffrey will be taught. Not just math and spelling and geography, but history, and, like, social studies, he calls it. Like how homosexuals are trying to lure our children to their side, how the Jews are running everything, how all this talk about the Holocaust is greatly exaggerated, how the Negro is an inferior race, how he has a greater sex drive"—at this she blushed a bit—"and how Negroes, black people, are not as advanced as the white race. I mean, I've met Negroes, and I don't know about their sex drives, but, Mr. Walker, do you believe that sort of stuff?"

She asked it innocently, like she was asking whether I thought it might rain tomorrow.

"No," I said. "I don't."

"Well, I don't either. I listened to my father say these things for years, and then I was gone away for a while, I was out on my own, and I learned that so many of the things my father had taught me, they just didn't seem true. I hate to say this, but I think my father may be something of a, well, a racist."

"I guess that's something you'd have to consider," I said.

"Anyway, I've kind of had a lot of sadness in my life, going way back. I got pregnant eleven years ago, with Jeffrey, of course."

"He seems like a wonderful boy."

"Thank you. I was on my own then, I'd met this man, it was just a short-term thing, he wasn't the right man, you know? But I had the baby, on my own, and Daddy was very upset, he wanted me to come home and live with him. This was a few years after my mom died, and a few before he met Charlene. But I didn't want to go back and live with him, listen to all that hate that's bottled up in him."

"I can understand that."

"But he can be very forceful, you know? But I tried to make a go of it for a very long time, and it was hard, raising a small boy, getting jobs. And I'd no sooner get a job, it seemed, and then I'd lose it. About three years ago, I met this man named Gary. Gary Wolverton. A really wonderful man, and, we, you know, we became close. The thing is, he wanted to be a writer, a newspaper reporter? Like you? He cared about the way the world was, and wanted to write about things that were wrong and what could be done about it. Well, like I said, we were close, and he seemed to really like Jeffrey, which was terrific, because I so wanted a father for him. But Daddy, it was like he thought he should be Jeffrey's father figure. I mean, he's his grandfather, and that's great, but he wanted to be the main influence. Am I making any sense?"

"Sure," I said.

"So, Daddy made it very difficult when Gary and I decided to get married. Daddy figured I'd never come back home then."

"Well, of course not," I said. "You're entitled to make a life of your own."

May Wickens paused, took another sip of coffee. "Anyway, something happened. There was this accident? Gary was crossing the street, this was a couple blocks from where I lived in the city, we weren't actually living together yet, but he was coming to see me, and he'd stopped to get some wine, and that was when the car hit him."

"Oh my God," I said.

"It was one of the crazy things. A hit-and-run. He died instantly."

"I'm sorry," I said. "Did they arrest anyone?"

May shook her head. "No, they never did. They figured it was some drunk driver." She paused at the memory. "I took it bad, but so did Jeffrey, he really loved Gary. I tried to make a go of it, alone, and my father was really pressuring me then to come back and live with them, by this time he'd hooked up with Charlene and her boys, Dougie and Wendell. My stepbrothers, I guess, sort of. Anyway, he wanted me to move in with this new family of his, this was before we moved to your dad's farmhouse. And I really didn't want to, but I kept losing jobs. Things would be going great, and then they'd call me in and tell me I was fired."

"This happened a lot?"

"Like, three times in one year. I'd get accused of stealing, or they'd just fire me and wouldn't give any reason. I have, like, the worst luck."

"That's really tough."

"So I had no money, and I couldn't make my rent,

and Daddy kept telling me to come home, and finally, I really didn't have any other choice. I don't know, he finally wore me down. Jeffrey was nearly eight, I had to pull him out of school, and we moved in with Daddy, and he wouldn't even let me send him to a new school. He said we could look after that ourselves, that the schools were run by these secret societies and everything that wanted to brainwash children. And I realized, having been away for so long, how much I'd forgotten about what my father was like, the things he believes, the things he thinks need to be done."

She tried her coffee again. It had cooled down enough for her to take a sip.

"What sort of things does he think need to be done?" I asked. Even though it was warm enough in the café, I felt a brief chill at the memory of the McVeigh portrait hanging on Timmy Wickens's wall.

"Daddy wants a revolution. All these forces of darkness, he calls them, have to be stopped. Ordinary people have to rise up and stop the corruption of our society."

"What does that mean?"

"He doesn't, he doesn't talk to me as much about it. He talks to Dougie and Wendell, his little *soldiers*. They're on this mission. They hang on his every word." She looked down at the table. "And Jeffrey's starting to, too. I see how he looks up to them."

She linked her fingers together, entwining them so hard I thought they might snap.

"What about Morton?" I asked. "Was he on this mission, too?"

"I met Morton in the city about the time I decided to move back in with Daddy. He waited tables at this coffee place I would go to, and he'd been bouncing from job to job, he was kind of a lost puppy, you know what I mean?"

I nodded.

"There was something about him, I don't know. He was looking for something in his life, anything, to care about, to believe in, to belong to, and I wanted to be that for him, but it was hard, when I hardly had any money, and a little boy to raise. But when I moved back, and Morton came to visit, I think he found some of those things he'd been looking for. We were like a community for him, I think. He really got to know my father, listened to what he had to say, and I think he was kind of going along with it. About how all these special interest groups were hijacking the country, you know, about the *fags* and the *niggers* and the *liberal elite* and the *Jews* and the *Muslims*. But lately, it's like Morton was getting uncomfortable with it. I tried to get him to talk to me, but he was all wrapped up with himself, like he was struggling with something, like he was ashamed, or had this awful secret."

"What kind of secret?" I asked.

May shrugged. "I don't know. But I think he wanted my father to like him, because he loved me, and he liked Jeffrey, too. Jeffrey was warming to him, too, I could tell. Morton used to just visit every few weeks, but the last couple of months, he stayed with us, said he was going to find work up here, but Daddy said to him, don't worry, he could work around the place, do some things for him. And now . . ."

"What do you think happened to Morton?" I asked.

May blinked. "What do you mean?"

"The whole bear thing."

She wrapped her hands around the mug again, leaned in. "What are you saying?"

"I don't know," I said, backtracking, wondering whether to go there. "I mean, are you satisfied with the coroner's finding, that he was killed by a bear?"

She swallowed. "I'm not sure."

"Why?"

"Because, I don't know, because everyone's trying so hard to make me believe it was a bear. Dad and Charlene's boys, after this all happened, and they found Morton, they say Morton was talking about getting this bear, that he didn't want it going after Jeffrey, that he was going to kill it."

"Did that seem odd to you?"

She looked down into her cup. "Morton never once mentioned any bear to me. I've never seen one, I don't think anyone has ever seen one. If they have, they never talked about it until that day that they found Morton. I mean, I know there must be bears up here, but there are wolves and deer and everything else, too, but how often do you actually see them?"

"Anything else?" Lana said, appearing out of nowhere. "There's still a piece of that coconut cream pie left if you want it. I wouldn't breathe a word about you having two pieces in one day."

"No, thanks, that's everything, Lana."

She tore a check off a pad and slapped it on the table.

"Why are you telling me all this?" I asked.

May's eyes moistened. "For my son," she said. "Would you want to see a boy raised this way, on a daily diet of racism and hate?"

"Why don't you leave?" I asked. "Just get in your car with Jeffrey and keep on driving."

May swallowed. "Because he'd find us. He and Charlene, and those boys of hers. They'd find us. And they'd make us come back. Daddy said to me once, he said, 'Don't you go thinking about leaving, May,' he said, 'unless you're happy to leave Jeffrey behind.'"

I realized that my heart was pounding. "He threatened to hold your son."

May bit her lip. "I don't know what I'm going to do. I guess, I took a chance telling you because you might have some idea."

I had no idea whatsoever. The best idea I could come up with was to run back to the city as quickly as I could. To leave all these problems behind. Dad got himself into this mess, renting that house to the Wickenses, and he could just find a way out of it.

But looking into May Wickens's face, I knew I couldn't succumb to my first instinct to cut and run.

"Let me think about this," I said, tossing a couple of bills onto the table. "Right now, I have to get Dad back—"

"Oh my God," May said. "What time is it?"

I glanced at my watch. I told her it was nearly noon.

"I have to go," she said, her voice laced with panic. She shifted out to the edge of the seat, and as she did her sleeve caught on a chip in the tabletop. There was a red welt on her arm, a couple of inches above her wrist.

"Did you hurt yourself?" I asked.

She quickly pulled down her sleeve. "It's nothing," she said. She got out of the booth and headed for the door, with me right behind. "He'll start looking for us if we're gone too long," she said. "I've got to get Jeffrey and—"

Timmy Wickens was standing outside the café door, looking inside at us, and he was clutching the hand of young Jeffrey, who stood obediently at his side.

15

"HEY, MR. WICKENS," I said. "Timmy." I extended a hand. "Good to see you. Thanks again for dinner last night."

Timmy Wickens wasn't buying it. His face seemed made of stone. He wasn't even interested in talking to me, at least not yet. He had his eyes on May.

"You know where I found this boy of yours?" he said.

"I ran into Mr. Walker," she said.

"Do you know where he was?"

"I had to go to the drugstore," May said. "I had," and she lowered her voice to a whisper, "some personal, feminine things to buy."

"Where are they?" Timmy Wickens asked. "I don't see a bag. Where's the stuff you bought?"

"Do I have to empty my purse?" she said, trying to be indignant. "You want to haul out my box of tampons right here on the main street?"

He recoiled a bit at that, but he was ready to go in a different direction. He yanked on Jeffrey's arm for dramatic effect. "I found him playing video games," Timmy said, tightening his grip on the boy. I tried to catch the boy's eye, but he was looking at the sidewalk.

"I gave him a few quarters," May explained. "So I could run my errand. I didn't think it would do any harm."

"You know I won't have him hanging around places like that. And this don't exactly look like the drugstore to me," he said, casting his eye across the front of Lana's.

"I just ran in to get a coffee," she said. "To go. To drink on the way home. And I saw Mr. Walker here."

"That's right, Timmy," I said. "May was just—"

Timmy turned on me. "Am I talking to you right now?"

I took half a step back. "Hey, listen, back off—"

"Because I'm pretty sure I'm talking to her. When I'm talking to you, you'll know it."

Up the street, a horn honked. I could see Dad leaning over in the front of his truck, hitting the steering wheel.

"Daddy, stop being so rude to Mr. Walker. He just offered to buy me a coffee as a way of saying thank you for our having him and his father to dinner last night."

"You been in there a long time being thanked," Timmy said. "I been up and down this street twice looking for you. When you weren't back soon, I went looking, and can you imagine what I thought when I saw my grandson standing in the doorway of a video game parlor? Can you?"

"I was just play—"

"Shut up, Jeffrey," his grandfather said. "Don't interrupt me when I'm talking to your mother."

"Honest to God, Dad," May whispered. "We're in public. Let's just forget about this and go home."

She grabbed Jeffrey's hand out of her father's and started down the sidewalk. She'd gone about five steps when she stopped and turned to say, "Thank you, Mr. Walker, for your kindness."

I started to go, too, but Timmy Wickens suddenly had hold of my upper arm. His hand felt like a vise.

"Let go of me," I said. I was full of rage, but a good part of me was rapidly turning to jelly.

With his free hand, Timmy made a fist with his index finger sticking out. "You want to talk to my daughter, you go through me."

"Why should I do that?" I asked. I don't know what part of my brain, exactly, made me say such a thing, when I was just as inclined to say "Okey dokey."

"Excuse me?" Timmy said.

"She's a grown woman. She's got a son. Why should it be up to you who she talks to and who she doesn't? If she doesn't want to talk to me, she doesn't have to."

Timmy's hand squeezed harder on my bicep. It hurt. He leaned in close to me, and his breath was hot and foul. His teeth were brown at the gum line, and for a moment, he reminded me of Gristle. Or maybe Bone. Or some creature that hides in the forest at night, waiting for you to walk past.

"I look out for her," he said. "I take care of her,

and I take care of her boy. And that gives me the right, way I see it."

"Sure," I said, deciding it might be wise to back down not for my own protection, but to mitigate whatever punishment Timmy might decide to mete out to his daughter once they all got back home. "Whatever you say."

Timmy's grip on my arm relaxed and he nodded slowly. "Good. Now, in the future, I think it would be best if you didn't talk to my daughter or my grandson. That way, I think we can continue to remain good neighbors with your pa. Because I figure you'll be going back home pretty soon, wouldn't you say?"

"Soon as Dad's ankle gets better, I guess I will."

Timmy nodded agreeably. "That's great. I bet they miss you back home. You got a wife, right, and kids?"

My mouth was getting very dry. "Yes," I said.

"I'll bet they want to see you just as much as you want to see them. Hey, you know what might be fun? Maybe sometime, I'll drop by and have a coffee with them when you're not around. Works both ways, you know."

He let go of my arm, but not without tossing me up against the window of the café at the same time. "Oh, sorry," he said. "Sometimes I don't know my own strength." And with that he walked off in the same direction that his daughter had gone.

Lana stepped outside. "What the hell was that all about?"

"Nothing," I said, and headed back to Dad's truck.

I was shaken. My legs felt wobbly, my heart was pounding, things seemed to be spinning around me.

I paused by the phone booth, put my hand up against the glass, but it felt papery under my hand. It was another flyer for the fall fair, taped to the glass. And below it, another one of those flyers, plastered on with duct tape, that said "Keep Our Parade Straight."

My only purpose in coming up here had been to make sure Dad was okay. Aside from a twisted ankle, he was okay. But now I felt held here, as stuck to Braynor as those flyers were to the phone booth. Bad things had already happened up here. A man ripped to shreds in the woods. Another man fatally stabbed. A lawyer's house burned to the ground.

A farmhouse full of nutjobs.

And a young woman and her son trying to escape.

I got to the truck without even glancing at Dad, turned the ignition, threw the gearshift into drive, and shot out of Braynor like the entire town was rigged to explode at any moment.

"Jesus H. Christ," Dad said. "You took long enough. Where's Leonard the Diaper King when you need him? I'm about to wet my pants."

"I think I beat you to it," I said.

16

THERE WERE CHORES TO BE DONE when we got back to Denny's Cabins. Given how rattled I was, it was good to have something to do. I emptied cans of garbage, hauled a pail full of fish guts up to the pit in the woods and buried it, cut some grass on Dad's racing tractor, taking care to go easy on the throttle. Sitting on the mower, the vibrations from the engine and the three rapidly rotating blades in the housing below my feet had a calming effect on me that was not unlike a massage. The constant buzz from the steering wheel traveled up my arms and into my shoulders like magic fingers.

I said barely a word to Dad on the drive back from town. Sometimes, I think, when I'm scared—and I'll be totally honest with you here and tell you I was plenty scared—the things I'm afraid of seem more real if I start talking about them. I ground my teeth until we got back to the camp, bolted from the truck, forgetting to go around the other side to help Dad get out, and went about my duties.

There'd been plenty to unnerve me since arriving here earlier in the week. The shredded body of Morton Dewart. The bizarre dinner at the Wickenses. Those dogs. The murder of Tiff at the co-op, which might or might not have anything whatsoever to do with the events of the last few days.

But nothing had shaken me as much as my run-in with Timmy Wickens on the main drag of Braynor. There'd been menace in the air before, but now I felt it directed at me personally. And I am not, as you may have gathered by now, what you might call a heroic figure.

I believe the term I used in my conversation with Trixie Snelling was "weenie-like."

It's a terrible thing to be weenie-like and still have, at some level, some commitment to do the right thing. A moral conscience matched with physical cowardice is not a winning combination.

"How's it going?" Bob Spooner asked, poking his head into the storeroom, where I was checking to see how the worm supply was going. Betty and Hank Wrigley had helped themselves to a couple dozen that morning while Dad and I were in town, and left a note to that effect so that we could add it to their bill.

I jumped. "Jesus, Bob, you scared me half to death."

"What's with you? You seem a bit on edge."

I just waved my hand in the air in frustration. "Long story, Bob."

"Hey," he said. "You'll never guess who I had on my line this morning."

"What?" I said. "Who?"

"She took another run at me. Audrey. Saw her break the surface, knew it was her. Almost had her in the boat this time before she spit the plug out." He rubbed his hands together.

"One of these days, Bob," I said.

"You know what I think?" Bob said, leaning in the doorway. "I think she knows. I think she knows it's me. She's a smart fish, and she's a mean fish, and she's playing with me. I can feel it."

"Maybe," I said. I dug my fingers through the dirt, drew them up. Still lots of little wiggly guys in there.

"You ever have a goal like that? Something you've waited years to achieve? That's what Audrey is to me. Hauling her into the boat, that's my ultimate dream. I get her, I could give up fishing after that. It wouldn't matter anymore. They could put me in a box, drop me six feet into ground, toss the dirt in."

"My goals these days are rather short-term, Bob," I said. "I want to see Dad get back on his two feet and me get the hell out of here."

Bob cocked his head curiously. "What's up?"

I shook my head. "I'm not going to dump all this stuff on you. This is your vacation up here. Enjoy it. Go fishing. Hunt down Audrey. Whatever problems Dad and I have to deal with, well, we'll deal with them."

Bob shrugged. "You need to talk things over, you know where to find me. Think I'll grab myself a nap, go back out again this aft. Leonard keeps wanting to hang out, go fishing or hiking. All he wants to do is talk about this goddamn resort of his. If he actually gets to build that thing, this lake won't be worth a shit anymore. Your dad thought of lodging any sort of objection with the Braynor council?"

"I think Dad sort of has his hands full at the moment."

"Well, if he gets a minute, he should do that. The only way you can stop something like that is to mount some sort of opposition."

"Bob, I hear ya. You might want to mention it to Dad yourself."

He mulled that one over. "Yeah, good idea."

Bob stepped aside to let me out of the storeroom. I strode over to Dad's cabin, throwing the door open so hard it hit the wall. "Dad!"

"In here," he said. He was in his study, hanging up the phone. "I've been calling some other lawyers. I tried two other ones in Braynor, figuring I'd try to get someone close before going to other towns, and the moment I mention who I want them to send a letter to, they say they're too busy."

"This town's scared of the Wickenses," I said. "I'm scared of the Wickenses."

"Maybe I should drop it. If those people really had anything to do with setting that other lawyer's house on fire, I mean, do I need those kinds of problems?"

"I don't know, Dad."

"And by the way, what the hell happened out front of Lana's, anyway?"

I ignored the question. I didn't want to talk about it. "Here's an idea, Dad. Why don't you put this place on the market and sell? Get the hell out of here. Fast as possible. Buy another fishing camp someplace else."

"That's your plan? To run away? And who do you think would buy this place, knowing they were going to inherit tenants like the Wickenses?"

I ran a hand over the back of my neck, tried to massage it. I was feeling a bit tense.

"I think we need to have another chat with Orville," I said. "A really serious chat. I'm willing to put aside the fact that he seems to be a total asshole to see if we can get something done here. There are more things going on than I realized at first."

"Like what?"

I told him about May Wickens and her son. How she desperately wanted to get away from her father. How her son was on a daily curriculum of hate and prejudice.

"How's that your problem?" Dad asked. "Don't we have enough problems without taking on hers? I want them all out of there, and I guess that would include her and her boy. She can figure out how to get away once they've moved someplace else."

I was silent. There wasn't much to admire in what Dad said, but it made a lot of sense just the same.

"You got a number for Orville?" I asked.

Dad dug out an address book next to his computer, folded it open to a particular page, and handed it to me. "This his cell?" I asked, and Dad nodded. I punched the number into the phone on Dad's desk.

"Hello?"

"Orville? Zack Walker."

"What," he said flatly.

"Listen, I'm sorry about everything at the café. I think you and I need to get past all that crap, because there's a real problem out here, has to do with the daughter at the Wickens place. May. That's her name. I think she's in real trouble and I think we need to find some way to help her out. I'm willing to stop being a pain in the ass to you if you'll come out so we can talk about this."

"I kinda got my hands full with a murder investigation," he said. "Remember?"

"I understand. Are you still coming out here tomorrow morning to look for the bear?" I kept any skeptical tone out of my voice.

"Depends. On how things go with Tiff's murder. But if I get a chance, I'll swing by later this afternoon, about this other problem of yours."

"Okay," I said. "Thanks." And I hung up. I picked up the phone again, impulsively, and dialed Sarah's number at *The Metropolitan*.

"Hey," I said.

"How's your dad?"

"Okay."

"Say hi to him for me."

"Sarah says hi."

"Hi," said Dad. He got out of his chair and, using his crutches, edged past me. "I'm making coffee," he whispered to me. "Want some?"

I nodded. What would we do without coffee? "How're the kids?" I asked Sarah.

"Same old same old," Sarah said. "Fights over the car, seeing as how we're down one with you up there. Paul's ignoring curfew, Angie would rather date than study, I want to kill myself. There was a story on the wires the other day, mother kills her entire family. I thought: Been there. How 'bout with you?"

"Okay. Listen, you got Lawrence Jones's number there?"

There was an instant chill from the other end of the line. "What do you want Lawrence for?"

"There's kind of a situation up here I'd like to bounce off him."

"Bad things happen to you when you associate with Lawrence," Sarah said, using the voice she did with the children when they misbehaved.

"That's not totally true," I objected. "Bad things happen to Lawrence when he associates with me." It was true that, the first time Lawrence and I had worked together—he was doing his thing as a private detective and I was writing about it—he'd taken a knife in the gut and nearly died. But it was also true that the reason he hadn't died was that I'd shown up at the right place at the right time.

Arguing these points with Sarah, however, was unlikely to score me any.

"That's not very funny," Sarah said. "What could possibly be going on up there that you'd need Lawrence's help for? You want him to do a stakeout on a bear?"

"There's no bear," I said.

"There's no bear? Tracy didn't say that in the story

she filed. She says the coroner said the guy, what was his name?"

"Dewart."

"That a bear killed him."

"It's a long, long story, Sarah. Have you got Lawrence's number in your book or not?"

She gave me two. His home/office and his cell.

"A couple other things," I said. "I know we've probably run a million stories on this, but can you look up what sort of services there are for women? Like shelters?"

"Abused women?"

"Well, sort of. I mean, I don't know if there's actual physical violence, but—"

"Zack. What the hell are you getting into? I thought you were helping your father run the camp?"

"There's a woman up here, her name's May Wickens, and she's got a son, and she's kind of under the thumb of her father, who doesn't want to let her move out, and has threatened to hold on to her son if she tries."

"Jesus. And what does this have to do with you?"

"Sarah."

"Look, tell her to get a good lawyer."

I laughed. "Yeah, fat chance in this town."

"Okay, okay, I'll see what there is, but the services are probably mostly in the city. I can't imagine there's much like that up in Braynor."

"And one last thing."

"Shoot."

"Does the name Orville Thorne mean anything to you?"

Sarah took a moment. "No. Should it?"

"He's the local police chief, and from the moment I've gotten here it's been bugging me. He reminds me of someone, and I can't figure out who. I feel like maybe I've run into him before someplace, like maybe doing a story for the paper, or something. I thought, if that was the case, maybe you'd recognize it."

"Hang on," Sarah said. I could hear her tapping some keys. "I'm just keying the name into the system." She was referring to the paper's library system. If we'd ever run a story with Thorne's name in it, it would come up. "Is that Thorne with an 'e'?"

"Yeah."

"There's nothing," she said.

"Google?" I said, glancing at Dad's computer. I could have checked myself. But Sarah was already on it.

"Absolutely nothing," Sarah said.

"Okay, thanks. It was worth a shot."

"Can you send me a picture?" Sarah said.

"What?"

"A picture. Maybe I'd recognize him, too, even if the name doesn't ring a bell."

I glanced over to the shelf where Dad's digital camera sat. I knew Dad used his computer to send guests pictures he'd taken of them with their catch.

"I might be able to pull off something like that," I said. "Leave it with me. Listen, while you're keying in names, I've got another one for you."

"Fire away."

"Timmy Wickens. Maybe Timothy Wickens. Or Tim Wickens. If he'd ever been arrested, it'd probably be Timothy."

"Arrested?"

"Sarah."

"Okay, hang on. Nothing in our own files. Let me check Google. . . . Okay, there's a writer . . ."

"I don't think that's him."

"And a hairdresser in Reno."

"Definitely not."

"And a story here, from, like, five, six years ago, it's just one name among a dozen, bunch of people arrested for causing a disturbance at a Holocaust memorial event in Pittsburgh. They were Holocaust deniers."

"Read me some of the names." I grabbed a pen and Dad's yellow legal pad and began scribbling.

"Uh, other than Wickens, there's Randall Stilton, Gregory Bent, Michael Decker, Charlene Zundman—"

"Hang on. Charlene? What was that?"

Sarah repeated it. Then she read the rest of the names, all of which I made note of, but no other ones rang any bells.

"Anything else come up?"

"Nothing," Sarah said. Then, with more gentleness in her voice than before, "Zack, you're being careful, right?"

"Of course," I said.

"There's nothing dangerous going on up there, is there?"

"Of course not," I lied.

"Because, I've had enough, you know?"

"Sure," I said. "You don't have to tell me."

"Lately, you seem to have this knack for attracting trouble."

"Yeah, well," I said, "those days are over."

17

My next call was to Lawrence Jones.

I got his machine when I phoned his home/office. I left a message, saying I would try his cell, which I then did.

"Jones," he said.

"It's Zack," I said.

"Zack, my man, how's it going?" In the background I could hear some piano, probably one of Lawrence's jazz CDs.

"Pretty good, you know, more or less."

"Yeah, well, people don't usually call me unless they've got a problem, so I'm guessing you're going to work up to it slowly."

"Am I catching you at a bad time?"

"Just sitting in my car, listening to some Oscar Peterson, parked down the street from a motel where Mr. Corporate Executive is boffing his secretary, and by the time I get the photos back to his missus he's going to be a lot more agreeable when it comes to working out the terms of the divorce."

"I didn't know you did that kind of work."

"Oh, Zack, I bet you still believe there's a tooth fairy, too."

"This is a long-term job you're working on?"

"I'll be done soon as this guy walks out and gives his sweetie a kiss goodbye for the camera."

"You got anything lined up next?"

"Zack, there's always work. We live in cynical times. Did you know that people don't trust each other anymore? It's a very disturbing development, but it pays the bills. What's on your mind?"

"I'm up in Braynor. You know Braynor."

"I know I got called one all the time when I was in high school. The teachers thought I might be gifted, and I always did my homework. Of course, I also got 'browner,' but that might have had more to do with my skin tone."

"Braynor's an hour and a half north of the city. Lakes and mountains. Fishing. Wildlife."

"Sounds nice. I'm not due for a vacation."

"I'm up here at my dad's place. He's got some cabins he rents out. Lawrence, there's a whole lot of shit going on up here and I think I could use your help."

"I see. What sort of shit?"

"Well, there's some people up here you might find interesting. They think the world's going to hell in a handcart because of blacks and gays."

"Hmmm," said Lawrence. "That makes me a kind of double-header worst nightmare for them. Tell me more."

I did.

"I could come up tonight, maybe tomorrow," Lawrence said.

"I haven't cleared this with Dad," I said. "But I think he'd be prepared to hire you. He was ready to pay a lawyer. And if he's a bit short, I can—"

"Zack, shut up. Every day I get, I thank you."

I swallowed. "Okay."

When I was finished talking to Lawrence, I found Dad plopped onto the couch, reading the *Braynor Times* I'd bought him at the grocery store.

"Poured you your coffee," he said, nose in the paper. "Cream and sugar's already in it."

I grabbed my mug off the counter and sat down opposite him. "I've called in the cavalry," I said.

"I figured, with your newspaper connections, it'd be Superman," Dad said.

I told him about Lawrence Jones. That he was an ex-cop, an experienced private investigator, and, as a bonus in dealing with whatever the Wickenses might throw at us, black and gay.

"That's comforting," Dad said. "We're gonna be rescued by a poofster." I decided to let that one go, figuring Lawrence himself would be able to dispel the stereotypes once he got here.

As I took a sip of my coffee, Dad said, "I did a little checking on the Internet while you were outside."

"Yeah?" The notion of Dad surfing the net was still difficult to imagine.

"I looked up ammonium nitrate. Fertilizer."

I said, "Go on."

"What McVeigh did was, he used four thousand

pounds of the stuff and mixed it with diesel fuel, and some blasting caps, then put everything in fifty-five-gallon plastic drums, loaded it up into that Ryder truck, lit a fuse, and ran like stink."

"I'll bet," I said, "even if you stole a lot less than four thousand pounds of that stuff, you could still make a hell of an explosion."

"I suspect," Dad said.

"A day ago, you didn't even want to consider the possibility that something other than a bear ripped that man apart, and now look where your mind's taking you."

"You haven't thought the same thing?"

"Of course I've thought the same thing. You know what kind of paranoid I am. I'm this close to pinning the Lindbergh kidnapping on the Wickenses. But we don't have anything to suggest that Wickens had a thing to do with the murder of Tiff Riley. If we hadn't seen that picture of Timothy McVeigh on their wall, hanging where most people might hang a picture of Jesus Christ, we wouldn't even be having this conversation. You know, the Wickenses aren't the only crazy people in the world, probably not the only crazy people in this county."

"That's comforting."

"Maybe we should be calling the FBI or something," I said. "Don't they handle this sort of thing? Or Homeland Security? What color alert are we at when the neighbors have murderous pit bulls?"

"Let's give Orville another chance," Dad said. "You were almost nice to him on the phone, which must have nearly killed you. We'll lay it all out for him. You know, you really haven't given him a chance. From the moment you got here you've been picking on him. And by the way, who loaded that dishwasher last? You or Lana?"

"Wasn't me," I said.

Dad shook his head. "She put the knives in blade up. Almost slit my wrist unloading it."

"So many faults, so little time to correct them," I said.

Dad tossed the paper at me. "Read the piece on the front."

I grabbed the paper off the coffee table that separated us. "Which?" I said.

"The main piece."

Had I bothered to read the headlines before asking Dad, I would have been able to figure out which one he meant. The headline on the lead story, written by Tracy, who also had all the other bylines on the front page, was "Mayor Mulls Canceling Parade." It read:

Braynor mayor Alice Holland says she may cancel the fall fair parade on Saturday if she thinks the appearance of a gay activist group could lead to violence.

"Either the Fifty Lakes Gay and Lesbian Coalition will be in the parade," the mayor said, "or there won't be any parade at all."

Mayor Holland said to exclude the coalition from the parade, something many people in

Braynor want, would subject the town to a potential civil rights suit that could bankrupt the municipality.

"People are going around collecting names on petitions to keep the parade straight, and if they don't mind seeing their property taxes double to pay the costs of going to court to defend a foolhardy decision, well then, fine. But if they have a problem with that, and still want the coalition banned from walking down Main Street, then we don't have to have a parade at all."

Charles Henry, manager of Henry's Grocery, which puts a float in the parade every year, has been spearheading the petition to "Keep the Parade Straight" and he reacted angrily to the mayor's comments.

"I can't help but wonder," he said, "whether the mayor is a lesbian. It would explain a lot."

Henry said the mayor may not need to cancel the parade, that many of the participants may back out instead. "She can ride in her convertible all alone," he said, but refused to say whether Henry's Grocery would withdraw its own float, which this year was to depict a large cow, its body covered with dotted lines to depict different cuts of meat.

Stuart Lethbridge, of Red Lake, who heads the Fifty Lakes Gay and Lesbian Coalition, promises a tasteful display. "There'll be a good crowd of people in the parade, carrying the Rainbow Flag, plus we'll be displaying the number for our counseling line, which, as you can imagine in a community like Braynor, gets a lot of calls from gays and lesbians looking for a sympathetic ear." Lethbridge said the coalition would not back out of the parade, even if that's the only way it can be saved.

The Braynor council is divided on what to do. Most members are united in wanting to avoid a lawsuit, but a number are in favor of scrapping the parade altogether, even though it is a tradition.

But even if the parade is canceled, all other fall fair activities, including the pie-eating contest, the lawn tractor races, chainsaw competition, and cow-pie-tossing contest, will go ahead as planned.

"What's a cow pie?" I asked.

"Shit," Dad said.

I nodded. "And this chainsaw competition. What do they do? Juggle them?"

"You're starting to annoy me."

"And I see the lawn tractor races are still on. Too bad I won't be able to help you there. I have a predisposition to whiplash."

"I might be well enough by then," Dad said. "I was putting some weight on my ankle today, and it didn't seem that bad."

"You think the mayor's a lesbian?" I asked. "There's no picture of her here."

Dad started to answer, then could tell by the look on my face that I was still working at being annoying.

"But seriously," I said. "Have you met her? She a nice lady?"

"Yes, and yes. She's a bit too reasonable for this crowd up here. She moved up here from the city a few years ago, and she's still a bit too sophisticated for her own good."

"I wonder if she'd be worth talking to," I said quietly, almost to myself. "Are you okay with gays in the parade?"

"I don't give a shit," Dad said. "You think we could look any more foolish when we've already got a marked-up cow in it?"

"How about Lana?" I asked. "Her business is on Main Street, right by Henry's Grocery. She signed the petition yet?"

"Lana, and I, are a lot more tolerant, and forgiving, than you'll ever know," Dad said.

There was something in the way he'd said that that stayed with me for the rest of the afternoon, which I spent doing more chores around the camp. I felt we were in a holding pattern, waiting for Orville Thorne to show up, and, with any luck, Lawrence the next morning.

I was down by the docks, replacing a board that looked like it was about to break through, when Bob Spooner returned from an afternoon out on the lake. Once he'd killed the motor, I said, "Get anything?"

Bob lifted up the stringer from the bottom of the boat, revealing two good-sized pickerel and a large-mouth bass.

"Not bad," I said. Beyond Dad's cabin, I could hear

a car approaching. I looked back and saw that it was a police car.

"The law," Bob said ominously.

"I got an idea," I said to Bob. "Let me get your picture with your catch."

"Oh, I've done better than this."

"No, come on. I want to get some pictures with Dad's digital camera, send a couple snaps back to my wife, Sarah."

Bob shrugged and secured the boat to the dock while I ran back for the camera. Orville was out of his car and walking toward the cabin. "Two seconds!" I shouted to him, burst into the cabin, grabbed Dad's camera from the study, and ran back out the front door for the shoreline.

Chief Thorne, curious about what was going on, which seemed so unlike him, followed. Dad, on crutches, was coming down as well.

The commotion was attracting others. Leonard Colebert had been inside making himself some dinner, and Betty and Hank Wrigley were sitting on their porch, reading, but as is generally the case at a fishing camp, when someone comes in with a good catch, everyone wants to pass judgment.

Bob, his arm in a muscle-making position that kept the stringerful of fish from dragging on the ground, smiled proudly as I held up the camera.

"Nice!" said Leonard.

"Where'd you get 'em?" Betty wanted to know.

"What were ya using?" Orville asked.

I took a couple of shots, then said, "Hey, let's get

some other people in here." I moved Betty into the frame on one side of Bob, then Hank on the other, and took a picture. Leonard took no persuading at all to have his picture taken with Bob.

"Tomorrow morning, early, we go on our hike, right?" Leonard said. Bob nodded resignedly.

"Hey, Chief, how about you?" I said, bringing Orville forward.

"No no, that's okay."

"No, come on, come on." I had my hand around his back and was moving him up next to Bob.

"Hey, Orville, think you could lose the hat for a second?" I said. "The way the sun is, your whole face is in shadow."

Orville obediently removed his hat. I fired off a series of shots. For a couple, I used the zoom lens, cropping out Bob and his fish and coming in tight on Orville Thorne's face.

"Hey. That's great," I said. "Thanks, everyone. Don't forget to leave me your e-mail addresses before you go home so I can send you all—"

The sound of something being knocked over caught us all by surprise. Over at the fish-cleaning table, the bucket of guts underneath, which couldn't have had much in it since I'd emptied it only a few hours earlier, had been tipped over.

The Wickenses' two pit bulls, Gristle and Bone, had their heads jammed into it, and their maniacal snarls and growls echoed within the metal chamber.

I turned to Bob, standing there with his fish. "Get inside as fast as you can," I said. But he was already making a beeline for his cabin, and just as he had his hand on the porch door, the two dogs withdrew their heads from the bucket, their fish-finding sonar evidently beeping in their thick skulls.

Gristle and Bone both looked about for a second, slobber and fish innards dripping from their massive jaws, and then, in a shot, they were on the move, their legs like pistons. Even though they barely came up above my knee, I could feel their charge through the ground, like a pair of horses running past.

Betty screamed. Leonard, figuring the dogs wouldn't go after him in the lake, ran off the end of a dock. Hank put himself in front of Betty. And Orville was unholstering his weapon.

The dogs didn't care about us, however. They were after Bob Spooner, who was inside now and putting his weight against the flimsy wooden screen door. The dogs hit it like a pair of battering rams, growling, trying to bite at the wood.

"Help!" Bob shouted. "Get back, you fucking monsters!"

"Shoot them," I said to Orville.

He had his gun out and was running toward Bob's cabin when we heard someone shout: "Bone! Gristle! Stop!"

The dogs were making such a racket they didn't hear the command. Timmy Wickens' stepson Wendell came around the corner of the cabin and shouted at them again, louder this time, and the dogs suddenly stopped barking, panting heavily, their tongues hanging over their jagged teeth.

Two leather leashes dangled from Wendell's hand.

He hooked them back up to the dogs and grinned stupidly at the rest of us.

"They kind of got away from me there," he said, and laughed.

18

"**Bad dog!**" Wendell scolded Bone. Then, to Gristle, "You too, bad dog!"

Bad? *Bad?* How about fucking terrifying?

Even though Wendell had the two leashes reattached, and the grips looped securely around his wrist, Bob Spooner stayed behind the slightly chewed screen door of his cabin, and Betty and Hank were slowly moving toward theirs, no doubt thinking that if the dogs could get away from Wendell once, they could get away from him again.

Orville had not yet holstered his weapon, but was holding it at his side, pointed toward the ground. Neither he nor I had moved for the past half a minute, waiting to be certain Wendell had control of those two beasts.

Dad was the one most at risk. Probably none of us could outrun those pooches, but Dad didn't stand a chance. I glanced back at him, saw the fear in his eyes.

"Well, sorry about that," said Wendell offhandedly.

The dogs kept swiveling their heads around, looking back at Bob's cabin, whimpering, knowing there were goodies in there they couldn't get. Wendell gave a tug on their leashes and started walking back to the road that would take him back to the Wickens farmhouse.

We all stood for another moment, shell-shocked. It was Dad who spoke first. "Orville, why don't you come in."

Chief Thorne slipped the gun back into its holster and he and I followed Dad into the cabin. I slipped into the study to leave the digital camera by the computer, then took a seat with Dad and Orville in the living room.

Orville forced out a laugh, and said, "Well, that was a bit of excitement, wasn't it? Good thing he got those dogs back on the leash. I'm sure Wendell won't let something like that happen again. They probably just got away from him for a second there."

"Great," I said. "We haven't even got started, and you're already making excuses for them."

"I'm doing no such thing," Orville objected.

"Zachary," Dad warned, "I want you two to be nice."

Nice?

"I think," Dad said slowly, "that we've got some real problems here."

"Yeah, well, I've got a few problems of my own," said Orville. "I'm investigating a murder, you know." He made it sound like bragging. Like "I got an A+ on my paper, you know."

"And how's that investigation coming?" I asked, struggling not to add "Sherlock."

"Well, not great," said Orville. "There's no witnesses, of course. It happened after the co-op was closed. And the owners never felt there's been enough of a crime problem up here to justify putting security cameras in, so we've got nothing to look at there. But we're asking around, checking into Tiff's friends, seeing if anyone of them might have had a grudge against him, you know?"

"You think it's personal?" I asked.

"You have to be thorough," said Orville authoritatively, like he had a clue what he was doing. "We're looking into all the angles, even if we're not convinced they'll pan out. That's just good police work."

Hold the tongue. Hold the tongue.

"What about the missing fertilizer?" Dad asked.

"Yup, for sure, it's missing, but then again, they can't be sure it went missing last night. It might have gone missing earlier, who knows? So we can't even say for sure it has anything to do with Tiff's death."

"But," I said, "you're considering that there might be a connection, right? I mean, that would just be good police work."

Orville gave me a look. "Of course we are. And what's it to you, anyway? You didn't say you wanted to talk about Tiff Riley's murder. What business have you got asking me about the progress of an investigation that has nothing to do with either one of you?"

"Now just hear me out here, Orville," said Dad. "And I'd be the first to admit that we've not got a lot to go on here, not what you'd call proof, but have you ever been inside the Wickenses' place up there?"

Orville eyed Dad suspiciously. "No."

"So you haven't seen whose picture they've got up on their wall?"

"No."

"Timothy McVeigh."

Orville waited, like this was supposed to be some great revelation, then looked at me. "You mentioned that name this morning."

"It rings a bell, right?" I said. "Oklahoma City, big big bomb, the perp walk in the orange jumpsuit?"

"Okay," Orville said evenly. "Now I know who you mean."

Would he know the name Lee Harvey Oswald? Charles Manson? Son of Sam? Should I put a quiz together?

"Don't you think it's odd, that they'd have his picture on the wall, that they'd see him as some kind of hero?" Dad said.

"This is it," Orville said. "You want me to go arrest Timmy Wickens and the rest of his family because of a picture on the wall." He looked, in turn, at both of us.

"Well, it is kind of odd," Dad said, a bit defensively.

"Yeah," I said.

"I'd have to look that one up in the statutes," Orville said. "Being odd. Maybe I should get together a posse, we'll round up everyone in the county who's odd. Hey!" He smiled. "We could call it The Odd Squad."

This hurt. Orville was right. We had nothing. What an unexpected and unwelcome turn of events.

"Okay," I said, wanting to move on. "But couldn't you look around their place anyway? See if they have the fertilizer? Because if they do, well, they'd have a lot of explaining to do."

"You want me to search their place. You've got no evidence, no witnesses, nothing. What sort of judge would give me a warrant based on what you're telling me here?"

"Well, couldn't you tell him we've got a feeling?" Dad said.

Don't give Orville the easy ones, I thought.

"And besides," Dad continued, "would you even need a warrant? I mean, I own the place. If I say it's okay, can't you go ahead and do it, even if they object?"

I could see Orville's discomfort growing. I suspect the last thing he wanted was to confront the Wickenses. "I'm not sure," he said hesitantly, which I took to mean that yes, he could search. "But what am I going to say? I'm just going to walk up there and start snooping around?"

"You've got another reason to go up there," I said. "You could go up and talk to them about their dogs. Remind them that they have to be penned up, kept on a leash, kept on a chain for fuck's sake, so that they don't come down here and bother Dad's guests again."

"I suppose," Orville said, looking at his hands.

"And here's the other thing," I said. "It's about May Wickens and her son, Jeffrey."

"What the hell have *they* done?" Orville asked.

"Nothing. But I had coffee with May this morning, and she kind of poured out her heart to me, at some considerable risk, I think. She wants to get away from her father, to get her son away from him. Timmy Wickens is feeding that boy's mind a daily diet of poison."

Orville Thorne shrugged. "So, she should leave. She's free, white, and twenty-one, isn't she?"

"Timmy Wickens has this kind of hold on her. She said if she tries to leave, he'll hold on to the boy. He won't let her take him."

For the first time, Orville almost looked concerned. "He can't do that."

"I know. She says if she tries to leave, with Jeffrey, that Timmy and those two stepsons of his, Charlene's boys, will track her down wherever she goes and bring her back."

"That's crazy."

"Just go up and talk to them," Dad said. "Just get a feel of what's going on."

"But you can't let on that you know what May told me," I said. "I think that could be bad for her."

Orville collapsed into total frustration. "Just what the hell is it you want me to do? Hunt for stolen fertilizer when you don't have a shred of evidence that Wickens had a thing to do with it? Try to get the daughter and her boy out when she's made no official complaint whatsoever? Honest to God, what do you want from me?"

Dad and I looked at each other.

"Also," I said, "he assaulted me."

"What?"

"On Main Street. When he found me having coffee with May, Timmy Wickens grabbed my arm and squeezed it."

Now it was Orville's turn to try not to laugh. "Did he squeeze it really hard?" His voice dripped with concern. "Go ahead, grab my arm and show me how hard he squeezed. I can take it."

"Fuck it, never mind," I said. "Let's just go up and talk to them about the dogs."

"The dogs."

"They have to keep them tied up. Plain and simple. Then, while we're up there, we play the rest by ear."

Orville said, "We?"

Dad begged off, saying his ankle was throbbing. I think he was glad for an excuse not to go.

So Orville and I walked up the road to the Wickenses' gate. I knew enough now not to hop it. Orville shouted, "Mr. Wickens! Hello?"

Timmy appeared, followed by Wendell and Dougie, who, at that moment, really did remind me of the Darryl and Darryl characters from that long-ago sitcom. The three of them walked, casually, taking their time, down the drive to the gate.

"Yeah?" said Timmy. Not nearly as friendly as at dinner the night before.

"We wonder if we could come in and talk for a moment," Orville said. "Provided your dogs is someplace safe."

"They're in the barn," said Wendell, grinning.

"You're sure?" I said.

"If the boy says they're in the barn, they're in the barn," Timmy Wickens said, unlatching the gate and opening it wide enough to admit me and Orville. We started walking slowly, walking and talking at the same time, toward the house.

"What's this about?" Timmy asked.

"Your dogs got a bit out of control today," Orville said.

"Wendell told me." Wendell nodded at this. "Didn't he say he was sorry?"

"Well, you see," Orville said, feeling his way, "it's not just a problem of an apology."

"What then?" said Dougie.

Charlene, in a grease-stained football jersey, had come out onto the porch to see what the commotion was. I could make out May Wickens at the window.

"Those dogs are dangerous," Orville said.

"Did they bite anyone?" Timmy Wickens asked.

"No, no they didn't."

"Well then. Every dog's allowed its first bite, and they ain't even done that yet."

"They're vicious animals, Mr. Wickens. If you can't control them, the town will seize them."

Timmy bristled. "Will they now? I'd like to see them try something like that."

"It won't be necessary so long as you keep them tied up," Orville said.

May had stepped out onto the porch, walked over to the railing. Our eyes met.

"Hello, ladies," Orville said. "Nice to see you." Charlene glared at him. There was something in

May's expression that seemed to reach out. Orville looked directly at her. "How are you doing, Ms. Wickens?"

"I'm fine, thank you," she said quietly.

"Everything's okay with you, is it?"

Timmy face darkened, and he looked from Orville to his daughter and back again. "Yes," May said. "Everything is fine."

"That's terrific, I'm glad to hear that. That's wonderful." Orville cleared his throat nervously. "Well, that's good. Isn't that good that everyone's fine?"

"Is there anything else?" Timmy asked.

"Well, as a matter of fact," Orville said. "I wonder if you'd mind if we just had a look around the place?"

Whoa. I couldn't believe it. Maybe Orville actually had some balls. One, at least.

"What?" said Timmy. "You want to search my place? On what grounds? Do you have a warrant for that?"

"He doesn't really need one," I said. "Because this property belongs to—"

"Hey, look," said Orville, "I just wanted to look around, that's all. You don't have anything to hide, do you, Timmy? Because—"

"Ha-ha!" said Wendell. "I got it!"

He'd come up around Orville from behind and grabbed the police chief's gun right out of his holster. Orville must have failed to snap the safety cover back on after the dog incident, making it easy for Wendell to snatch. Wendell waved it playfully in the air, dancing as he did so.

"I got your gun! I got your gun!" He singsonged, like he was chanting a nursery rhyme.

"Hey!" Orville said. "You give that back!"

Dougie was laughing, and Timmy had a big smirk on his face, too. "Hey," Wendell said, pointing the gun at his brother. "I'm gonna shoot ya!"

"No!" I said.

"Bang!" Wendell shouted, and Dougie dropped to the ground comically, engaging in a set of ridiculous spasms on the grass.

"You got me!" he cried.

"You give that back to me right now!" Orville said, running after Wendell, who'd begun skipping away. Dougie was back on his feet now, running behind Orville.

"Here!" Wendell shouted at Dougie. "Catch!"

Dear God no.

Surely they would have enough sense not to toss around a loaded gun. But they did. It sailed through the air, up and over Orville, who reached futilely into the air to catch it. The gun arced earthward, and Dougie caught it handily, running off in the other direction.

"Now, boys," Timmy said, smiling. Charlene was laughing now, too. May was the only member of the Wickens family not to find this amusing. She looked on in horror. Jeffrey slipped outside and sidled up next to his mom.

"What are they playing?" the boy asked.

"Go inside right now," she said. May must have known what could happen if a loaded gun landed on the ground. "Now!"

Orville was running back and forth between Wendell and Dougie as they tossed the gun between themselves. "Stop it!" he shouted. "Stop it!"

"Come on, fellas," Timmy said. "You better give him back his gun."

But the boys paid him no mind. It was Charlene who brought things to an end.

"Boys!" she bellowed. They both whirled around and looked at her. She smiled at them. "I think it's time to stop."

"Do we have to?" Wendell asked. He and Dougie looked so terribly disappointed.

"Your mom's right," said Timmy. "Time to call it quits. So long as Orville here agrees to one condition."

Orville stared at Timmy.

"Chief Thorne, I'll ask my boys to give you back your gun, but you're going to have to promise to leave us alone."

Orville said nothing. Timmy walked over to Dougie, the current possessor of the weapon, and took it gently from his hands.

"We were just having some fun," Dougie said.

Then Timmy slowly walked over to Orville, and before handing him the gun, he leaned in close to the chief's face and said, "Now, Orville, you just walk away, now. Okay?"

Orville stared into Timmy's face.

"You understand, Orville?" Timmy said, smiling. "Just. Walk. Away."

Orville, his face ablaze with shame, took the weapon

and slid it back into his holster. Then he turned and started walking back to the gate.

"Hold on," I said. "Aren't we—"

"You better go with him," Timmy said, feigning concern. "You know what? Take him into town, get him an ice cream. Make it all better."

19

ORVILLE WAS MOVING so quickly I had to run to catch up with him. "Orville, wait," I said. He was out the Wickenses' gate and walking down the hill toward his patrol car. "Would you hold up for a minute?" I shouted.

He stopped abruptly and whirled around. "You wanna make a joke? You wanna have a good laugh? Go ahead. Laugh. And then just keep the fuck away from me."

"Orville," I said. "Listen, I don't know what to say." And I didn't. I knew I didn't want to make fun of him. I had no smartass remarks ready to go. Maybe, being a cop in Braynor, you didn't have to deal with that many like Timmy Wickens. And when you ran up against one, you didn't know what the hell to do.

It was clear Orville Thorne wasn't much of a cop. It wasn't that he was a cop on the take, as far as I knew. I'd had to deal with at least one of those in the past. Thorne just didn't have the stuff. Which made him, in many ways, a lot like me. At some level, I was sharing his shame.

"Why don't we go talk to my dad," I said gently. "Those guys, look, those guys are nuts. If I'd been you, I don't know what I would have done. I mean, it wasn't like you could just shoot them all dead, as much as you might have liked to. We just, we just need to figure out another way to—"

"Shut up, Walker," Orville said. "Just shut the fuck up."

I felt badly for him. You couldn't watch someone get humiliated like that and get any pleasure out of making it any worse. Orville Thorne knew what he'd failed to do, and he didn't need me to remind him of it. Back up the hill, beyond the gate, we could hear Dougie and Wendell laughing, making whooping sounds.

"Orville," I said, "I have a friend coming up, some-one who's had some experience dealing with all kinds of things and—"

"That's great," Orville said. "It'll be great, won't it, to get someone up here who knows what he's doing. You'd like that, wouldn't you? Someone who can show me up real good."

I held my arms out at my sides in a gesture of sur-render. "I'm not trying to give you a hard time. I'm just saying this guy might be able to give all of us some ideas about a fresh approach, is all."

Orville reached his car, got inside, turned it around, and stopped as he passed me. "Tell your dad we'll be out in the morning to look for the bear."

"Sure," I said. "I'll tell—"

And then he hit the gas, kicking up gravel on his way out.

I went back into Dad's cabin. "How'd it go?" he asked.

I ignored him and went into his study and downloaded the shots I'd just taken from the digital camera to Dad's computer. "Hey," he called out. "Are you gonna tell me what happened up there or not? Where's Orville?"

I found two good pictures of Orville, one straight on, the other a three-quarters shot, and e-mailed them to Sarah's work address with a note. *This is the police chief, Orville Thorne. Does he look familiar to you?*

I closed the mail program and went back into the main room.

"Would you tell me what in the hell is going on?" Dad said, anger creeping into his voice. "Every time I ask you about things, like what happened out front of Lana's, what happened up there just now, you don't tell me a damn thing."

I decided it was time to start doing a bit of work on my own. I dug out the phone book he kept in a drawer in the kitchen area. "What's that mayor's name again?" I asked.

"Huh? What do you want her name for?"

"The name?"

"Holland. Alice Holland. She's mayor for Braynor and the surrounding county. Are you calling her? What are you doing?"

I ran my finger down through the listings of the slender phone book. There was only one Holland, but no A. Holland. "There's only a G. Holland here," I said. "On Connor Bay Road."

"That's her husband. George Holland."

"So she's not a lesbian," I said.

"Far as I know," Dad said.

I asked Dad where Connor Bay Road was. "North side of town, half a mile or so, road runs off to the east, you hang a right, it's kind of windy," he said. "Are you just going to go out there? You're just gonna show up? Don't you think that's a bit rude? Shouldn't you call first?"

I grabbed my car keys off the counter and was out the door, Dad calling out, "What's going on?" I got in my Virtue and headed into town. The only traffic light on Main Street was green, allowing me to sail through Braynor in under a minute. As the houses on the north side began to thin, I looked for Connor Bay Road.

I hung a right. The town was only a quarter mile behind me, but I was back in the woods, tall pines crowding up to the shoulders of the road. I watched the mailboxes, each of them named, and when I saw "Holland" I put on my blinker and turned in.

The trees opened up about fifty yards in, revealing a chalet-like home with pine board siding, a peaked roof, and enough glass that I could see right through the first floor to the bay on the other side. There were a couple of SUVs parked off to the side, and I pulled in behind them.

A large, bearded black man, six feet easy, a couple hundred pounds, emerged from a separate double-wide garage, wiping his hand on a rag. It looked like he'd been doing some mechanical kind of work, but he didn't have a mechanic's look about him. He was wearing pleated khakis and an Eddie Bauer–like shirt. He eyed me warily, stepped back into the garage for a moment, and reappeared with a baseball bat in his hand.

Not a good sign.

"Can I help you?" he asked, lightly tapping the bat with his right arm into his left palm.

"My name is Zack Walker," I said. "I'm a reporter for *The Metropolitan*. I was looking for Mayor Holland. Are you Mr. Holland?"

"I am. So what do you want the mayor for?" The bat was hanging down at his side now, swinging ever so gently.

"I just wanted to ask her a few questions, that's all." He kept swinging the bat. "I'm not here to cause trouble."

"We don't get *The Metropolitan* up here much. There's one place in town I think you can buy it. Why's someone from a big paper like that interested in talking to a small-town mayor like my wife?"

"Look, is she around?"

"I'll let her know you're here." He stopped swinging the bat, disappeared into the house, and a moment later, Alice Holland appeared at the door.

"Why don't you come in?" she said, waving me toward her.

"Thanks for seeing me," I said, stepping in. "I took a chance that you might be home. Your husband doesn't seem very eager for you to have visitors."

At a glance, I could see this was no cottage.

Modern, Swedish-style furniture, abstract art on what few walls weren't made of glass, art books and copies of *The New Yorker* and *Harper's* on the coffee table.

"You've come a long way to see me," Alice Holland said. She was a small woman, mid-fifties, I figured, barely five feet. She'd have looked even tinier had she been standing right next to her husband, but he held back, by the door.

"You want me to hang around, hon?" he asked.

"No, George, it's okay." He slipped out, and she smiled at me. "He just wants to be sure I'm okay. He'll be happy to go back to work on his snowmobile anyway," she said. "Another two or three months and we could have two feet of snow on the ground." She had a pretty face, even without any makeup. But when she brushed some of her silver hair away from her eyes, I could see how weary they looked.

"I was already in the neighborhood," I said. "And I'm not sure whether I'm speaking to you as a reporter or as a concerned citizen."

"Why don't you sit down," she said, gesturing toward one of the two leather couches.

"My father owns Denny's Cabins, south of town. Arlen Walker."

Alice Holland brightened. "Oh yes, I'm sure I've met Arlen once or twice. And I've probably been into his place at some point, maybe when I was campaigning. I've certainly seen the sign on the highway." She put her hands on her knees, leaned forward, as if we were sharing a secret. "Isn't that where the man was killed by the bear? Tracy had a story in the *Times*."

I hesitated. "Yes, that's right."

She nodded thoughtfully. "Actually, I think Tracy writes every story in *The Braynor Times*. I wouldn't be surprised they make her deliver it, too. Your father, I trust he's okay? He wasn't attacked as well?"

"No, well, he sprained his ankle, which is why I've been hanging around for a few days, to help him with the camp." I cleared my throat. "For a small town like Braynor, there seems to be a lot going on."

"Yes," she said. "A man killed by a bear, and then that horrible thing down at the co-op. Did you know Tiff Riley?"

"No."

"He was a charming man. Not the sharpest knife in the drawer, but nice. And that's off the record, by the way. I wouldn't want to be quoted saying something unflattering about the man, especially one who's just passed on."

"I'm not taking notes," I said. "Braynor also seems to be caught up in a bit of controversy at the moment."

Now the weariness fell over Alice Holland like a blanket. "Oh yes. Will we or will we not let the gays into our parade?" She moved her hand across the air, like she was pasting up a headline. "The world waits with bated breath."

"Well, will you?"

"Of course we will. Unless this town wants to be buried in lawsuits."

"So the gay and lesbian organization, they have your support?"

"Ha!" said Alice Holland. "They're nothing but a bunch of shit disturbers, pardon my French. Honestly, can you imagine any gay and lesbian group even wanting to be part of a fall fair parade that features lawn tractor racing? It's all I can do to sit in the back of the convertible from Braynor Ford. Those gay activists'll have the Braynor High School band in front of them performing 'Feelings' with trombones and tubas and coming from behind will be Eagleton's Bait and Tackle, which, last I heard, was going to have choreographed, dancing night crawlers. People in worm suits. I mean, isn't the gay community a tad too sophisticated for something like that? The only reason they want to be in the parade is because there are so many people who *don't* want them in the parade. If Charles Henry, who, by the way, can kiss my skinny white ass, got rid of his petition and put a sign out front of his grocery store saying "Welcome Homos!" they'd pack up and go back to the city and forget this whole damn thing."

I said, "You don't sound like you're from around here."

Alice Holland smiled. "You're very astute."

"How long have you lived in Braynor?"

"George and I moved up here from the city almost fifteen years ago. He was a set designer, and I practiced law, and then we came into a shitload of money when his mother died, and we figured, let's get out. We moved up here, didn't have to work right away, but then we got interested in the area, about attempts to overdevelop it, and I ran for a seat on council and won, and then a couple of elections later, ran for mayor, and won. Who'd have thunk it?"

"Don't suppose you ever thought of opening a law office up here?"

She shrugged. "Not really."

"Think about it," I said. "Some of the local talent leaves something to be desired."

"Yeah, well, what can you do? You should meet our chief of police."

It was my turn to smile. "I've had the pleasure. Speaking of overdevelopment, which way's council leaning on that big fishing-resort proposal south of town? The one Leonard Colebert's pitching?"

"Oh, that," Mayor Holland said. "I was looking at the plans for that again only yesterday. Every time he submits new ones, there's something new added. Another floor on the hotel, or a new outbuilding, or a casino. The day that goes in is the day I let them run over me with an Evinrude."

"So council's unlikely to approve it?"

"Well, there are a few members, they're tempted by the extra jobs, the increased tax base. But they'd bring in a fucking nuclear waste dump if it brought in enough taxes to buy a new snowplow."

I really liked this woman.

She leaned back on her couch. "So, what the hell are you actually doing here, anyway? I mean, I'm having a lovely chat and all, but are you doing a story, or what?"

I paused. "I have a bad feeling," I said with some hesitation.

Mayor Holland's eyebrows went up a notch. "Really?"

"Yes."

"And why do you have this bad feeling?"

I sensed that part of her was humoring me, that she was starting to find me amusing.

"I have to tell you, first of all, that I'm something of a worrier. I'm a worst-case-scenario kind of guy. I'm not some kind of conspiracy nut. I just think that if there's a chance that things might go really bad, they will."

Alice Holland said, "Some people would call that being a realist."

"Yes, well, I can appreciate that. It's just that, the things I've seen happening in Braynor, and out at my dad's place, I have a sense that these events are linked and leading toward something very bad."

Alice Holland said nothing.

"Are you familiar with the people who've rented the farmhouse out on my dad's property?"

"Refresh my memory," she said.

"Timmy Wickens. And his family. A wife, her two sons, his daughter and grandson."

"Ah yes. Are they friends of yours?"

I was taken aback. "Not at all."

"Then you won't be offended if I categorize them as a bunch of whacko-nutcase-racist-survivalists."

"So you've heard of them."

"They have a bit of a reputation in the Fifty Lakes District. They've moved around a couple of times, they're known to police. Some people think they burned down a lawyer's house up in Red Lake, but nothing was ever proved. So what about them?"

"Do you know what was stolen at the co-op?" I asked.

"No."

I told her. And I told her what it could be used for.

"You're making quite a leap," the mayor said.

"I appreciate that."

"Have you discussed your suspicions with Chief Thorne?" she asked.

"I have. These, and others. He's not been particularly receptive."

Again, a small smile. "No, I don't imagine he would be. One of the things I've learned, when I was in a law firm, and being mayor of a town as small as Braynor, your personnel problems are always your biggest headaches."

"I don't know what the protocol might be, but you might want to see whether you can get any help from other law enforcement agencies. And I don't mean this as a slap at Orville. There may be things going on that are beyond the expertise of any small-town police chief."

"Well, all I can say is—"

The phone rang. The look on Alice Holland's face suggested that her heart had stopped. She looked at the phone mounted on the wall next to the door, let it ring once without getting up. Let it ring a second time.

It wasn't any of my business whether she answered her phone or not, but I couldn't help watching her while she let it ring.

Then the door burst open and George grabbed the receiver. "Hello?" He only listened a moment, then slammed the phone back down.

"Death to the dyke bitch again?" the mayor asked.

George nodded once.

"What's going on?" I asked.

"All this over a goddamn fucking parade," Alice Holland said.

20

"HAVE YOU TOLD HIM?" George Holland asked his wife. "About the other calls? This nonstop harassment?"

Braynor mayor Alice Holland sighed and settled back into the couch. "George is very worried about this," she told me.

"There's so many freaks living up here, it could be anybody," George said. "But I tell you who I blame. I blame that crazy redneck son of a bitch Charles Henry for stirring things up with his petition, that's who I blame. That motherfucking bastard, I'll never buy so much as a carton of milk in his store again. I don't care if we have to drive an hour to get our groceries, he won't be getting a dime from us."

"I don't think I can go in there either," I said, not bothering to explain.

"He *has* stirred things up," Alice said. "But that doesn't mean it's him who's been calling here."

"Is it the same person every time, or different callers?" I asked.

George said, "I think there's a couple of them, but

I can't be sure. Now, we just hang up soon as we know what kind of call it is. And I always answer the phone now."

"What kind of threats?"

Alice Holland, very matter-of-factly, said, "Sometimes, they just say I should die. Other times they call me a lesbian, ask me the name of my girlfriend. One gentleman offered to use a lit stick of dynamite on me in a very personal manner."

George, seething, looked ready to kill somebody.

"So, Mr. Walker," Alice said, "I would have to say I share your sense of foreboding, that there's something in the air, something not very good."

"I think you should cancel the parade," I said.

Alice Holland considered that for a moment. "I don't like caving. Although it would be nice if Mr. Lethbridge would offer to back out. I wouldn't ask him to, but it would be worth pointing out the risks."

For a moment I'd forgotten the name. Then I remembered the story in *The Braynor Times*. Stuart Lethbridge, head of the Fifty Lakes Gay and Lesbian Coalition.

George said, "The more risk, the less likely he'd be to pull out. It's like he wants something to happen, so he can be a martyr."

Mayor Holland nodded. "I suspect there's some truth to that. Any other suggestions, Mr. Walker?"

"I have a friend coming up tomorrow. He might have some ideas. And like I said earlier, you might want to make some calls to other agencies, see if you can get Orville some help."

She nodded, then stood up. This, I quickly understood, was my invitation to leave.

"Keep in touch," the mayor said. "But don't be surprised if we don't always answer the phone."

The morning of my fourth day at Denny's Cabins, I was up early, and when I emerged from my cabin to head over to Dad's for breakfast, I spotted Bob Spooner and diaper magnate Leonard Colebert getting ready to go hiking. I was guessing Bob had run out of ways to say no to him.

"Thing is," he said to me quietly while Leonard went back into his cabin for another water bottle to tuck into his backpack, "he's not that bad a guy, once you get past his extremely annoying personality."

"I saw the mayor last night," I said to Leonard when he came back out with a couple of bottles of Evian in his hands. "She doesn't seem all that fired up about your resort proposal. She seems to think it's a bit over the top."

Leonard was either in denial, or knew something I didn't, because he had a broad grin on his face. "Oh, she'll come around. And she's still just one vote on council. If the others go for it, there won't be any way she can stop it. This town hasn't even got a community center. Now suppose someone was willing to pay for one in return for getting approval for his project, what do you think might happen then? Especially when everyone in town finds out they could get a center for nothing?"

Bob shook his head. "Leonard, I really think you

need to reconsider some of this. You know, take into account the character of the area, the beauty of it, and just how your place might impact on—"

Leonard slapped Bob on the back. "Come on, let's go. You think I don't love nature? I love nature! In fact, why don't we drive down the highway and we'll hike into the woods where I'm gonna build my dream. You'll come around, I know you will, when I show you what I'm actually going to do."

Bob looked at me and rolled his eyes. "We'll take my truck," he said, and off they went.

Lana Gantry's car, which I'd failed to notice the other morning when I'd walked in and embarrassed myself and everyone else, was parked behind Dad's cabin, so I rapped lightly on the door before opening it.

"Just me," I said softly, but loud enough that I could be heard in Dad's bedroom.

The bathroom door opened and Lana walked out, clothes and makeup and hair all in place. She strode over and gave me a peck on the cheek. "Hi, sweetie," she said. "Your dad's still in bed. I'd love to make you breakfast, but you'll have to come down to the café to get it. I got to head straight in. One of my girls is off today."

It's difficult to get used to the notion that your father is sleeping with a woman who's not your mother, even when your mother has been gone for several years. I peeked in on Dad, who was snoring, and went back to the fridge, getting out some orange juice and cream for coffee. Lana was looking in her purse for her car keys.

"So who was that you were having coffee with yesterday?" she asked. "And wasn't that Timmy Wickens you were talking to on the sidewalk?"

"Hmm?" I said.

"Yesterday. At the café."

"That was his daughter, May."

"She lives up there at the house with the rest of them?" she asked.

I nodded.

"Well, if I were you," she said, "I wouldn't be getting involved with some woman from a family like that."

"Lana," I said, "we were just having a coffee."

"Oh, listen, I know you and Sarah are okay, your dad's told me that. I'm just saying, don't get mixed up trying to help anybody from a family like the Wickenses. You'll get your ass shot off for the trouble." She discovered her keys, gave them a shake, and smiled on the way out.

A few minutes later, I glanced out the window over the sink and saw two vehicles swoop down over the hill and brake abruptly, tires slipping in gravel. One was Orville's cruiser, and the second, a blue pickup I didn't recognize. Orville jumped out of his car and two men hopped out of the pickup.

They were all carrying rifles.

I peaked in on Dad again. "Hey," I said. "Cavalry's here."

Dad opened one eye. "What?"

"Orville. And others. All armed. Come to hunt bear."

"Jesus." He opened his other eye, threw back the covers. "Where's Lana?"

"She left. Not before dispensing a little advice." I looked at the mess of bed covers, the indentation in the pillow next to Dad's. "Good to see that bad ankle hasn't curtailed all your activities."

Dad sat up in bed. "Where the hell were you last night? Did you really go see the mayor?"

"Yeah. Nice lady. Why don't you get dressed while I go say hello to our rescuers?"

I walked outside, hands in pockets, and strolled over to Orville Thorne, who was talking to the two other men, both dressed in hunting jackets and caps, looking like maybe, after they got our bear, they were off to audition for *Deliverance 2*.

"Morning," I said.

Orville glanced my way. "Your father here?"

"Just getting up."

"You can tell him we're here. To get the bear. We see it, we're going to kill it."

"Super," I said. "Knock yourself out."

"What do you mean, knock ourselves out?" asked one of the hunters. He turned to his buddy. "He wants us to make ourselves unconscious?"

Orville approached, coming up almost nose to nose with me. "I know you've got your own crazy ideas about how Morton Dewart died, but I have a responsibility to protect this community, and if there's a chance he was killed by a bear, I have to go looking for it."

"Absolutely," I said. "But I think you may have bigger things to worry about."

"Like what?"

"You know the mayor's getting death threats?"

Orville's eyeballs danced for a second. "She may have mentioned something about that to me. How do you know about that?"

"I went to see her last night. Her husband greets visitors with a baseball bat. They're on edge."

"I'll talk to her."

"And how's your investigation of Tiff's murder coming along?" I asked.

"We're making inquiries," he said, trying to sound confident. "His wife, she might have had a boyfriend who did it."

"Really?" I said. "So he's a suspect?"

"Well, not exactly. We don't know yet whether Tiff's wife actually had, or has, a boyfriend, but once we find that out, and if she did, then of course, he'd be of interest to our investigation."

"Especially if this boyfriend, if there is one," I said, "ever said to Tiff, 'I'm going to stab you one day,' and if he doesn't have an alibi for the time in question, and if you go to his house and find him holding a bloody knife that matches Tiff's DNA," I said. "Sounds like you've practically got the whole thing wrapped up."

"I don't owe you any explanation of how I conduct my job," Chief Thorne said.

"I think those threats the mayor's getting might be more than just crank calls," I said. "Some people are getting pretty agitated about this parade on Saturday. This Charles Henry, who owns the grocery? He's been stirring up a lot of shit with his petition."

"And so's that guy who wants to be in the parade. Maybe he should do everyone a favor and take a hike."

"Maybe so," I said. "You want to know what I think?"

Orville said nothing, breathed through his nostrils.

"I think you're a good guy, but I think you'd rather chase a bear, a real one or an imaginary one, than confront some of the people in this town. You're running off into the woods to avoid problems, not deal with them."

Orville shook his head. "Gee, thanks, Dr. Phil."

The two hunting buddies snickered. "Let's go, guys," he said to them, and they marched off together into the forest.

Dad opened the cabin door halfway and asked me, "Do they want some coffee first?"

After breakfast I went about my camp chores, collecting garbage, burying fish guts, cutting some grass. Around eleven I went inside to check Dad's computer, see whether Sarah had gotten back to me after I'd e-mailed her the picture of Orville Thorne. She hadn't. I surfed a bit, read *The Metropolitan*'s website to see what was happening back in the city, then checked some of my favorite sci-fi sites, learned that some new kits from the old *Lost in Space* TV show were being issued. I still hadn't gotten around to replacing my model of the *Jupiter II*, the saucer-like ship the Robinson family used to travel around the galaxy, that had been smashed to pieces a couple of years ago.

Outside, I heard voices.

I looked out the window and saw Thorne and his two helpers emerging from the woods, looking discouraged and bedraggled. I didn't have the energy to go outside and rub it in, so I stayed in front of the computer while Dad, crutches tucked under his arm, went to meet them. The conversation was subdued, but I could make out enough to know that they hadn't spotted a bear, but were prepared to come back the next morning.

"Just because we didn't see him doesn't mean he's not out there," I heard Orville say, loud enough, I figured, so that I would hear him through the wall.

I heard a car coming down the hill and moved my head closer to the window so I could get a better look. A shiny blue Jaguar sedan.

Lawrence Jones had arrived.

I went out to greet him. He got out of his car slowly, taking in the scene from behind his shades. He had on a black leather bomber jacket and jeans that looked like they cost a lot more than the Gap variety I was wearing. He nodded when he saw me, then cast his eye over the three men with rifles.

I shook Lawrence's hand. "Hey," I said.

I nodded my head in the direction of the others and Lawrence closed the door of the Jaguar and walked along with me to where Dad was talking to Orville and his two hunting assistants.

"Dad, Orville, fellas," I said, "I'd like you to meet my friend Lawrence. Lawrence Jones."

Orville glared. "Hey there, Larry."

"It's Lawrence," he said, extending a hand. Orville took it reluctantly, probably figuring that refusing it would cause a greater scene. Everyone shook hands.

"This the guy going to solve all our problems?" Orville asked.

Lawrence said nothing. I said, "Lawrence has some experience that might be helpful."

Orville grinned. "Well, I think we've all been waiting for someone with an expensive car and pretty clothes. I know I feel safer already." The hunters chuckled.

"Orville," Dad said reproachfully.

"I take it you're coming back tomorrow," I said to Orville.

"We did what we could today," he said. "We're not going to give up."

"Of course not," I said. "Come back as often as—"

Bob Spooner's truck came over the hill with a roar. It was moving so quickly, skittering across the gravel, I wondered whether it was out of control. Through the windshield I caught a glimpse of Bob, his face bloodied, his eyes wild. We took a few steps back, thinking we might have to run for cover, but then Bob slammed on the brakes, the truck lurching to a stop, gravel dust engulfing the vehicle.

Bob threw open the door, nearly fell out. There was blood streaming from his face, blood on the palms of his hands. "Call an ambulance!" he shouted. "You gotta follow me! We gotta go back! Bring your guns!"

"What is it?" Dad shouted.

"The bear!" he shouted. "I think he's got Leonard! Jesus Christ, follow me!"

Lawrence Jones, taking off his glasses and looking at me, said quietly, "Is it always this busy around here?"

21

BEFORE ANY OF US COULD ASK BOB anything else, or suggest he not drive in his excited state, he'd turned his truck around and was racing back up the drive. Dad and I got into Lawrence's Jaguar while Orville and his two pals piled into his cruiser. Orville was talking on his radio at the same time as he was turning the car around, calling for an ambulance to meet them up the highway.

Bob's truck jerked forward as it hit the highway, the wheels hitting pavement after spinning on gravel.

"Bob shouldn't be driving," Dad said. "He looked like he was in shock or something. Why didn't he take some bear spray? I thought we had another can of the stuff. What the hell was he thinking?"

The Jaguar's engine hummed as Lawrence pushed down on the accelerator.

"You know what I bet he was thinking?" Dad said, answering his own question. "I bet he was thinking there was no bear. And you know why he'd be thinking something like that?"

Dad was sitting in the back, so I didn't have to look at him.

"Because of all your crazy talk, that's why."

"My crazy talk? You've been thinking something different? After our dinner at the Wickenses? You mean to tell me you haven't been thinking the same thing I've been thinking?"

"I'm just saying."

"And besides," I said, "I don't think I've ever even told Bob my theories about what happened. It's one thing to involve you and Orville in conjecture, but it's quite another burdening your guests with all this shit."

"So," Lawrence said, his eyes darting back and forth between Bob's truck and Orville's police car in the rear-view mirror. "It sure is beautiful up here."

Dad said, "My son tells me you're homosexual." Lawrence took a long breath. "You don't look homosexual," Dad said. "Of course, that might be because you're black. Most of the homosexuals you see on TV are white. Isn't that right, Zack?"

Orville had put the siren on. I glanced back and saw that he had the flashing red light going, too. I had a pretty good feeling that he was going to be insufferable very soon. And I had a pretty good feeling I was going to have to endure it.

Ahead, Bob's brake lights came on and the truck skittered over to the shoulder. The truck was barely stopped before he had the door open and was running back to us, pointing into the forest.

"I think it was here!" he shouted as Lawrence pulled the Jag over. Bob was an older guy, and he was looking winded.

Lawrence and I got out. Dad, who'd hopped into the car and come on this adventure without crutches, opened his door but made no move to get out.

"Bob," I said, as calmly as possible. "You have to slow down. You're going to have a heart attack."

He put his hands on the Jag hood to steady himself. Lawrence glanced down at the bloody smudges being left on his sheet metal.

Bob took a couple of breaths. "We might," he said, gasping for air, "already be too late."

Orville and company bolted from the police car like it was rigged to explode, running forward, rifles held across their chests. "Which way?" Orville asked.

Bob pointed again toward the forest. "I'm gonna have to lead you in, show you where I last saw him. Jesus, I don't believe this."

I put an arm around Bob's shoulder. "First of all, how badly hurt are you?" Bob's face was cluttered with several cuts and scrapes and smudges of dirt. The skin was scraped in several places on his hands.

"I fell," he said. "Couple of times, I think. I was running fast as I could. I didn't want him to get me. Jesus, he was huge."

"Okay, but you haven't broken anything, right?"

"I, I don't think so, no."

"Okay." I looked into the back of the Jag. "Dad, you can't walk anyway, so you watch for the ambulance, all right?"

Dad gave me a thumbs-up as Orville brushed up next to me. "I'm in charge here," he said. "And you've got a lot to answer for."

We all started following Bob through the high grass at the edge of the road and into the woods. Orville had taken a position next to Bob.

"Mr. Spooner, isn't it?"

"Yes, that's right."

"What happened exactly?"

"Um, Leonard and I, we were hiking through here, this is the land where he wants to build his fishing resort, you know? He was showing me around, and we heard this rustling behind us, and we turned around, and there it was."

"The bear."

"Fucking right, the bear. He was standing on his back legs, kind of rearing up, you know, and he roared, Jesus, I never heard anything like it in my life."

"Did he attack you? Did he go after you and Leonard?"

"We must have been in shock for a second, I guess we must have just stood there. And I noticed, I saw that one of the bear's ears was clipped, like it was sort of torn off."

I thought back to what Timmy Wickens had said. That the bear they'd seen, the one Morton Dewart had supposedly gone after, had a torn ear.

Orville picked up on that, too, glanced back at me and shook his head.

"Then what happened?"

"We both turned and started to run. I went one

way, Leonard started off in another. I shouted to him, I said, 'Come on! The road's this way!' But then I wondered, maybe he was right, maybe the road was the other way. All I could think to do was keep running, and hope to Christ I was heading for the road, and not deeper into the woods. I glanced back once, tripped over something and scraped myself up a bit, figured the bear would be right on me, because they say you can't outrun a bear, but you can't think of anything else to do, you know?"

"Sure," said Orville, nodding, lots of sympathy. His two buddies, their rifles drawn, were scanning the woods. One caught his rifle on a tree branch and stumbled back. "Was the bear right behind you?"

"No. So I figured it must have gone after Leonard, and I started calling out for him, going back the way I'd come. I was screaming till I nearly lost my voice, but I didn't see any sign of him, or the bear. Jesus, this is terrible."

"It's okay, Mr. Spooner. Did you ever find him?"

"No, no, I never did. I found my way back to the highway, maybe a quarter mile down from where I'd left my truck, ran down to it and went back to the camp, figuring I could get more help, that we could come back and find Leonard." Impulsively, he shouted, "Leonaaard!"

Then we all started doing it. "Leonard!" I shouted. The two hunters called out, even Lawrence cupped his hands around his mouth and called. We were all shouting at once, and then, as if on cue, we all stopped.

No one answered.

This was, I was pretty sure, the same part of the woods Leonard had led me into when he wanted to show me where he was going to build his dream.

"He got him," Bob said, shaking his head. "The bastard must have got him."

He stopped, looked around. "I'm pretty sure it was around here where we encountered him," Bob said. He pointed to the right, raising his arm halfway, as if he wasn't totally sure. "I think I went this way, and Leonard"—he pointed in the other direction—"went thataway. We should probably look over there."

We all kept fairly close together, the six of us, maybe twenty to thirty feet apart, looking down and up and from side to side. Up by the highway, we could hear the wail of an ambulance.

Lawrence moved in close to me, whispered, "I thought you said on the phone there was no bear. That that other guy was killed by dogs, you thought. That that Wickens guy had the dogs kill him for some reason."

"Yeah, well, that was kind of one of the theories I was tossing around."

"So now it looks like you dragged my ass up here to go after a real bear. I have to tell you, that's really not my area. You want Grizzly Adams."

"I thought he liked bears."

"Fuck, I don't know."

"Listen, there's more to what's going on up here besides the bear," I said, pointing my finger into the air in front of me. "Even if Dewart was killed by a bear, it doesn't change all the other stuff."

"Yeah, well, I'm sure you'll bring me up to speed later." Lawrence ducked under a pine branch. "Your dad, he's fun."

"I think he was hoping you'd be a bit swishier."

"Maybe later I'll do some show tunes."

Bob and Orville had pulled farther ahead, then stopped. Bob was looking around, seemingly bewildered. I was thinking maybe, once that ambulance arrived, they should have a look at him while we kept looking for Leonard. Bob might have suffered injuries he wasn't even aware of.

"Hello?" From the road.

My heart stopped. Leonard?

We all looked back, and saw an ambulance attendant in the distance. "We haven't found him yet!" Orville called back. "Soon as we know, we'll give you a shout!"

Lawrence and I had wandered a bit off to the right of everyone else, where the ground gradually sloped up through the trees. I remembered this climb. It led up to the cliff, which overlooked the area where Leonard had talked about putting in a fake whale for kids to play in.

When we got to the top, Lawrence said, "Whoa."

It was a sharp dropoff down onto jagged rocks and then more forest below. Lawrence nudged me in the shoulder and pointed.

Down at the bottom, off to the left, was the twisted body of a man.

"Oh shit," I said. "Hey!" I shouted. "Over here! Over here!"

Everyone came running, Orville in the lead.

When he reached the edge, he reeled back a bit, like he thought he was going to fall over. Lawrence pointed.

"We have to find a way down there," Orville said.

I looked off to the right, where the ground appeared to slope down less precariously. "That way," I said.

Orville shouted back toward the highway. "Back here!" In the distance, a muffled "Coming!"

Lawrence was well ahead of everyone else, hopping over fallen limbs, skittering down the edge of the hill, his arms out for support. He got to Leonard Colebert about ten seconds ahead of the rest of us and was kneeling over him when Orville rushed up.

"Don't touch him!" he said.

Leonard Colebert's body lay flat, on its back, on the forest floor, but his head was twisted nearly 180 degrees, like he was looking over his shoulder when he hit the ground, and his neck stayed that way. His eyes were open and blank. The fall had torn his down-filled jacket, and his pants had slipped partway down his butt.

It seemed apparent to everyone that he was dead, but he still looked in a lot better shape than Morton Dewart did when he was found.

"Oh my God," Bob said. "He's dead, isn't he?"

No one said anything, but everyone was nodding.

"Why isn't he, I mean, he doesn't look like the bear got to him, does it?" Bob said.

Orville was shaking his head, looking back up the hill. "My guess is, he was running, looking behind him to see if the bear was gaining, went right off the cliff before he even knew it was there." Orville paused. "All things considered, it was probably a lot better way to go."

I couldn't argue with that.

One of the two hunters with Orville pointed to Leonard Colebert's partially dropped pants. "Look," he said. "The guy was wearing a fucking diaper."

His friend giggled and said, "I guess, if I ran into a bear in the woods, I'd wanna be wearing one of those, too."

22

SOMEONE PUT IN A CALL to the local general practi-
tioner/coroner, my good friend Dr. Heath, and being
the oldest of all of us out there, even if Dad had been
with us and not stuck back up there on the highway,
he was offered some assistance navigating his way
down the steep hill to examine Leonard Colebert
and declare him officially dead. I offered my arm,
but when the doctor saw who it was attached to, he
pulled back and clung to someone else, a gesture
Lawrence Jones didn't fail to pick up on.

Lawrence said, under his breath, "How many days
you been up here? And how many people have you
already managed to piss off?"

"You don't know the half of it," I said.

The ambulance attendants didn't mind accepting
my help, and that of others, getting Leonard's body,
once it was on the gurney, back out to the ambulance. It took a good ten minutes to carry him up the
hill and through the woods to the road. Dad was out

of the car, leaning against it without his crutches, watching the action.

"What happened?" he asked when I walked up onto the shoulder of the highway. I brought him up to speed, including Orville's theory, which, it pained me to realize, seemed to make a lot of sense. Leonard had been looking for what was behind him, instead of what was in front of him, and taken a header over the edge. The bear must have decided it was too much trouble to go down there and make a meal of him, and maybe had gone looking for Bob instead.

One of the ambulance attendants came up to us, a backpack hanging from one hand, and said, "This was Mr. Colebert's."

I reached out to take it as Dad said, "We can take that back and put it with his other stuff. I don't know what family he has, but I guess they'll be coming up to claim his things."

The attendant said, "We think Mr. Spooner should come to the hospital to have those cuts and scrapes looked at, but we don't want to make him ride in the ambulance with the deceased. Would one of you be able to take him in? We don't think he should drive his truck."

I offered to take Bob, in his own pickup, into Braynor. I made this proposal to him as he stood at the back of the ambulance, watching them load Leonard. He still appeared to be in a mild state of shock.

"I think I'm okay," he said, looking numbly at the palms of his hands.

"You should go have those cuts checked," I said. "You might get an infection if they don't treat them. Why don't you get in the truck."

Chief Orville Thorne strode up to me, his finger pointing. "Not so fast with the smart remarks now, are you?"

I said nothing.

"You come up here from the city, bring along your fancy smart friends"—he nodded in Lawrence's direction—"because we don't know anything, we're just a bunch of hicks, right? You think Dr. Heath and me don't know what we're doing, you have the nerve to cast doubt on his conclusions, suggesting he didn't know a bear attack when he saw it. You tell me how to do my job. You really take the cake, you know that? You have any idea how much trouble you've caused? You probably got this man killed, telling him there really was no bear. Maybe, if he hadn't listened to you, he'd still be alive."

"I never told him anything," I said.

"Yeah, well, whatever," Orville said.

I said, "I'm going to drive Bob into town. Nice talking to you, Orville."

I got Bob into the passenger seat and got myself back in behind the wheel. The keys were still in the ignition. The steering wheel was smeared with blood, and I tried to wipe most of it off with a tissue from my pocket. Once we were on the road and heading into Braynor, Bob said to me, "What was he talking about?"

"Nothing," I said. "He just thinks I'm an asshole."

"What did he mean, that you questioned the findings of the coroner, Dr. Heath? That he was wrong thinking it was a bear that killed that man at the camp?"

"It doesn't matter anymore, Bob. It's just, I always had my doubts, because of those damn dogs. And how weird the Wickenses are, and what Betty had to say."

"Betty? What did Betty have to say?"

"She used to be a nurse, and she saw Morton Dewart's body, and she just didn't think he looked like he'd been torn apart by a bear. She thought it looked more like the work of those pit bulls. And then, the other night, Dad and I went up there for dinner."

"Up where?"

"The Wickenses."

"You had dinner with them?"

"Yeah, well, we didn't have seconds, I can tell you that. But yeah, we did, and everyone went out of their way to tell us how Dewart had seen this bear, and decided to go after it, and how he must have had a run-in with it. It just all seemed a bit rehearsed, you know? Like they were putting on a show for us."

I glanced in my rear-view mirror, saw Lawrence's blue Jag following us. Bob stared straight ahead. "So what do you think now?"

"I guess there's a bear in the woods, Bob. I still don't know for sure that one killed Dewart, but I'm not going to get anyone to listen to my suspicions, certainly not Orville, who doesn't give a shit what I say anyway. And the fact is, your description of the bear, with the torn ear, matches the description the Wickenses gave of the bear that Dewart went after."

Bob nodded tiredly. "I feel kind of sick," he said.

"You've been through a traumatic incident, Bob. We need to get you looked after, and then get you back to the camp."

"I need to lie down," he said.

"Just hang in till we get to the hospital. They'll get you patched up and then you can come back, sack out in the cabin. We'll have you back out on the lake in no time."

"The lake," Bob said dreamily.

"Yeah. Maybe you can take me out with you."

"Did Leonard, did he have a wife, a family?"

"I don't know. I don't think so."

Bob put his head back against the headrest and kept his eyes closed until we pulled into the driveway of the emergency ward.

I left Bob with the nurse at reception and went out to talk to Lawrence and Dad, who now was in the front seat. Dad hit the power window. "How is he?"

"Shook up, but he'll be okay. I better hang in to drive him back. Once they bandage his hands it may be hard for him to steer."

Dad said he'd have some lunch ready for when I got back, and Lawrence's Jag pulled away. By the time I walked back into the ER, Bob was already with a doctor. This wasn't exactly like going to a big-city hospital, where they kept you waiting for hours.

"Hey, Mr. Walker."

I whirled around. It was Tracy, pen and notepad in hand.

"You're everywhere," I said. "I guess you heard about what happened."

"The bear got another one."

"Well, yes and no. Looks like Leonard Colebert died trying to get away from him. But you should talk to the chief. This is his thing. I'm out of it."

"Is there some kind of trouble between you two?" Tracy asked.

I shrugged, not eager to get into it. Tracy presented me with a brown business envelope. "Could you give this to your wife, Mr. Walker? It's a resumé? My work experience, some clippings?"

"Why don't you fax it to her directly," I said. "I may still be up here for a few days."

"And I heard a rumor the mayor's getting death threats. Is that true? Is that why you were up talking to her?"

"I'm out of this, Tracy. Talk to the chief."

I felt I really was out of it. What did my suspicions amount to, really? Betty could be wrong in her assessment of how Morton Dewart died. Tiff, at the co-op, could have been killed for any number of reasons. And all that fertilizer could have been stolen by a farmer looking to save a few bucks.

And the Wickenses might have a framed picture of Timothy McVeigh on their wall because they were nuts. Simple as that. It didn't mean they were up to anything particularly sinister.

And Alice Holland's refusal to kick a gay rights group out of the fall fair parade could be expected to produce some nasty crank calls. People were always tough when they were anonymous. It didn't have to mean the mayor was in any real danger.

With any luck, Dad's ankle was nearly healed. Maybe, by the next day, or the day after that, he'd be well enough to get back to running the camp on his own.

I was ready to go home.

I grabbed a seat in the waiting room and was glancing through a hunting magazine that I cared nothing about when Bob reappeared. His hands were wrapped in gauze, and he had a couple of small bandages on his cheeks, and a third on his forehead.

"Ready?" I said.

"Ready," Bob said.

He said nothing the whole way home, and once we were back at the camp, he said a simple "Thanks" as he got out of the truck and walked over to his cabin.

"You want to come over, have a drink, something to eat?" I asked.

Bob shook his head no and went inside.

There were tuna sandwiches on the table when I walked into Dad's cabin. "I didn't do a thing," Dad said. "Lawrence here made lunch."

I suddenly realized I was starving, and sat at the table and practically inhaled the sandwich.

Lawrence said, "Your father's kinda been filling me in. The stuff you already told me, plus some other stuff."

"I don't know whether there's anything here for you to do or not," I said. "I'm sorry if I dragged you up here for nothing."

"Well, from the sounds of it, these folks renting the farmhouse from your dad are bad news, no matter how you look at it. I think we start by trying to find out more about them."

I shrugged. I just didn't know anymore.

"I do know one thing that hasn't changed," I said. "And that's May Wickens, and her boy, Jeffrey. They still need to get away from her father, Timmy. No boy should be growing up, getting indoctrinated in the kind of hate that's preached up there by that man."

"So this Timmy, he hates fags and niggers and Jews and probably the New York Philharmonic as well," Lawrence Jones said thoughtfully.

"Yeah. And he decides what lessons his daughter should teach his grandson."

He pursed his lips, nodded. "Doesn't sound to me like a very enlightened curriculum."

"What are you going to do?" I asked him, taking another bite of my sandwich and feeling a bit apprehensive.

"We'll see," Lawrence said.

When I finished my lunch, I went into Dad's study to see whether Sarah had gotten back to me.

I signed on to the mail program. Bingo.

Sarah wrote:

When are you coming home? Angie and Paul are starting to drive me crazy. No, I take that back. They've always driven me crazy, but when you're home, at least you can take some of the brunt of it. I've spent $60 on taxis just so I won't have to referee all these fights over the car. I don't want to give you something else to worry about, but the dishwasher is making a really weird noise, it goes chugga-chugga halfway through the cycle, sounds like there's a cat in there. The dishes are coming out dirty, which means they have to be done by hand, which means I have to ask Paul or Angie to do them in the sink, which sets off World War Three because they each think it's the other person's turn. And while I'm on the subject of cats (see dishwasher, above), both the kids are talking about getting a dog. Where did that come from? I don't want any part of it.

They're making some noises around the offices about when you're coming back. There's a Star Trek convention in town this week and the features editor figured you'd be the perfect guy to cover it, which I happen to disagree with. I say you send someone who DOESN'T know the first thing about Star Trek, and can take a look at these sci-fi nuts, no offense intended, and offer an unbiased perspective, but what the hell do I know.

Now, your requests. I made some calls about women's shelters. A place where this woman and her kid could go. I've got a contact at Kelly's Place, the one that was named in honor of that woman whose husband killed her with a crossbow. They've got a spot, if you think she's interested.

And on the other thing, the picture you sent me, of Orville Thorne, the police chief. Nice fish, by the way. I'm pretty sure I've never seen this guy before, but if you're wondering why he looks so familiar, maybe you should go stand in front of a mirror. The guy looks just like you. You could be brothers, for crying out loud.

All for now. Love, Sarah.

I stared out the window, and into the woods, for a good five minutes.

23

I REMEMBER IT like it was yesterday.

I am twelve years old.

My mother is standing just inside the front door, looking back into the house, two suitcases packed and at her side, my father at the top of the stairs, saying, "Evelyn, don't go."

It is raining outside, and Mom is wearing her tan raincoat, with the long dangly belt that is always slipping out of the loops, over a blue striped dress, and if she had just come in from the outside, you might have thought those were two raindrops running down her cheeks.

I am standing next to my sister, Cindy, who's fourteen. Mom looks at me and tries to smile and says, "You two look after each other, okay? Your dad's going to be busy and won't be able to look after everything."

I am numb. What is going on here? Why does Mom have suitcases packed? Where is she going? How long is she going to be gone? I get this horrible feeling that if she goes, she is not coming back. That she is leaving forever. What has Dad done to make her so angry she has to leave?

"Where are you going?" Cindy asks. "Will you bring me something back?"

"Don't be an idiot," I snap at her. "She's not coming back."

Cindy shouts at me. "Shut up! You don't know anything!" She's so angry, she must have some idea that this is actually the truth.

Mom swallows. She is crying. "I'll send you something," she says. "And I'll call you all the time."

Dad shakes his head. "This is crazy. You can't do this. We can figure out something else."

Mom looks at him. "Arlen, I think you know why I have to do this."

There are tears in his eyes, too. He turns away so we can't see him wiping them away.

There have been arguments in the night. For a few weeks now, it seems. Sometimes, in bed, I pull the pillow over my head so I won't hear their muffled voices through the wall.

I know Dad drives her crazy on occasion, but I've never thought his behavior would drive her out of the house. I mean, he drives me and Cindy crazy, too, but we aren't leaving. It seems no more a choice for Mom than it does for us, as children.

It has not been that long since the infamous Emergency Brake Incident. Five or six months, maybe.

We have a white Volkswagen Beetle, with the motor in the back, and it distresses Dad to no end that his wife can't remember to pull up on the emergency brake when she parks the car. She figures leaving the gearshift engaged holds the car in place, and on level ground, you can get away with that, I suppose, but there is a slight incline to our driveway, which means that if the shifter were to somehow become disengaged, our Bug would roll back and out into the street.

Dad reminds her time and again that she has to put the emergency brake on, and sometimes she remembers, but most times she forgets. Mom is a bit forgetful at times, easily distracted. She explains that she's the one who keeps the house running, that she has a lot to keep track of, and if she can manage to make twenty-one meals a week and change the sheets and do the laundry, can't she be forgiven if she doesn't always remember to put on the emergency brake?

It doesn't help that our other car, a 1965 Dodge Polara, has automatic transmission, and even Dad rarely bothers to shove the emergency brake foot pedal down in it. Mom must figure, if she doesn't have to remember it in the Dodge, why does she have to remember it in the Volkswagen?

One day, Dad decides to teach her a lesson.

She's returned from grocery shopping, and Dad slips out to see whether she's remembered to put the brake on. He does this almost every time she comes home, and if she's slipped up, he'll come in right away and let her know. If she's remembered, he says nothing. Sometimes, soon as Mom gets home,

I'd slip out before Dad can and if Mom has forgotten to pull the brake on, I'll do it.

This one particular day, I guess he's had enough.

He gets into the Beetle and coasts it back, just far enough that the back end is hanging into the street about a foot. Then he slips it back into gear, resists the temptation to put the emergency brake on, and goes back up into our garage, where he finds Cindy's red and white tricycle, which we still have, even though she hasn't ridden it in six years or more. The garage is filled with stuff we've outgrown, including a turquoise pedal car I once used to tour the neighborhood and pick up hot four-year-olds.

Dad takes the tricycle and carefully wedges it, tipped onto its side, under the back of the car. The handlebar he links in with the bumper.

Dad has staged the event in such a way that it can be seen from our front door.

He comes back inside and walks into the kitchen, where I am making a peanut butter sandwich, and Mom is glancing at that day's paper. He says, casually, "Did you hear something?"

Mom says, "What?"

"Out front. I thought I heard something a second ago."

Mom decides to go check. I don't think it even occurs to her that there is a problem with the car. Maybe she's thinking Dad heard the mailman arrive. Dad waits in the kitchen. He's grinning, and at this point, I have no idea why. It's only later I learn how he's set this all up.

So I have no idea why Mom is suddenly screaming, "Oh my God!"

I bolt from the table, ahead of Dad, and when I got to the front door I can see Mom running flat out to the end of the driveway. I see the trike jammed under the back of the car, and I recognize it as Cindy's, and even though I know she doesn't ride it anymore, I feel this jolt. I guess Mom felt it, too. I shudder at the thought of what else might be found under the car, in addition to a tricycle.

Mom drops to her knees, looks under the car, gets up, looks around, as if maybe she might spot some injured child attempting to crawl home.

Dad is leaning in the doorway, arms folded, looking unbearably satisfied with himself. As Mom walks back across the lawn, saying something about maybe they should call the police, there might be a hurt child wandering the neighborhood, Dad says, "Looks like maybe you forgot to put on the e-brake."

That stops her cold. Not, I suspect, because she is trying to remember whether she did apply the brake or not, but because at that moment she realizes what has actually happened. That her husband has staged this event. That he has allowed her to think, if only for a moment, that she is responsible for a monstrous tragedy.

She walks up the steps to the house and, in a blinding flash, slaps my father across the face.

I have never seen my mother hit my father. Nor have I ever seen him hit her. For all his faults, he is not that kind of man.

This is not some little slap, either. It actually

knocks him off his feet and into the shrubs at the side of the door. And then she goes inside, and doesn't speak to him for three days.

Dad apologizes endlessly. It doesn't take him long to figure out that he may have crossed the line here.

It is painful to recall this incident, not just because it shows my father, basically a good man, in such a bad light. It also shows how little we can learn from our parents' mistakes, how we can know, even as children, that what they've done is wrong, and then, when we grow up ourselves, we go along and make the same kinds of mistakes. I had to make my own, with disastrous consequences, before I learned to tone it down.

Looking out the window of Dad's cabin, one memory links to another, and then, suddenly, there is Lana Gantry.

Not outside the cabin, but in my memories.

The Gantrys live up the street. I hadn't remembered it all that clearly when I'd been reintroduced to Lana earlier in the week, but now things started coming back. Mr. and Mrs. Gantry. His name is Walter. He works at the Ford plant. He's the first person in the neighborhood to have one of the new Mustangs. My parents get together with them once in a while. They play bridge, or barbecue out back. One time, they actually play charades.

After three days, Mom starts talking to Dad again. It is summer, and they've already invited the Gantrys over for dinner that weekend, so some sort of peace accord is reached.

I see the four of them out back, Dad and Mr.

Gantry with beers in their hands, laughing, the women shaking their heads and smiling, sharing jokes about their husbands' foolishness. They are all friendly together. Mr. Gantry talking to Mom. Dad talking to Lana.

Sometimes, slipping his arm around her waist. Surely, I think, this does not mean anything.

And then, not long after, Mom at the door with her suitcases.

And not long after that, the Gantrys move away.

And the four of them never get together again.

But now, a decade after my mother's death, here is Lana Gantry again. Back in my father's life.

Living in the same town as a young man she refers to as her nephew. Orville Thorne. Who, I guess, is about thirteen years younger than I.

And who, I now realize, looks an awful lot like me.

It doesn't seem possible that Mom would walk out on Dad for the better part of half a year over the Emergency Brake Incident. But I can imagine her leaving him for fathering a child with a woman from down the street.

The night before she leaves, I hear snippets of her argument with my father in their bedroom, snippets which, up until now, more than three decades later, never meant anything to me. I hear the name "Gantry." And I hear the word "baby."

"I can't live here," I hear my mother say.

"The shame," I hear her say.

And then I pull the pillow down harder on my head so I won't have to hear any more. There isn't anything else from that argument to recall now.

She keeps her word, though. She does call all the time. She talks to Cindy, and then my sister hands the phone to me, and she asks me what is going on at school, and whether I am doing my homework, and what I am doing with my friends, and I tell her everything I can think of, about *Star Trek* and this episode where Kirk and Spock go back to Earth in the 1920s to find Dr. McCoy, who's met this woman who will change the course of history, and I am ready to tell her every detail of the entire episode because I want to talk to her for as long as possible, but finally, Dad nudges me aside, mumbles something about long distance, because Mom is staying with her sister in Toronto, but what he really wants is to talk to her himself.

Once he has the phone, he asks me and Cindy to leave the kitchen, to go watch TV or something, but sometimes I hide around the corner and hear my father say, "I still love you. It's my fault, not yours. I'm ready to start all over again. How are you feeling? Are you feeling okay?"

After six months of this, Mom comes home, and our house is whole again.

They are both different after that, but especially Dad. He still has his quirks and phobias. He gets the oil changed in the Dodge every four thousand miles, and if he's even a hundred miles overdue he can't sleep at night for fear the engine will seize up and cost him a thousand dollars to fix. He still drives me and Cindy nuts, but he is never so critical of Mom again. He lets stuff go. He even trades Mom's Volkswagen in on a compact Ford with automatic transmission, doesn't care anymore whether she uses the emergency brake. And maybe, after a year or two, they are signs that they actually love each other.

But there are also times when I notice a faraway look in Mom's eyes, and I will ask her what she is thinking.

"Oh, nothing," she says. "Nothing at all."

It's the day she leaves that stays with me. Her standing in the door, waiting to leave, the suitcases at her side. The rain coming down outside.

Cindy rushes to give her a hug, but I hold back. I am so angry that she's going. That no matter what Dad has done, she can't put it aside to take care of us.

"Zachary," she says, "can you give Mom a kiss good-bye?"

I run to my room and watch from my window as Dad helps Mom take her bags to the car and toss them into the back seat of the Volkswagen. And then she gets in, Dad standing next to the car as though he expects her to roll down the window and say one final thing to him. But she does not.

The Bug comes to life with its distinctive, throaty roar. She puts the wipers on, then backs out of the drive.

That's when I notice that one end of the belt to her raincoat has become caught in the bottom of the door, and is dangling down, swinging an inch above the wet pavement.

I run from my room and descend the flight of stairs in two jumps, burst out the front door, run past Dad standing in the driveway, and after my mom's car, screaming, "Your belt! Your belt!" But Mom does not look back, and then the Volkswagen turns the corner and is gone.

Standing there, in the rain, I cry enough tears to drown the world.

24

I CAME OUT OF DAD'S STUDY and walked past him and Lawrence at the kitchen table. I couldn't bring myself to look at Dad, not directly, anyway. I reached into the fridge, found some orange juice, and poured myself a glass.

"Lawrence here was saying," Dad said, "that you don't really choose to be gay. You're born that way."

I said nothing. I looked at Lawrence, who was smiling at me.

"That's kind of interesting, don't you think?" Dad said. "Maybe it doesn't make a lot of sense to pick on gay people if they can't help it."

"That's very charitable," Lawrence said.

"Well," said Dad, who'd evidently detected some sarcasm in the air, "you know what I mean."

I leaned up against the counter. "You're not joining us?" Dad asked, nodding toward an empty chair. "What's with you?"

"Nothing," I said.

"It's this Leonard thing," Dad said, happy to

provide me with an excuse for my unwillingness to participate in the conversation. "I'm upset, too. Shit, I'm the one, I guess, who's going to have to find some sort of family, have them come up here and pick up his car and his stuff. Hey, where's Leonard's backpack?"

"My car," Lawrence said. "I can go get it for you."

"No hurry. I just don't want to forget about it."

"What do you want to do?" Lawrence asked me. I was looking at the floor, and when I didn't say something right away, Lawrence said, "Hello? Earth to Zack?"

I raised my head slowly. "So, Dad," I said, "I finally remembered Lana Gantry."

Dad looked around. "Hmm?"

"From when I was a kid. I didn't remember her at first, but it came back to me today. All kinds of memories."

"Oh," Dad said. "Okay."

"She and her husband, they used to come over, right? I can remember you guys barbecuing in the backyard. Coming over to play cards, watch stuff on TV."

Dad made an effort at trying to recall. "Yeah, yeah, I think we did, now that you mention it."

"I seem to remember you guys laughing, having a good time. There was even a time, I think, when I walked into the living room and you were all playing charades."

"Charades," Lawrence said. "People really did that, huh?"

I said, "You all seemed to get along really well. You

and Lana, you were friends years ago before you reconnected up here."

Dad swallowed. "We all got along very well."

"So, what happened? Did they move away?"

"That's what Lana told you the other day," Dad said. "Weren't you listening? They sold their house, moved away, and years later, I ran into Lana in town here, and we kind of renewed old acquaintances. Her husband's long since dead, you know." Getting a bit defensive. "And your mother's been gone a long time, too, Zachary."

"Did I say something?" I said. I looked at Lawrence. "Did you hear me say something?"

"Hey, man, I don't know where you're going with this."

"I'm entitled to a life," Dad said. "Who I see is none of your goddamn business."

"Did I say it was? Of course, who you see *now* is none of my business. I couldn't agree more. But what about when I was a kid? Still living at home. Under your roof. Would it be any of my business then?"

Dad's mouth opened, but nothing came out. He was getting ready to say something, but then stopped himself.

"Tell me about Orville," I said. "I'm a bit curious about him. You go out of your way to defend him sometimes. Have you noticed that? You tell me I'm being too hard on him. Why do you do that? What do you care? What's he to you?"

"He's Lana's nephew," Dad said quietly. "I just want you to show a bit of respect, that's all."

"Is that really what he is? Lana's nephew? She's his aunt?"

Now it was Dad's turn to be sarcastic. "That's sort of how it works, Zachary. If you're my nephew, I'm your uncle, or aunt."

"It's not possible that he's something other than Lana's nephew?"

Dad stared at me, hard. "Zachary," he said slowly, "I don't know what you're thinking, or what you're getting at, but you need to leave this alone. It's none of your business. It's not any of your concern. I'm telling you, don't go stirring up all kinds of shit. It's not going to help anyone."

I looked Dad in the eye. My mouth felt dry.

"Here's my other question," I said. "About Orville." I took a breath. "What exactly are *you* to Orville?"

"Zachary, for Christ's sake, what the hell are you talking about?"

"I guess what I'm wondering is, if Lana's not exactly his aunt—"

"I never said that."

"—if Lana's not exactly his aunt, and I'm just supposing here, isn't it possible that you're more than just some citizen of Braynor that Orville's sworn an oath to protect?"

Again Dad started to say something, then stopped himself.

"I sent Sarah a picture of Orville," I said.

"You what?"

"On the computer. I told her that ever since I've arrived, there's been something about him that seemed familiar to me. Couldn't put my finger on it."

Shouting. "You had no business using my computer!"

"Dad, I've been using it since I got here. And I didn't snoop around in it. I downloaded the picture into it. That's what I sent Sarah. And you know what she said? I felt like an idiot when I read her note, it suddenly seemed so obvious."

Dad waited, thinking he knew what I was going to say, but not sure. Lawrence was looking pretty interested, too.

"She said he looked just like me. That we could be brothers."

Dad glared at me, and then, in a flash, he swept his arm across the top of the table, sending his and Lawrence's cups and plates and cutlery and the salt and pepper shakers and napkin holder crashing onto the floor.

"You don't know what the fuck you're talking about!" he bellowed. "Mind your own fucking business!"

Lawrence had jumped back in his chair when everything hit the floor, and now he was on his feet, looking at Dad, then at me, then back at Dad again. He stooped to start picking things up off the floor.

"Leave it!" Dad said, and Lawrence straightened. No one moved, no one said a word for several moments.

Dad eyes were welling up, and he put his hands over them so we couldn't see.

"Dad," I said.

He took one hand away and waved me off, then put it back over his face. Lawrence took a step toward me, caught my eye, and said quietly, "Come on. Let's take a walk."

I felt this was the wrong time to walk out, that we were on the verge of something here.

"Dad, I just want to know—"

"Get out," he said to me. The tone suggested he was not in a mood to debate it.

I slipped out the door with Lawrence. We started walking, with no particular destination in mind.

"Well," said Lawrence. "I don't know whether I've had a chance yet to thank you for inviting me up here. I've only been here for, what, three hours, and we've already had a guy killed by a bear and you're having a family meltdown. What's happening after dinner?"

I picked up a stone from the gravel lane that led up to the highway, threw it into the trees. "I think I have a right to know about these things," I said.

"Yeah, well, I'm sure that right is enshrined somewhere," Lawrence Jones said.

"Don't you think, if Orville Thorne is my half brother, that I have a right to know that?"

Lawrence raised his face to the sun. "I don't honestly know whether I'd want to find out Orville Thorne was related to me. Although, from what I've seen and what you've told me, he's inept, easily intimidated, and totally unsure of himself. So I guess it's possible."

We were coming to the bend, where the lane branched off to the Wickens place.

"Sorry," I said. "I didn't ask you up here to get in the middle of a dispute between me and my father. I didn't expect that e-mail from Sarah, what she'd say, but when I read it, pieces started fitting together."

"What sort of pieces?" Lawrence asked.

"There's the whole thing with my mother, how she was so angry with Dad that she left home when I was twelve. Then, Lana and her husband moving out of the neighborhood, after they'd been so close to my parents. And now, years later, with her husband dead and my mother passed on, it's like they're picking up where they left off years ago. And look at Orville, he's about twelve, thirteen years younger than I am. It's been bugging me from the first moment I saw him, thinking that he looked like somebody I knew. He looks like me, Lawrence. The son of a bitch looks like me."

Lawrence thought about that. "Yeah, there's a passing resemblance, I admit. It's not really obvious, but if you know there's a connection, you can see it."

"No wonder I've been wanting to give him a wedgie since the moment I first met him," I said. "I just want to put him a headlock and run my knuckles over his head."

We were twenty feet away from the Wickens gate. Lawrence took in all the threatening signs. No Trespassing. Beware of Dogs. "So these are your friends," he said. He looked into the yard, at the abandoned appliances, the piles of wood, the old white van with blacked-out windows, a couple of beat-up trucks, an old four-door Pontiac economy car.

"Looks like they're going to open a used-car dealership," he quipped.

"Dad's got so much work ahead of him, if he ever gets them out of there."

We'd been spotted. Gristle and Bone appeared from around the far side of the house and were running toward the gate, their paws pounding the dirt, propelling them forward, their hackles raised. Their chorus of angry growls sounded like broken gears trying to mesh together. They locked their jaws on a gate board, went berserk chewing on it, splinters of wood dropping to the ground. They seemed to think they could eat their way through to get to us, and given enough time, probably could.

"Cute," Lawrence said. "What do you think you'd have to do to dogs to make them this mean?"

"Let's walk back," I said.

The dogs remained in their frenzied state until we'd disappeared behind the trees. "Think they could eat someone?" I asked.

"Yeah," said Lawrence. "But then, so could a bear. Actually, those dogs could probably eat a bear."

We headed down to the lake and perched ourselves on a large rock at the water's edge, upwind from the fish bucket.

"What should I do, Lawrence?" I asked.

"About your dad, or about everything else?"

"My dad is my problem. How about everything else?"

"Well, even if there really is a bear, and Morton Dewart was killed by one and not by Satan's puppies up there, it doesn't change the fact that you've still got a bunch of McVeigh worshippers living on your dad's property. You've got another dead guy and a shitload of missing fertilizer that's ideal for making things blow up good, your mayor's getting death threats, and you've got a public event coming up, what, tomorrow, that has a lot of people riled."

"Yeah."

"It's like when they issue a tornado watch. It's not a warning. There's no tornado on the horizon. But all the conditions are right for one."

"You think there might be a tornado coming."

"The conditions are right."

"So, what next?"

"I guess we start doing a little surveillance, talk to the people involved. I need to get to know these Wickenses a little better."

I heard a plop in the water, and craned my neck around to look farther up the shore. It was ten-year-old Jeffrey Wickens, his jeans rolled up, standing in six inches of water, tossing stones.

"I guess we could start right now," I said. "Come on. I'll introduce you."

We got off the rock and ambled along the shore-line. Jeffrey was hunting around in the water, look-ing for flat stones, then attempting to skip them. He got his index finger wrapped around the edge of a stone, then flicked it out across the water, but he couldn't seem to manage more than a single skip.

"Maybe the water needs to be a little calmer," I said, and Jeffrey whirled around. He smiled warmly enough at me, but as soon as he noticed Lawrence, his expression turned wary.

"Hi, Mr. Walker," he said.

"Hope you're not still in trouble about going to

play video games," I said, thinking back to when I was having the coffee with his mother.

"Grandpa was mad for a while, but not anymore," he said. His eyes kept darting to Lawrence.

"I'd like you to meet my friend," I said. "Lawrence Jones."

"Hi," Lawrence said, and extended a hand out over the water. Tentatively, Jeffrey took a couple of steps and shook it, then withdrew his hand quickly, like he might lose it if he didn't act quickly enough. I saw him glance at Lawrence's light-colored palm.

To Lawrence, he said, "Do you know about Lando Calrissian?"

"Yeah," he said. "I think. From *Star Wars*, right?"

"I don't have him anymore," Jeffrey said. "How about Mace Windu?"

Lawrence looked doubtful. "You got me there."

I stepped in. "The new crop of *Star Wars* movies. Starting with *Phantom Menace*. Played by Samuel L. Jackson."

Lawrence nodded, getting it now. The black contingent from *Star Wars*.

"Would those be real Negroes?" Jeffrey asked. "I mean, because it's another galaxy, and there's no Earth there, if there are Negroes, are they really the same as Negroes here on this planet? Because they'd have different origins, right? And blood? And wouldn't they have different DNA and stuff?"

Lawrence looked at me, but I figured he could handle this one, even if he wasn't as well versed in science fiction lore.

"Those are actors," Lawrence told Jeffrey. "Black actors."

Jeffrey rolled his eyes. "I know *that*. But if they're playing people from other planets, are they still Negroes in the movie?"

Lawrence paused. "What makes you ask?"

"Well, if I could explain to my grandpa that they're not really colored people, because they're from another planet, then maybe he would let me have their figures."

"Figures?"

"Action figures," I told Lawrence. "They're very collectible." I paused. "I have a number of them."

"Okay," he said. "Jeffrey, why wouldn't your grandpa want you to have those figures, regardless of whether they're . . . Negroes or not?"

"Because they're an inferior race," he said innocently. He added, with the utmost politeness, "I don't mean that personally."

"Of course not," Lawrence said.

"I mean, you might be the exception," Jeffrey said.

"You never know," Lawrence said.

"I'm really lucky," Jeffrey said, shifting gears, "because I don't have to go to school. I go to school at home. I'm kind of on a recess break now, but I have to go back soon. I love to skip stones."

"Do you learn about these things at home?" Lawrence asked. "About which races are inferior, and which ones are superior?"

Jeffrey nodded. "My grandpa helps my mom figure out what to teach. My mom mostly does the spelling and arithmetic and geography, and my grandpa does a lot of the other stuff. Like how a lot of stuff they teach in history class in regular schools is wrong or never even happened. He gets really upset about that. One time I was telling him about my friend Richard? When I still went to regular school? And Richard's grandfather, or his great-grandfather, I don't remember, but when he was a kid he was in this huge prison camp where they put people in ovens and burned them all up. It was called Awwshits."

"Close enough," Lawrence said.

"So I told my grandpa, and he made me go to bed without any supper and when I snuck down later? To the kitchen to make a sandwich? He caught me and gave me a whooping."

He said this without an ounce of malice or sorrow. He was just making conversation.

"So that's why he helps me with history, because he knows that a lot of stuff that some people say happened never did."

"Well," Lawrence said, glancing at me. "Aren't you lucky that he takes such an interest. So, Jeffrey, you got any friends up here?"

"Not so much," he said. "I used to, before Mom and I moved up here, when I went to that real school. But up here, there aren't even any neighbors. But Grandpa says that's okay, because it reduces the number of bad influences." As he said it, he blinked, suddenly realizing that he might be talking to one. "There are bad influences all over the place, even in Braynor."

Lawrence reached down and ran his fingers through the wet stones. He found a smooth, flat one. "Try this," he said, handing it to Jeffrey. "But when you throw it, try to tip it up a bit, so you can skip it right over the waves."

Jeffrey took the stone and looked back out to the lake. He took a moment to get his grasp right, leaned into it, then snapped his arm.

The stone hit the water, skipped once, skipped twice, then disappeared under the water.

"Not bad," Lawrence said. "Not bad at all."

"Thanks," Jeffrey said. He looked at me. "I didn't know you had any Negro friends."

"I got all kinds of friends," I said.

"Well," he said, stepping out of the water and finding a pair of shoes that he'd left behind a tree, "I better get back. Mom'll get mad if I'm late for my lesson. If I'm late, Grandpa might take the strap to both of us, and I always feel bad if Mom gets it because of me."

I thought of the red welt I'd seen on May Wickens's arm as she was leaving the coffee shop. "Sure," I said.

"Nice to meet you," Lawrence said.

Jeffrey slipped on his shoes. "Bye!" he said, and ran back up the road to the Wickens place.

Lawrence watched him run off, and I looked for a trace of anger in his eyes, but all I saw was sadness.

25

Our previous surveillance work together, when I was doing a feature for *The Metropolitan* on what it was like to be a detective and was hanging out with Lawrence waiting for some bad guys to rob a high-end men's store, did not go particularly well. Lawrence would be the first to admit this. But at least attempting surveillance in the city has its advantages. It's a lot easier to spy on people when you have side streets and alleys to hide in, and plenty of other cars on the road to blend in with.

But up here in the country, well, that was an altogether different thing. "You try to follow somebody on these roads," Lawrence said, "it's not going to take your subject long to figure out what you're up to. You're the only two out there." And as far as sneaking up on the Wickenses' farmhouse went, well, that presented a host of difficulties, it struck me, night or day. You couldn't get inside the fence without being seen or running into the dogs. We could probably stay hidden on the other side of the fence, in the woods, where all we had to worry about now, evidently, was the bear.

"No, we'll be better off watching them at night," Lawrence said. "We'll go through the woods, come around the back way."

"I don't know," I said. "I can see a whole bunch of problems."

"And your idea would be?" Lawrence asked.

"You know, there's a lot less chance of being spotted if there's one of us instead of two," I said. "You could head off into the forest, and I could hang in back here, with the cell phone, and you could call me if you needed backup." As soon as I'd said it, I recalled you could barely get a cell signal up here, but I didn't want to confuse Lawrence with useless details.

"Backup," Lawrence said. "That's what you are."

"Hey, I can do backup. I was born to do backup."

Lawrence gave that some thought, but not for long. "It's not that I don't see merit in your idea. Taking you along is a bit like having to take your little sister on a date because your mom feels sorry for her."

I didn't much like the comparison, but felt this was not the time to take offense. Enduring some insults seemed a small price to pay if it meant I wouldn't have to go anywhere near the Wickens place. "You see?" I said. "I knew you'd agree."

"But seeing as how I've taken this project on for somewhat less than my usual fee, and by somewhat less I mean sweet fuck all, I think I'm entitled to a bit of assistance."

"Like?"

Lawrence shrugged. "I might need you to take a bullet for me at some point."

"Maybe if we just paid you."

"Won't hear of it," Lawrence said. "Now that we've got that settled, we need to decide how to use our time most productively before it gets dark."

"What's the plan, Stan?"

"Okay, there are a number of things going on in this town that may or may not be related. Why don't we assume, just for fun, that they are, which means if we make progress in one area, it might end up benefiting us in another."

"Okay."

"Why don't you show me the co-op, where this Tiff Riley was killed, then the mayor, and then we can pay a visit to your local gay rights leader."

"Fine. Just as soon as I bury the fish guts and make sure we're not low on worms."

I returned to the cabin, with some trepidation, to tell Dad that Lawrence and I were heading off to do real live detective work, but he was in his study, on the phone, speaking in low tones. The mess on the floor had been cleaned up, the salt and pepper shakers put back on the kitchen table. I tried to get his attention, poking my head in, but he swiveled in his office chair so he wouldn't have to look at me.

"I'll catch you later," I said to his back, and left.

We took Lawrence's Jag, which was not exactly an undercover car. In Braynor, you saw a lot of Fords and Chevys and Dodges, often in the shape of pickups and SUVs, but not a great many Beemers, Saabs, or Jags. There was a small Ford dealer on the south side of town, heading in, with a one-bay service garage and barely half a dozen new vehicles out front, and the GM dealership on the north side wasn't much grander.

At the co-op, we found the owner, a woman named Grace. I introduced myself as a reporter, and Lawrence identified himself as a private detective, but artfully declined to divulge on whose behalf he was working. We were, truth be known, just being nosy.

"This was where Tiff died," Grace said, taking us out to the warehouse and leading us down an aisle where stacks of bagged goods—topsoil, feed, and fertilizer—were stored on pallets. There was nothing much to suggest that this had been a murder scene only a day and a half earlier. Traces of sawdust, presumably remnants of what was used to soak up Tiff's blood, dusted the concrete floor. There wasn't a lot to see.

"What have the police told you?" I asked Grace.

"Orville?" she said. "Are you kidding? He couldn't find his ass in a snowstorm, let alone Tiff's killer."

"You got any ideas of your own?" Lawrence asked.

Grace shook her head sadly. "I don't know. A few bags of fertilizer, a plastic drum, why the hell would you kill someone to get that?"

Lawrence cocked his head. "A plastic drum?"

Grace nodded. "Well, we noticed one missing. Can't say for sure it was taken that night, but we had five of them out back, fifty-five-gallon ones, and now there's only four."

"Did you tell the police about that?" he asked.

"What would be the point? I mean, so we lost a drum. You think Orville's really going to care about that?"

Back in the car, Lawrence asked me to direct him to the mayor's house.

"What was that about the drum?" I asked.

"If you're going to make a bomb out of fertilizer and diesel fuel, you need something to put it in," Lawrence said.

I said nothing.

A few minutes later, we were sitting where I'd been the day before, Alice Holland on the couch, her black husband, George, leaning up against the wall. I thought George and Lawrence exchanged some sort of glance as we walked inside, a shared-history thing, I don't know.

"I understand," the mayor said, "that the fishing-resort proposal is no longer on the table."

"You heard about Leonard Colebert," I said.

"Another bear attack. I heard about it on the radio. It's a terrible tragedy. It's really quite astonishing. All the years I've lived here, I've never known anyone to be killed by a bear. And now, two in a week."

"Technically speaking," I said, "the bear didn't kill him. But the fall running away from it did."

George Holland said, "That resort would have been a terrible thing for that lake. And how long would it have taken, once it had been built, for that lake to have been totally fished out? Who'd come up to the resort then?"

Alice Holland said, "I would never have wished the man dead, and I think we could have somehow stopped that project, but Braynor's certainly better off without it. What do you suppose it is, this bear? A grizzly?"

"Well," I said, "I don't really know my bears, but the man who saw it, Bob Spooner—he's a friend of my father's and a guest at his camp—didn't give me the impression that it was as large as a grizzly. It looked to him like the bear that we'd heard about earlier. Similar markings."

"I suppose I'll have to speak to Chief Thorne. He may need to organize some hunters, go in and kill this bear before it strikes again."

"He's ahead of you there. He was out in the woods this morning, brought two men with him who looked like they'd just come from a casting call for *Elmer Fudd, the Movie*. They were looking for the bear when the incident happened, but they were in a different part of the woods."

The mayor shook her head sadly, then studied us. "But that's not why you're here, is it?"

"No," I said.

"This is the friend you mentioned yesterday."

Lawrence said, "I used to be a cop. Now I'm private."

Alice leaned forward on the couch. "Interesting."

"Zack told me about your phone calls. They're still coming?"

She nodded. "Another one last night, after you

left"—she nodded toward me—"and one today. There'll be at least one more before the day's over, I'm sure. Especially with the parade being tomorrow."

"We just hang up, soon as we know what it is," her husband said.

"I brought some equipment along," Lawrence said. "In my trunk. It may help in a number of ways. We might be able to trace the call, get a number, maybe determine whether it's a pay phone, but best of all, we'll have a recording of the caller's voice. You get a chance to listen to it a few times, you might figure out who it is, if it's someone you already know."

George's eyebrows went up. "So you want to hook this up to our phone? Don't you need a warrant for something like that?"

"Well, first of all, I'm not the police, and second, it's your phone, and you know about it."

George looked at Alice who said, "What do you think?"

He nodded. "Sure, if you think it will do some good."

"Don't know, yet, for sure," said Lawrence. "The main thing is, keep him on the phone this time instead of hanging up on him. Keep him talking awhile. It might even be better"—he was talking specifically to George now—"if you let your wife take the call, even though I can understand you wanting to take it instead, spare her the abuse."

"It's okay, George," Alice said. "If it helps."

He nodded regretfully. "I guess."

"I'll get the stuff," Lawrence said. Then, to me,

"Maybe you can find out the other thing while I'm doing that." Lawrence left.

"Ms. Holland, do you know where I can find the head of the Fifty Lakes Gay and Lesbian Coalition?"

"Stuart Lethbridge?"

"That's the guy."

"He doesn't live in Braynor. He's over in Red Lake, about ten miles west. I think he runs a comic book store just off the main street."

"A comics store?"

I must have looked more than just surprised. I guess I looked interested, because Alice nodded and asked, "You like comic books?"

I smiled. "Sort of."

Lawrence was back with a couple of hard plastic, high-tech-looking cases. He opened them up on the kitchen counter and I went over to peek inside. There were headphones and mini tape recorders and larger tape recorders, and something that looked like a gun with a furry barrel. I saw some small black things that looked like buttons.

"What are these?" I asked.

"Microphones," Lawrence said. "You plant them, you listen in from afar. But I don't need those right now."

He gently lifted out some other devices, packed into the case in gray foam, and put them on the counter by the phone. To Alice and George, he said, "I'll get this set up, then show you what to do. And I'll leave you my cell number, and Zack's, and his dad's, so you can get in touch when you've got something for us to listen to. When he's called before, have you recognized the voice?"

"I don't think so," Alice said, "but I think he's disguising it, going really low."

"I'd like to get my hands on this bastard," George Holland said. "I'd like five minutes alone with him."

"If it's up to me," Lawrence said, "I'll give you ten."

"So why do you want to see Lethbridge?" I asked once we were back in the Jag and on our way to Red Lake.

"Just nice to get to know all the players," he said. "If he weren't pushing to be included in the parade, a lot of this other shit wouldn't even be happening."

"But does this have anything to do with the Wickenses?"

Lawrence took the Jag through a tight turn, barely slowing down. "I dunno. If we knew all that, I could go home."

Red Lake, even though it sounded like nothing more than a hunting lodge, was actually a slightly larger town than Braynor, maybe a couple of thousand people or so. The main street was lined with small, independent stores. No Gap here. No American Eagle. No Home Depot. But there was Onley's Men's Wear, and Katie's Wool Bin, and Red Lake Hardware with a display of snowblowers on the sidewalk out front.

"There," I said, pointing.

Just in from the corner at the second cross street,

small shop with one big sign in the window:
"Comics."

"Think a town like this could support two comic
stores?" Lawrence asked.

"I'm kind of surprised it can support one."

Lawrence parked out front. It was a pretty dingy
storefront, the paint peeling, the "Comics" sign
slightly askew. There were bits of what looked like
eggshell stuck to the window and the frame, dried
yolk cemented on.

"Looks like someone doesn't like this place," said
Lawrence, picking at the egg with his finger.

Behind the dirty window a few comics in plastic
sleeves were displayed. A Flash comic that must
have come out when I was a kid caught my eye.

"DC or Marvel?" Lawrence asked.

"When I was a kid, DC," I said. "Superman,
Batman, Justice League. Actually, that's still my
thing. You?"

"Marvel. When I was a kid. Fantastic Four,
Spider-Man, Hulk."

"It's amazing we can be friends," I said.

Lawrence opened the door and I followed him inside. Two narrow aisles surrounded on all sides by
boxes jammed with used comic books. The walls
were covered with movie posters, collectible toys
hanging from hooks, more comics.

From the back of the store, a voice: "Help you?"

He appeared from behind a display case filled
with little statuettes of superheroes like Wonder
Woman, Green Lantern, and some newer SF characters, like Hellboy and the characters from the

animated movie *The Incredibles*. I guessed he was in his late twenties, about six feet, and not much more than 140 pounds. Wispy. His black hair hung down to his shoulders, and he eyed us through a pair of glasses with thick black frames. This was the guy who'd stirred up so much trouble?

"Are you Stuart Lethbridge?" I asked.

"Yeah."

We introduced ourselves.

"So what do you guys want?" Stuart asked.

"You're the head of the Fifty Lakes Gay and Lesbian Coalition, right?" I asked.

"Yeah. So?"

"We just came from Mayor Holland's place," Lawrence said. "You know Alice Holland?"

"Sure. She's okay. She's letting us in the parade tomorrow. Unless she decides to cancel the whole thing at the last minute. Because we're not pulling out."

"Who's we?" I asked. "How many you got in the parade?" I wondered just how many members of his group were at risk if something very bad should go down.

Lethbridge's eyes rolled up into his head as he did some mental counting. "Okay, hang on," he said. "Counting me, I guess there's four."

Lawrence eyes danced for a moment. "Four?"

Lethbridge was defensive. "Yeah. So? Okay, we're not exactly San Francisco. What of it?"

"You've got *four* people?" Lawrence asked. "Is that even enough to hold a banner?"

"It's only about fifteen feet wide. So yeah, four will hold it fine."

Lawrence looked at me. "Four." I shrugged. Lawrence continued, "So, if you've got four, what's the breakdown? Gays to lesbians."

Lethbridge cleared his throat. "There's three gays, and one lesbian, but, well, my sister is representing the lesbian community, except she's not, technically, a lesbian."

Lawrence ran his hand over his face. "So, does this mean there *are* no lesbians in these here parts?"

"I'm sure there are, but it's probably because of people like you, who are so contemptuous of the gay and lesbian community, that they don't come forward."

"Uh," I said, not sure whether I was stepping out of line here, "it just so happens that Mr. Jones here is, well . . ."

Lawrence looked at me as if to say, "I can handle this, Zack, thank you very much."

"You're gay?" Stuart Lethbridge asked skeptically. "Are you going to be around tomorrow? Would you be interested in being part of the parade? I think we could find a spot for you."

"I'll have to pass."

"Oh, I get it. When it comes to standing up for your rights, for supporting others in the community, you can't be bothered."

"Stuart," Lawrence said, "it's just possible you have an inflated sense of what will be accomplished by being in the Braynor fall fair parade. I mean, why do you even want to be *in* this parade? With school bands and cheerleaders and the 4-H Club? It's very uncool. And for that matter, what are you doing running a comic book shop? I figured, at the very least, it would be a bed-and-breakfast place."

"What's wrong with a comics store?"

"Yeah," I said. "What's wrong with a comics store?"

"Whatever I do, I have a right to raise awareness about gay and lesbian issues," Stuart said.

"Yeah, for all three of you," Lawrence said, shaking his head. "Listen, Stuart, I'm sorry. Aside from me, is anyone else giving you a hard time about this? I notice someone's been trying to redecorate the front of your store."

"I've gotten egged so much, I've given up trying to get it off," he said. "Plus there's the petitions and the hate mail."

"How about threatening phone calls? Death threats?"

"Well, I might be getting them, if the phone worked. I couldn't pay the bill last month and they cut it off. The store hasn't been doing that well, and I still got to get someone to run it tomorrow, when the parade's on. Saturday's the only busy day, when kids living out in the country come into town."

Lawrence sighed and said, "Stuart, do you have any idea how much shit you've stirred up? And all to be in a parade no one with a dime's worth of sense would want to see anyway?"

"There's going to be racing lawn tractors," I reminded him.

"Let's go," Lawrence said to me.

But before we left, there was something important I needed to know. "That Flash comic in the window. How much is that?"

While Stuart went to check, something under the tables that supported all the boxes of comics caught Lawrence's attention. He bent over and dragged it out. "What is this?"

"Are you kidding?" Lethbridge said, like he couldn't believe someone wouldn't instantly know. "Those are *Star Wars* figures."

"No shit? Like from all the different movies? Okay, you got a Lando Calrissian here? And a— Zack, what's the other guy?"

I had to think for a moment. "Mace Windu."

"Yeah, that guy."

Lethbridge said, "They might be in there somewhere, but I don't have the original boxes or anything. Some kid brought those in, traded them for some *Alien* figures."

Lawrence started picking through the box, tossing aside several figures, including a weapon-wielding Boba Fett and a gold-colored C3PO. There were so many figures in the box, and they were all a mystery to Lawrence, who was quickly getting frustrated.

"I know I'm looking for a couple of brothers, but could I get some fucking help here?"

Lethbridge found him a used Lando, and a new Mace, still in the packaging, from the display case. "Twenty-five dollars," he said.

Lawrence didn't argue, handed over the cash.

"A gay nerd," said Lawrence as we got back into the Jag. "Who'd of thunk it?"

26

DRIVING BACK TO BRAYNOR, Lawrence slipped a Miles Davis CD into the dash. He said, "When you fight for the right to do things that don't matter, it diminishes your fight for the right to do things that do."

"Okay," I said.

"You think I shoulda bitch-slapped him?"

He'd tucked the plastic bag containing two *Star Wars* figures into the center console. I said, "A little something for Jeffrey."

"I knew you were the guy to bring along. You figure out everything."

"You haven't said anything about him. Not even after what he said to you."

"About inferior races," Lawrence said, hunting for a track on the Davis CD.

"Yeah."

"It's not his fault. I guess you could argue it's not his grandpa Timmy's fault either. Maybe he was raised that way, too. But Timmy Wickens is older now, he's had time to figure things out, and he's got no excuse for being an ignorant, racist pinhead. But Jeffrey, he's what again?"

"Ten."

"Yeah, well, there still might be time to save him."

"And his mother?"

"That'd be nice, too," Lawrence said.

"You heard him talking about Timmy taking a belt to them, sending him to bed with no food."

"I heard it." Lawrence seemed to grip the wheel a little tighter. He turned up the volume a notch. "Listen to this."

I listened to Miles for a while, then turned to Lawrence and asked, "How's the thing?"

"The thing?"

I pointed to my own abdomen, in roughly about the same spot where Lawrence had been stabbed the year before. "Here. Where you got stabbed."

Lawrence thought a moment. "Changes your outlook," he said. I waited for him to elaborate, but instead, he skipped ahead to a different Miles Davis track. "Listen to this."

I listened.

We were heading down the road into Denny's Cabins, passing by the gate to the Wickenses, when Lawrence spotted Jeffrey. He was sitting on the top of the gate, one leg on each side, and bumping up and down, like he was pretending it was a horse.

Lawrence stopped the Jag, lowered the window.

"Hey," Lawrence said. "Whatcha doing?"

"Nothing."

"You got a sec?"

Jeffrey hopped down and approached the car, staying about ten feet away from the door. "Yeah?"

Lawrence tossed the bag from the comics store at him. "Found those. They're yours."

Jeffrey looked into the bag and his eyes went wide. He quickly had the two *Star Wars* figures in his hand, a broad smile on his face.

"This is great!" he said. "Where did you get these?"

"Comic store in Red Lake. One of them's used, but I figured you wouldn't care."

"Wow!" He took a couple of steps closer to the car. "Thanks," he said.

"No sweat," said Lawrence, holding his foot on the brake.

Jeffrey gave him a cautious look. "I've been told to watch out for strangers with gifts."

"That's a good rule," Lawrence said. "Sometimes, people give you stuff and want something in return. Sometimes things that are bad."

Jeffrey nodded. "Why'd you get me these? You want something bad?"

"All I want is for you to make judgments for yourself, not let others make them for you. You understand?"

Jeffrey took a moment. "Maybe."

"Good enough," Lawrence said. "We gotta go." The window went back up and he shifted his foot to the gas. As we came round the bend and the cabins came into view, I saw Lana's car parked next to Dad's truck.

"Uh-oh," I said.

"What?" Lawrence didn't know the car. I told him whose it was.

"Maybe she's just visiting," I said, "and Dad hasn't told her what happened. Or maybe they're just getting their stories straight, before I walk in." I paused. "I guess I kind of precipitated a crisis."

"Hard to believe, you doing something like that," Lawrence said. He parked the Jag by my Virtue out back of cabin 3. As he was getting out, he noticed the late Leonard Colebert's backpack in the back seat, and grabbed it.

"Your dad wants this to give back to that guy's family when they get here."

Lawrence popped the trunk and grabbed his overnight bag. "Where am I staying?"

"You're bunking in with me," I said. I had the screen door open for Lawrence when I saw Lana Gantry pop her head out of cabin 1.

"Hey, Zack," she said. "Got a minute?"

"I'll be back," I whispered to Lawrence. I reached for Colebert's backpack. "I'll drop that off for you, too." As I walked over, I said, all innocent, "How are you, Lana?"

"Your dad and I wondered if you'd have a moment, in a little bit, to talk about some things."

"Sure, that would be great." My mouth felt dry again. "When were you thinking?"

"We're just waiting till Orville gets here."

"Oh," I said. "Great."

"I just got off the phone with him. He figures half an hour, maybe an hour, before he can get here."

Super, I thought. A big family get-together.

"Okay," I said. I handed the backpack to her. "Could you give this to Dad? It was Leonard Colebert's. I think Dad's arranging for Leonard's family to come up here and get his things."

"Yeah, they've been in touch. I think they're coming up tomorrow afternoon."

I nodded, smiled, backed away and returned to cabin 3. Lawrence had found his bed and was taking out some shirts from his bag, carefully refolding them, smoothing the creases, and slipping them into the empty dresser.

"Nothing like roughing it," I said.

"What's up?"

"Cards-on-the-table time, I think."

"Better you than me. If my dad knocked up anybody other than my mom, I never knew about it, and don't figure I ever will now. Which is just fine."

"Thanks, Lawrence. That's just—"

There was a bang at the door. I stepped out of the bedroom and saw, through the screen, that the neighbors had come to visit.

Wendell and Dougie.

Wendell said, "Where's the colored guy?"

I pushed open the screen. "Hi, fellas," I said. "Can I help you with something?"

Wendell said, "I just told you, we want to see the colored guy. The one who gave Jeffrey those toys."

Lawrence emerged from the bedroom and came up alongside me at the door. "Are these gentlemen the neighbors you've been telling me about, Zack?"

"Yeah," I said, easing the door open farther so the

two of us could step outside. "This is Dougie, and this here is Wendell."

Lawrence nodded, but did not offer a hand. "My name is Lawrence Jones," he said.

"Yeah, well," said Dougie, "don't be giving no stuff to Jeffrey."

Coming down the lane were Jeffrey, running, and trailing behind, his mother, May. She looked stricken.

"It was a couple of *Star Wars* figures," Lawrence said. "Jeffrey had mentioned he was looking for those ones, and I found them in a comics store. Just thought he might like them. No obligation. And no disrespect intended."

Jeffrey, barely out of breath even though he'd run the whole way, said, "Come on, guys, let me keep them."

Wendell said, "Jeffrey, you know what your grandpa said. You're not having those things."

Jeffrey's eyes were red, and it was clear he'd been crying. "What does it matter?"

But now Wendell was talking to Lawrence, and had taken a step closer to him. "We don't like strangers interfering. You understand?"

"I'm getting the picture."

"Everybody here lately is interfering in our affairs. So just butt the fuck out," Wendell said. "Dougie, give the man back his little toys."

Dougie frowned. "Shit. I forgot them. I thought you were bringing them."

"They were right on the kitchen table, you dumb-ass," Wendell said.

"I'm sorry, I just thought you had them."

Now that he knew the toys were still back in the house, Jeffrey looked like he was getting ready to turn and sprint back toward the farmhouse before Wendell and Dougie could get there.

"Don't you be hiding those things, you little fucker," Wendell told Jeffrey.

"Don't call him that," Lawrence said.

"Huh?" Wendell looked stunned.

"Don't call Jeffrey names like that. He deserves as much respect as either one of you fellows." Lawrence paused. "Probably more."

Jeffrey watched.

Wendell started to laugh. "You hear that, Dougie? Now he's telling us what we can and cannot call members of our own family?"

May had arrived. She looked at me first, shook her head in frustration. "I'm so sorry," she said. "Leave these people alone," she told the two young men. She placed her hands on her son's shoulders. "You go back to the house," she said.

He twisted away. "In a minute," he said.

"We're kind of in the middle of something here, May," Dougie said, grinning.

"Yeah," said Wendell. "This boy here," and he tapped Lawrence's chest with his index finger, "is giving us a bit of atti—"

Lawrence's arm came up and he took hold of Wendell's finger, and in a move that Lawrence made look effortless, had Wendell twisting backwards and sideways, and then heading straight to the ground.

"Owwww!" Wendell said. "Jesus! You're breaking my fucking finger!"

Dougie stood, openmouthed, watching the attack on his brother unfold. May took a step back, but Jeffrey stood transfixed.

In a second, Wendell was flat on his back, wailing about his finger, and then Lawrence had his foot on the man's neck.

"Apologize to the boy," Lawrence said. He wasn't even winded. I, however, was breathing rapidly.

Wendell coughed, tried to catch his breath.

"I asked you to do something," Lawrence said.

"Get your foot off my neck, man! Jesus, Dougie, do something!"

Dougie rushed Lawrence. The detective took his foot off Wendell's neck long enough to use Dougie's forward momentum against him, stepping into his stride and tossing him over his hip. Dougie hit the ground with a thud, and as Wendell turned his head to see where he'd landed, he found Lawrence's foot bearing down on his neck again.

Lawrence increased the pressure on Wendell's neck, ever so slightly. "Apologize to the boy."

Wendell coughed. "I'm sorry, Jeffrey."

The boy turned and ran.

Dougie was struggling to his feet, dusting himself off. Lawrence took his foot off Wendell and stepped back. Wendell sat up, rubbed his neck with his hand, and slowly got to his feet.

"Get lost," Lawrence said.

They both turned and started shuffling back toward their farmhouse. May looked at us, shocked, but for a second, I thought I saw her dead eyes sparkle.

"I'm sorry about them," she said. To Lawrence, she said, "Thank you for standing up for my son." She turned and started back to the farmhouse.

"Well," I said. "That was just great. Be interesting to see Timmy's reaction. I'm guessing we've got about an hour left to live."

27

LAWRENCE PATTED ME on the shoulder. "Everything'll be fine," he said. "You worry too much about things."

"Oh," I said. "You noticed. You think those bozos aren't going to run right back and tell their stepdaddy what happened? You think there won't be some fallout from that?"

Another pat. "Maybe. Maybe not. And if there is, maybe that'll be a good thing. It's like shaking the trees."

I was less sure. I was okay with doing things to the Wickenses that they didn't find out about, but beating the snot out of two of them, that was kind of out in the open.

Lana popped her head out of cabin 1 again. "Zack? You wanna come over? Orville just called and said he'll be out in a few minutes."

Lawrence said quietly, "You go have fun. It's still a few hours till it's dark, can't start watching the Wickens place till then anyway."

So I went over to Dad's cabin, Lana Gantry still

holding the door open for me, and stepped inside. Dad was at the kitchen table, Leonard's backpack in front of him.

"Guess I owe you an apology," he said.

Well, I thought, at least we're getting off on the right foot.

He held up one of the cans of bear spray we'd bought in town back on Tuesday. "I'd offered one of these to Leonard and figured he hadn't taken it, but it was right here in his backpack. You know how I blamed you, said he'd left himself undefended because you'd convinced him there was no need to take this along?"

Slowly, I said, "Yeah."

"Well, turns out he had it after all, tucked in here. Musta never had a chance to get it out when he got surprised by that bear."

"I guess," I said. "Can I have that?" I was thinking ahead, to the hours I would be spending sitting in the woods at night with Lawrence. A can of bear spray might be handy to have along.

Dad handed it over, and I left it on the kitchen counter right by the door so I'd remember to take it when I left.

"Sit down," Dad said.

"Yes, please," said Lana. "I've made some coffee."

I sat down.

"This is, uh, this is kind of hard for me," Dad said. "Telling you what I'm about to tell you."

Lana put cups and cream and sugar and a pot full of coffee on the table.

"Maybe, if you hadn't sent that picture to Sarah,

and she hadn't pointed out the resemblance, we wouldn't be doing this," Dad said. "But I'm not blaming you. This always stood the chance of coming out."

I spooned some sugar into my coffee, poured in some cream.

"Let's wait till Orville's here," Lana said.

"Sure," said Dad. "But I just want you to understand, Zack, that yeah, part of what you've suspected is true. You and Orville, you're, well, you're sort of related."

"Sort of related," I said.

Lana sat down.

"But I'm not Orville's father."

Wait a minute, I thought. This was how it was going to go? They were going to start with denials? I cocked my head. "Well, hang on. Then—"

"And Lana here, Lana is not Orville's mother."

I'd only been sitting down for a minute, and already I was getting a headache. What kind of cock-and-bull story had the two of them concocted? Here they were, years later, boffing their brains out in Dad's cabin, and they thought I was going to believe that they weren't up to the same thing years ago?

What other possible explanation could there be?

There was a rapping at the door.

"That must be Orville," Lana said, and got up to see. She opened the door, and said, "Oh, hello."

I looked around. It was not Orville.

It was Timmy Wickens. This is it, I thought. We're all going to die.

"Won't you come in?" Lana said, and Timmy did.

He nodded courteously at Lana, my father, and then at me.

"Good day," he said. "Is the other gentleman around?"

"Lawrence?" I said.

"I believe so. The, uh, the black gentleman."

"I'll go get him," I said, and bolted. I found Lawrence in the cabin, examining the rest of his surveillance equipment. "It's Timmy," I said. "Wants to see you."

"Okey doke," Lawrence said, closing the case.

"Aren't you going to get your gun? You're gonna bring a gun, right?"

Lawrence brushed past me on the way out, walked over to Dad's cabin, and stepped inside. Timmy nodded at him when he came in, although he didn't offer a hand to shake.

"I believe," said Timmy, "that my boys may have caused a bit of a kerfuffle here a few minutes ago."

Dad and Lana looked questioningly at all of us. Had they missed something?

Lawrence and I said nothing. Timmy continued. "Anyway, I'd just like to offer my apologies on their behalf."

Now Lawrence and I really had nothing to say. "Sometimes," Timmy said, "they get a little carried away, and I suspect that's what happened." He looked right at Lawrence. "That was very thoughtful of you, getting those toys for my grandson."

Lawrence nodded.

"Anyway, I'm sorry if I interrupted anything here." And he did a little bow, and let himself out.

Lawrence and I looked at each other. "What do you make of that?" I asked.

"I don't know," he said. "I think it's bad news."

"Hold on," Dad said. "The man apologizes and you think it's bad news? What the hell happened, anyway?"

"Why bad?" I asked.

"He doesn't want to rock the boat," Lawrence said. "Because he's already up to something, and he doesn't want to screw it up. He wanted to smooth this over so it wouldn't mess up his other plans."

"Is anyone going to tell us what the hell you're talking about?" Dad asked.

Before either of us could reply, there was another knock at the door.

Orville Thorne had arrived.

The four of us were seated at the table. Lawrence had excused himself. Orville was annoyed before a single word had been said. It might have been for the reason he gave, that he was very busy hunting down Tiff Riley's killer. But I suspected it had more to do with the fact that he was having to sit at the same table with me.

And I was thinking, *I know something you don't know.*

But then again, how much did I know, really? Dad and Lana had turned my assumptions upside down when they claimed not to be Orville's parents. But Dad had still said we were "sort of related." How could that be?

"Aunt Lana," he said, "whatever this is about, could we make it quick?"

She pulled out a pack of cigarettes. Up to now, I hadn't even known she smoked. She lit one, took a long drag on it, and blew the smoke out. "We might as well start there, Orville," she said. "There's a lot of things that you don't know, that I haven't explained to you. And the first thing is, I'm not, I'm not technically your aunt."

Orville shook his head. "What do you mean, you're not my aunt? What's that supposed to mean? Is this a joke?"

My thoughts exactly.

"Your uncle Walter, my dear husband, he, he wasn't your uncle, either."

"What in the hell are you talking about? Why are we talking about this? And whatever it is, why are you talking about it in front of these two?"

"Because it involves them," Lana said gently.

"So you're saying what? That you and Uncle— that you and Walter, that you're not even related to me? That I'm not your nephew?"

"Not exactly. I love you very much, Orville. You've actually been more to me than a nephew. You've been like a son to me. But we're not really related." She took another drag on the cigarette. "But you and Walter, that's different."

Wait a minute, I thought.

"Well, but, if," Orville stammered. "If Walter wasn't my uncle, but he was related to me, then what was he?"

I had it half right, I thought. But I had it backward.

"He was your father," Lana Gantry said.

Orville looked stunned. If I'd had a mirror, I could have checked to see whether I did, too. The room was quiet for a moment.

"But," said Orville, "you'd always said my father was Bert Thorne, that my mother was Katrina Thorne. That they were killed in a car accident right after I was born. If Walter was my father, what about Katrina? Was she my mother?"

No, I almost said.

"No," Lana Gantry said. "She wasn't. I'm sorry, Orville, we had to tell you things that were not . . . It was a different time. . . . People were much more secretive about indiscretions. . . . I'm so very sorry."

Orville's eyes were turning red. "Then who is my mother?" he asked.

Lana turned and looked at Arlen Walker, my father. He said, very quietly, "Your mother was Evelyn Walker." He swallowed. "My wife." He paused again. "Zachary's mother."

Orville looked across the table at me, stared, the realization sinking in. And it was sinking in for me, as well.

"They had an . . . affair," Dad said to Orville, but he was saying this for my benefit, too. "Lana's husband and my wife. She became pregnant. And there were people who knew it couldn't be my child. After Zack was born, I'd had, you know, the snip. It was . . . it would have been a scandal, I guess. In our neighborhood, we'd been friends, the four of us . . ."

The cabin seemed to be spinning.

"William," Lana said, "wanted you. He wanted a son. We had no children."

"And Evelyn, she . . . did not want another child," Dad said. "She went away, for six months, she lived with her sister in Toronto, she had you. We got a lawyer, he did the paperwork, and Lana, and Walter, they took the baby, and they moved away, to another part of the city where no one knew them, knew their history, and they raised you."

"But there were still people we saw," Lana said. "Coworkers of your father's, we didn't know how to explain your sudden appearance, so we came up with a story. That you were our nephew, that Walter had had a sister, and a brother-in-law, who'd been killed in an accident. And that we had agreed to raise you."

Orville said, "I don't believe any of this."

I said, "Look at us."

"What?"

"Look at us. Look at me. Look at my face. When I first got up here, I felt I knew you from someplace. There was something familiar about you. And then I sent your picture to my wife, Sarah."

"My picture? Where did you get my picture?"

"I took it. When I was taking pictures of the fish. And I sent it to my wife. And she spotted the resemblance immediately. I couldn't believe it at first, but I started putting things together, how my parents and the Gantrys had been friends, how my mother had left home, although I had the reason for it all wrong."

Orville said, "My whole life is a lie. The person I am, that's a lie."

No one said anything. He was right.

I said, to my father, "I don't understand. How did this happen? Why, how did you and Mom stay together?"

Dad looked down at the table. "I was a bastard," he said.

"What do you mean?" The use of the term, in these circumstances, threw me.

"I was a prick. A miserable son of a bitch. Always finding fault, always picking on her. I drove her away. I drove her into the arms of another man. It was as much my fault as hers. I realized one day, I saw myself for what I was. Thank God I had the sense to see what kind of person I'd been, and to try to do something about it."

"You actually forgave her?"

"Like I forgave Walter," Lana said. "It took a long time, but that boy, you, Orville, that baby was part of my husband, and I still loved him. And because I"— her voice became very quiet—"wasn't able to have children of my own, I decided to put the best face on the situation that I could."

"It was a rough time for us, I won't kid you," Dad said. "But we got through it. Maybe it was easier for us, because your mother gave her child away. But there was always a part of her, for the rest of her life, that was missing. Part of her died when she gave you up, Orville."

I recalled Mom's faraway looks, how she would sit

and stare out the window. Maybe she was looking for that other son that she knew would never show up.

"And the two of you," I said, indicating Dad and Lana. "Today."

Dad shifted in his chair uncomfortably as Lana reached over and touched his hand. "We didn't keep in touch. It really was a coincidence. When Walter retired early, we moved up here, with Orville, and bought the café. I kept it after Walter died. It was my own retirement plan. And then, years later, your father buys this camp, and he comes in for breakfast one day, and well, there he was, sitting there. I couldn't believe it. I wondered if it was some kind of a sign."

"We had a lot in common," Dad said. "Our spouses had a child together. Our spouses had both passed on. We both learned to forgive. And we were both looking for someone in our lives."

"Jesus Christ," Orville said. "This is just, this is too much to deal with."

"And Orville here," Dad said. "When I see him, I see your mother in him. And I think about how I still love her."

I had to get up and walk around the room. I was having as much trouble taking it all in as Orville.

"Orville," Lana said. "Orville. The thing is, Orville, you have a brother. A sister, too, Zack's sister, Cindy. You and Zachary share a mother. You're half brothers."

Orville was on his feet now, too. He backed away from the table, shook his head again. His eyes went from Lana, then to Dad, and finally landed on me.

"All these years, never having a brother or a sister," he said. "And so now, it turns out I actually have a big brother."

I felt a lump in my throat.

"Imagine. All your life, you wish you had a brother, and then, you finally find out you've got one, and he's the biggest asshole in the world."

Orville turned and left.

28

LAWRENCE WAS JUST COMING INTO THE CABIN as Orville stormed out to his patrol car. Lawrence caught the screen door before it slammed shut, then beckoned me with his index finger. I excused myself from the table.

"What is it?"

"Alice Holland called my cell," he said. "It broke up a lot, the reception's lousy up there, but her secret admirer got in touch again."

"Did she say whether she recognized him?"

"She said we had to hear it for ourselves. She was sounding, I would have say to the word is 'bemused.'"

"Bemused?"

"Bemused."

"I'll be out in a second," I said.

Dad and Lana were sitting quietly at the table. She was on her second or third cigarette, and Dad had opened a bottle of red wine and filled to the rim a glass that once held peanut butter.

"Thanks for telling me," I said. I looked at Dad. "I had it figured all wrong. I'm sorry."

"I couldn't have cared less if you thought less of me. I didn't ever want you to think badly of your mother. But it was taking too much effort to keep this a secret any longer."

"I'm gonna go," Lana said. "I've got a feeling Orville will drop by later, to talk about this, and I want to be there in case he does."

"Sure," Dad said.

"I've gotta take off, too," I said. "Lawrence and I have to go see the mayor."

"Alice?" said Lana. "You say hi to her for me."

I grabbed my jacket, and grabbed the can of bear spray by the door as I went out, slipping it into the inside pocket.

When I went outside, Lawrence was sitting in his Jag, the motor running. I got in, closed the door. We drove out to the highway, neither of us saying a word. Finally, Lawrence said, "So, what's up with your brother? He didn't look very happy at the news when he left."

I almost smiled. "I feel a bit numb."

Lawrence nodded slowly. "You gonna have to start sending Orville Christmas cards now?"

"I thought I had it all figured out," I said. I filled Lawrence in. "I imagined Dad was this two-timing son of a bitch, but he's not. In fact, I don't know who the hell he is, exactly. I find out he's not the bastard I suspected, and now I have to consider that he may be a better person than I ever realized." I paused, thinking back. "He said to me a couple of days ago that he and Lana were a lot more forgiving than I'd ever know. Now I understand what he was talking about."

"And Orville? His reaction?"

"He's a bit disappointed to learn that his new big brother is a major asshole."

Lawrence mulled that one over. "Yeah, that would be hard to take."

We drove through Braynor, turned down the mayor's road, and as we pulled up behind her house she opened the door. It was just getting toward dusk, and she flicked on the back light.

"Welcome back," she said. "I hadn't expected to call you quite so soon."

George was pacing in the kitchen, his hands made into fists. When he saw us come in, he said, "Alice, we don't even need their help now. We know who it is. I want him. I want to rip his fucking head off."

"You *know* who it is?" I said.

"You've been so helpful," she said to me and Lawrence, "that I thought you should have the opportunity to enjoy this. But I don't know the first thing about this machine. Can you replay the calls?"

"Of course," Lawrence said, and proceeded to work his magic with the device he'd hooked up to the Hollands' phone by attaching it to a laptop. "This shows you've had three calls since we were here."

"It's the last one. The first was from the town clerk, the second a call from my daughter in Argentina. Play the third one."

"Okay," Lawrence said. "Here we go." Everything was digital, with no actual tape to rewind, but

Lawrence was still hitting Rewind and Play buttons on the laptop screen with his mouse.

Alice Holland: Hello?

Man: Mayor Holland?

Alice: Yes, this is the mayor.

Man: You haven't got much time left to do the right thing. The parade's only a few hours away.

Alice: Who is this?

Man: This is the voice of reason, bitch. Are you going to get those perverts out of the parade or not?

Alice: What if I don't? What do you propose to do?

Lawrence nodded approvingly at the way Alice had kept her caller talking.

Man: Something awful might happen to you. Is that what you want? All so a bunch of queers can walk in the parade?

Alice: You know what? I'll bet even the lesbians in that parade have more balls than a guy who phones people up anonymously and threatens them. Have you looked in your shorts lately? Is there anything down there at all?

Man: You bitch! How dare you—

Voice: (from afar) Hi, Mr. Henry!

Man: Shit! (hangs up)

Lawrence looked at me and I smiled. Lawrence smiled. Alice Holland smiled. Only her husband George still looked angry.

"Fuck me," said Lawrence.

I said, "Now, is this where you use your years of police training and honing your deductive skills to try to figure out who the caller is?"

Now Alice was laughing, and Lawrence was starting to laugh. Even George was starting to loosen up, unclenching his fists.

The voice in the background had sounded like a teenage girl. Alice, imitating the voice, said, "Hi, Mr. Henry!"

Now I was starting to laugh, and pretty soon, all of us were clutching our stomachs, clutching the kitchen counter to keep from collapsing.

"Oh God," said Alice. "This is too much."

"I think I've figured it out," Lawrence said, deadpan. "But I have to hear it one more time to be sure."

He cued up the call again, played the last part of the exchange between Alice and the caller again.

"Hi, Mr. Henry!"

"Stop it," I said. "I'm gonna die."

Slowly, we all pulled ourselves together.

"Oh man," said Alice. "Whoo."

"Okay," said George, who had completely regained his composure. "Now let's go kill him."

We took two cars. George Holland led the way in theirs, taking us back through Braynor, past Henry's Grocery and the phone booth just down from it, then a left down a street of boring, boxy brick houses that were probably built in the sixties. George put on his blinker and turned into the driveway of a two-story red brick house, blocking in a black Ford Taurus sedan. Lawrence pulled over onto the shoulder and we all got out.

As we walked up the drive, Lawrence, small briefcase in hand, glanced into the back windows of the Taurus and said, "Hello."

"What?" I said.

"Check it out," he said, and opened the back door on the passenger side. He reached down behind the seat to the floor and brought up a container of eggs.

"Odd place for eggs," I said.

Alice and George watched with interest.

Lawrence opened the top of the cardboard container. Five of the dozen eggs were missing. "Now, I could see forgetting some of your groceries in the car when you came home, but I can't see taking your eggs into the house one at a time." He handed me the carton to carry.

Alice went on ahead and rang the doorbell. An overweight frizzy-haired woman opened the door, and when she saw who it was, said, "Oh, hello, Mayor."

"We're here to see Charles," she said.

The woman looked back into the house. "Chuck!" she screamed. "Visitors!"

By the time Braynor grocery store magnate Charles Henry was at the door, all four of us were standing there, looking, I suspect, fairly intimidating.

"What's this about?" he said nervously, half standing behind the door. You could tell, just looking at him, the way he was sweating already, that he knew the jig was up.

"I thought maybe you'd like to talk to the bitch in person," Alice said.

"What? What's that supposed to mean? Alice, I don't know what you're talking about."

Lawrence held up his case. "We've got it all, man. You want to hear it? The last part, where the kid shouts 'Hi, Mr. Henry!'? You have to hear that for yourself. You'll bust a fucking gut."

George moved forward. "I ought to take your head off, you miserable little worm."

Henry tried to close the door but George shoved it back and walked in, the rest of us following. Down at the end of the hall I could see Mrs. Henry in the kitchen, cleaning up after dinner. Two girls, about eight and ten, ran giggling from the kitchen, down the hall and up the stairs.

"Maybe we should play it for them," I taunted Henry. "Here's how Daddy talks to grown-up girls."

"Shhhh," he said, running a hand over the top of his head. "Just, just come downstairs."

He led us down into a rec room that didn't appear to have been changed since the 1960s. Brown shag carpeting, dark paneled walls, a pool table covered with boxes of Christmas decorations that had evidently been sitting there for months. With Christmas only a few months away, there wasn't much point putting them away now.

"Chuck?" his wife shouted downstairs. "What's going on?"

"Shut the damn door!" he shouted at her. The door slammed shut. He said to us, "What do you want?"

Lawrence found a corner of the pool table on

which to rest his laptop, opened it up, and played the recording of his call to Alice Holland's house, finishing with "Hi, Mr. Henry!"

Henry shook his head. "Goddamn that Violet."

"Violet?" I said.

"Cashier," said Alice, who clearly knew everyone in town. "Grade 12 student, works part-time for Charles. She see you at the pay phone after her shift?"

Charles Henry said nothing.

"First thing I want is," said Alice, "I want you to own up to what you've been doing."

I held up the egg carton from the car. "And we're not talking just the phone calls. You've been paying some visits to the comics store in Red Lake."

It was cool in the basement, but Charles Henry was still sweating.

"I don't know anything about any comics store."

"Really?" said Lawrence. "What do you think will happen when I give this carton of eggs to my friends at the forensic lab, and they compare the DNA of these eggs to the DNA of the eggs splattered all over Stuart Lethbridge's store?"

I looked at Lawrence.

"Oh my God," Henry said, clearly overwhelmed by what science apparently could do. "Okay, okay, I egged the place. And I'm really sorry about the phone calls."

George Holland made a snorting noise. "He's fucking sorry."

"You're sorry you got caught," Alice Holland said. "This is what I want you to do. I want you to call Tracy over at the *Times*. Tell her you're withdrawing the petition. Tell her you think it's time to let things calm down. Tell her yeah, people have differences of opinion about who should and shouldn't be in the parade, but tempers are flaring, and it's time for people to cool off."

Charles Henry nodded, swallowed. "Okay," he squeaked.

"The *Times*'s next edition doesn't come out for a few more days," I said. "You need to get the message out now."

Alice nodded. "Charles, you're going to call Andy at FL Radio and offer him an interview that he can get on the next newscast. Tell him what you're going to tell Tracy. You can tell them you don't want gays and lesbians in the parade, I don't care, but make it clear that the parade needs to be peaceful, that this is an issue that can be taken up at a later date."

Henry looked hopeful. "We can still have discussions about this?"

Alice leaned in close to Henry, forcing him up against the pool table. "Not you, Charles. Never. Your opinion in this town counts for nothing from this day forward. You give me one moment's trouble, and I'll give that recording not only to the police, but the radio station. I'll put it on a loudspeaker and drive around town playing it at full volume. Let people find out what you're really like. That you're a little, little man."

Henry seemed to shrink.

"I have some questions," Lawrence said. Alice stepped aside and Lawrence moved forward. "What do you know about what's going to go down at the parade tomorrow?"

"Huh?" Henry said, surprised. "What do you mean?"

"If you know about anything that's going to happen, something bad, you better tell us now."

"I don't know what you're talking about!"

Lawrence turned to George. "You know how you were asking for ten minutes alone with this guy?"

George brightened. "Yeah."

"This seems as good a time as any."

"No! No!" Charles Henry whined. "I swear, I don't know anything!"

"What about the Wickenses?" Lawrence said. "Timmy Wickens and his crew?"

"Timmy Wickens? Are you kidding? That guy's crazy! Him and those boys, his wife's two? They're a bunch of psychos!"

Well. Something we could all agree on.

We were all quiet for a moment. For a few seconds, all we could hear was a dishwasher running upstairs, and Henry's rapid breathing.

"I don't think he's in on anything else," Lawrence said.

"I'm not! Honestly!"

"I don't think he's got the balls for it," Lawrence said. "A little man like you, dirty phone calls and eggs, that's about all you're capable of."

"I think you're right," Alice said.

"Does this mean I can't have some time alone with him?" George asked.

"I'm sorry, honey," Alice said, patting her husband on the arm.

As we were heading back to the car, I said to Lawrence, "Match the DNA from the eggs on the comics store with the eggs still left in the carton?"

Lawrence opened his door. "I couldn't believe I was actually saying it. Sometimes I get swept away in the moment."

29

BY THE TIME LAWRENCE AND I got back to our cabin, it was dark.

He went into his bedroom and opened the top dresser drawer, where he'd carefully tucked his clothes earlier, and pulled out a black, long-sleeved pullover shirt with a high, almost turtle-like neck.

"What are you doing?" I asked.

"I'm getting changed," Lawrence said. "You might want to do the same."

"What? Spying on the Wickenses, this is a formal affair?"

Lawrence was stripping off his slacks and pulling on black jeans, tucking in the black shirt. He pulled at the shirt, tenting the fabric. "This kind of thing," he said. It occurred to me that even his surveillance clothes looked more expensive than the stuff I wore in to the newsroom. "Dark clothes? So you won't be seen? You're new at this, aren't you?"

"I didn't exactly pack for hiding in the forest," I said. "In fact, I didn't get a chance to pack at all."

Lawrence made a face. "How long you been wearing these clothes?"

I shrugged.

Lawrence sighed and tossed me an extra dark shirt. "Your jeans will be okay," he said. "This shirt'll help, but I don't know what we're going to do with that Ivory Snow face of yours."

I unbuttoned the shirt I was wearing, slipped into Lawrence's, which smelled of fabric softener or something. "This smells nice," I said. "You do your own laundry?"

"What of it?"

"Okay, tell me this," I said. "Can you iron?"

"You working up to some sort of gay joke?"

"No no," I protested. "I just wanted to know whether I could add ironing to the list of things you can do that I can't. With beating the snot out of people at the top, and ironing at the bottom. God knows how many things in between."

Lawrence buckled his belt. "Let's talk about the dogs," he said.

"Well, you saw them this aft. There's two. Gristle and Bone. And I'm not even sure, technically speaking, that they're dogs. They may be very short velociraptors. All muscles and teeth. And from what I've seen, as deranged as they are dangerous. The other day, they tried to eat through one of the cabin doors. If your plan is to get into the Wickenses' house to plant some bugs, you're out of your mind." The very thought was making my skin crawl, although that might have been the high neck on the shirt Lawrence had lent me.

"I mean, think about it," I said. "If the dogs are outside, roaming about the property, you'll never make it from the fence to the house, and if the dogs are in the kitchen there, where they eat and sleep, there's no way you're going to get inside the house."

Lawrence said nothing.

"And," I continued, "if it's your plan to poison the dogs, which, even though I am not the sort of person who condones the murder of house pets, in this case I'd be willing to make an exception, that's going to arouse their suspicions, don't you think? Their dogs turn up dead, they're going to be asking some questions, and I imagine the first people they're going to ask are me and Dad, and now you, since you've made such a terrific first impression on them. And Timmy Wickens does not seem to be the kind of guy who asks questions nicely, even though he didn't make a fuss about how you got the drop on his boys. Hello? You're not saying a lot. Do you understand what I'm saying here? Am I coming through?"

Lawrence nodded. "Yes," he said.

"Tell me you're not going to poison the dogs."

Slowly, and thoughtfully, Lawrence said, "I am not going to poison the dogs. If I have to, I'll shoot them." My eyebrows went up. "But that's not my plan at the moment."

"So what are you going to do?"

Lawrence led me into the main room and opened up his cases filled with surveillance gear. He pulled out a gadget I'd noticed earlier, at the mayor's place, that looked similar to a gun, but the entire barrel was covered in a soft, black, spongy material.

"Shotgun microphone," Lawrence said. "You point at something, off in the distance, it picks up those sounds. But I don't know just how effective it will be. Whether they'll have their windows open at all. Whether they'll come outside."

Then Lawrence picked up those button-like microphones I'd spotted earlier. Each one was about as thick as three pennies, one side smooth, the other dense mesh.

"These are bugs?" I asked.

"Yeah. New model, pretty effective, they advertise that they can withstand moisture, pick up sounds through walls, but the walls have to be pretty thin, in my experience."

"So, what, we stick it to the outside of the house, hear what's inside?"

Lawrence shook his head. "No, I don't think it would be strong enough to work through an outside wall. But I'm wondering . . ."

"What?"

"If we got one or two of these into the kitchen . . ."

"Lawrence," I said, exasperated. "Were you listening two seconds ago? That's where the dogs stay. You're not going to get into that kitchen with those dogs there. And besides, there are six people living in that house. Maybe, just maybe, if I got to know May Wickens better . . . No, even though she wants to get herself and her son away, that doesn't mean she'd be willing to plant a bug on her own father, and it's pretty hard to get near her anyway, her dad's watching her pretty closely."

"What if," Lawrence said, "we could use the dogs?"

"Huh?" I stared at him. "What are you talking about?"

"The dogs are our biggest problem. Why not make them part of the solution?"

"I still don't get you. What, we hook them up with a Dog Cam? Like on Letterman? Sure, why don't you do that. I'm sure they'd hold still while you rigged them up."

Lawrence shook his head. "Nothing that obvious. What if we got some of these little guys"—he held the button-sized mike up between his thumb and index finger—"into the dogs?"

I smiled. "You're kidding me."

"I've never tried something like this before, but what the hey, it might be worth a shot. We give the dogs something to eat, we shove the mikes into the food, hope they swallow them whole. Dogs go lie down in the kitchen, bugs in their tummy, we listen in."

"You're serious."

Lawrence smiled. "I've never been more so."

I couldn't conceal my admiration. "You know, at this very moment, I find you very hot."

Lawrence studied the mike in his hand. "I've told you before, you're not my type."

"How many of these are you going to need? How many do you have?"

"I've got a half dozen of them. We get some Alpo, slip it into bowls and set it over the fence, they're bound to sniff it out. We hide the mikes in the dog food, we might get lucky."

"You know," I said, "I can get something those dogs like better than Alpo."

It took me a while to find the fish guts burial ground in the dark, but when the trees opened up and my flashlight caught the cottage shutter on the forest floor and the pile of dirt with a shovel already sticking out of it, I whispered to Lawrence, "Welcome to my new job."

We'd found two metal galvanized pails back in the open garage that was attached to the workshed, tucked in behind Dad's souped-up lawn tractor. I flipped the shutter off the hole, and about two feet down a layer of dirt covered the last load I'd dumped in. I'd gone first to the can of fish guts down by the lake, but recalled that I had emptied it earlier in the day, and when I lifted off the lid I saw there was nothing in it but a single filleted perch. It had been, evidently, a lousy fishing day at Denny's Cabins. Not hard to understand, given that we'd lost one guest fleeing a bear, and Bob was probably too traumatized to do anything but sit in his cabin. Betty and Hank Wrigley just weren't able to pick up the slack.

I yanked the shovel out of the dirt pile and drove it into the top layer of dirt. There was a soft, squooshy noise. I brought up a couple shovels full of dirt, then the main event.

"Oh my God," Lawrence said as I displayed for him the array of guts and fins and scales and eyeballs on the shovel blade. "That is, without a doubt, just about the most horrible mess I have ever seen in my entire life, except for maybe *Eyes Wide Shut*. You see that movie?"

"Hold out the buckets."

"Fuck no. I'll set them down here. You fill 'em up. I think I'll just wander over there and vomit."

The guts slid off the shovel and into the first pail.

"You're telling me these dogs love this stuff?"

"Like candy," I said.

I worked the shovel into the hole again, got a load for the second bucket, and dumped it in.

"Alpo would've worked fine," Lawrence said. "And it wouldn't have stunk anywhere near as bad."

"This stuff'll slide right down their throats like Jell-O," I said. "They won't even have to chew it."

"I really don't feel well," Lawrence said.

"Drop the mikes in."

Lawrence tossed one into each bucket.

"They expensive?" I asked.

"Don't even ask."

"And you say they're moisture resistant?"

"Supposed to be. Although I doubt the prototypes were ever subjected to this kind of test."

"If it works, how long do you think they'll be useful?" I asked.

In the moonlight, I could see Lawrence shrug. "How long's it take for something to go through a dog?"

"Twelve hours maybe? I hate to tell you, but the Wickenses don't strike me as stoop-and-scoop people. You're not gonna be getting these back."

"Your loss. I was going to give them to you."

Once I had a couple of inches in guts in each pail,

I shoved the shovel blade back into the dirt pile. Lawrence was being so squeamish, I didn't bother to ask him to grab the pails.

"Let's go feed our puppies," I said. "Do you think you could manage to throw some dirt over those exposed guts and drag the shutter back over the hole?"

"Uh, no thanks," said Lawrence. "I don't mind offering my detection services for free, but there are limits to what I'll do."

I decided I could deal with the hole later and led Lawrence through the trees toward the wire fence that surrounded the farmhouse. The house sat about thirty yards away, and we were looking at it from the side. It looked peaceful and ominous at the same time. Lights were on downstairs and up, and even from here, you could hear the soft sounds of people talking inside. The barn, off to the right, was a black square on a black canvas, large and foreboding. The only outside light was over the door on the front porch to our left.

"What if the dogs aren't outside to eat this shit?" I said.

"They gotta let them out at some point before they all go to bed," Lawrence figured.

We'd also brought along a wire coat hanger that I'd untwisted so I had a long hook with which to lower the pails over the fence. Carefully, I set them into position without letting them tip over. Lawrence and I moved a few feet back from the fence, stood there in the quiet night, and stared at the house.

"Come on," Lawrence said under his breath. "Let those bastards out."

Every minute or so, a light wind would come up, and the smell of fish guts would waft our way.

After five minutes of staring at the house, I said, "It's going to take me a while to get my head around this thing with Dad, and Orville. You think you know everything, then you realize you don't know shit. My mother, she was a good person."

"I'll bet she was."

"But she kept secrets her whole life."

"That's what people do," Lawrence said.

I thought about that. "Even you?"

In the moonlight, I could see the corners of his mouth go up a notch. "Especially me. My dad, he never knew my full story."

I remembered my visit to the hospital, when Lawrence lay near death in the intensive care ward, and the chat I'd had with his sister Letitia. "Your sister made mention of that. She gave me the sense that you kept your secret from your father not so much to protect yourself as to spare him."

"He was a good man," Lawrence said. "He just wouldn't have understood. I'm who I am. I don't expect the whole world to change to suit me." Lawrence squinted. "Door's opening."

I trained my eyes on the farmhouse. The porch door swung open, a woman's voice. Charlene, I thought.

"Away ya go," she said.

And out bolted Gristle and Bone. The huffed and snorted as they bounded down the steps, each starting to go his separate way, and then, almost simultaneously, they froze.

"Jesus," said Lawrence. "Look. They've caught the scent already."

The dogs, still standing in the glow of the porch light, a couple of nightmarish beasts of the night, raised up their heads, sniffed the air. Gristle glanced at Bone (or the other way around, I couldn't be certain), and then, as if on cue, they started running in tandem.

Right toward us. Or at least, I hoped, the two buckets that were between them and us, on the other side of the fence.

Once they were on the move, we could barely see them, just dark shadows barreling quickly across the ground, closing the distance. They were to the buckets in seconds, both going to the one on the left at the same time, trying to jam their heads into it. But then Bone pulled his head out, saw the other bucket only a few feet away, and shifted over.

They had their heads in the pails for nearly a minute, slopping up the guts and bones and fins, these canine garbage suckers. Gristle knocked his bucket over, pushed it around with his head, trying to get every last morsel.

"Shit," said Lawrence. "If he pushes that bucket too far, we won't be able to retrieve it. We can't have anyone seeing those buckets there in the morning."

When Bone was done, he ran off in the direction of the barn, and his buddy followed. I used the straightened coat hanger and managed to get both pails back over the fence. Carefully, so as not to be seen from the farmhouse, I shone the light into both of them.

"Nothing left," Lawrence said, rubbing his hands together. "Not a scrap, not a single bone, and no mikes. I'll get my toys set up and we'll see if this is going to work."

"You know, this is crazy," I said. "But I'm just a tiny bit hungry. Did we even have dinner?"

30

I KEPT MY SPOT by the fence while Lawrence ran back to the cabin for the tools of his trade. He was back in under ten minutes with his two cases. From the larger one he pulled out the laptop, which he made sure, when he opened it, wasn't facing the house. Didn't want them seeing a tiny square of blue light off in the distance. In the same case he had two sets of headphones and some other gear. He handed me one set of phones, which I slipped around my neck, and he did the same with his. He got his shotgun microphone from the other case and gave it to me.

"Point that at the house, holding it steady as you can. I'm not quite ready yet, but it'll help me do other stuff if you can do that."

"Sure," I said, holding the gun with both hands. "This is about my skill level right here."

Lawrence began tapping away at the laptop, moving the cursor around, opening boxes. I didn't have the foggiest idea what he was doing. "Do I need to have any of this explained to me?" I asked.

Lawrence didn't even look at me. "No." He slipped on his headphones, as if doing a test, then took them back off. "The first thing we're going to want to know is whether the dogs scarfed down those bugs without destroying them."

I watched the farmhouse. Soft sounds emanating from within, a shadow passing by a window. The dogs appeared out of the darkness, bounding up the porch steps and scratching at the front door, bumping into one another. Someone, I couldn't tell who, opened the screen enough to let them slip inside. "Hey, boys!"

"They're back in," I said.

"I think we've only got one," Lawrence said, pulling one side of the headphones away from his ear. "I'm picking up one mike, but not the other. It must have got chewed right through."

"Can I listen?"

Lawrence told me to slip my phones on. This is what I heard:

"Pa-thump, pa-thump, pa-thump, pa-thump."

"What the hell is that?" I whispered. There was another background sound, too, harder to pin down, but regular, almost a whistle.

"That would be DOS," Lawrence said. "Dog Operating System. Heartbeat, breathing. I'm gonna see what I can do to filter some of that out."

I listened some more. *"Pa-thump, pa-thump, pa-hump* and that's all *pa-thump, pa-thump* homework *pa-thump* dishes, beer over here *pa-thump, pa-hump."*

"This is crazy," I said. "You can't hear a damn thing for the heartbeat. And it sounds like whichever dog swallowed the mike is roaming from room to room."

"Zack, just chill," Lawrence said, fiddling some more with his computer. "Okay, I've got your shotgun mike working now, so just focus it on the house. I'll start coordinating the mikes, aim for the same thing from different directions. The dogs have had a good runaround. At some point, they should collapse and snooze. If one does, the other probably will."

"They do share a brain," I said.

On the headphones: "Hey, boy, howya doing. Fuck, what did you get into?"

Slightly muffled, but an actual entire sentence. Timmy, I figured, or one of Charlene's sons. Commenting, no doubt, on the dog's breath. After a meal of fish guts, you really needed a mint.

"There's a blanket on the floor in the kitchen," I whispered. "They curl up there."

Lawrence stayed focused on his screen, which looked like a graph with different bars sliding up and down depending on what sounds came through the headphones. He made some adjustments with the cursor. The heartbeats, while still there, receded faintly into the background.

With the headphones on, my hands wrapped tightly around the shotgun mike, and watching the house so intently, I jumped when Lawrence tapped my knee. "Shit!" I said. "You just gave me a fucking heart attack."

"Aim the mike more toward the back of the house. I think that's where the kitchen is."

"That's right," I said, recalling the layout from the dinner. I adjusted my aim ever so slightly. Lawrence held up his hand, indicating I should stop.

"Jeffrey!" Timmy, no doubt about it. Some shuffling, footsteps.

"Yeah?"

" . . . what . . . you . . . doing out of your room?"

" . . . get some water . . ."

"You're grounded, buster . . . want out, you'll hand over those figures."

Lawrence shook his head. "Aww man, I never meant to get the kid in trouble," he said softly. "Couldn't he have just hid them from the get-go? Shit . . ."

Jeffrey again. "But I really like them."

"Yeah, well, no water, no dessert, no nothing for you till you hand them over to me."

"Jeez, Dad." A different voice, not so deep, softer. This had to be May, unless Charlene liked to call her husband "Dad," which seemed unlikely. I whispered to Lawrence, "The daughter, Jeffrey's mom."

May said, "What's the big deal about a couple of little figures? So what if they're black? They're just—"

"As long as he's . . . my roof, he's going to live by my rules, and that . . . for you, too. Am I gonna have to take . . . belt to ya?"

"It's . . . fucking nigger's fault."

Wendell or Dougie.

" . . . go back and kick his black ass . . ."

Lawrence didn't flinch, just kept listening.

"No," said Timmy. "We got more important things . . . do."

"It's not right, him gettin' away with that. My neck's still hurtin'."

"Yeah." The other brother. "And my back, I think it might be broken or something."

"If your back was broken, you wouldn't be standing there." Timmy.

"You shoulda seen it," Jeffrey said. "He had both of them on the ground in like seconds." I thought I could detect a hint of admiration coming through.

Then some shouting. "Sorry," Jeffrey said.

"It was wrong, what he did." Another woman, but not May. Charlene. "You can't tell my boys they can't make this right. It's their pride."

A bang. Someone bringing a fist down on a table, maybe. "Not now!" Timmy, for sure.

I whispered to Lawrence, "You're always causing trouble. I thought it was just me." Lawrence waved at me to shut up.

"Put him to bed," Timmy said. "Little shit's gonna learn . . . for . . . all . . ."

Lawrence fiddled with his settings. We were losing the conversation. "Dog's on the move," Lawrence said. "Come on, boy, go back to the kitchen. Shit!"

The voices largely faded away. The little bit we were getting, I guessed, was from the shotgun mike in my hand.

For the next five minutes we got little more than the sounds of a dog patting around the house, a voice occasionally coming in, then fading out. We each had one ear covered with a headphone, the other exposed so we could talk more easily to one another.

"This is hopeless," Lawrence said. "We're going to have to come up with another plan."

"Like what? Wanna say sorry to the boys with a delivery of Big Macs, you can sneak some bugs into the special sauce?"

Lawrence looked pissed and frustrated. And then, from the headphones, clear as a bell:

"I'm gonna head out to the barn." Wendell, I thought. "I could use a hand."

"Yeah," said Timmy.

The dog had returned to the kitchen, and was, I suspected, curled up again on the rug. I was steadying the shotgun mike, about to slip the other half of the headphones into place, when I heard some rustling behind me.

"Lawrence," I said.

A few feet off, something bumping into branches. I set the shotgun mike onto the forest floor and reached slowly into my inside jacket pocket, where I'd tucked the can of bear spray Dad had found in Leonard Colebert's backpack.

"There's something out there," I whispered. I was holding my breath, and I was betting Lawrence was, too. More rustling in the trees, about fifteen yards off to the left, it sounded like. The idea of encountering the bear in the daytime was scary enough. But the thought of running into him at night, that was truly terrifying.

Lawrence was reaching into his jacket for something, too. If he'd brought along bear spray, I was unaware of it. But then I saw the moonlight glinting off something metallic, and it became evident that Lawrence had something more powerful than a small can of spray. He had a gun.

He wouldn't want to be using it, I was pretty sure of that. The sound of a gun going off, that could draw the attention of the Wickenses in a hurry, possibly before we'd had a chance to clear away the surveillance equipment. If we were busy fending off a bear, we weren't going to have much else to think about.

More rustling this time, a few steps closer.

Lawrence whispered. "Spray first. Then gun."

I understood the reasoning, but didn't much like the idea that I was to take the lead here. Wasn't Lawrence the more likely man of action? And didn't you have to get a lot closer to spray?

I raised my arm, my finger poised above the button that would release the noxious spray.

The trees rustled again, and then there was a thud, like whatever was out there had just taken a tumble.

And then: "Shit."

Lawrence and I looked at each other. I'd seen a lot of bears perform tricks in circus acts, but I'd never heard one use foul language.

"Oh man," the voice said again.

"For crying out loud," I whispered. "It's my dad."

I slipped the bear spray back into my jacket, noticed Lawrence putting away his gun, then move through the trees in the direction the sounds had come from.

"Dad?"

"Zachary?"

I found him on his knees, patting the ground, looking for the crutches he'd lost when he'd fallen.

"What the hell are you doing?" I asked. "Dad, we thought you were a goddamn bear. I almost nailed you with bear spray. If that hadn't worked, Lawrence was ready to shoot you."

"I saw you two heading out here and wondered what was going on."

"Are you out of your mind? Trying to walk up here?"

"My ankle's been feeling a lot better lately and I thought I could make it without much trouble."

"Have you twisted it again?"

"I don't think so. I just got a branch in the face is all. Lost my balance."

"Dad, go back to the cabin."

He reached out a hand so that I'd help him up. "I wanted to talk to you," he said when he had hold of me.

"Listen, Dad—"

"I haven't had a chance to talk to you since Lana and I, since we tried to explain things, and, well, I don't know. I wondered if you were okay."

"I'm okay, Dad."

"Because, I wouldn't want you to . . . I guess what I'm saying is, it's been nice."

"Nice? What's been nice?"

"Having you up here. It's been nice having you up

here this week. I mean, it's been kind of crazy around here, but it's been nice. That's all."

We were both quiet for a moment, listening to the sounds of the night. The odd cricket, the breeze blowing through the branches.

"I've liked it, too, Dad." I paused. "I've got to go back and help Lawrence."

"Sure. What are you two doing?"

"We're listening to the Wickenses."

"Really?" Surprised, and intrigued.

"Shhh! Keep your voice down."

"Can you do that? Listen in on them, without their permission?"

"Dad, if we got their permission, wouldn't that sort of defeat the exercise?"

"Oh yeah, I suppose."

"Listen, Dad, head back to the cabin. We can talk some more later, okay?"

"Zack!"

Lawrence was whispering at top volume. "Zack, Jesus, get back here!"

"Okay," Dad said, "I'm going. But we'll talk later, right?"

"Yeah. Get home without getting eaten, okay?" I reached into my pocket to offer him my bear spray.

"No," he said. "I got my hands busy with crutches. I'll be okay."

He turned and started hobbling back. I watched him until he was swallowed up by the trees and the darkness.

A moment later, I was squatting down next to

Lawrence again, slipping my headphones back on, pointing the shotgun mike at the house.

"What I miss?" I said.

"Shut up," Lawrence said, trying to listen.

There was still the faint dog heartbeat in the background, and its breathing. But the voices were coming in pretty clear again.

"I can do it, Timmy." Dougie, I thought.

"I don't know."

"Trust me, I can do it. I'll show you. I won't forget anything. And I'll find a good parking spot for the van, then find a good spot to watch from."

A chair squeak blocked out Timmy's reply. All I heard was " . . . parade to remember . . ."

"Yeah, for sure." Wendell. "The remote, I think the button's a bit sticky."

"It's fine." Timmy. "Want to double-check the . . . though."

"I get to take the remote." Dougie.

"Yeah, if you don't fucking forget it." Wendell.

"Fuck you."

"What kind of sandwiches you want?" Charlene again.

"Ham," said one.

"With cheese," said another.

"No mustard on mine." Timmy, I thought.

Whatever they planned to do at tomorrow's parade, I guessed no one wanted to do it on an empty stomach.

"Okay, let's get this done." Timmy Wickens.

More chair scraping, people getting up from the table. Seconds later, the back door of the farmhouse swung open and three figures made their way across the yard to the barn. A large door, big enough to admit a vehicle, was slid open, and someone flicked on a light, and once the three of them were inside, the door was slid almost all the way shut with just enough space left for someone to squeeze through.

"You heard that?" I said. "Remote? And parade?"

Lawrence nodded solemnly. "We need to get a look at what they've got inside that barn. Whatever they're putting together, it's in there."

"So, how do you propose to do that?"

Lawrence smiled. "We'll sneak over."

"Across the yard? You're joking, right?"

"The dogs are inside. They're probably asleep now. It's late. We should be fine."

"Lawrence, really, there has to be another way to—"

"We need to know what's in that barn. And we haven't got that building bugged, the dogs aren't there, and it's even farther away from here than the farmhouse. The shotgun's not going to work. We need to hear what's going on in there."

I patted my jacket, felt the can of bear spray inside it.

"I guess if this stuff will slow down a bear, it ought to slow down a dog," I said.

"Maybe," Lawrence said. "Those dogs, they might be too dumb to know they've been hit."

Lawrence removed his headphones, folded up his laptop, placed his equipment in their cases. Then he had his foot into a gap in the wire fence, and it sagged under his weight as he got his other foot into a higher opening. In a moment, he was over the top and hopping down onto the other side.

He looked at me on the other side of the fence, his fingers wrapped around the top wire. "Are you coming?" he asked.

I sighed, and started climbing.

31

WE HUGGED THE INSIDE OF THE FENCE that ran along the edge of the forest. Taking it to the right would get us closer to the barn, so that when we had to walk across open territory, there wouldn't be as much of it. We were worried that, with the moon shining down the way it was, there was a chance someone looking out a window of the Wickens place might catch a glimpse of us.

We crept, and raised our feet with each step. If we came across a stick or small stone, we'd be stepping on it from above, rather than tripping over it. I resisted all temptation to say anything to Lawrence, who was ahead of me by about two yards.

We heard a door and froze. Together, we craned our necks around to look back at the farmhouse. The back screen door swung open, and there was Charlene, silhouetted in light from the kitchen, a washbowl of some kind in her hands. She tossed some water from the top step, then slipped back inside.

As best as we could tell, no little critters had taken the opportunity to scoot out the door.

Lawrence and I exchanged glances, nodded in silence, and kept on moving.

In a few minutes, we were around the far side of the barn, the farmhouse now obscured from view. If we couldn't see it, no one in it, we figured, could see us. Pencil-thin slivers of light seeped out from between the barnboards, offering us a number of places where we could peek inside. We approached the side of the barn, a step at a time, mindful of the grasses and twigs and stones beneath our feet. We were more worried than ever now about making any sounds. Tentatively, I reached out and touched the barn with the tips of my fingers, like a tired climber reaching his hand over the crest of the cliff. We sidled up close to the building, each of us putting an eye to a crack.

I didn't have much of a view. The back third of an old white van, the one I'd seen in the yard earlier in the week, with its back door open. Wendell, Dougie, or Tim, passing through the scene. Lawrence, only three feet down from me, must have had pretty much the same view.

The good thing was, even if we couldn't see them all that well, we could hear them perfectly, a nice change from our pit bull mike.

"What about the water tower?" Wendell said. "Wouldn't that be a good place to watch from?"

"Too out of the way, perfect place to get caught, too," Timmy said. "You get spotted up there, what are you going to do? No, stick with the original plan,

Dougie. Couple blocks off Main, that seniors complex, you get up on the roof, you can see from there, press the button whenever you want. Boom it goes."

"That's way better than a fuse," Dougie said. "A fuse, you gotta run, hope it goes off at the right time."

"Did you bring out those wiring diagrams?" Timmy asked.

"Oh shit," said Dougie. "I left them in the house."

"Honest to God, Dougie," Timmy said.

"I can go get 'em."

"Never mind, I don't think I really need them."

Timmy passed by the end of the van, appeared to go in the open back door. From inside, his voice slightly muffled: "This looks fine. You did this, Wendell?"

"Yep."

"I think that'll work just fine."

"Fucker's gonna blow huge," Dougie said. "It's gonna be awesome."

"Are people gonna know why we did it?" Wendell asked Timmy, still inside the van.

"They'll figure it out. Especially if we set it off right when the gay float goes by."

Float? Would you believe four people and a banner?

"Hey, Timmy," said Dougie. "How'm I gonna know, exactly, just when they're going by the town hall so I know when to hit the button?"

"I told you, they're supposed to be right behind the high school band, and ahead of the grocery store float, which is the huge piece of beef or something."

"Okay, that should be easy."

"Thing is," Wendell said, "parade's probably so fucking small, wouldn't matter when you hit the button, you'll take everyone out. It isn't just about the fags. It's a bigger statement, about the town government and the mayor, right, Timmy?"

"Dougie," said Timmy, "I'm thinking, maybe I should let Wendell handle this part."

"Come on! Mom said I could do this. She said you *promised* her."

"I know, it's just . . ."

"She said you need to show more confidence in me." He paused. "You know, for my self-esteem."

"Jesus," Timmy muttered as he hopped back out of the van. "Fine. Just so you remember, be very careful with the remote. You press down on that button, the van blows, right then. That's why I've made a little box for the remote, with foam all around it, so even if the thing falls off the dashboard when you're driving into town, you're not going to blow yourself up. But once it's out of the box, it's very sensitive."

"I'm not stupid," Dougie said. "I just forget things once in a while. But that don't make me dumb. I've even been writin' some of this stuff down, so I won't forget any of it. Mom's idea."

"He'll be okay, Timmy," Wendell said. "I'll be driving in after him, if he has any problems, I can help him out."

I couldn't see Timmy, but I could sense him mulling it over. Out of the corner of my eye, I saw Lawrence's arm moving. He tapped me lightly, motioned me toward him.

He put his mouth right up to my ear. "A lone wolf," he whispered.

I looked around, expecting to see a large, dog-like creature sneaking up on me.

"No no," Lawrence said. "It's an FBI term. A lone terrorist. Timmy's out to make a statement of his own. Not part of a larger group."

"A lone wolf with family support," I whispered back.

"We have to get help, do something right away. We need everybody. Forget Orville. I'm talking the feds. Now."

I nodded. Then Lawrence did a series of motions—pointing to himself, then pointing around the barn, then pointing at me, and finally, pointing at the ground. I thought I got the message. He wanted to get a peek inside the barn from the other side, and I was to stay put.

As he crept away, I put my eye back to the crack and heard Wendell say, "I'm starving."

"When's Mom coming with sandwiches?"

Jesus. I didn't figure Lawrence had heard that. He was on the move, slipping around the corner of the barn. Timmy and the boys were expecting a visit from Charlene, any moment now.

"She'll be out soon enough," Timmy said.

"I hope she doesn't put cheese on mine," Dougie said. "I think I forgot to ask."

Wendell said, "Jesus, she's only been making you sandwiches for twenty years. I think she knows you don't like cheese on ham, even if the rest of the entire fucking world does."

I took a step, thinking that maybe I should go after Lawrence, but then thought, Lawrence was no fool. He had to know something like that was possible. One of the men in the barn could decide to head back to the farmhouse, the dogs might get let out. Any number of things could happen. He might—

Through the crack, I saw guns.

Big guns. Long ones.

Wendell was standing next to Dougie, at the back of the van, each holding a shotgun of some kind. I've never, and still don't, know much about guns, even though I'd fired a couple in recent years, even shot a man in the leg not that long ago, but guns are not my thing. I don't like them, I don't own them. A gun in our house, if I were the incompetent wielding it, would undoubtedly put my family at greater risk, not less.

But even though I didn't know much about guns, I thought I recognized the weapon in the hands of those young men. Pump action shotguns. With double barrels.

Bad bad guns.

Maybe, by now, Lawrence had staked out a new position on another side of the barn, and had peered through a crack and seen these guns.

An image of Dick Tracy flashed in my mind. If only Lawrence and I had two-way wrist radios. Cell phones that could text message would have done the trick.

I couldn't stay put. I had to join Lawrence.

I moved up to the corner of the barn he'd disappeared around, stuck my head around it, let my eyes

adjust. Crossing along that side, he would hav
scooted past the big barn door, which had been
pulled shut about ninety percent of the way. Ther
was no Lawrence. So he must have gone aroun
the next corner, and was peering in from the oppo
site side.

From this vantage point, I could see the farm
house, and as I started to make my move to the nex
corner, the back door of the house swung open, an
out stepped Charlene, a tray in her hands.

The sandwiches were on their way.

I couldn't go around the barn that way without be
ing seen by Charlene, so I doubled back to the othe
corner, all the while aware of the murmurings o
Timmy and Wendell and Dougie inside. I peere
around it, and again, no sign of Lawrence. Which
only left one side of the barn for him to be on.

I tiptoed through the tall grass, sidestepped a
rusting plough blade from God knew how man
decades ago, and when I reached the end of the wall
tipped my head beyond the edge.

No Lawrence.

Pressing myself up close to the barn, I move
along the wall, wondering what could have hap
pened to him. He couldn't have gone the other wa
That would have exposed him to the house, an
Charlene the Sandwich Lady.

The ground was built up on this side, and I real
ized it was a ramp leading to the upper part of th
barn. My eye followed the ramp up to a narro
opening, a door that was only slightly ajar.

Lawrence had gone into the barn. What the hell was Lawrence doing in the—

"Okay, nobody move!"

Oh shit.

I ran up the ramp, squeezed in the doorway, my shoes kicking old hay and stones out of the way. Once in, I found that this upper level of the barn afforded a view into the lower area, where the Wickens crew had been occupied with the white van. And down there, I could see Lawrence, doing the cop stance, both hands on his gun, barking commands at Timmy and Wendell and Dougie.

"Put the guns down," Lawrence said.

"The fuck?" said Wendell.

"Jesus, *you*," said Dougie. "That's the guy, Timmy. He's the one was so mean to me."

"I know, Dougie," said Timmy. "I talked to him. Remember?"

So Lawrence had snuck in from above and gotten the drop on them. I sure hoped he had a plan for subduing the three of them. Was he carrying several sets of handcuffs I didn't know about? And if not, where was my friend Trixie when you really needed her?

And where, exactly, was Charlene?

She should have been to the barn by now. It wasn't a long walk. Which meant she must have been almost to the barn with her tray of sandwiches when she heard Lawrence's voice, and knew there was trouble inside. So where had she gone? Was she running back to the farmhouse? Going for help?

What to do? Shout to Lawrence? But would that

distract him, give the others a chance to get the jump on him? Maybe if—

"Drop it."

Off to Lawrence's left, standing in the narrow opening of the big barn door, stood Charlene, a long-barreled gun in hand, a goddamn six-shooter it looked like from my hiding spot up in the barn, pointed straight at Lawrence's head.

Fucking Ma Barker.

32

NO ONE MOVED.

Not Wendell or Dougie. Not Lawrence. Not Charlene. Lawrence had his gun aimed at the three men, who were clustered together at the back of the van, and had, I could see from my hiding spot, put down their weapons. But Charlene Wickens had her gun firmly in her grip, and it was trained on Lawrence.

"Put your gun away, Mrs. Wickens," Lawrence said evenly. "Drop it."

"I don't think so, boy," she said. She practically spat out the last word.

"Mrs. Wickens," Lawrence said, his eyes darting back and forth between her and the men in front of him, "I'm sure you don't want to see one of your sons, or your husband, hurt."

"And I'm sure you don't want your fucking head shot off." She held the gun with such confidence, I had the sense she could do it.

Lawrence persisted. "Mrs. Wickens. If you don't

put down your gun and stand over here with the rest
of your family, I may have no choice but to use my
weapon. Who do you want to see die first? One of
your boys, or your husband?"

"Well," Charlene Wickens said, appearing rather
thoughtful, "I guess if you gotta take one of them,
best it be my husband. I wouldn't feel good about
you taking one of my own flesh and blood." I wished
I could see Timmy Wickens's expression, but
Wendell was standing to this side of him, and his
face was obscured.

Charlene Wickens continued, "But the way I see
it, the best you might be able to do is get one of
the three, and by then, I'll have put a bullet of my
own into you. And if you figure it makes sense to
shoot me first, since I'm the one holding a gun, lot
of luck there, pardner. The moment I see your muscles twitch to start aiming in my direction, I'm dropping you."

There was one thing Lawrence had on his side
that none of the Wickenses knew about, and that
was me. He must have figured that I was watching
this, not from inside the barn, perhaps, but at least
from the spot outside where he'd left me. And he'd
know that, even if I lacked the requisite heroic skill
to turn the tables on the Wickenses at this moment,
I could at least run like hell for help.

If only my bear spray had a range of forty feet.

"Maybe," said Lawrence, "I'm willing to see how
many of you I can take out before you shoot me. I'm
betting I can kill at least two of you before you k

me. And that ought to be enough to disrupt your plans for tomorrow's parade."

Everyone thought about that for a few seconds.

Then Charlene said, "We do it your way, then after, whoever's left standing here is going to take a walk down the road and get rid of every possible witness who could ever tell the police anything about what's been going on around here. Walker, and that meddlesome son of his, and whoever else is down there. We'll take care of all of them. And then we'll pack up and move on."

That didn't sound good at all. And I could tell, from Lawrence's expression, that it didn't sound very good to him, either.

So, slowly and deliberately, he bent down and set his gun on the barn floor. And Dougie walked over and kicked him in the balls.

Lawrence dropped like a bag of cement. He lay on the floor, writhing.

Timmy shook his head, walked over to Charlene. "Nice going, honey."

She smiled, gave him a peck on the cheek. "I hope you know I didn't mean nothing by telling him to shoot you first. You know I love you, even if not quite as much as I love my boys."

"I know," Timmy said. "You did what you had to do."

Wendell said, "Were you still making sandwiches, Mom?"

"Oh, almost forgot," she said. "I was bringing the tray over, and when I heard the commotion going on in here, I put it down outside, ran back and got my gun. Just a sec." She slipped out the door and was back ten seconds later, the tray of sandwiches untouched by any creatures of the night.

Wendell and Dougie rushed her. "Which one's without cheese?" asked Dougie, who was already lifting the lids of the various sandwiches to check.

"This one," Charlene said.

Dougie grabbed it, shoved a quarter of the sandwich into his mouth, his cheeks bulging out. Wendell did the same.

"Nothing for you?" Charlene asked her husband. "I made you one without mustard, just like you asked."

Timmy shook his head, glanced back at Lawrence Jones on the floor, slowly twisting and turning. "I'm a bit worried about him. I don't figure he'd be out here working alone. It was Walker's son brought him up here from the city."

Wendell and Dougie, looking like squirrels hiding nuts to take back to the nest, stopped chewing a moment to take in the significance of this comment. Charlene said, "You think he might be around here, too?"

"Why don't we go ask?" Timmy said, and walked back over to Lawrence. He bent over slightly, and said, "Who else is out here with you?"

I began slipping back toward the open door, which meant I couldn't see what was going on, but I could still hear.

"I said, who else is out here with you?"

Quietly, "Nobody."

"I don't believe you. Dougie, come over here and give this man another taste of your boot."

Up above them, nearing the door, I could hear the kick.

Lawrence said, "Unnhhh."

"Now let me ask you again. Are you out here alone, or is there someone with you?"

As it turned out, Lawrence didn't really need to answer the question. I answered it for them when, as I slipped out the door, my foot pressed down on a twig and snapped it.

It wasn't a loud sound. It was hardly anything at all. But it must have been enough to prick some-one's ears.

"Up there," Charlene Wickens said. "Someone's up there!"

"Wendell!" Timmy shouted. "Dougie! Go! Go!"

I now embarked on the "run like hell" part of my plan. My legs started pumping, carrying me back in the direction I'd come from, along the inside of the fence, looking for the place where I'd hopped over, because I knew the terrain back down toward the cabins from there pretty well.

I glanced back briefly, and when I saw the shad-ows of the two brothers appear in the light of the barn door, I dropped to the ground, flattening myself to it. Each of them was armed with a shotgun, and as soon as they were standing outside the barn, they stopped momentarily, reminding me of the pit bulls when they stopped to determine where the smell of fish was coming from. They hadn't seen me, didn't know where I might be, and were wondering which way to go. There were a lot of choices, standing under that starry sky.

One of them, I couldn't tell which, pointed and said to the other, "You go that way!" That one disappeared behind the far side of the barn. The one I could still see, and it was beginning to look to me now like it was Wendell, started off, slowly, in my direction.

As long as I pressed myself to the ground, I felt he couldn't see me. Unless of course, he happened to come right toward me.

Charlene Wickens came out of the barn, an empty tray in her hand, and walked briskly back to the farmhouse.

Don't let the dogs out, I thought. *Please, please, please do not let those dogs out.* Wendell might not be able to see me in the dark, but I had every confidence in the dogs' collective ability to sniff me out.

She went into the house, let the door slam shut behind her. Upstairs, a light went on.

Wendell was moving my way.

I felt a small rock under my right hand, gripped it. I rolled over onto my back and threw it, as best I could from that position, back toward the barn. It hit the ground, and just as I'd hoped, Wendell stopped and turned. He was holding his breath same as I was, I suspected, listening for any sound. He decided the noise was worth investigating, and went slowly in that direction.

I got to my knees, almost in a sprinter's starting position, and then bolted, trying to keep low. I got to the spot where I'd hopped the fence, grabbed hold of it, and the metal wire twanged softly as I got my feet into the openings and threw myself over.

Once my feet were planted on the other side, I looked back, and saw that Wendell was running my way now. Running hard, the barrel of the shotgun wavering back and forth in front of him as he ran toward me.

I ran into the woods wildly, not as sure of my bearings as I'd thought I would be. And even had I known exactly where I was, I couldn't decide where to go, or what to do. I could run back to Dad's cabin, but he wasn't going to be able to protect me from a guy with a shotgun. We could put in a frantic call to Orville, but how long would it take him to get out here? And once he'd arrived, how much help would he be? Hadn't the Wickenses intimidated him more than once before? Could you expect your life to be saved by a guy who couldn't even hang on to his hat? Or his gun? If Timmy Wickens told him to take a walk again, wasn't there a good chance he would?

And what could Betty or Hank Wrigley do, or Bob Spooner, who was—

Wait a minute.

Hadn't Bob mentioned having a gun in his tackle box? Hadn't he made a comment about a Smith & Wesson? Could I make it down to his boat before Wendell caught up with me? If I could get my hands on the gun, would I have a chance of being able to use it against him? And would it even be there? Wasn't it likely Bob took his tackle box into the cabin at night? Well then, couldn't I burst in there and get it from him?

And would I be able to get back to the barn before the rest of the Wickenses did any more damage to Lawrence Jones?

I kept running, branches armed with pine needles coming out of nowhere, slapping my face, disorienting me. I thought I could hear footsteps coming behind me. I reached into my pocket for the bear spray, and without even looking back, started shooting it over my shoulder, hoping that if Wendell was back there, some of the pepper would waft into his face somehow.

I came upon an opening and there, in front of me, was the open pit of fish guts, which Lawrence had refused to cover with the cottage shutter. I leapt over it at the last second, nearly falling in, started stumbling headlong, then regained my footing and kept going.

I was cutting left, then right, looking for the lights from the cabins, still spraying wildly over my shoulder, and somewhere behind me I heard, "Shit!"

It sounded a ways off, so I slowed, listened some more. "Fuck! What the fuck is this?"

Wendell, evidently, had not navigated the pit of guts as well as I had. I gave myself the luxury of a half-second smile, then kept on for the cabins, thinking of nothing else but getting my hand on Bob's Smith & Wesson and—

"Hold it."

My heart felt like it had been struck with a sledgehammer. There, in the darkness, was Dougie. Standing directly ahead of me, the shotgun raised and pointed straight at my forehead.

I stopped.

"Wendell!" he shouted. "I got him! Over here!"

The can of bear spray was still tucked into my hand. I slipped my index finger over the button at the top, kept it there.

Dougie stepped forward. He had a dopey grin on his face, and his dirty teeth glowed in the moonlight.

"You put your hands up," he said.

I did as I was told. As my arm went up, I aimed the spray at Dougie's face and hit the button.

The can went *phisss* briefly, and then died.

"What's that?" Dougie asked.

I let the empty can drop to the ground. "My last hope," I said.

33

"I FOUND HIM!" Dougie told his mother and Timmy after he and Wendell had marched me back to the barn.

"I sent him right to you," Wendell said. "I flushed the fucker out."

"Yeah, well, I'm the one that actually got him, that's all I'm saying. I'm not saying you didn't have anything to do with it."

"Boys," Charlene Wickens, who'd returned to the barn when she heard the commotion, said, "you've both done a very good job, and both deserve a lot of credit."

The brothers smiled.

"Does anyone want ice cream?" she asked.

"Oh yeah, I'd love some ice cream," Wendell said.

"Do we have chocolate sauce?" Dougie asked.

"I'm pretty sure we do," Charlene said. "How about you, Timmy?"

Timmy, who had just closed the gate on a stall that contained me and Lawrence, said, "Maybe just a little. But no sauce. Just plain."

Everyone was in a mood for celebrating. They had me, and they had Lawrence. And they had his gun, our cell phones for whatever they were worth out here, and our keys. After a minor setback, they were able to continue with their plans.

I was thinking of asking whether I could have a bowl of ice cream, but the fact was, I was just too scared shitless to crack wise.

Lawrence was sitting in the corner, his butt on the floor, his legs stretched out in front of him, his back against the wall. "So," he said to me, "I presume you're here to rescue me." Evidently Lawrence was not having the same problem.

"How badly did they hurt you?" I asked.

Lawrence shrugged. "I couldn't ride a horse right now, but I'm okay. I've had worse. Pride's a bit bent out of shape."

"What were you thinking? Going it alone?"

He closed his eyes, shook his head sadly. "There's a huge fucking bomb in that van, Zack. I didn't feel we could afford to wait to bring in the troops. If it hadn't been for Bonnie Parker there—"

"I was thinking more along the lines of Ma Barker."

"Yeah, even better. If it hadn't been for her unexpected arrival, things might be a bit different now. How about you? You okay?"

I nodded.

"Man, you stink," I heard Dougie say to Wendell.

"I fell in something fucking awful," Wendell said.

Charlene said, "I'll get the ice cream ready." She left the barn.

Timmy stood on the other side of the gate that

closed off our stall, which at some time must have been home to a horse or cow or two. It wasn't like we were in a prison cell—the stall wasn't locked and the gate would have taken a second to climb over. But it wasn't the sort of thing you could do without being noticed.

"So," Timmy said. "You boys put a bit of a wrinkle into things there for a while."

I took a couple of steps his way, but once I was within three feet of him he waved the shotgun over the top of the gate. "You just stay there."

I stayed there.

But from where I stood I could see into the back of the van. There were no seats in it but the two front ones, and a large blue plastic drum sat in the middle, on the floor. Atop it was a black plastic device, about the size of a shoebox, and some wires. Beside the van, on the barn floor, were several emptied fertilizer bags and three red plastic gas cans.

Timmy smiled. "I see you admiring my handiwork."

I swallowed. "I don't know a lot about explosives, but that looks big."

"Well, not as huge as some. We're not trying to bring down the Alfred P. Murrah, but it'll do."

Lawrence slowly got to his feet, came up alongside me. "Looks like you did a pretty good job of it," he said. "Clean, simple."

Timmy nodded. "Thanks."

"How many people you figure you'll end up killing?"

Timmy's lips puckered while he thought about it.

"Don't really know. But that's not important. What's important is the message."

"And what," Lawrence asked, "would that message be?"

"That this country has to get back on the right track. That we have to stomp out immorality. That we have to put an end to state interference. That we have to keep this country pure, and good, and not turn it over to a bunch of special interests, that's what the fucking message is, my friend."

"Okay," said Lawrence. "For a while there, I thought maybe you all were just a bunch of nuts. But now I understand."

"Lawrence," I whispered.

"I wouldn't expect you to get it, anyway," Timmy said to Lawrence. "You're as much a part of the problem as anyone. I don't know why you people don't just hurry up and kill each other off, either with guns or with your addiction to drugs, and be done with it. If it wasn't for good, decent folks getting caught in the crossfire, it wouldn't matter so much, but sometimes you people take your battles outside your own neighborhoods and innocent people get killed."

"Yeah," said Lawrence. "We're a bit thoughtless that way."

"So blowing up a parade, that'll get your message across," I said.

"The parade, the town hall, and the faggot float," Timmy said.

Lawrence grinned, and then the grin turned into a low-level chuckle.

"What?" Timmy asked. "What's so funny?"

"You don't even know, do you?" Lawrence asked.

"Know what?"

"Your so-called faggot float is a total joke. Four people carrying a banner. Three guys, one girl, and she's not even lesbian. She's faking it."

Timmy looked dismayed. "Are you serious?"

"Yup. Hardly worth the trouble, when you think about it."

"I'm sure you're wrong about this," he said. "I'm sure it's going to be bigger than that. It said in the paper. It said at least a dozen."

"Hey, you can't believe what you read in the papers," I said. I figured I should know better than anyone here.

Lawrence said, "We saw Lethbridge today. Stuart Lethbridge. He wanted the right to be in the parade, and he got it, but he ain't got much to put in it."

"What's the problem, Timmy?" Dougie said, approaching.

"Never mind," he said, dismissing him. "Well, shit, it doesn't matter anyway. It doesn't make any difference."

"How's that?" I asked.

"Because the thing is, the mayor gave them the go-ahead, and that's the thing we're making a statement about. Even if they pulled out altogether, it wouldn't matter. And there's all the other things, about her own lifestyle, marrying outside her race, letting people do whatever the hell they please. That's what's wrong with the world now, you know. Life's just one big party. Do whatever you want, sleep with whoever you want, it doesn't matter anymore."

"So," Lawrence said, "bombing whoever you want, that's a solution?"

Timmy smiled at Lawrence, like the detective was a simple child. "You can't change the world overnight, but every little bit helps. You bring awareness and enlightenment to people one person at a time."

I said, "How about Morton Dewart? Did he like your brand of awareness and enlightenment?"

Timmy shook his head. "That was too bad."

"What do you mean by that?"

"It was just too bad, that's all."

"There was no bear, was there, Timmy?" I said. "That was all bullshit, wasn't it?"

Timmy chuckled. "I thought it was, until one of your dad's guests got killed by one."

"But Morton. He didn't meet up with any bear, did he? He had a run-in with Gristle and Bone."

"Hey, Timmy," said Wendell, his voice tinged with caution. "I don't know if Mom wants you talking about that."

"It's okay, Wendell," Timmy said. "It's not going to make any difference."

I felt a chill.

"So it *was* the dogs," I said. For a fleeting second, I felt some sense of satisfaction. Then I reminded myself of my current situation, and got over it.

"Morton," Timmy began slowly, "had become a bit of a problem. The boys and I, we thought, when May brought him up here, that maybe he was kind of on the same wavelength with us, you know? And so, slowly, we started taking him into our confidence, letting him know what we planned to do, because he was a bright boy. He'd taken electronics at college, knew lots of helpful stuff we thought we could use." Timmy paused. "But it didn't work out."

"Two for two, huh, Timmy?" Dougie said, and laughed.

"What's that mean?" I asked.

Before Timmy could respond, Dougie said, "May has kind of bad luck with men."

I cocked my head. "May had a boyfriend before, who died in an accident."

Timmy said, "She told you about that, did she?"

"Yes," I said.

Timmy said, "I felt, we felt, that it was best for May to come home. To be with her family. With me, and Charlene and the boys. It's a nasty world out there, and home, well, that's the best place to be." Timmy paused. "We just had to establish the right conditions that made it conducive for May to return to the fold."

I wasn't sure I was really hearing what I thought I was hearing.

"I'm not sure I'm following, Timmy," I said. "What do you mean, establish the right conditions?"

"I got to drive," Dougie said, beaming.

"You guys should really shut up, you know," Wendell said.

"You ran him down?" I said to Dougie. "You ran down May's other boyfriend? A hit-and-run?"

"But Timmy and Mom made the phone calls," Dougie said. "They're better at that sort of thing. But you put me behind the wheel, and I know what to do."

"You made anonymous calls to May's employers," I said. "So she'd lose her jobs, one after another, run out of money, and have to come back here and live with you."

"It had to be done," Timmy said. "I was thinking of the boy. Of Jeffrey. It's not right, him growing up in a world like that. He's much better off with us. He's a wonderful young lad. So the odd call here, suggesting May might have stolen from a company, or that she was giving secrets to competing firms, in the long run, it was to help Jeffrey. And her, too."

"Is sending Jeffrey to his room without dinner helping him?" I asked. "Striking him with a belt? Is that helping him? And how about when he sees his own mother take a whipping from you? You think that's going to make him into the kind of man you want him to be?"

Timmy's eyes were full of fury and they bore into mine. "That's the whole problem with the world today. Everyone's afraid to discipline anymore. Kids need a firm hand. They *want* a firm hand. And it doesn't stop when they get older. As long as they're your own, you have a right to set them straight. I'll bet your father never took a hand to you. I'll bet you never got so much as a little pat on the ass, did you? And that's why now you're nothing but a big pussy, has to call a nigger up here to help you out. Imagine being that weak."

I never broke his stare. I said, "So maybe all I can hope then is that Jeffrey grows up big and strong so that someday, he can get justice for his mother by taking care of you."

And then Timmy spat at me. His spittle shot over the top of the gate fast as a bullet, landing on my right cheek just under my eye. I blinked, looked away, and used my sleeve to wipe it off.

I turned away, clenching my fists so tightly my nails left marks on my palms.

Lawrence, either to defuse the situation or get more information, or both, asked, "But what about Morton? What happened there?"

"You could tell," Timmy said. "There were signs. He wasn't with us. He wasn't prepared to do what was necessary. He was talking about going back to the city, just for a visit, see his family, but it was pretty obvious to me that he was going to talk. He was going to tell the authorities. He was going to tell them about our revolution."

A revolution. A bunch of nuts with a bomb and a van.

"So you decided to do something about it," I said.

"The boys and I invited Morton to come along with us when we took the dogs for a late-night walk. I think he must have thought something was up, but he came along, and we talked about this and that, it didn't really matter, because no matter what he told us then, we wouldn't have believed it. He was going to leave. And he was probably going to take May and Jeffrey with him." Timmy sighed. "No way I was going to allow that to happen."

"Of course not," Lawrence said.

"And so you took him into the woods," I said, "and sicked the dogs on him."

Timmy shrugged.

"What about the bear story?" I asked. "Where did that come from?"

"Well, once it was over, we started thinking, someone might come looking for him, or find him, which did happen the very next morning. And the first thing we thought of was the first thing everyone else thought of. That it had been a bear."

"And you came up with that story about Morton seeing a bear, and going off after it."

"We figured, if anyone came around asking questions, that was the story we'd stick with. And that's what we told May and Jeffrey, too."

I leaned up against the side of the pen, kicked at some old hay with my shoes. "Have you ever actually seen a bear around here, Timmy? Because you gave Orville and everyone a pretty good description of it."

"Nope. There's obviously some in these hills, but I've never laid eyes on one." He smirked. "I guess that's what you'd call ironic, huh? Considering."

"So what's your plan for us?" Lawrence asked. I wasn't so sure I wanted the answer to that question. "You going to turn the dogs loose on us, blame it on a bear again?"

Timmy gave that some thought. "I don't think so," he said. "I think we'll just shoot you."

34

CHARLENE RETURNED WITH ICE CREAM. Three bowls of vanilla, two with chocolate syrup on top. She handed them out to Wendell, Dougie, and Timmy.

Dougie spooned into his, looked contemplative, and asked his mother, "Do we have any sprinkles?"

"I think so," she said. "You want me to go get some?"

Timmy said, "Stop making your mother make so many trips. If you want sprinkles, go back and get them yourself."

Dougie set his bowl just inside the back of the van, on the floor, and said, "I'm gonna get some."

Timmy said, "You know what? I think I would like some chocolate sauce after all. Bring some back with you. The stuff in that little squeeze jar." Dougie nodded and ran out of the barn.

I said, "What about Tiff Riley?"

"Huh?"

"The guy at the co-op," I reminded him. "The one who was stabbed to death."

Timmy's eyes lit up. "What about him?"

"Did you kill him, too? You broke into the place to steal fertilizer and a barrel after hours, not expecting anyone to be there, and he got in the way. That about right, Timmy?"

"Wendell took care of that," Timmy said. "It's good to be giving the boys more responsibility. That's what their mom wants. Although I have to tell you"—he leaned toward the gate conspiratorially—"I'm not so sure about Dougie. I want to give him a little more to do, but I don't know that I'll ever be convinced that he's ready to handle the big stuff. But you can't argue with his mother, you know what I mean?"

"You talking about me?" asked Wendell, leaning up against the far side of the van. I could hear him scraping the bowl with his spoon, trying to get the last of the syrup.

It must have occurred to me before this, at some subconscious level, but it wasn't until this moment that it fully hit me.

This was an entire family of psychopaths.

Dougie had mowed down May's previous boyfriend with a car. He and his brother and Timmy had set the dogs on her next boyfriend, Morton. Wendell had murdered Tiff Riley. They'd set a lawyer's house on fire. Timmy had already indicated he was going to shoot me and Lawrence. They were preparing to set off a bomb in the middle of a small-town parade, an act that could kill any number of innocents. And all Charlene was worried about was that none of her men be hungry when they embarked on a killing spree. They were a family without a single conscience to share between themselves.

Except for May and, if it wasn't too late, her son, Jeffrey.

Dougie reappeared with a small glass bottle, about the size of a salt shaker, filled with multicolored sprinkles. He grabbed his bowl and covered his ice cream liberally with the dessert garnish.

"Where's my chocolate sauce?" Timmy asked.

Dougie winced. "Shit, sorry, I forgot."

"Honest to fucking Christ, Dougie," Timmy said.

"I can go back."

"Never mind."

"No, really, I can go back."

"My ice cream's almost totally melted anyway, so it's not worth it," Timmy said angrily. He shook his head in disgust.

"I'll go get you some syrup," Charlene said.

"I said it's not worth it!" Timmy shouted. "If your stupid son could just remember one goddamn thing . . ."

"Don't you talk about Dougie that way," Charlene said. She had a tone, like she was giving her husband, the boy's stepfather, a serious warning. "The reason he forgets things is because you pick on him and make him nervous."

"Yeah, it's all my fault."

Dougie's gaze moved between Timmy and his mother. He had a smudge of chocolate sauce, with sprinkles in it, on his chin.

Wendell said, "I think I'm gonna go get changed."

He left the barn, but was back only a few seconds later. "There's a guy down by the gate," he said worriedly.

"At this time of night?" Timmy said. "It's got to be long after midnight, isn't it?"

"Who is it?" Charlene asked.

"It looks like maybe he's on crutches or something."

Oh no.

"Crutches?" said Timmy, looking at me. "That must be Mr. Walker."

"I'm sure he's just getting some air," I said. "He likes to walk at night."

Timmy shook his head slowly. "A man on crutches doesn't go out for a midnight stroll. My guess is he's out looking for you."

"I'm not lying," I said. "He's just looking at the stars, I'll bet."

Timmy gave Wendell a nod. "Get him." Wendell grabbed his shotgun and slipped out the door.

"No!" I said. "Timmy, come on, leave him alone. He's just an old guy."

"If he's looking for you, and can't find you, then he goes back, starts making phone calls. That's not good. Can't have that." Timmy suddenly looked very serious, as though something had just occurred to him.

"What?" I said. "What are you thinking?"

"It's just . . . You see, you go missing, and your father comes looking for you. And now your father's going to go missing, and who's going to come looking for him?"

"No one," I said.

"What about the people at the camp? How many people are staying in those cabins?"

"Everyone's checked out," I lied. "After our guest got killed running away from that bear, they all got spooked and went home."

Timmy thought about that. "I don't think I believe you."

"It's true," Lawrence said. "I tried to talk a couple of them into staying, but they wouldn't hear of it."

Outside, in the distance, I could hear shouting, an argument. Gradually, the voices grew louder, more distinct, as they approached the barn.

"Jeez, old man, can you not move a little faster on those things?"

"Goddamn it, I'm going as fast as I can!"

Lawrence whispered to me, "We'll figure a way out of this."

"You have a plan?" I whispered back.

Lawrence said nothing.

Dad appeared first in the doorway, and one of his crutches got caught on the latch, sending him falling to the barn floor.

"Dad!" I said.

"Zachary?" he said, raising himself up and looking over at me through the slats of the stall gate.

"Dad, are you okay?"

"Yeah, yeah, I'm okay."

Wendell stepped in behind him, pointing the shotgun downwards, in Dad's direction.

"Mr. Walker," Timmy said, "you've had quite the week, haven't you? A body found on your property three days ago, a guest killed by a bear today. It's no wonder all your guests have packed their bags and taken off."

"Huh?" said Dad. "Where'd you hear that?"

I looked down at the floor, shook my head. Lawrence laid a consoling hand on my back.

Timmy strolled back over to the gate and said to me, "This is becoming a much fucking bigger problem by the moment. How long before someone else comes looking for you or your friend or your father?"

"It's late," I said. "People are asleep. No one will be looking for us."

The hell of it was, that was probably all too true. The Wrigleys were in their sixties and turned in early, and Bob was their age, too. Lana had gone back into town, figuring Orville might need to talk. And the next closest set of neighbors was probably half a mile away, at least.

"I don't know whether we can take that chance," Timmy said. "Wendell."

"Yeah?"

"You're going to have to go down to the cabins. Round up anyone staying in them, bring them all back here."

"How many's that?" he asked.

"I don't know. Three, four, something like that."

Three. Bob and Betty and Hank.

"Okay."

"You need your brother?"

Dougie, wiping his chin with his shirttail, looked up.

"No, I think I can handle it," Wendell said. "Long

as I have this." He waved the shotgun. "I'll be back in a bit," he said, and disappeared into the night.

So now Timmy was prepared to kill me and Lawrence, my father, Bob Spooner, and Betty and Hank Wrigley. There was no way he could leave any of us behind, not once he'd brought off his parade surprise.

Timmy went over to my father, put his hand under his arm, and hauled him over to the stall. "Stand back there," he ordered me and Lawrence. "Dougie, cover them."

Dougie grabbed a shotgun and held it on us as Timmy opened the gate and shoved my father in with us. His crutches were back on the floor where he'd fallen, and he limped over to us.

I hugged him.

"I was worried," Dad said. "You'd been gone a long time."

"Yeah, well, we're sort of in a situation," I said. "You hurt?"

"Uh, I don't think so," Dad said.

"How's your ankle?"

"Not too bad." He glanced back into the open area of the barn, took in the van, the blue drum in the back, the device perched atop it. "Is that what I think it is?" he asked.

Lawrence and I both nodded.

"Timmy," Lawrence said, "just where do you plan to be twenty-four hours from now?"

"Huh?"

"Tomorrow night. You're not planning on still being here, are you? Living in this farmhouse?"

Charlene gave him a sly, questioning look. Dougie, not capable of that, just looked, as did Timmy.

"I mean, come on," Lawrence said. "You're going to kill all of us, kill God knows how many at the parade, you think people aren't going to be looking for you? I don't think something this big is going to be left for Chief Orville Thorne to figure out." Lawrence glanced at me, did something with his eyebrows that seemed to say "No disrespect intended to your new stepbrother."

Lawrence continued. "This county, this town, it's going to be swarming with every law official imaginable, from Homeland Security to the Mounties. What happens when they find no one at Denny's Cabins? No. One. Not even the owner. You think you can pretend not to know what happened to all of us? We're just over the fucking hill."

"Maybe," said Charlene slowly, "I should start packing a few things."

"Yeah," Timmy agreed, nodding. "We might want to go away for a while."

"A while?" said Lawrence. "How about forever? Don't you have some like-minded brethren, committed to the same whacko causes, who'll hide you for a while?"

"Jesus, Timmy," said Dougie. "You don't think we could get caught for this, do you?"

"Look," Timmy said, working up some courage, "we do what we have to do. We're fighting for ideals that are bigger than just us, okay? We're sticking with this, we're not going to turn back now. But yeah, Charlene, you might want to throw a few things together."

"I want to take my Hot Wheels collection," Dougie said.

"What's going on?"

We all turned our attention to the open doorway. There stood Jeffrey, in slippers and a pair of striped pajamas, his hair all tousled.

"Why's everybody out here?" he said. "What's everybody doing?"

"Get back to bed!" Timmy shouted. That prompted Jeffrey to look over Timmy's way, and then his eyes landed on me, and Lawrence, and Dad.

"What are they doing in there?" Jeffrey said. He smiled at Lawrence. "Hi," he said, and made a small wave.

"Hi, Jeffrey," Lawrence said. "How's it going?"

"Okay," he said, quietly. He could tell something was going on. Something bad. "Why are they all locked up?" he asked his grandfather.

"Jeffrey, go back to the house. Charlene, take him back to the house."

"But I don't get it. Why are they there? Did they try to steal something?"

Timmy pounced on that. "That's right. They were trying to steal some tools. These are actually very bad men."

"That's not true, Jeffrey," I said.

"Jeffrey?" It was May, just outside the barn. "Jeffrey, are you in there?"

The boy looked back as his mother, wearing a long pink housecoat, stepped inside. It took her a second to take in the scene. Dougie, Charlene, Timmy, the three of us in the stall. The white van in the middle of the barn.

"What the hell is going on here?" she asked.

Timmy said, "May, take your boy and put him to bed. You know he's not ever supposed to be out here. You too, for that matter."

Jeffrey said, "Grandpa, these aren't bad men! They're good men! Even that one!" He pointed at Lawrence.

Timmy shook his head in anger. "Jeffrey, I've had just about enough—"

"He was really nice to me! He isn't mean like you!"

Timmy grabbed the boy by the arm and started shaking him. "Why, you little shit, I oughta—"

"Daddy!" May screamed. "Leave him alone!"

Jeffrey was leaning back, trying to break free of his grandfather, who was holding on to him with one hand and trying to swat his cheek with the other. Jeffrey was waving frantically with his free arm, working to deflect the blows.

May ran forward, grabbed her father, which allowed Jeffrey to wriggle free. Now Timmy had to wrestle with his daughter, whom he grabbed by the shoulders and flung to the barn floor.

"I hate you!" Jeffrey screamed at him, and burst into tears.

Timmy stood there, looking down at his daughter, wondering whether he should offer to help her up or not. May was looking from him to Jeffrey and, finally, to me. In addition to this domestic crisis she was having, she seemed to be trying to get her head around why the hell I was penned in with my father and Lawrence.

"Mr. Walker?" she said. I wasn't sure whether she meant me or my father. She got to her feet, ignoring her father's outstretched arm, and took three steps toward the stall. "Mr. Walker, what's going on?" She was directing the question at me, not Dad.

I was thinking, the way things were going, that maybe May was our new last hope. That if she knew the truth, if she knew the extent of her father's evil, maybe she could do something. That if she were presented with the truth, and could throw it back in Timmy's face, maybe he'd reconsider what he was going to do.

I said, evenly, "Your father's getting ready to kill us and a whole lot of other people, May, that's what's going on."

"Shut up!" Timmy shouted at me. "May, get out of here!" He grabbed her by the shoulders and started turning her away.

"Don't touch her!" Jeffrey shouted, still crying.

"Ask him about your boyfriends!" I shouted. "Ask him what happened to Morton, and Gary!"

May twisted out of her father's grip, looked back at me. "What?"

"I told you to shut up," Timmy said.

"What's he talking about, my boyfriends?"

"It's not a coincidence," I said. "First one gets hit by a car, then another gets killed in the woods."

"Gary?" May said, looking at Timmy. "The hit-and-run?"

Timmy tried to adopt a gentler stance, reachin

his hands out to May's shoulders, but she took a step back. "Honey, you and Jeffrey need to go back to the house. We can talk about this later. We've all said a few things that we're probably going to regret later. And we're kind of busy out here, in case you hadn't noticed."

"Busy doing what? What have you been doing out here? You've been out here for days, working on something." She caught a glimpse inside the van. "What's all this?" She whirled around. "What was he talking about, my boyfriends?"

"He killed them both," I said. "With help from Wendell and Dougie. And sabotaged your jobs with anonymous phone calls. So you'd have no choice but to come back home."

May was stupefied. Jeffrey, who had stopped crying, was looking a bit baffled as well.

"That's not true," Timmy said softly. "You know I'd never do anything like that."

May looked at her father as though seeing him for the first time. "You're a monster," she whispered. "I guess I've always known it, but I've never known until now just how big a monster you really are."

She turned and reached out her hand to grab Jeffrey's hand. She was about to exit the barn when Charlene stood in her path.

"What?" May said. "Get out of my way."

Charlene looked over at Timmy, her look cold and dispassionate. Her eyes had no life in them.

Timmy shook his head slowly. "Son of a bitch." He and Charlene looked into each other's eyes, neither of them saying a word, but there was plenty of information being exchanged. They were making some hard decisions. Facing up to some cold realities.

"Jesus," Timmy said, and shook his head again. "Charlene, put the two of them—Jesus H. Christ—put them in the pantry at the back of the house, I don't know. Lock them in there, and we'll sort this out later."

"You're going to lock up your own daughter?" May asked. "Your own grandson?" Then, screaming, "What are you! What the fuck are you?"

Charlene had the gun in her hand that she'd had earlier, and she nudged May with it. "Come on," she said. "You and your boy, you got none of my blood, so pulling this trigger wouldn't be all that hard for me."

Timmy started to say something, then stopped himself.

Charlene motioned for May and Jeffrey to go through the door ahead of her. She gave May's shoulder a shove on the way out.

A look of resignation had come over Timmy's face. What chance did we have, I thought, if he was already considering the possibility of killing his own daughter and grandson?

"That was a stupid, stupid thing to do, telling her those things," he said to me.

"She should know," I said. "She should know just what kind of loving father she has."

Timmy simmered, the air whistling in and out of nostrils.

"It'll be easier when Wendell gets back here with the others," he said, as much to himself as to me. "Then we can do everybody at once."

35

I WANDERED TOWARD THE BACK CORNER of the stall, leaned my head in close to Lawrence's.

"Wendell's going to be back here any minute with Bob and Betty and Hank," I said. "Then he's going to kill the whole lot of us."

"Yeah," said Lawrence. "I've been following."

"What if we hop the gate, rush Timmy, maybe one of us gets to a gun before Dougie does?"

Lawrence thought. "What about your bear spray?"

"Used up," I said. "All gone."

He sighed. "Rushing Timmy may be our only option. But I don't think we'll all survive it. He'll get at least one of us before the other two can take him. And that's only if Dougie's slow off the mark."

"I'll go first," said Dad, who had edged close enough to hear what we were talking about.

"No, Dad," I said.

"Look, I'm the old guy, I've had a good run. Let me go first, and while he's dealing with me, you two grab him."

The thing was, even if I liked the idea, which I didn't, it would take Dad, in his condition, so much longer to hop the gate that there wouldn't be the slightest element of surprise.

"Something you'd like to share with the class?" Timmy said. We broke apart. "A little less chatter, okay?"

We said nothing. Timmy called Dougie over to the back of the van.

"Okay," Timmy said. "I know the parade's not till morning, but I want you in position early, before the sun comes up. You got to be somewhere that's close to the parade route, and close to the town hall, because I want both of them taken out. You understand?"

"Sure, Timmy."

"Good. Before you go, I'll set the bomb so it's ready to receive the signal from the remote detonator, so you won't have to worry about doing that."

"Okay. That's good, because you're better at that stuff than me."

"No kidding," Timmy said. Dougie's brow furrowed, like maybe he was picking something up on his sarcasm detector.

"Now this," Timmy said, holding up what looked like a walkie-talkie, with a short stubby antenna and a number of buttons on front, "is your remote detonator. It couldn't be simpler. See this red button here?"

Dougie examined it. "Yes."

"You press it, the bomb goes off."

"I can do that." He held the device in his hand. "But I won't press it now."

"It wouldn't matter if you did, because the bomb's not turned on. But once it is on, you have to be careful."

"What if I drop it or something?"

"Remember I mentioned the box?" Timmy led him over to the nearby workbench and showed Dougie a small plastic case, about the size a soldering gun comes in. He opened it up, and it was filled with spongy foam, the same kind of stuff that held the surveillance gear in Lawrence's equipment case. A recess, cut the same shape as the detonator, was cut into the foam.

"You carry the detonator in here, and take it out when you need it. That way, even if you dropped this case, or smashed it up against a wall, the red button can't go down."

"Whew," said Dougie, grinning. "That's a relief."

"You're *sure* you can handle all this?"

"Oh yeah, no problem."

"Because, and I have to be honest with you here, Dougie, I'd normally do this myself, or trust it to Wendell, but your mother thinks it's time you were given more responsibility. And she wants you to take on something big, like this."

"I know. It's for my self-esteem. I think it's already starting to feel bigger."

"That's really terrific," Timmy said.

Lawrence was watching Dougie and Timmy, and I knew he was doing mental calculations. Distance and time. Time and distance.

"We gonna put it in there now?" Dougie asked, pointing to the detonator and the foam-filled box on the workbench.

"Soon enough," Timmy said. "Soon enough."

"I'm back!"

It was Wendell's voice, but it wasn't Wendell who made the first entrance. Bob Spooner stepped in, wearing a pair of boxers, a jacket, and a pair of work-boots without socks. Betty and Hank hadn't been given any time to get dressed either. She was in a long blue flannel nightgown and slippers, and Hank was in blue pajamas and bare feet. Wendell came in last, the shotgun leveled at their backs.

"Oh man," Lawrence whispered.

"Over this way, folks!" Timmy said, greeting them with a wave of the hand and directing them to the stall. "Welcome!" He unlatched the gate and swung it wide enough to admit the new prisoners. Hank's face was wild with fear. Betty looked scared, too, but at the same time there was a calmness about her. And Bob looked dazed, as if this were all some sort of dream, that he'd wake up a few hours later and none of this would have happened.

I hardly knew what to say to them as Timmy closed the gate.

"Things are starting to come together," he said.

"So," said Wendell. "I got 'em. Good, huh?"

"Yeah. You done good."

He reached into his pocket, pulled out several sets of car keys. "And I got everybody's keys, in case any one thought of trying to get away, they wouldn't ge very far. And I even yanked out the phone line in the first cabin. It was the only cabin with one, I checked."

Timmy nodded happily. "Wendell, that was good thinking. Really good thinking. I hadn't thought of that."

Wendell blushed. "It was no big deal."

"I'd have thought of that," Dougie said. "If you'd told me."

Timmy, his back to Dougie, looked at Wendell and rolled his eyes. He pulled Wendell to one side, close enough to the gate that I could hear their discussion.

"I'm a little worried about Dougie," Timmy said. "You think he can do this?"

"I guess," Wendell said.

"I was thinking, what might make sense would be, you drive into town a little later after Dougie goes, stick with him till the sun comes up, in case he gets nervous or anything, and then after he blows up the van, you can give him a lift back out here."

"Yeah, I can do that. But it might make Mom mad. She wants him to do this alone."

"Okay, fine. I've also got another little problem."

"What's that?"

Timmy's voice got even quieter. "I'm gonna need a place to put all these bodies."

"How many?"

Timmy took a few steps back, his face appearing round the corner of the stall. He was counting us. Then he disappeared from view. He whispered to Wendell, "At least six." He paused. "Maybe a couple more. I don't know. I gotta sort that out later."

"Gee, where we gonna do that? I don't have to dig a hole, do I? I mean, if it was just a couple, that would be okay, but that many? That'll take forever."

I knew something about the frustrations associated with getting your kids to do chores, but this was a bit beyond my realm of experience.

"Any other ideas?" Timmy asked.

"What if I put them in the lake? Like, we put their bodies in a boat and sink the boat?"

"I don't know. Won't they just float back up?"

"What if it's a boat with a deck, and we stuff them under the deck?"

"Any boats like that down at Walker's place?"

"I don't know. I never looked."

"Why don't you go check it out. See if any other ideas present themselves to you."

"Okay."

"Oh, and wish Dougie good luck. He might be gone before you get back."

Wendell went over to his brother, patted him on the back, said, "Good luck, man. I'll see you later, okay?"

Dougie gave him a thumbs-up, and then Wendell slipped away.

"Did you hear any of that?" Bob Spooner whispered to me.

"All of it," I said.

"They're talking about how to get rid of our bodies!"

"Shhh!" I said. "I know. I know."

"Dougie!" Timmy said. "I'm getting a bit tired watching our guests all the time. And you're going be heading off soon, so I wonder if you could do me a favor before you go."

"Yeah, Timmy?"

"Why don't you get the dogs and bring them over?"

"Sure thing," Dougie said. As if things weren't already bad enough, we were about to get Gristle and Bone as babysitters.

"Do you believe in luck?" Lawrence whispered.

"Why?" I said.

"Because we sure could use some now."

36

TIMMY PICKED UP A SHOTGUN and kept it trained on all of us, the barrel aimed through the boards of the gate, while Dougie left to get the pups.

There were six of us. And one of him.

Lawrence shot me a look. I had a pretty good idea what he was thinking. This might be our only chance alone with Timmy. Our last chance to do anything before the others came back. Before the dogs arrived.

We knew now, as if there had ever been any doubt, what the dogs were capable of.

Lawrence stood at the back of the pen. From there, if he took a run at the gate, given the kind of shape he was in, he could put his hands on top of it, pitch his legs up to one side, and vault over in one smooth motion. But Timmy would see him coming no matter how quickly, and be able to get off a shot.

What if two of us tried it, at the same time? Well, the stall was only about six feet across, and if two of us tried to vault over the gate at the same time, w might present a more complicated target for Timmy, but we'd also get our legs tangled together at the same time.

Okay, what if—

"You cocksucking bastard!" Hank Wrigley charged the gate, hooking his bare foot on the bottom board, trying to get his other leg over. But Hank was no Lawrence. He was probably my father's age, and there was no way he was going to leap over that gate in a hurry.

"Hank!" Betty screamed. *"Hank!"*

It was almost leisurely, the way Timmy tipped his shotgun up, pumped it, and pulled the trigger. The blast was deafening.

Hank came flying off the gate toward us, and Lawrence tried to break his fall. Hank fell into his arms, and once he had him, Lawrence laid him down on the floor, gently. His left pajama sleeve was torn and bloody.

"My God, Hank!" Betty said, dropping to her knees to see how badly he was hurt. "You stupid son of a bitch!"

I thought she might have thrown her arms around him, but Betty, even as shocked as she had to be, was all business. It hadn't been that long since she'd retired from nursing, and I was guessing she hadn't forgotten a thing. She started tearing away his sleeve.

"Ohhhh," Hank said. "Ohhhh."

I looked at Timmy, who shrugged. "What's he been smokin'?" he said.

Bob said, "How is he? Is he going to be okay?"

"It's his arm," Betty said, already ripping Hank's sleeve right off and turning it into a tourniquet. "If we can get him to a hospital," she said, breathlessly, "he'll be okay."

"Ohhhh," Hank said again. "I'm sorry. I'm sorry. I just wanted to . . ."

"Stupid old man," Betty said.

"We need to get this guy to a hospital," I said to Timmy.

He looked at me, grinned, shook his head. "That's a good one."

"Timmy," I said, "can I ask you something?" He shrugged. "What's going to happen to May? And Jeffrey?" He was silent. "You going to kill them, too?"

"Shut up," he said.

"If you don't, I'm sure Charlene will. May and Jeffrey aren't *her blood*, you know. What's it to her if they die?"

Timmy frowned, took a step closer to the gate. "Don't you think you've got enough to worry about without worrying about my family problems?"

There was the sound of snarling and growling outside, and then the dogs made their entrance. Gristle and Bone dashed around the barn, running here and there, bumping into each other, sticking their snouts into mounds of hay, under the van, over by the work bench, then the gate.

When they got to us, they shoved their jagged snouts between the boards and started acting like they were on crack. They barked and snarled incessantly, chewed the boards, broke off bits of wood with their large, viselike jaws.

"Settle down, settle down," Timmy said.

The dogs ignored him. In the stall, Bob, Lawrence, Dad, and I moved to the far end. Betty held her spot, tending to her husband.

"Settle down!" Timmy shouted, and the dogs fell silent. "That's better. Sit."

The dogs sat.

"Stay."

The dogs stayed. The two of them sat, side by side, panting lawn ornaments from hell, staring between the boards at us with their dark, pit bull eyes.

Timmy said, "Any of you folks move suddenly, and the dogs, they're gonna go nuts. Understand?" Our collective silence was taken as a yes. "Good. I've got a couple things to do." He crawled back into the van.

Dougie entered the barn. "They kind of got away from me," he said.

From inside the van, Timmy said, "It's okay. I got them on guard duty."

For the next quarter of an hour or so, not much happened. We sat quietly in our pen while Timmy did some final tinkering with the van. He hopped out the back and closed the tailgate, pulling on the handle once to satisfy himself that it was shut securely.

"I think we're ready," Timmy said. "The device is all ready to go. You push the button, it does its job."

Dougie smiled. "I guess I'm a little nervous, if you want to know the truth."

"That's understandable. It's like you're going on a great mission. Actually, you are going on a great mission."

Dougie, embarrassed, looked at the floor.

"You ready?" Timmy asked.

"Yeah."

"You remember everything you have to do? You've got everything you need?"

"I do," Dougie said. "I really do. Park the van near the town hall, along the parade route. Find a place on high ground where I have a good view. Meet up later with Wendell, he'll give me a ride back."

"And then we're going to have to get out of here," Timmy said. "We're going to have to leave this place."

Dougie nodded. "I'll miss it. I've liked it here. It's real pretty." He called over in our direction. "Mr. Walker? Like, the older one?"

Dad said, "Yes?"

"Thanks for letting us rent your farmhouse. We've really liked it here."

Dad looked at me, speechless.

"Okay," said Timmy. "That's it, then."

"I really appreciate you letting me do this," Dougie said, and he threw his arms around his stepfather and hugged him. Timmy patted the young man's back a couple of times, with some reluctance, it seemed, and pulled away.

Dougie opened the van door, got into the driver's seat. He put on his seatbelt, turned the key in the ignition. The engine caught, and exhaust billowed out the tailpipe almost immediately, in the direction of the stall.

"Timmy? The door?"

Timmy Wickens ran around to the front of the van and pushed the barn door, which had only been wid-

enough to allow a person through, all the way open. For the first time, from our spot in the pen, we could see the yard, the farmhouse off in the distance to the left, the gate to the driveway just beyond that to the right. I thought I could see, walking toward the barn, Wendell. Coming back from the cabins with some plan for getting rid of our dead bodies, no doubt.

Dougie put the van in drive and began to pull out just as Wendell was reaching the barn.

Timmy gave a small wave goodbye, in case Dougie might see him in his rear-view mirror. Timmy turned around as the van pulled away, and his eyes landed on the walkie-talkie-like detonator, still sitting atop its plastic carrying case, over on the workbench.

"For fuck's sake," he said. "Can't that boy remember anything?"

He ran over to the workbench, just as Wendell was entering the barn. "Hey!" he said, cheerful. "So Dougie's on his way!"

Gristle and Bone put their noses to the air.

Timmy Wickens turned, the detonator in his hand, and said, "The stupid idiot forgot this! Get this to him!"

Wendell ran over to the workbench and grabbed the detonator, still not in its box, from his father, then turned to run after the van.

What happened next happened very, very fast.

37

THE VAN, its rear red taillights coming on as Dougie
tapped the brakes going across the bumpy yard, was
nearing the house when Charlene stepped out to
wave goodbye.

Then, as I strained to peer harder into the distance, I saw that she wasn't just waving. She had
something in her hand. A brown lunch bag.

Wendell took the detonator from his father's hand
like a relay runner grasping a baton. He pivoted,
started running after his brother.

"Don't hit the red button!" Timmy warned.

"Don't worry!" Wendell shouted back. "I know
how it works!"

The pit bulls, Gristle and Bone, raised their snouts
again. Something had caught their attention and was
distracting them from their task of guarding the prisoners. Their hindquarters lifted from the floor, and
they turned about, attempting to track down the
source of what was wafting up their nostrils.

They fixed their eyes on Wendell, and their heads turned with him as he ran from the barn.

I knew then what had sparked their interest. It was the scent of fish guts, smeared all over Wendell's pants and the front of his shirt from his plunge into the pit.

The dogs were transformed into low-flying missiles.

"Hey!" Timmy shouted at the dogs. "Get back to your post!"

They were oblivious. Nothing else mattered now. They were on a mission to find their dinner. Their paws pounded the floor as they took off after Wendell, their jaws already open in anticipation, the gums pulling back away from their teeth through the sheer force of their acceleration.

Wendell never saw them coming. He was running, and then he wasn't, as each dog grabbed hold of a leg, like a pair of lions bringing down a gazelle.

Wendell screamed.

"Hey!" Timmy shouted again at the dogs. "Halt!"

"Let's move," Lawrence whispered. With Timmy occupied by the dogs and what they were evidently about to do to Wendell, he wasn't watching the stall. Lawrence hopped the gate, slid back the bolt, and opened it wide for the rest of us.

"An ambulance," said Betty, still kneeling over and tending to her husband. "We need an ambulance."

Wendell's screams were unlike anything I'd ever heard before. I'd once heard a man trapped in a car trunk with a python, but even that was nothing like this. As the dogs brought him down they ripped into his legs with an insane ferocity. Wendell pitched forward, the detonator still gripped tightly in his right hand.

At the house, Charlene turned her head to see what the fuss was about.

I saw Wendell's hand fall toward the ground.

The van slowed as it passed the farmhouse. Charlene held out the lunchbag as Dougie stuck his hand out the window to grab it.

The dogs, frenzied, ripped away chunks of Wendell's jeans. And, judging from the blood that was instantly appearing, chunks of him, too.

His hand, still clutching the detonator, slammed into the ground.

The van blew up.

The explosion was so intense, the fireball so massive, I never even saw scraps of sheet metal or glass blowing outwards. One second there was a van, and the next, this huge orange ball.

Timmy, who was out of the barn and about ten yards away from the dogs and Wendell, was blown back by the force of the explosion. In the barn, we could feel the shock wave of heat blast past us.

I turned away, fearful that some bits of debris might strike me, get in my eye. When I looked back a second later, I couldn't see the farmhouse. At first I thought it was obscured by the flames and smoke. But then I realized the farmhouse was gone.

No, not all of it, as it turned out. There was a small part, at the back, still standing. The rest of the building—a pile of rubble with a few timbers and beams poking out of it—was ablaze.

"Ahhhh!" Wendell screamed. "Mommmmm!"

There appeared to be no mother left to hear Wendell's cries.

Lawrence said to Betty, "Can he move?"

She looked at Hank, whose eyes were drifting open and then shut. "I don't think it's a good idea."

Lawrence ran over to the workbench, where two shotguns were leaned up. He grabbed one, returned to the stall, and handed it to Betty. "In case Timmy comes back," Lawrence said. "I think he's the only one left we have to worry about."

I grabbed Dad by the arm, started leading him out, and he did his best on the healing ankle, skipping and hopping.

"We need to get help," I said.

"They took the car keys, they cut the phone line," Dad reminded me. The keys to the other vehicles outside the Wickens place would probably be inside the house that didn't exist anymore.

"Can you hop your way back to the cabin?" I asked.

"I think so."

"Take the tractor," I said. "You leave the key in it, right?"

Dad said, "Yes."

"Go into Braynor, or the closest house with a phone."

Dad nodded, and was about to start hopping and skipping off into the night, when Bob Spooner slapped his hand over Dad's shoulder and said, "I can get there faster."

Dad looked at me. "You think?"

I smiled at Bob. "Yeah, you go. Get an ambulance, get Orville, get the fire department, get everybody."

"Got it," Bob said.

"And tomorrow, you can take me fishing."

Bob managed a smile back. "Sounds good." He ran off into the night.

I turned to Lawrence. "May," I said. "And Jeffrey."

Lawrence took a look at the house, at how little was left of it, saw the back part, where the kitchen was, still standing. But the flames were quickly spreading to it.

We ran, side by side, past the dogs, who had somehow managed to nudge Wendell over and were ripping into his belly.

Wendell was no longer screaming.

"Get off him, you fuckers!" Timmy screamed. He barely glanced at Lawrence and me as we ran past. I looked back, saw Timmy run back into the barn. He was heading, I guessed, for the other shotgun.

Lawrence and I reached the back door of the farmhouse together, and he hopped up the steps to open the door. Some smoke billowed out, but the room wasn't fully engulfed yet. What hindered our efforts, however, was that the explosion had cut off power to the house, and there were no lights.

"May!" I shouted as loud as I could. "Jeffrey!"

Lawrence shouted, too. "Where are you?"

We held our breath a moment, not wanting to miss their call back. The only sound, and it was considerable, was the fire.

"In here!" May.

"Help!" Jeffrey.

Their voices came from the left, and we worked our way over, bumping into kitchen chairs, knocking things off the table until our eyes adjusted to the dim moonlight coming through the window. I found a narrow door, with a padlock attached.

It was getting unbearably hot in the kitchen.

"It's locked," I told Lawrence.

"Help!" May screamed. They would have heard the explosion, be feeling the heat from the fire that was sure to spread into this room any second.

"Hang on!" I shouted.

Outside, I heard a shotgun blast. I looked out the window, saw Timmy standing over Wendell, pump the gun, then another blast. A third, and a fourth.

Lawrence grabbed something off the kitchen counter, an appliance of some kind. An electric can opener. He bashed the lock with it. Five, eight, ten times, until the can opener's plastic casing shattered into half a dozen pieces.

"Hang on!" Lawrence shouted. He was opening drawers now, rummaging around in the dark. "Shit!" he said. He drew out a hand, shook it as though trying to dry it. Fleck of something dark flew off. Blood. He'd encountered a drawerful of knives.

Then he was into another drawer, and came out with a short silver mallet, the kind used to flatten meat.

He swung at the lock like a madman, and finally, the hardware that the padlock snapped onto came free. Lawrence got the pantry door open a crack, worked his fingers in, and broke the door open.

May pushed Jeffrey out first, then followed. "What's happened?" she asked. "What was that noise?"

"Later," I said. "We're going down to my father's place."

The four of us went out the door as the roof caved in on the kitchen. Smoke and sparks billowed out around us.

In the light of the fire, Timmy stood, motionless, over the bodies of Wendell and the two pit bulls.

"This way," Lawrence said, moving May and Jeffrey toward the gate and the lane that would lead us back to the cabins. Jeffrey had, clutched in one hand, the two *Star Wars* figures Lawrence had purchased for him that afternoon.

When he caught me noticing, he said, "I hid 'em in the pantry."

We were all running now, and as we passed the gate, there was a loud racket coming from around the bend that led down to the cottages. Suddenly, Dad's customized tractor appeared, Bob Spooner at the wheel. He saluted us as he blasted past for the highway.

May looked, agog, at the front of the farmhouse. Bits and pieces of van, no doubt mixed with bits and pieces of Dougie, were scattered as far as we could see in the moonlight.

It was anyone's guess where the remains of Charlene had been scattered to.

We ran down the lane and around the bend, and when I saw the light over the back door of Dad's cabin, it was like a beacon of hope, a sign that maybe, just maybe, we were going to get out of this alive.

We filed into Dad's cabin, Lawrence first, then May and Jeffrey. I waited for Dad to catch up, held the door for him.

"Betty and Hank," I said.

"Bob'll get help," Dad assured me. "You can count on him."

"He's still out there," I told Lawrence. "Timmy's still out there, with a shotgun."

He nodded. "We have to hide everyone until help arrives."

Dad said, "A boat. Why don't we take a boat?"

Lawrence and I liked that idea, and ushered everyone out the front door of the cabin and down to the water.

Somewhere, off in the distance, I thought I heard a siren.

Dad had a small fishing boat like Bob's, and we got May and Jeffrey into it. Dad, with some difficulty, got himself straddled over the back bench, and started pulling the outboard motor cord while Lawrence and I untied the boat from the dock.

"When it's safe," I said, "I'll keep flashing your cabin lights on and off. Just go out there and sit until the signal."

Dad gave me a thumbs-up, gently turned the throttle on the outboard, and the boat glided away over the dark lake.

"I want to sneak back, keep an eye on Betty and

Hank," Lawrence said. "Why don't you wait here for the troops to arrive."

I nodded as Lawrence ran off.

And then, for the first time in several hours, I was alone. I stood at the end of the dock, listening to the receding sound of Dad's boat as he took May and Jeffrey to temporary safety.

The sirens sounded as though they were getting closer. Bob had done good.

I slipped into Dad's cabin and turned off all the lights. No sense advertising to Timmy Wickens, wherever he might be, that anyone was here. In the dark, I ran some water at the sink and filled a glass. I drank it down fast, filled the glass a second time.

I wanted to call Sarah, but with the phone line cut, there wasn't much I could do there. Our cells, our keys, were all with Wendell. In his jacket. So long as the dogs hadn't eaten them, we'd probably be able to retrieve them from his body when the sun came up.

I went back outside, walked down to the water's edge and gazed up at the stars. There was a glow in the sky beyond the trees. The last of the farmhouse hadn't quite burned to the ground yet.

So much chaos, so much death, and now, things seemed almost peaceful.

My shirt—Lawrence's shirt—reeked of smoke, and I felt confident I could slip into cabin 3, strip off and find a fresh one, without having to turn on any lights. I walked over to the cabin, went in from the lake side.

Once the door had closed behind me and I was in the main room, the lights flashed on.

I blinked a couple of times, trying to adjust my eyes more quickly than they wanted to.

Standing by the other door, with his shotgun aimed straight at my chest, was Timmy Wickens.

38

"WHERE ARE MY DAUGHTER AND GRANDSON?" Timmy asked, the shotgun still raised and staring me in the face.

"They're okay," I said. "We got them out of the farmhouse just before the rest of it went." I paused. "I don't know if that's good news or bad news as far as you're concerned."

He ignored that. "The rest of them," he said. "They're all dead."

I nodded. "So it would seem. Dougie couldn't have survived that explosion. Same with Charlene. And I'm guessing the dogs finished off Wendell."

Timmy remained stone-faced. "The dogs are dead too," he said.

I nodded again. It would have been hard to offer condolences and sound sincere about all the lives lost, so I opted to say nothing.

"Where are they now?" Timmy asked. "My daughter. Jeffrey."

"They're safe," I said.

"I asked you where they are."

"They're already miles from here," I said. "Getting as far away as possible, as fast as possible."

"I didn't see any cars leave here," he said. "Wendell got all the keys."

"He missed a set," I said, and swallowed. The sirens sounded closer. "They're gone, and there isn't anything I can do about it. Even if I wanted to. Wendell collected cell phones, too. I can't call them, and if I could, they haven't got a phone."

Timmy Wickens thought about that, ran his tongue over his teeth. Then he sucked the spit off them, hissing, and bared his teeth like one of his now dead pit bulls.

Or a wolf.

"It's your fault," he said, and pulled the trigger.

The bullet went past my left ear and blew a hole in the wall. It was like thunder. It couldn't have been meant to hit me. I was too close for him to miss.

"Everything's gone wrong since you came up here. Started nosing around. Talking to May behind my back."

He fired again. This time the bullet went past my right ear and blew out a window. I was cold with fear.

But I managed to find some words in my throat. I needed time for help to arrive, and talking might stretch things out.

"I think things went wrong when you let your dogs kill Morton Dewart," I said, and swallowed. "That's what got people asking questions. That, and killing off Riley, stealing the fertilizer, those kinds of things."

I thought I heard the sound of crunching gravel, of a car coming down the hill to the cabins.

Timmy motioned for me to move toward the center of the room. He took three steps in, away from the door.

"I was going to be somebody," Timmy said.

"Excuse me?"

"I was going to be somebody. People would've talked about me. I'd have gone into the history books."

"I suppose that's true," I said. "Just like McVeigh."

Timmy nodded.

"But people would have had to find out," I said. "You'd have to be caught for the world to know what you'd done."

Timmy thought about that. "Eventually. I wouldn't have minded waiting a little while. Turning on the news, hearing about them looking for me. Other people, cheering me on." He moved forward and pushed the barrel of the gun up against my neck. "Except not people like you. People who don' give a fuck about how this country is going into the toilet."

Unless I stepped back, I couldn't talk or swallow. I inched backwards, but Timmy moved with me, the barrel pushing into the flesh of my neck. Before I knew it, I was up against the wall.

"Why don't you make a run for it?" I said, my chin raised, head tilted to one side. "Just go. Disappear into the woods."

He grinned. "There's still a nasty bear out there."

No, I thought. There isn't.

Timmy forced the gun a little harder into my

neck. "But with this, I guess I'd stand a pretty good chance, wouldn't I?"

"So go," I said, shifting my neck a bit to the right to keep from choking. "Take off."

Timmy stared at me. "I got just one thing left to do," he said. "And that's deal with you."

Could I run? Could I rush him? Was there anything I could do to avoid getting shot by Timmy Wickens? With the barrel of a gun already pressed up against my neck?

I thought of Sarah. And Paul, and Angie.

"Hear those sirens?" I asked Timmy. "Sounds like they're already up at your place. Fire department, ambulance. Police. They're going to be down here soon. You don't have much time."

The door he'd been standing by when I came in suddenly swung open. Chief Orville Thorne stepped in, his pistol drawn.

Even though Orville had a gun and I didn't, Timmy Wickens kept his weapon fixed on me.

"Timmy, Mr. Wickens," Orville said. "Put down your weapon."

Timmy grinned, and showed his teeth again. "Well, look who's here to save the day. How's that make you feel, Mr. Walker? You're waiting for help to arrive, and look who shows."

"Hi, Orville," I said, and tried to swallow my fear.

Orville didn't look at me. He raised his pistol, wrapped both hands around it.

"Come on, Timmy," he said, almost pleading. "Put your gun down."

"Orville, take a walk," Timmy said, his voice

confident. He'd been in this place before. "Go home. Go home before I take away your hat *and* your gun."

Orville kept his pistol aimed at Timmy. But he kept blinking, like he had sweat or tears in his eyes.

"Maybe I'm not getting through to you, Orville," Timmy said. "You walk away and you don't even see what it is I have to do. You can say you came in just a minute too late, that Mr. Walker was already dead, that I was gone. You've always been a reasonable sort, Orville, and this would be the wrong time to be stupid."

Timmy glanced at Orville, just for a moment, long enough to see that Orville was scared. Maybe not as scared as I was. But scared.

"Orville," Timmy said. "Take. A. Walk."

I stared down the barrel of the shotgun. Timmy smiled, shook his head at Orville's foolishness, and squeezed his finger around the trigger.

Orville Thorne shot Timmy Wickens in the neck.

Timmy said, "Ack."

The shotgun fell away from me.

His mouth stayed open, but all that could be heard was a faint gurgling sound. He clamped one hand to the wound, blood spilling out between his fingers. He held on to the shotgun with the other hand, turned it toward Orville. Before he could fire Orville shot him again, this time in the chest, and Timmy dropped to the floor.

Orville took a step forward and in the moment before Timmy Wickens closed his eyes, Orville said, "He's my brother."

39

Y THE TIME THE SUN CAME UP, Hank Wrigley was in
aynor District Hospital getting patched up, Betty
his side. What was once a farmhouse was nothing
t a pile of smoldering embers. A pumper from the
aynor Fire Department was still pouring water
to the site. They'd run a hose down to the lake and
re pumping from there.

After Orville shot Timmy Wickens, I flicked the
hts at Dad's cabin on and off until he came back
the boat with May and Jeffrey. Lawrence showed
not long after that, once the ambulance atten-
nts had arrived and left with Betty and Hank. We
th made a point of keeping May and her son away
m cabin 3, where Timmy lay in a pool of his own
od.

Dr. Heath was roused from his slumber so that he
ld pronounce Timmy Wickens and Wendell
d. Nobody was able to find enough of Dougie or
arlene to make a similar assessment.

The coroner was good enough to retrieve our car

keys from what was left of Wendell's jacket and
pants. The dogs had chewed through them, and him
pretty thoroughly.

The phone company even sent someone out to get
the line to Dad's cabin reconnected. The cops—and
they were from every level imaginable—were turning
Dad's place into a temporary command center, and
wanted the phone operating pronto.

Once the phone was working, I called Sarah and
gave her the short version. I told her I'd be home
sometime in the late afternoon, and would write
something for the next day's edition of *The
Metropolitan*. About a family of homicidal psychos
who'd planned to blow up a parade.

"You still want this other information you were
asking me about the other day?" she said. About a
shelter, where a woman with a child on the run
could go.

"She's not exactly on the run now," I said. "But
she's going to need some help. Everything she had is
gone. No clothes, nothing."

"I'll start making some calls," Sarah said.

"See if we have some old stuff of Paul's that would
fit a ten-year-old."

Lawrence, who'd walked into Dad's study in the
middle of my conversation, said, "They can stay with
me till we get them set up someplace."

"That'd be great," I said to Lawrence. I told Sarah
of Lawrence's offer and added, "She's a nice woman.
She's been through a lot. And she and Jeffrey are on
their own now. That's actually going to be a plus

given who she was with, but she's still going to be traumatized for a while."

"Sure," said Sarah. "And you? Are you okay?"

I smiled. "I'm a complete disaster."

"Get home safely."

I hung up and found Dad in the kitchen, sitting at the table, looking dazed and tired. I asked him about the ankle, and he said it was a bit swollen again.

"But I don't need you here anymore," he said. "I'm closing the place for the rest of the season. Soon as Hank's released, he and Betty are going. Bob's taking off end of the day. Leonard Colebert's family is due here today to pick up his things. And there's a lot of stuff to deal with, of course. Insurance, for one thing."

"Well, at least you don't have to worry anymore about finding a way to get the Wickenses out of your house."

Dad gave me a tired smile. "No Wickenses. No house. No problem."

I found Bob Spooner down by the water, sitting in his boat, just looking out over the lake.

"How was the tractor?" I asked.

"Fast," he said.

"I was serious, what I said last night," I said.

"About what?"

"About going fishing. Are you packing up yet?"

"Not till the end of the day. I might even hang in till tomorrow. Are you serious? After all that's happened? You want to go out one last time?"

"Yeah," I said. "If you don't mind. Something a bit restful, for a change."

"Sure."

"In an hour?"

Bob said sure, again.

The parade, we heard later, went off without a
hitch. Stuart Lethbridge and the rest of the Fifty
Lakes Gay and Lesbian Coalition failed to show
Turns out Stuart couldn't get anyone to run the
comics shop, and Saturday being his busiest day, he
couldn't afford to close.

May and Jeffrey were going back to the city i
Lawrence's Jag. They'd given statements to the po
lice, and Lawrence had let them know that they'd b
staying at his place, at least for a while.

Lawrence had finished packing all his stuff an
tossed it into the trunk. Jeffrey, still holding on
what was now his entire *Star Wars* collection, Mac
Windu and Lando Calrissian, was getting into th
backseat.

"You take care," I said. "Lawrence will look aft
you."

Jeffrey was dazed and tired. "I know," he said.
like him."

"I like him, too," I said. I shook Jeffrey's han
then went over to say goodbye to May.

She gave me a hug. "Thank you," she said quiet

"I'm sorry about your father," I said. For any pa
she felt, I really was.

"I had no idea," she said. "Not that he'd killed t
men in my life. Sabotaged my jobs. And then he
lowed us to be locked up. Would he have killed

My own father? Would he have killed me and his grandson?"

"I don't know," I said. "But if he couldn't have brought himself to do it, I think Charlene would have."

She looked like she was going to cry. She gave me a kiss, thanked me again, and got into the Jag.

"Thanks," I said to Lawrence as he opened his door.

He put his arms around me, patted my back, and whispered into my ear, "The shit you get into. I do declare."

As they drove up the hill and disappeared around the bend, I noticed Orville Thorne standing not far away.

"I owe you," I said.

He gave me a half smile. "I may not be cut out for this," he said. "Maybe I should think about doing something else."

"Well," I said, "you were there for me when I needed it most, and I thank you. When you're in the city, I want you to come by. My wife Sarah, my kids Paul and Angie, they'd be honored to meet you."

"I'd like that," he said.

"How are you and Lana?" I asked.

Orville sighed tiredly. "We talked a lot last night. She's not my aunt, she's not my mother, but she loves me as much as either."

"Hold on to that."

"I wish," he said, working to get the words out, "that I had had a chance to meet your mother."

"Our mother," I said.

He nodded. His eyes were wet.

"I'll do what I can to tell you everything about he that I can."

He smiled sadly. "I'd appreciate that. And, I'ı sorry."

"Sorry?"

"About what I said before, when I found ou about you being my half brother, what I called you

"Oh, the asshole thing?" I said. "Don't worry. Yc wouldn't be the first one in the family to make th assessment."

"**A**ll set?" Bob Spooner asked. He was already in t boat, doing an inventory of the lures in his tacl box, when I walked out onto the dock.

"Ready," I said. I untied the bow, got in, took t middle seat, and Bob unhooked the stern. I pushed the boat out with an oar, lowered the pr into the water, and started the motor. Shouting ov it, he said, "I thought I'd take us where we went t other day."

Rather than shout back, I gave him a thumbs-ı There was almost no breeze, no chop on the wa and hardly any other boats out. It was nearing end of the season. It was an overcast day, but li chance of rain. The sound of water rushing agaı the metal hull was therapeutic.

We were in our spot in about five minutes, ; Bob killed the outboard. He handed me a pole which he'd already attached a lure.

"You can pick something different if you want," he said.

"No, that's good," I said. "Besides, it's not about the fishing. It's about being out here."

"Ain't that the truth," Bob said. "There's no more beautiful spot on Earth."

"Tell me again how long you've been coming up here?"

"Thirty-two years. Never missed a summer."

I cast out between some weeds. "Amazing. And the lake, it's as beautiful up here as it was when you first came up?"

"Pretty much. Just hope it stays that way as long as I'm coming up here." Bob cast out, reeled in slowly, then repeated the process.

"At least," I said, "we won't be seeing a huge fishing resort going in. At least not from Leonard. But you never know, there may be another developer just around the corner."

Bob nodded without looking at me. "Yeah, well, that's true. But it was still an awful thing, what happened to Leonard. I'll never forget it as long as I live, Zack, I'm tellin' you."

I reeled in, then cast out again. I asked the question I'd been wanting to ask since the night before.

"So, Bob," I said, "what really happened when you and Leonard went on your hike?"

"Hmm?" he said, pretending not to hear, glancing down into his tackle box.

"When you were out with Leonard Colebert. I was wondering, maybe you could tell me what really happened."

Bob stopped reeling in for a moment and looked at me. "What are you talking about, Zack? You know what happened. For Christ's sake, you were out there. You saw what happened to him. Jesus."

We were quiet for a moment, the only sound the lapping of the waves against the metal hull.

"There was no bear," I said. "Certainly not where Morton Dewart was concerned. Timmy Wickens admitted that to me. But not with Leonard Colebert either."

Bob Spooner, both hands on the pole, looked at me.

"I swear to God, Zack, I don't know what you're talking about," Bob said.

"I guess the first thing was, why didn't the bear eat him?" I asked.

"Christ, you want me to make excuses for a bear? Leonard was running away, he fell down the side of a hill, the bear must have decided it was too much work to go down there."

"That's possible," I said. "And if that had been the only thing, I might have let it go."

Bob waited.

"But then, Dad found bear spray in Leonard's backpack. It was sitting right there, near the top."

"Leonard must have dropped his backpack," Bob said.

"It was found with his body," I said. "Why didn't he try to spray the bear? Why couldn't he have slipped the backpack off, reached in while he was running? Even if he didn't want to stop and face the bear, he could have sprayed wildly over his shoulder

That's what I did last night, when Wendell was chasing me through the woods. I never got a good shot at him, but at least I tried."

"All I can think," Bob said, "is that he just never had a chance. The bear was closing in on him. That had to be the way it was."

"I suppose," I said, lifting the lure out of the water and casting out again. "Maybe, if it had just been the bear not eating him, and the bear spray in his backpack, maybe even then, I might have let it go."

Bob's eyes moved about. He had to be wondering what else I had.

"Remember," I said, "when you came back, and you described the bear?"

Bob, slowly, said, "Sure, I guess."

"You said the bear had one torn ear, like it was clipped off."

"I think, I guess I remember that."

"That day, when we first met Timmy Wickens, when everyone was trying to figure out whose body that was in the woods by the cabins, Wickens said Morton Dewart was looking for a bear, a bear that had an ear torn off. So when you told us about the ear that chased you and Leonard, the one that chased Leonard off the side of the cliff, and said it had an ear torn off, we all figured, hey, it had to be the same bear that killed Dewart."

Bob started to say something, then stopped himself.

"But Timmy Wickens made up the bear story. Made it all up that a bear killed Dewart, made up the story that Dewart was going out to track down a

bear. Even made up a description of the bear, because, as he told me last night, he's never even seen
a bear around here. There may be some, but he's
never actually laid eyes on one."

Bob said, "I see."

"So you pinned Leonard's death on an animal that
doesn't exist. You built your lie upon another lie.
When the first one fell apart, so did yours."

"That's how you see it," Bob said.

"So my question is, what really happened out
there?"

Bob took his right hand off the reel, holding the
line in place with the thumb of his left hand, and
rubbed his gray whiskers. He hadn't shaved this
morning. Who had?

"We had an argument," Bob said.

"Okay."

"We were hiking through there, and I'd been talk
ing to him about his proposal, this stupid fishing re
sort, told him it was all wrong, that it would ruin the
area, that he should forget about it, that bringing in
hundreds of fishermen would clean this lake out o
fish in a couple of years. Told him he was out of hi
fucking mind."

"How did he like that?"

"He didn't like it much. He said he had powerfu
lawyers, that they'd find a way to get the council t
approve it. That Mayor Holland would have to agre
or she'd have to spend millions to fight it."

"Not good," I said.

"We kept walking, arguing, and we got to the to
of this ridge, the cliff, and he told me to come loo

that this was part of the property he was going to develop, and that down at the bottom of the ridge, he
was going to take down all those trees, mow everything down, and put in some huge whale for kids to
play in."

"Yeah," I said.

"And then he said I shouldn't even worry about
the fish being depleted, that he'd stock the lake,
maybe bring in fish from other places. Starts talking
about bringing in swordfish, for Christ's sake. Those
aren't freshwater fish, I told him. You can't put goddamn swordfish in a lake with muskie and pickerel. I
asked him if he was out of his fucking mind, even
suggesting something that stupid."

"That's pretty crazy," I said.

Bob's cheeks got red. "I swear to you! He was going to destroy this lake, that's what he was going to
do. This is God's country, Zachary. Look around."
Bob's eyes got misty. "This is paradise."

It was hard for me, just yet, after the kind of night
I'd put in, to think of this as paradise, but Bob was
right. If there was a more beautiful part of the world,
I hadn't seen it yet.

"So," Bob said, "I guess I said something I shouldn't
have."

"What was that?" I asked.

"I called him a fucking idiot. Plain as that. I said,
'Leonard, you are a complete, total fucking idiot.'"

"How'd he take that?"

"He hit me. Well, shoved me, I guess. Told me I
was a stupid old coot, standing in the way of

progress. So, I don't know, I guess I shoved him back."

"And over?"

Bob nodded slowly, once.

"Leonard went off the edge, tumbled. Rolled down, ass over teakettle. Around the second time he rolled over, I swear, I thought I heard something snap. His neck, I guess." Bob paused, breathed in. "He rolled to the bottom, and I called down to him. Jesus, I musta called down to him ten times. But he didn't answer. So, I found a way down, the same way we all found our way down later, to check on him."

"And he was dead," I said.

Bob looked out over the water, looking for some thing that wasn't there. Some sort of salvation maybe.

"No," Bob said.

Maybe my mouth dropped open, I'm not sure, bu it wasn't the answer I was expecting.

"He was alive?" I asked.

"I guess, just barely. He was breathing, but he wa twisted up something awful. He managed, sort c whispered, something about not being able to fee anything. At all."

A slight breeze caught the bow of the boat an gently turned us. I felt cold.

"What happened then, Bob?"

"I"—and the words were catching in his throat— "I, I started thinking about what had happened him. How he'd probably busted his spine, do something horrible, how he'd never walk again, an

I thought of my wife, how her life dragged on, how Leonard didn't deserve something like that."

"Is that really all you were thinking?" I asked.

Bob was quiet for a moment. "I suppose I was thinking a few other things, too." He paused. "About what was going to happen. About how, once I got help, and we got Leonard to a hospital, and he told the police what had happened, that I had pushed him over the edge, that even if I didn't get convicted of anything, even if I could somehow convince them that Leonard slipped, that his lawyers, these goddamn lawyers of his, they'd find a way to ruin me. To destroy me."

"Probably," I said.

"And so, I put my . . . I put my hand over his mouth, and I pinched his nose, and I pressed really hard, and he couldn't do anything, he couldn't move his arms, he couldn't twist away or anything. It took, I don't know, a minute or so, maybe more. I think I kept my hand there a lot longer than I needed to. I was scared, that maybe I wouldn't have done it for long enough."

Now neither of us spoke for a minute.

"That's cold, Bob," I said, finally. "Getting into a shoving match, accidentally knocking Leonard over the cliff, I could see that. But the finishing him off, the smothering him, I have to be honest. That surprises me."

Bob kept looking away. "Me too." He paused. "I'm not proud of what I did."

"So what happened then?"

"Once I knew, knew that he was dead, I tried to

think of what to do. And I thought about the bear that, supposedly, was roaming the woods. I thought up a story, about how we'd run into it, made a run for it and got split up. When I got back up top, I really did run, deliberately tripped, let myself get pretty scraped up, to make the story as believable as possible."

"You had us all fooled, Bob," I said. "You did a darn good job of that."

"I was already scared about what really did happen. But I just pretended it was something else that scared me."

I shook my head sadly, turned the reel a couple of cranks.

"Zachary, are you taping this?" Bob asked, eyeing me suspiciously.

"No, Bob," I said. "I'm not wired, if that's what you're thinking. I just wanted to know what happened."

Bob, one hand still holding his fishing pole, opened his tackle box and reached inside with his right hand. When it came back out, it was holding a gun. His Smith & Wesson pistol.

He pointed it in my direction.

"Oh, come on, Bob," I said. "You're not going to kill me."

He swallowed. "I don't know as you leave me much choice, Zack. I'd hate to do it. I like you. You're a good kid. And I think the world of your father."

I said, "There's not just that. A guy falls and breaks his neck, you can call that an accident and get away with it. But you shoot a guy, how you going to explain that?"

"I don't know," Bob said. "I guess I could say you drowned, fell overboard. Weigh your body down, let it sink to the bottom. I could tip the boat over, there could be an accident."

"They'd find my body, Bob. This isn't that big a lake. And even Dr. Heath could probably find a bullet hole. And the other thing is, I don't think you're a bad person. I admit, what you did, smothering Leonard, I'm a bit taken aback by that, but you were a desperate man in a desperate circumstance. It was wrong, but I know how you must have been thinking at the time. And I know how badly you must feel about it now."

He still had the gun pointed at me. "I do," he said.

I said, "Honestly, Bob, I don't know what to do. I could tell them what I know, but I don't think you'd ever spend a day in jail. You could deny telling me his story. You could stick with your original version. Maybe there really is a bear out there with a clipped ear. How would they prove there isn't? There are no witnesses. And it's only my word about what Timmy Wickens said, and he's dead. I wouldn't be surprised if they didn't even file charges. They'd realize, from the get-go, that they'd never get a conviction."

"So then what's the point of telling them?" he asked, resting the arm that was holding the gun on his knee, but still keeping me in his sights.

"Because that's what you did," I said.

"So you're going to tell them."

I sighed. It should have been an easy question. I

knew Bob Spooner had killed a man. But it had started out as an accident. I knew Bob Spooner was basically a good person. A good man on the verge of being what's known as an "old man." I am not what you'd call a moral absolutist. There are a lot of shades in my world.

And yet.

"I don't know, Bob," I said, being honest. "If you're worried about what will happen if I do, then you'll have to shoot me. Now."

I could see he was thinking about it. Thinking about it pretty hard.

Bob's line started to go out.

"What the . . ." he said, looking down at his reel, the spool of white filament spinning away.

Twenty feet off our port side, a fish broke the surface, briefly. A muskie, a big one at that. The fish disappeared, then came up again, its head poking out of the water, trying to shake the lure from its mouth. Its cold black eye caught a brief glimpse of us before it went back under.

"Oh no," Bob said, staring at the ripples where the fish had gone back under.

"What?" I said.

"It's Audrey," he said. "I saw the scar." The scar under the eye. The scar that marked the fish that had been toying with Bob for years.

He didn't have a chance of reeling her in, however. Not with one hand holding a gun on me.

"You're going to need both hands," I said. "And me holding the net, if you can get her close enough to the boat."

More and more line was being fed out. Audrey was getting farther and farther away.

It was a hell of a choice for Bob. Take a chance at finally getting the fish he'd been trying to catch for so many summers, and risk spending the rest of his life in jail. Or take care of me, make sure I never told my story to anyone, and lose any chance of landing Audrey.

"Take this," Bob said, handing me the gun.

I took it from him carefully, then laid it on the bottom of the boat, ahead of the middle seat, where I was perched.

The moment he'd given up the gun, Bob went into action, reeling in, bending the pole back toward him, horsing it, then easing it forward and reeling in the slack.

I grabbed the net, got ready to scoop Audrey.

"The hook's really into her," I said. "Way more than when she hit my line."

"Looks like it," Bob said. "But she's spit it out before when I was sure I had her." He glanced at me, just for a second, and said, "I couldn't have done it."

"I know," I said.

He reeled in Audrey a bit more. "Are you going to tell?" he asked, watching where the line vanished into the black.

I kept watching for the fish. "I don't know."

Bob nodded. "Maybe, if you tell, and they do convict me, they'd let me hang Audrey on the wall of my cell."

I smiled at that. The metal handle of the net was cold in my hands. I could see a shape in the water, something moving under the surface, darting left and then right. I leaned over the edge of the boat, let the net slip into the water. My hands dipped below the surface.

"Are you ready?" Bob said.

"I think so. Just lead her this way."

When the fish was almost into the net, Bob said "I'm not a bad man, Zack."

"I know, Bob," I said. "I've met bad men, and you're not one of them."

40

IT WAS A LONG DRIVE HOME.

I got in the car after saying my farewells to Dad.

"Thanks," he said, leaning up against my Virtue's fender. The ankle was bugging him a bit, and he was using his crutches. "For a lot of things."

"It's okay."

"Bob's pretty excited, coming in with Audrey. I'm gonna take some pictures."

"E-mail me one," I said.

"He seemed kind of troubled," Dad said.

I nodded. "He's got a lot on his mind," I said. "He's been through a lot this week, like all of us." I thought for a moment. "Tell him not to worry. Tell him I said not to worry."

Dad nodded. "Listen, promise me you won't think less of your mother."

"I won't."

"People make mistakes, but they often have help. I helped her make hers. Remember that, with you and Sarah. You be good to her."

I gave him a hug. "We'll be talking," I said.

Dad peeked into the back seat, saw something wrapped in a blanket. "What's that?" It was a Smith & Wesson. I'd kept it, and when I got back to the city, intended to get rid of it. I hadn't taken it so much for my own personal security, as to put my mind at ease over what Bob Spooner might do with it. I had a fear that he might find an expedient solution to his dilemma.

"So long, Dad," I said.

"Bye, son," he said.

I got in the car and as I headed up the drive back to the highway, I slowed and took one last look at the smoldering ruins of the Wickens farmhouse. There was nothing much left but a foundation and a few blackened timbers at what was once the back of the structure.

Something caught my eye. Something large, and black, and lumbering, moving amidst the debris that was once the farmhouse.

It was a bear.

I stopped the car, opened the door, and stood by the car, one foot on the rocker panel, a hand on the roof, ready to jump back in if I needed to.

The bear was rummaging around, hunting for food, I figured. Suddenly aware of my presence, he rose up on his haunches, sniffed the air, looked in my direction. He stared at me lazily for a moment, then, quickly losing interest, he dropped back down onto all fours, and wandered off into the woods.

———————

There was a lot to think about on the ride back. About Dad, Dad and Lana. The revelations about my mother, and Lana's husband. About Orville. About Bob, and what he'd done.

About evil.

Sarah met me at the door. After we kissed, and held each other for at least a minute, she said, "It's all over the news. There was even something on CNN. But their details are really sketchy. And the office has called. Three times."

"It's already written," I said. "In my head. They say how much they want?"

"They can go three thousand words, starting on front, turning inside. They hired a helicopter, took lots of the site from the air. And Lawrence called. He's got May and Jeffrey settled in. Monday morning, they're going to meet with some social service types, see what they can do for them. I've got some clothes, too, that we can drop off. And linens, stuff like that. I've got clothes I could give May, but I don't know what size she is."

"You're pretty close," I said. "Why not throw some stuff in, we'll take it over. I've got some old *Star Wars* toys tucked away that I'm going to take as well."

"You look tired."

"Yeah." I slipped my arms around her, and for a moment or so, I cried.

She made me a bacon sandwich. As I sat at the kitchen table eating, my seventeen-year-old son, Paul, breezed through long enough to grab a Coke from the fridge. "Hey, Dad," he said, and disappeared. The

phone rang while Sarah was out of the room, and
grabbed it. It was Angie, calling from the library a
Mackenzie University, working on that second year c
her psychology major.

"Oh, hi, Dad. I didn't know you were back
Everything go okay up at your dad's place? Mon
didn't say a lot."

"Pretty much."

"Is Mom there? I need to ask her something abou
what to get for a friend of mine who's getting en
gaged."

"Hang on."

"Oh, and Dad? What do you think about us ge
ting a dog? Paul and I were talking. We think
would be neat."

I called Sarah to the phone and took my sandwi
upstairs to my study, fired up my computer, an
started writing. Ninety minutes later, I had it dor
The broad strokes. The Wickenses, what they we
planning, how it went wrong.

Nothing about Bob Spooner.

I phoned the city desk and said I was e-maili
them the story.

I recalled that this had all begun with a phone c
while I was having lunch with my friend Tri
Snelling, and how it had seemed, up until the n
ment when I got word that there was a very go
chance my father had been eaten by a bear, t
she'd had something important on her mi
Something she was working up to telling me.

So now that my story was filed to the office, I
I needed to make amends. I went into the kitc

and poured myself some coffee. Sarah came up to me, hugged me from the side, leaned her head into my shoulder. I gave her a squeeze back.

"You've filed?"

I said yes. "I figure I've got about a half hour before they start calling with stupid questions."

"At the outside," Sarah said.

"I'll take advantage of the lull before the storm to give Trixie a call."

"She called, while you were away, to ask about your father. To see if he'd really been eaten by a bear. I set her straight."

"Good."

"Zack?"

"Yes, hon?"

"Promise me. No more of this. This is not our life."

"Yeah," I said.

"Promise?"

"I promise."

I nodded and glanced at the clock on the wall. Saturday night, eight o'clock. There was a very good chance Trixie might be with a client, but if she didn't answer, I'd just leave a message.

I went back into the study, dialed Trixie's personal number. She picked up on the second ring.

"Hey," I said.

"Zack," Trixie said. "How's your dad?"

"He's okay."

"Sarah said. But she said there were some other problems. Did everything go okay?"

"Things . . . are okay. If I weren't so tired, I'd tell

you all about it now, but as they say in the newspaper biz, you can read all about it tomorrow."

"Okay."

"Listen," I said. "I kind of had to rush off when we were having lunch Tuesday, and maybe I'm wrong, but I had the feeling there was something you wanted to talk to me about."

It was quiet at the other end of the line.

"Trixie?"

"Yeah?"

"If I'm sticking my nose in where it doesn't belong, tell me. You just seemed, I don't know, like there was something you wanted to get off your chest."

Another long pause. Finally, she spoke.

"I'm in trouble," Trixie said.

ACKNOWLEDGMENTS

Thanks, as always, to my agent, Helen Heller, and the Bantam Dell gang, particularly Irwyn Applebaum, Nita Taublib, Micahlyn Whitt, and Shawn O'Gallagher. And to Neetha, Paige, and Spencer, best gang ever.

ABOUT THE AUTHOR

LINWOOD BARCLAY is a former columnist for the *Toronto Star*. He is the author of several critically acclaimed novels, including *No Time for Goodbye*, a #1 bestseller in Britain. He lives near Toronto with his wife and has two grown children. His website is www.linwoodbarclay.com.

Don't miss Linwood Barclay's
next electrifying thriller

FEAR THE WORST

Available now in hardcover
from Bantam Books!